MEN OF HONOR SERIES

FIGHTING
Temptation

BESTSELLING AUTHOR
K.C. LYNN

This story is dedicated to my grandma who had a love for romance novels. I hope you have been wrapped in eternal love and sunshine since you left this world. Jaxson and Julia's story is for you.

MEN OF HONOR SERIES

FIGHTING
Temptation

1

A Glimpse Of Our Beginning

Julia

I knew something was wrong the moment he said to meet him at our special place. My heart hasn't stopped twisting since I received his text a half hour ago. It's not uncommon for us to meet like this but his message was abrupt, said we needed to talk.

Please, God, whatever he's going to tell me, please don't let it be bad.

Reaching the beach, I slip off my sandals and start across the cool sand to where I can see a fire being started in the distance. I lift my long, white maxi dress as I walk along the shore, wetting my feet. Each step brings me closer to the man I'm secretly in love with, my best friend Jaxson.

We met when I moved here to Sunset Bay, South Carolina, just a little over two years ago. My mother had just passed away from cancer and I came to live with my grams. It still amazes me how fast I fell in love with this town, and how quickly I made some of the best friends I'll ever have.

A smile touches my lips as I recall the first time I laid eyes on Jaxson. My best friend, Kayla and I, had been sitting outside the ice cream shop, on a sweltering hot summer afternoon, when he came riding in on his motorcycle…

"Well, it looks like today is your lucky day, you're finally going to get to see the famous Jaxson Reid." Kayla's voice fades away as I watch him park across the lot, becoming captivated by the mysterious bad boy I've heard so much about.

He's dressed in loose, dark, faded jeans that have a few holes in them, and a snug black T-shirt that molds to his lean, muscular frame in all the right places. My eyes draw to the erotic display of tribal tattoos that are woven up his arms, getting cut off by the sleeves of his T-shirt. He takes his helmet off, and all the air sucks out of my lungs, my entire world tilting on its axis. Thick, dark lashes frame magnificent ice-blue eyes, his olive-colored complexion complemented by shaggy, dark brown hair. It's the kind of hair that makes my fingers itch to run through it, just to see if it feels as soft as it looks. His strong jaw is graced with a sexy five o'clock shadow.

I'd heard a lot about Jaxson since moving here, all the girls spoke about him as if he was some sort of god, and now I know why.

He unleashes a sexy smirk on me, and I soon realize that I've been busted openly ogling him. Heat invades my cheeks as I look away, only to receive the same knowing smile from Kayla.

"I know, right? If sex could walk, he would be it. Don't feel bad; you're not the only one who drools around him. Most do, well, except for me. As sexy as he is, I have the major hots for his friend Cooper. I have big plans for that boy, just you wait."

She goes on to tell me that Jaxson is two years older than my sixteen and that he just graduated before the summer. I'm disappointed to learn that I won't see him around school.

"He did live with Cooper's family for a while, but now they have an apartment of their own," she explains.

"What about his parents?"

"His mom left when he was a kid, his dad a few years ago. I don't know where; he was a real asshole—the town drunk."

That information explained a lot later on. Little had I realized at the time, but Kayla really did have a plan laid out for her and Cooper. A year later, and they're still dating.

Unfortunately, I didn't get to meet Jaxson that day, he was there meeting Melissa Carmichael. My blood heats just thinking her name. She's always been such a bitch to me, especially after I became close with Jaxson. I hate to even think about what they did together after they left the ice cream shop that day. Although, that's been the story of my life for the last two years—watching Jaxson with random girls. He's not the relationship type, or so he says. I have a sneaking suspicion his mom leaving has something to do with that.

The night I finally did get to meet him, well… it was the scariest night of my life.

It was two weeks after seeing him at the ice cream shop. I had snuck out of my bedroom window after Grams went to sleep and walked to the cemetery to visit my mom. I had sat at her grave and talked to her. It was something I always found comforting and still do. I told her how scared I was to be starting a new school, worried people weren't going to like me, and more than anything, I told her how much I missed her. My mother was my best friend. The pain I felt when she passed hadn't faded, and I'd wondered if it ever would. I don't remember how long I'd been crying for before I heard some rustling and laughter...

I turn around to find two guys stumbling up behind me. They're big, their builds reminding me of linebackers. By looking at them, I guess they're a couple of years older than me. They smile as they approach; smiles that have terror skittering down my spine. I stand up quickly, my shaky legs barely able to hold me up.

"Well aren't you pretty. Isn't she, Jace?"

Suddenly feeling exposed in my yoga tank and shorts, I fold my cardigan over my breasts that they are openly staring at; the action only seems to amuse them.

"Yeah, she's really pretty, I'm glad we happened upon her."

Ignoring them, I start forward, but the one referred to as Jace steps out in front of me, blocking my escape. I attempt to calm my wild heartbeat while figuring out how to get out of this mess I've found myself in. I know I won't be able to outrun them, but my hope is to at least make it to the street and pray someone hears me scream for help.

Unfortunately, it's exactly what they anticipate. I don't make it far before one grabs a fistful of my hair and yanks me back against him. His hand clamps over my mouth with brutal force, muffling my screams.

"You stupid bitch. Shut the fuck up!"

With every bit of strength I possess, I fight against him, kicking and shifting, trying to break the hold he has on me, but none of it makes a difference; he's too strong.

He drags me back to my mom's grave while his friend Jace watches, his hand stroking over the front of his jeans.

My eyes close in disgust as bile inches up my throat.

"Come on, fucking help me, man! This bitch is squirmy."

Jace snaps to attention and grabs my kicking legs to help carry me. They drop me on my mother's grave, the hard impact knocking the breath from my lungs. The one behind me pins my struggling arms above my head while Jace sits on my legs, restraining them. His hand wraps around my throat as he leans in close, a malicious smile curling his lips. "I'm going to fuck you right here on your mother's grave, you little bitch."

It's now, I realize they must have been watching me for some time to know this is my mother's grave. For the first time since they showed up I feel something other than fear. Anger swells inside of me, bubbling over, and I spit in his face.

It's my first mistake.

Fury washes over his expression, his fingers tightening on my throat. "You're a brave little whore." He rears back and slaps me, the impact is so hard that blood pools in my mouth and black spots dance before my eyes. "After I'm done fucking you, my buddy is going to get a turn, then we're going to beat some manners into you."

He tears at my tank top, ripping the strap from my shoulder.

"No! Please don't do this," I beg, but quiet quickly when I realize my pleas only excite him further.

As his hand moves to his belt, I close my eyes and begin to pray. It's the first time I've prayed since my mom died. I am praying so hard that I don't realize my legs are suddenly free. Soon though, I clue in to the sound of shouting and painful grunts.

My eyes spring open and I see Jace on the ground with another guy on top of him, beating the ever-livin' crap out of him.

The guy holding my arms eventually releases me to help his friend.

"Watch out!" I scream, warning the mystery guy.

He turns around just in time to land a solid right hook, causing my attacker to hit the ground unconscious.

This guy packs a serious punch.

As he rises to his full height and turns toward me, I realize the dark avenging angel is none other than the town's bad boy, Jaxson Reid.

Rage twists his expression as he starts toward me.

I cower against my mother's headstone, fear gripping me for a second time. He's so fierce, it frightens me.

When he senses my alarm, he slows his steps and approaches me with more caution, lifting his hands in the air. "I'm not going to hurt you. Everything is going to be okay. I'm calling the police now."

After calling it in, he sits a short distance away and waits with me. Awkward silence fills the air around us. I want to thank him, but I can't form words, my teeth are chattering like crazy, my body shaking.

He catches me off guard when he leans over and gently brushes his fingers *across my bruised cheek. "Sorry I didn't make it before this happened," he says quietly.*

His tenderness surprises me. I've been told Jaxson was dangerous, and someone you don't want to screw with. After witnessing what he did to my two attackers, I can see why.

"Don't be sorry. Thank you for coming when you did, because if you hadn't, well… you know what was about to happen."

The horrific event comes rushing back with a vengeance. I wrap my arms around my legs, hugging my knees to my chest and begin sobbing.

He moves a little closer to me and awkwardly pats my shoulder. "Everything is fine now."

I can tell he's uncomfortable trying to console me and doesn't know what to say.

"Listen, I know now is not the time to be a dick, but what the hell were you thinking coming to a graveyard this late at night by yourself?"

His disapproving tone has my back going up. "I was visiting my mother. I didn't think coming here would almost get me raped," I snap, then feel bad, especially after everything he's done for me. "I'm sorry, you're right, it was stupid. I won't be doing it again, at least not in the middle of the night."

"I don't recognize those assholes. I'm assuming they were driving through, maybe back to Charleston." He shrugs. "Either way, probably a good idea if you come during daylight."

"I will," I say quietly.

He extends his battered hand to me. "I'm Jaxson Reid."

I put my shaking one in his. "Julia. Julia Sinclair."

Pulling myself back to the present, I try to shake the memory. What had started out to be one of the most awful nights of my life turned into one of the best. Because the sexy, dark, and mysterious bad boy I was warned to steer clear of became my best friend. Since that night, Jaxson has taken care of me—protected me. He brought me back from the brink of pain and heartbreak after losing my mother. He reminded me what it was like to be happy again.

People have a misperception about him, mainly due to the reputation of his father. Grams once told me his father was a terrible man and Jaxson was better off without him. That's all she had said but I didn't need her to elaborate, because I can tell just how deeply his father had hurt him. At times when his guard slips for a brief moment, I can see flashes of it, and he doesn't realize anyone is looking. I know any physical scars he bears are nothing compared to the ones left on his heart.

Don't get me wrong, Jaxson has earned some of his reputation. He can be arrogant, aggressive, and angry. He's guarded and damaged yet he's also beautiful, strong, and honorable. Our friendship surprises a lot of people because, other than Cooper, he has never befriended anyone else, and he definitely doesn't have any friends that are girls. But Jaxson and I formed a bond, one so strong, it is unbreakable. I unconditionally and irrevocably love every damaged part of him. And for the boy who doesn't believe in love, he will always and forever have mine.

My steps slow as I come up to him sitting by the fire; he stares into the bright flames, lost in thought. I watch him for a moment, his troubled expression glowing from the firelight.

When he hears my approach, his eyes lift to mine and his expression softens; he looks almost relieved to see me. Sometimes when he looks at me the way he is now, I think maybe he does love me the way I love him. But whenever I let the silly thought in, I shove it away and remember whom I'm talking about.

Flashing me a sexy smirk, he stands and walks over, pulling me into his arms. "Hey, Jules." He greets me with a familiar kiss to my forehead.

For whatever reason, he has kissed my forehead from the moment we became friends. It's something that he's reserved just for me, and I savor the intimate contact with him.

"Hey, Jax." I hug him back tightly, breathing in his comforting scent.

He breaks the connection much too soon, his hand grasping mine as he leads me to sit next to the fire. We rest back against the log behind us; both of my arms wrapping around one of his as I lean into him, seeking his warmth.

The tense silence filling the air has lead settling in my stomach and my earlier fear comes rushing back swiftly. "You're going to tell me something bad, aren't you?"

His somber expression says it all. "It'll be all right. It's not that bad." He pauses, expelling a heavy breath. "I'm leaving town. I've decided to enlist in the Navy. I want to be a SEAL."

My heart plummets, a million questions plaguing me at once. "Okay, and what does that mean exactly? Where would you go? Don't you have to qualify first, before you can even be accepted?"

"I already have been," he admits quietly. "I had to do some written exams and evaluations, but I passed. I'm going to their training facility in Coronado, California."

"What? Just how long have you thought about this?"

He clears his throat. "I started the process about six months ago."

"Six months?" I shriek, rearing back. "How could you keep this from me?" Betrayal thickens my throat, a sharp pain infiltrating my chest.

He blows out a breath, his eyes turning to me, pleading with me to understand. "I'm sorry, Jules. I didn't want to upset you if I wasn't going to make it," he apologizes, his words heavy with regret. "Please understand. I need to do this. I need to get out of this fucking town; I don't belong here. The only thing that kept me here as long as it has is you."

"How can you say that? This is your home, Jaxson. You grew up here."

"That's exactly my point. Everyone knows my shit. They know what I come from. Don't tell me you don't see how many people look down on me, especially when we're together. Everyone wonders why sweet little Margaret Sinclair's granddaughter is friends with a fuck-up like me."

I shake my head. "No you're wrong and even if you aren't, who cares what they think? Don't leave because you think you need to prove yourself."

"This has nothing to do with them. I don't give a shit what they think of me; I'm doing this for myself. I think I've found something that I'm going to be really good at. I did so well on the evaluation that the superior officers are excited to meet me."

"You're good at a lot of things. Can't you choose something else? Something that isn't so dangerous? How about being a mechanic? Or owning your own motorcycle shop? You would be really good at that, and that would be fun," I say, trying to sound upbeat.

Unfortunately, he doesn't take the bait. His eyes are lit with amusement as he stares down at me.

"It was worth a try," I grumble.

Chuckling, he slings his arm around my shoulders but sobers quickly, his blue irises holding mine. "I have a chance to do something good with my life. Tell me you understand."

"I'm trying, it's just hard. I don't want to lose you." My voice cracks as I struggle to hold onto my composure.

He rests his forehead against mine, his jaw flexing as he holds in his own emotions. "You won't lose me, Jules, we'll still see each other. Obviously not as much as we do now, but we'll figure something out."

"When do you leave?" I ask.

He straightens nervously, sending another dose of panic through me. "Jaxson?"

"Saturday morning. I take the ferry to Bradsford then fly out from there."

"This Saturday? As in three days from now?" I screech.

"I'm sorry. I just found out yesterday. They don't give you much time."

I shake my head, having a hard time grasping that any of this is happening right now. How am I supposed to go every day without seeing him?

His hand caresses my cheek, the touch pulling me from my torment. "Are we okay?" he asks.

We are okay, *I* am not. But I don't tell him that. Instead, I cover his hand with mine, and nod because my throat is too tight to speak.

"Listen, I have a lot to get done before I leave, but how about we go out on Friday? We'll grab supper then come hang out here for the night."

"Sure, that sounds good," I agree, wanting any time I can get. "Anyway, I better head home. I'm later than what I told Grams I would be, and I don't want her to worry."

And I really don't want to completely lose it in front of you.

"All right, come on, I'll walk you to your car."

I falter, knowing he's not going to like what he's about to hear. "Um, I didn't drive here, I walked."

His eyes narrow in disapproval. "Damn it, Julia. You know better."

"Relax. It's a beautiful night and I want the fresh air."

"You know the rules. No walking at night by yourself." Letting out a frustrated breath, he drives a hand through his hair. "Come on, I'll take you home."

"I don't have my helmet and I'm wearing a dress," I argue, but know it's pointless.

"I don't care. Either I drive you back or I follow you home, it's up to you."

My eyes roll at his bossy attitude but I relent and follow him to his bike.

He puts his black helmet on over my head, making sure the strap is tight then straddles the seat. When I don't follow suit, he tosses me an impatient look.

Geez, he can be grumpy.

I hike my dress up just enough to climb on behind him, my arms wrapping around his waist. My irritation quickly vanishes, peace invading my soul. One of my favorite things to do is ride with Jaxson. I love getting to be so close to him.

The bike roars to life, a second before it kicks forward, starting our short journey home.

I turn my face to the side, resting my cheek against his hard back and try really hard not to think about the fact that he's leaving me in just three days.

Three days.

Does Kayla know? I'm sure Coop does, but I would like to think that if Kayla knew she would have told me.

I don't get much time to think about it before we arrive at my house. Once Jaxson comes to a stop, I climb off the back, missing his warmth. I hand him back his helmet without making eye contact and flick him a quick wave, needing to get out of here. My fragile composure is close to shattering.

However, I don't get the opportunity, because as soon as I take that first step he grabs my wrist and yanks me against him, enveloping me in his arms. "It's going to be okay, Jules," he whispers into my hair. "I promise."

The tears I've managed to hold at bay finally unleash. "I'm going to miss you so much," I cry, burying my face into his neck.

"I'm going to miss you too, Jules." He holds me close, his large hand rubbing comforting circles on my back. Once my tears subside, he curls a finger under my chin, lifting my face to his. "I'll pick you up at six on Friday, okay?"

I offer him a small smile and nod. When he releases me, I walk into the house and decide that I can't let him leave without telling him how much I love him. Even if the consequences could potentially be damaging.

2

Jaxson

Once Julia's safely inside, I start my bike back up and take off. I knew that would be hard, but that fucking sucked. I hate that she's hurting because of me but I know I'm doing the right thing, not only for myself but her, too.

She thinks I don't know about the shit she gets from people for being friends with me, but I do. If it's not the rich assholes who think they're too good for someone like me, then it's the jealous bitches who hate the fact I'm close with Julia and not them. They don't understand that she's different; she always has been.

I'll never forget the first time I laid eyes on her. I had heard about the new girl, all the guys spoke about how hot she was, and even placed bets on who was going to fuck her first. When I found out she was at the ice cream shop with Kayla one night, I changed my plans and had Melissa meet me there instead. I had to get a look at the girl everyone was talking about. When I rode in, I immediately spotted her and Kayla sitting outside at one of the tables. I parked across the lot then took my helmet off to get a good look at her. It was like a jolt of electricity shot through my body and straight to my dick.

Julia was not *hot*, she was fucking beautiful.

Her gaze held me captive; her eyes, an exotic blue-green color that hid behind long, dark lashes, shone of beauty and innocence. Right then I knew she was not for me, but I couldn't stop myself from taking in the rest of her. She had long, brown hair that fell past her bare shoulders and laid against the best looking tits I'd ever seen. Her short yellow sundress enhanced her smooth, olive skin, and although there was nothing revealing about it, I still got a glimpse of her small, lithe body, one that I desperately wanted to feel wrapped around me.

She had stared back at me with appreciation, something that I was used to. Yet, she caused a strange sensation in my chest—one I'd never felt before, and I fucking hated it. I learned at a young age that feelings and emotions were dangerous; they only made you weak. So I gave myself a mental slap and acknowledged her appreciation with a cocky smirk. When Melissa climbed on the back of my bike I took off and fucked her all night, trying to get the new girl out of my head… It didn't work.

Two weeks later, I walked out of Big Mike's gym and heard a terrified scream echo from the graveyard across the street. A white-hot rage constricts my chest, just like it always does when I think about those fucking perverts on top of her, holding her down.

Little did I know, that night would change my life forever. The girl I had tried so hard to forget, the one I tried to stay away from, became my best friend. I knew she would be better off without me, but I couldn't stop myself from getting to know her. She was different from anyone I'd ever met. I never thought someone so good and genuine existed until her. The more I saw of her, the more addicted I became. Every time I was around her, she would destroy some of the darkness that lurked inside of me. She made the bad shit in my life seem not so terrible. Then before I knew it, I had fallen for a girl from another world.

As badly as I wanted her, I tamped down my feelings and kept my dick in my pants, because I knew I'd never be good enough for her. Unfortunately, my father's blood runs in me, and I refuse to taint her. She deserves everything good, everything I'm not.

Even though I didn't ever plan to take her, I made sure no one else had her either. I know it was an asshole move, but the thought of her with someone else rips my fucking guts out. So without her knowledge, I laid claim. I warned every guy to stay away from her, and they all did because no one was brave enough to fuck with me.

As much as I'm going to miss her, it's a good thing I'm leaving. My precious control is slipping and every day I'm finding it harder to be around her and not touch her the way I want to. The way I've dreamed about.

Relief surges through me when I pull up to the apartment I share with Cooper and don't see Kayla's car. Tonight, out of all nights, I don't feel like hearing the bed pound against the wall from the two of them fucking each other senseless.

Letting myself into the apartment, I find Cooper sitting on the couch, drinking a beer and watching TV. He looks up at me with a stupid grin. "Hey, SEAL boy."

My arms cross over my chest as I lean against the counter. "Not yet, but when I do pass, I'll put your rookie ass to shame," I fire back with a smirk.

He's gotten so cocky since he finished the police academy over a year ago. Graduated top of the class, as he always reminds everyone. He wants to be sheriff one day and knows the opportunity will arise when the current one retires in the next few years. He's the perfect guy for the job. He's more than my best friend, he's the best guy I know. If it weren't for him and his parents, I'm not sure where I'd be.

"No Kayla?" I ask.

"Not tonight. I told her I would meet up with her tomorrow. Figured you might need a beer, or four. Something you better appreciate, because not only will I not be getting laid tonight, I will probably lose my balls when she finds out I knew about you leaving and never told her."

I grunt. "Yeah, well, no need to keep it a secret anymore." Grabbing a beer from the fridge, I drop in the chair on the other side of the room.

"So how did Jules take it?"

"Pretty much as I expected. She was hurt, and pissed when she found out how long I have been planning it. She's still talking to me though." I feel uncomfortable confessing this to him, but I continue. "I didn't want to lose her over this."

"Did you really think you would? This is Julia we're talking about. That girl is as forgiving as they come."

He's right, she is, but I also know what it's like to have the people who you'd least expect abandon you. But she isn't one of them, and I should have known that.

"I need you to keep your promise to watch out for her and take care of her. I mean it, Coop, if something happens to her because I wasn't here, I'll never forgive myself."

He leans forward, his expression hard. "Have I ever broken a promise to you? I told you I'll watch out for her, and I will. Although, I can't promise I'll be able to control her dating life," he adds with a smirk.

I tense, my eyes narrowing. "Who in the hell said anything about dating?

She'll be too busy with school to worry about that. Besides, why would I care? As long as he's good to her, I don't give a shit who she sees." The lie flows easily from my lips.

He grunts, knowing I'm full of shit. "Yeah, right. You know Wyatt Jennings is going to move in on her as soon as your ass hits that ferry."

My stomach sinks like a heavy anchor, dread snaking around my chest at the thought. Wyatt has wanted Julia since she first moved here. I warned him long ago not to go anywhere near her. It's no secret the shit he's done to half the chicks in this town, I've seen the bruises. The thought of him laying one finger on her makes me fucking violent.

"He's already been warned to stay away from her. If he doesn't, you better remind him."

"I'm a local cop now, Jaxson. I hate the thought too, but I can't just beat the shit out of the guy. I'll do what I can to stop her though, and if he hurts her in any way, well, everything I just said to you goes out the window. I'll take him out. You know I will. I'll just need to do it more inconspicuously is all," he says matter of factly.

I nod. "Thanks for doing this. It makes it a little easier for me to leave, knowing you got her back."

"Jaxson, again this is Julia we're talking about. You don't need to thank me. She's my girl's best friend; I care about her, too. Don't worry about this. I'll take care of her. You're doing the right thing, man. Go for it, and show those fuckers at BUD/S what you're made of."

3

Julia

"I can't believe I am going through with this," I say to Kayla as I add the finishing touches to my hair while trying to calm the butterflies in my tummy.

"You can do this, Julia, don't chicken out now."

I've decided I'm going to tell Jaxson how I feel tonight and right now I am so thankful for Kayla's support. She's always known my feelings for him, and thinks I should have said something long ago, but I couldn't. Even now, I am so scared this is going to ruin our friendship.

No, I won't let that happen.

I know he probably doesn't feel the same way, and it will hurt to hear, but I can't let him go without telling him that I love him. I've thought long and hard about this. If something were to ever happen to him, I would always regret not telling him how I truly feel.

"If he tells you he doesn't feel the same way, he's lying," Kayla says, coming up behind me in the mirror. Leave it to her to say exactly what she thinks. It's something I've always admired about her.

"I'm not so sure about that, you know how Jaxson is, he doesn't believe in love."

"That's his daddy issues talking, Jules. Believe me, I have seen the way he looks at you. If he denies it, he's lying."

Letting out a nervous breath, I shrug. "I guess I'm not expecting him to say it back. I'm doing this so I have no regrets."

"Well, if he says he doesn't feel the same way, you could always say 'just kidding.'"

The suggestion has us both bursting into a fit of laughter.

Kayla sobers quickly, her laugh softening into a smile. "He's lucky to have you, Jules, and believe me, when he sees you tonight he's going to flip his shit. You look amazing."

"Thanks, Kayla," I reply softly, my throat feeling tight at her compliment. I decided on a short, faded denim skirt that shows off a little more leg than I'm used to. Soft pink lace edges the hemline which matches the tank top I borrowed from Kayla. I went against straightening my hair, letting my long, chestnut brown locks fall in loose waves past my shoulders. Kayla helped me with my makeup, making my aquamarine eyes really stand out with a smoky eye shadow. It made me think of my Mama. She always loved my eyes; said they reminded her of the Caribbean Sea.

Grams tells me all the time that I look like Mama, and although we do have some similarities, I don't hold a candle to her. I have yet to see anyone as beautiful as my mother.

Thinking about this, reminds me of the night I fell irrevocably in love with Jaxson. It was almost a year after we had met. We were at our usual spot on the beach, where I would sneak out at night to meet him. We'd hang out and talk, oftentimes until sunrise...

We're lying side by side, staring up at the stars, when out of the blue he asks if I'm happy living in Sunset Bay.

"Yeah, I am. I think it's a great town. I just wish the circumstances of what brought me here were different," I tell him, unable to hide the sadness in my voice.

"You've never mentioned your dad before. You can tell me to mind my own damn business, but I'm curious why you aren't living with him."

"Because I don't know who my father is." Before he is able to get the wrong idea about my mother, I rush to explain. "To make a long story short, my mother fell in love with my father in college and got pregnant. He didn't feel the same way, and didn't want a baby." I shrug, but can't deny the sting of abandonment I feel when thinking about him. "She said if I ever wanted to know anything about him I could ask, but, to be honest, I never thought too much about him. My mother was everything I needed. My pappi died before I was born and my mother never dated, so I never had any male figures growing up."

I shift, feeling nervous for what I'm about to share. He lays quietly, allowing me the time I need.

"But there were a few times I wondered if I was missing out. Like when I was young, living in our old house. There was a girl close to my age who lived next door.

She had this big tree in her front yard, and her dad hung a wooden swing from it for her. He would push her on it every night after supper; they would laugh, and she would beg him to go higher. Oftentimes I'd watch them out my window, and wonder what that felt like. But I wouldn't let myself dwell on it because no one had a mom out there like I did."

With a soft smile, I pull my gaze away from the stars to look at him and am surprised to find him staring at me, his intense blue eyes penetrating my soul.

Before I can ask what he's thinking, he looks away, breaking the connection. "Well trust me when I say, sometimes it's better not knowing who your father is." There's so much pain in those few words, and it's now I realize that he harbors something much greater than anyone knows.

As badly as I want to know more, I don't push. Family is territory that Cooper warned me to never step in and I'm happy that he has even divulged this much to me. Instead, I tentatively reach out to touch his hand, hoping to offer some comfort.

His fingers curl around mine, interlocking our hands. My heart dances in excitement, and butterflies flock in my tummy. It feels like the greatest victory I have ever achieved.

A few precious seconds pass before he changes the subject back to me. "What was your mom like?"

It's the first time he has ever asked about her. Even though we have become close, I haven't spoken much about her because it hurts too much. He knows she passed away from cancer, but that's about it. I decide it's time to share her with him.

"She was beautiful, Jax, and not just on the outside, but the inside, too," I start, feeling the sting of tears in my eyes. "She was graceful and sweet, she never judged anyone. She was the kindest and most forgiving woman you would ever meet. Sometimes I think God took her because he needed her as one of his angels." I realize how silly that probably sounds to him and shake my head. "I'm not making sense. I'm trying to describe how amazing she was, but no matter what I say, you will never fully understand how beautiful she was."

When a tear slips free, he leans over and wipes it away with his thumb. "Actually, I know exactly what you're saying, and I can picture it… because she sounds just like you."

Once again my eyes find his, the startling blue irises captivating me. In that moment, something shifted in me, something monumental, and I soon realize it's me giving Jaxson my entire heart.

I'm thrusted back to the present by Kayla ranting about Cooper. "I still can't believe that fucker kept this from me. He said he knew I would have told you. Can you believe that?"

"Well, would you have?"

"Of course!" she says, without missing a beat.

Her loyalty brings a smile to my face. "Then why are you mad at him?"

"Because he is supposed to tell me everything anyway, that's why," she replies, as if the answer is obvious. "I told him he isn't getting a piece of ass for at least a week. Although I may have to take that back, it's only been two days and I might die if I don't get him naked soon," she admits, making me chuckle.

Kayla and Cooper are the all-American couple. Kayla with her long, blonde hair, big blue eyes and witty personality. Before Cooper joined the sheriff's department he was the town's football hero, and let's just say that next to Jaxson, he is definitely the hottest guy I've ever laid eyes on. With his warm green eyes, brown hair and killer smile that girls fall all over themselves for, much to Kayla's dismay. I smile when I think of all the seductive tricks she used to snatch him.

"Don't be too hard on him, he was just being loyal to Jaxson. You would have done the same for me," I say, taking pity on Cooper.

"Yeah, you're right; I'm going to make him sweat it for a bit longer though," she snickers.

Smiling, I shake my head at her.

"Are you ready for this?" she asks.

I take a deep breath, nerves dancing in my belly. "As ready as I'm ever going to be."

Jaxson

I arrive at Julia's house just a few minutes before six and try to pull myself together. These past few days I've been in a shitty mood; leaving her is bothering me more than I thought it would. Even Coop has had enough of me.

Just as I lift my hand to knock, Julia's grandma, Margaret Sinclair, opens the door. "Jaxson, I thought that was your bike I heard. Come here and give me a hug."

I do so, awkwardly. I'm not used to affection, but she's a really affectionate lady and likes to hug a lot.

"How are you doing, Miss Margaret?" I've never cared much about my manners, but Margaret has been good to me. She's never treated me like I wasn't good enough to be friends with Julia.

"How many times do I have to tell you to stop with the 'Miss Margaret' and call me Grams?" She scolds lightheartedly.

"Sorry," I mumble.

"You're forgiven, handsome. Now come on into the kitchen, Julia will be down in a minute, Kayla's up there with her. They should be done soon." I follow her into the kitchen and sit at the table where she places a plate of cookies in front of me. "Julia and I baked them this morning."

I don't hesitate taking one, the lady makes the best cookies.

Sitting down next to me, she cuts right to the chase. "So I heard you're leaving us."

I nod. "I'm heading off for training and hoping to make it into the Navy."

She watches me silently, making me feel uncomfortable then silently gets up and walks into the living room. She grabs a big photo album, shifting through the pages, then pulls out a picture and brings it back to me. "Julia's Pappi, my Ben, was in the Navy. He was a sailor, a darn good one, too."

Sure enough, the black and white photograph is of a young man in a sailor suit who looks even younger than me. I turn the picture over and read: *Benjamin Sinclair, 1952, 18 years old.*

"He served ten years before he was honorably discharged. He could have stayed, but after I had Julia's mother, Annabelle, I wanted him home safe with us. Who knew it would end up being a drunk driver that took him from us."

I stare down at the picture, unsure of what to say. My eyes snap back up to her in surprise when she puts her hand on mine.

"You remind me a little of my Ben, Jaxson. You're fierce, loyal, and strong. I think the Navy would be lucky to have you help serve this country."

It was probably the nicest thing anyone has ever said to me. "Thank you."

"Now tell me, are you going to come back to my Julia?"

Jesus, speaking of Julia… Where the hell is she? What am I supposed to say to that when I don't know the answer?

"I'm not sure what will happen, but I do expect to see Julia again. I care about her; she's a good friend. I'll miss her, but it will be good for her, too. I know it's been tough at times for her to be friends with me."

Next thing I know, she comes to stand in front of me. I stare up at her warily, wondering what in the hell she's going to say now. This conversation is way too much for me.

She takes my face between both of her hands and gives me a kind smile. "You're a good boy, Jaxson, never think any differently. Julia is lucky to have you; she's much stronger than you give her credit for. She needs you in her life, though, you make sure you come home to her, you hear?"

I nod, but feel bad doing it because I'm not sure I will be able to keep that promise. Finally, I hear Kayla and Julia bound down the stairs.

"We're in the kitchen, girls!" Margaret yells, patting my shoulder.

I push to my feet and stand, thankful the conversation is over, and suck in a sharp breath when Julia walks in.

Ho-ly shit!

All the blood from my head rushes south to my cock, and I immediately regret that I'm standing. Every time I see Julia I'm always struck with the reminder of how beautiful she is, but right now it's more than that. I have never seen her look this way. She's showing way more skin than I have ever seen, and now I don't want anyone else to, either. The way her hair and makeup is fixed, she doesn't look like beautiful, wholesome Julia. No, she looks like a sexy vixen.

"Oh, Julia, dear, you look beautiful."

"Thanks, Grams." Julia kisses her on the cheek then looks at me. "Hey, Jax." She fidgets with the bottom of her skirt, and my eyes are drawn to her long, smooth legs. Legs that I want to feel wrapped around my waist while I drive myself into her.

Fuck me!

"Hi," I croak out then clear my throat when I hear how gruff I sound. "Hey, Jules, you look nice."

That's a fucking understatement.

My attention pulls to Kayla next and I find her watching me with a sassy smirk.

"Hey," she greets me with a small wave. "Well I'm outta here, folks. Have fun and call me later, Jules." She gives Julia a hug and whispers something in her ear before looking back at me. "Good luck with the Navy thing, Jaxson. I'm sure you'll do great."

"Thanks, Kayla. Make sure to keep Coop in check. Don't let him get too big of a head while I'm gone."

Laughing, she bids us all one more wave then heads out the door.

"Are you ready?" I ask Julia.

She nods. "Is it all right if we take my car instead? I'm not really dressed for the bike."

No shit.

"Yeah, that's fine."

"Where are you two headed tonight?" Margaret asks.

Julia looks over at me, unsure.

"I thought we'd go get a pizza at Antonio's. Then head to the beach later?"

"Sounds good to me." She gives me a smile, one that always hits me like a blow to the chest.

When we start to the front door, Margaret grabs me again and wraps her thin, wrinkly arms around my waist. "You take care of yourself now, Jaxson, I have no doubt you're going to do great. You remember what I said, okay?"

"Thanks, I will. You take care too...*Grams.*"

She smiles when I add that last part.

"I'm not sure what time I'll be home. Don't wait up for me, just in case I'm late," Julia says, her cheeks turning pink as she avoids eye contact with me.

What's up with her?

"Actually, dear, don't wait up for me. My knitting club and I are partying it up tonight at Joyce Becker's. She's making monster margaritas."

Julia snickers at her excitement. "Be careful, and call if you need a ride."

"Oh you know me, I'll be fine, and I have a ride home. You kids have a good night."

Once we step outside, Julia turns to me with a smile and hands me the keys. "I imagine you want to drive," she says, rolling her eyes playfully.

I never sit shotgun. I need the control in every aspect of my life.

My jeans tighten further at her sassiness. Before I can think better of it, I reach out and slip my finger in the waist band of her skirt and yank her against me.

She gasps at the feel of my hard cock against her stomach.

"You look really good tonight, Jules."

"Thanks." The response is breathless, her cheeks flushing with desire.

Leaning down, I press a hard kiss to her forehead then drag her to the car before I do something really dumb, like hike up that skirt of hers and fuck her right here on the front porch.

5

Julia

By the time we pull up to Antonio's Pizza Parlor, my senses are still reeling from what happened on my front porch, my skin burning from Jaxson's possessive touch.

Maybe tonight will go better than I anticipate.

"Did you want to order it to go and eat at the beach?" Jaxson asks as we get out of the car.

"Yeah, that sounds good." Smiling, I link my arm easily with his as we walk into the restaurant.

"Well, well, well, if it isn't my favorite customers," Antonio boasts loudly. He's a very loud, happy Italian man who makes the best pizza in the state.

"Hi, Antonio," I greet him with a smile, walking up to the counter.

"Come on over here, beautiful, and lay one on me." He pats the side of his face.

Pushing myself up on the counter, I give him a loud smooch on the cheek.

He turns to Jax next and shakes his hand. "How you doin', Jaxson? I hear you're leaving us to become a SEAL. Aren't you dangerous enough?"

"We all know you're the dangerous one in this town," Jax replies with a smirk.

Antonio proudly puffs out his chest. "You know it, kid. What can I get you two?"

Jaxson glances down at me. "A large cheese pizza, thin crust, to go."

I flash him an appreciative smile for ordering my favorite.

"Grab some drinks and take a seat. It'll be a few minutes."

We both grab a Coke then slide into an empty booth.

"Are you packed and ready for tomorrow?" I ask him, taking a sip of my soda.

"Yeah, mostly. Cooper is going to put the rest of my stuff in storage next week."

A moment of silence ensues, my heart heavy at the thought of him leaving. I'm not ready to lose him. I never will be.

The bell jingles above the door, announcing someone's arrival. Jaxson's gaze moves over my shoulder, and all easiness vanishes, his jaw tightening in anger.

"What is it?" I ask, glancing behind me. My body tenses when I see it's Wyatt Jennings. He looks directly at us, a cocky smirk curling his lips as he starts forward.

Oh shit!

Turning back around, I find Jaxson's eyes cold, fury pouring from him.

"Jaxson," I warn cautiously.

"Well hello, Miss Julia," Wyatt greets me, trying to get under Jaxson's skin.

"Hi, Wyatt," I respond for the sake of pleasantries, but my eyes remain on Jaxson. Wyatt has always been polite to me, so I would never be rude back.

"You look really nice tonight. Where are you headed?"

"None of your fucking business," Jaxson growls.

"I wasn't talking to you. I was asking her." Wyatt places his hand on my shoulder, his fingers caressing my bare skin.

Before I'm able to move away from his touch Jaxson is on his feet, knocking Wyatt's hand off of me. "Don't fucking touch her."

Oh god!

I stand up too, but neither of them notice. They're too busy glaring at each other, looking ready to strike at any given moment.

"I hear you're leaving soon, Reid. It'll be nice to finally get to know Julia. This town will be better off without you, and so will she."

I glare at Wyatt, angry on Jaxson's behalf. Right when I'm about to say something, Jaxson moves me to the side then grabs Wyatt by the shirt, slamming him into the wall.

Oh shit.

"Jaxson, don't!"

"I fucking warned you, Jennings, and I mean it. If you go anywhere near her, I promise you will live to regret it. Are you fucking listening to me?"

Everyone in the restaurant is quiet, watching the scene unfold. When I see someone grab their cellphone, I worry they're about to call the police.

"Jaxson, please. I don't want our night to end because of this. Let's grab our pizza and get out of here." I try to reason with him, not wanting him to spend his last night in jail instead of with me. Wyatt's father is on the city council and is very influential in this town.

Thankfully, Antonio walks out from the back and breaks them up. "Okay, you two, that's enough. Jennings, you got a death wish? Go get a table. Jaxson, let him go, son. Your pizza's ready, take Miss Julia and go wherever y'all are headed for the night."

Jaxson's fists remain curled in Wyatt's shirt, his furious face only a mere inch from his. "I mean it, you stay the fuck away from her." He releases Wyatt with a hard shove before stepping back.

Antonio hands me the pizza and puts his hand on Jaxson's shoulder, trying to calm him further.

"Let's go, Jax," I whisper, tugging on his arm.

His feet stay planted and he looks at Antonio. "How much do I owe you?"

"Nothing, it's on me. Good luck out there, kid, make sure you come back."

"Thanks, Antonio. Sorry about this."

Antonio accepts the apology with a nod then turns his attention to me. "Take care, Miss Julia, I'll see you soon."

Everyone's eyes are on us as we walk out the door. Once we get into my car, Jaxson loses control, his fists pounding on my steering wheel. "Fuck!"

I flinch, not expecting the outburst.

His hard eyes train on me, pinning me in place. "Jules, you have to promise me that you won't go anywhere near that asshole. Not ever."

"What is it with you two? Why do y'all hate each other so much?"

"Just promise me you'll stay away from him. If he gives you any problems you go to Cooper right away, okay?"

I'm a little surprised at how intense he is about this. "I'll be fine. I'm pretty sure he only talks to me now just to get under your skin. He's always been nothing but polite to me."

"That's because he wants in your fucking pants! Christ, Julia, will you just trust me on this? I know shit about him that you don't."

He looks so panicked that I lean over and hug him. "All right, I promise. Don't worry. I'll go to Cooper if I need to, but I'm sure it'll be fine."

He reaches over the console of the car and wraps his arms around me, pulling me to him and hugging me tightly. "I don't know what I'd do if something happened to you," he murmurs.

My heart warms, and throat tightens. I'm curious what he knows about Wyatt that has him so concerned for my safety. "Nothing is going to happen to me. You're the one who's going to be a SEAL, you're in more danger than I am." Sadness washes over me as I'm reminded about him leaving. It's easy to forget when I'm in his arms. "Come on, let's go, and in the future please don't beat my car again."

"Sorry." He smirks, not looking very apologetic.

I'm really going to miss that sexy smirk—I'm going to miss everything about him.

The evening is warm, the cool ocean breeze a welcome relief to my heated skin. We eat mostly in comfortable silence, the crash of the waves washing over me and soothing my nerves as I debate when to pour my heart out. Should I wait until the end of the night or do it soon? But what happens if it doesn't go well? I don't want our night to end too quickly.

I don't want it to end at all.

"When do classes start for you?" Jaxson asks, breaking into my tormented thoughts as he cleans up our garbage from supper.

"In three weeks. I just purchased my textbooks yesterday." I'm attending college in Charleston to get my teaching degree and am really excited about it. "I'm not really looking forward to four more years of school, but I'm hoping the elementary school will have a position for me when I'm done," I tell him.

"You're going to be a good teacher, Jules."

"Thanks," I say softly, giving him a smile. "So tell me what all this training is going to entail for you?"

He cocks a brow, looking at me doubtfully. "You really want to hear about it?"

"Of course I do." Scooting closer to him, I get into our usual position of me wrapping both my arms around his one, and lean back on the log behind us.

"Well BUD/S, which stands for Basic Underwater Demolition/SEAL, is a six month process with different stages. The first eight weeks are the roughest on recruits, both mentally and physically, or so I've heard. The third week being the toughest of all, which is why they call it 'hell week.' They put us through a lot of shit to see how much our mind and body can endure. I've heard a lot of people drop out before the first eight weeks are finished because they can't handle it. But—" His words stop abruptly when he looks down and sees my horrified expression. "Okay, that's enough info for you," he chuckles.

"Why would you put yourself through that? What if something happens to you?"

"Jules, they're not going to kill us. They're just going to make us wish we were dead." He jokes.

"It's not funny," I whisper, my heart heavy with worry.

He drops his arm around my shoulders, pulling me in close. "I'll be fine; I can handle it, Jules. Nothing is going to happen to me, I promise."

I turn my face up to his, our mouths so close that I can feel his breath on my lips. As if sensing my thoughts his eyes drop to my mouth. I think about making my move now, but he looks away, breaking the moment.

Things become kind of awkward, so I decide now is a good time to give him his present.

"I have something for you," I tell him, sitting up to reach for my purse.

"What? Why? I don't need anything," he grumbles.

He doesn't like receiving presents, but I don't care.

"Stop your grumbling, it's nothing big, and it's important to me for you to have this." Pulling out the small velvet black box, I hand it to him.

He eyes it for a long moment, looking uncomfortable.

"Don't worry, it's not an engagement ring," I tease.

Chuckling, he accepts the gift and opens it, revealing the stainless steel chain with the metal pendant.

"It's a medallion of Archangel Michael," I explain. "It's for protection. I had Father Gabriel bless it for you. Promise me you will always wear it, no matter what you're doing or where you are, you'll always have it with you."

He watches me with an emotion I can't decipher, and I start feeling unsure, thinking he might not like it.

"How much was this?" he asks oddly.

"Not much. I already had the pendant, I just bought the chain."

"The pendant was yours?"

I nod, knowing he's not going to like what I say next. "Yeah, my mom gave it to me."

He drops the necklace back in my hand so fast I barely have time to register it. "Fuck that, Julia. I'm not taking something your mom gave to you."

"Stop! It's my pendant, and I will do what I want with it. I know my mom would be okay that I'm giving this to you." I shift now so I'm sitting right in front of him. His ice-blue eyes are burning with frustration, and I'm worried he's not going to accept it. "Please take it, Jax, you need it more than I do. It gives me comfort knowing you'll have it."

"Damn it, Julia," he breathes, resting his forehead on mine.

I place the necklace back in his hand and close his fingers around it. With our faces so close, I know now's my chance. Before I can chicken out, I tentatively brush my lips across his, giving him a gentle kiss. His eyes flare in shock, but he doesn't pull away. Taking this as a good sign, I press my lips against his again, more firmly this time.

"Julia," he growls out the warning. "Ah, fuck it!" Grabbing the back of my head, he crushes his mouth to mine, kissing me with an intensity that steals my breath.

Oh god!

His tongue thrusts past my lips, taking what I so eagerly want to give him. My senses reel, head spinning as I become intoxicated with the taste of him. Gripping my hips, he lifts me to straddle him. My arms wind around his neck, fingers threading through his soft, messy hair as I match him stroke for stroke.

His warm hands glide up my bare thighs, slipping under my skirt to cup my bottom. A low growl rumbles from his chest, vibrating against my lips.

I move against him, feeling like I can't get close enough. That's when he reverses our positions, flipping me to my back, his hard body covering mine. I moan against his lips, feeling how hard he is between my legs. His rough jeans rub against my satin panties, causing the best sensations to ripple through my body. I raise my hips, craving more of him.

"You taste fucking incredible," he mumbles, his lips traveling down the column of my throat, nipping and tasting. I take the opportunity to suck in lungfuls of much needed air as he cherishes the skin he passes.

He slides the straps of my tank top down my shoulders until the lace material is bunched at my waist. His eyes ignite as he stares down at my hot pink, satin bra; his fierce expression robbing me of air.

"Touch me," I plead impatiently. I feel like I've been waiting my whole life for this moment.

"Oh, baby, don't worry, I fucking plan on it."

My stomach tightens at the erotic promise. Sliding his hand up my stomach, he grazes over one breast before flicking the front clasp of my bra. The cups fall open, baring me to his stare, the warm ocean breeze triggering yet another incredible sensation to my already aroused body.

"I knew you'd be beautiful." he murmurs. Leaning down, he closes his hot, wet mouth over my stiff nipple.

I gasp, feeling the delicious pull between my legs. "Jaxson." My back arches, offering him more. His hand cups my other breast, pinching and rolling the tight tip between his fingers. He gives just enough pressure that the pulse between my legs becomes agonizing.

Reaching between us, I start tugging up his shirt. "Please, I want to touch you, too."

He sits up, swiftly pulling the material over his head before taking his place once again. My gasp and his groan mingle in the air between us as his hot skin falls upon mine.

"Jesus, Julia, you have the softest skin I've ever felt."

His back ripples and flexes under my touch as I hold him desperately close; scared if I don't, this won't be real. Moving his hand down between our bodies, he gently runs one finger down the center of my panties.

"So fucking wet." Pulling my panties to the side, he runs his finger through my wet heat and stills. "You're bare?" he says, sounding surprised. "I might actually die from this."

A harsh cry parts my lips as his fingers begin stroking, skillfully massaging the bundle of nerves that ache for attention.

"I can't wait to feel you come," he growls.

"Jaxson." His name falls on a harsh whimper, my impending orgasm inching closer by the second. I wait for the mind numbing pleasure to take me but he moves his finger away, stealing my chance. "No, please don't stop!"

He reassures me by sticking one finger inside then quickly follows with another. I cry out at the beautiful invasion, my legs clamping around his arm, trapping his hand inside of me.

"Easy, baby, let me in. Trust me, I'm going to take care of you." He pushes my legs apart, pumping his fingers in and out of my wet heat. "Fuck. You're so hot, so tight."

His rough voice in my ear adds to the sensations overtaking my body. I grab his wrist, holding his arm in place and ride his skilled fingers, each thrust taking me higher and higher. He changes the position of his hand, his palm exerting the perfect amount of pressure.

"Open your eyes, Julia, I want to see you when you come."

My eyes snap open, his possessive gaze consuming me, stealing my heart a little more.

"Let go, baby, I've got you." Leaning down, he takes my nipple between his teeth, the sharp graze sending me hurtling over the edge of destruction.

Pleasure slams into me, an army of sensations exploding through my body as I soar to a place I've never been before. One so powerful and life changing, I know my heart will never recover from it. Jaxson holds me through it all, his fingers relentless until I'm limp and sated.

I become aware of my surroundings once again, hearing the crash of the waves against the shore as Jaxson's hard warm body keeps me anchored.

Lifting my face from his shoulder, I stare up into his ice blue eyes, my heart pinching at the vulnerability I see there. Before I lose the chance, I reach up, tracing the perfect outline of his lips and reveal the one secret I've been keeping from him. "I love you, Jaxson."

His body tenses above me, horror washing over his expression.

Uh-oh.

Dread twists my stomach into a painful knot, my heart sinking at the quick rejection.

Jaxson remains stock still; it's as if he's frozen in place.

"Say something," I choke out softly.

He pushes off the ground, jumping to his feet, my voice snapping him out of his shock. "Shit, shit, shit. What the fuck am I doing?" he mutters, pacing back and forth like a caged animal.

Feeling cold and exposed, I put my bra and shirt back into place then sit up, hugging my knees to my chest. Once he's done talking to himself, he finally turns to me, his expression full of regret.

Ouch.

"Jules, I'm so fucking sorry, I don't know what the hell I was thinking. I got carried away."

I stare back at him, wondering if he's serious. "That's what you have to say right now? What exactly are you sorry for?"

"What we just did... it shouldn't have happened," he says, shattering my soul into a thousand pieces. "Fuck, I can't believe I did this."

Anger begins to override my hurt, my teeth grinding. "Well, you know what? I think what just happened was pretty amazing, and I'm not sorry. Do you not recall it was me who kissed you first?"

"Listen, our emotions are all over the place right now. I should have stopped—"

"Do you really think I just told you I loved you because my emotions are all over the place? Seriously?"

He drives his hand through his hair in frustration. "I know you care about me but—"

"No, Jaxson, I told you 'I love you', there's a big difference!"

"You don't love me. My leaving is screwing with both our heads."

"Don't you dare tell me what I feel. If you think I said 'I love you' just because you had your fingers inside of me, then you don't know me as well as I thought you did."

"Damn it, Julia. Listen, you may *think* that you love me—"

"Don't fucking patronize me," I scream back, finally reaching my breaking point. Shaking my head, I begin packing up the blanket, realizing this was a huge mistake. "I've been in love with you since I was seventeen years old, but I kept it to myself because I didn't want to mess up our friendship." I turn on him, trying to mask my pain with anger. "Are you really that disgusted with me?"

Fury hardens his expression. "Watch it, Julia, you don't know what the fuck you're talking about."

"Oh really? I don't? Then tell me why you have screwed almost every girl in this town and act like it's no big deal, but then you touch me and you have so much regret and disgust on your face it looks like you're going to be sick."

"I do not feel disgust. You're different than everyone else!"

"Yeah, I finally figured that out." Turning my back, I start to walk away, not wanting him to see the tears building behind my eyes.

"Oh, for fuck's sake! I didn't mean it like that." He charges after me, his fingers gripping my arm as he spins me around to face him. "This is about me, Julia, not you. I'm too fucked-up to love you," he says, his voice completely broken. "Why tell me now, huh? Why would you tell me the night before I have to leave?"

"Because I didn't know if I would ever see you again, and I knew I'd always regret it if something happened to you and you never knew how much I loved you," the last of my words fall on a sob, my heart too broken to hide my pain any longer.

The agony that reflects back at me, has me crying harder. "I'm so sorry, Jul—"

"Whatever, I just want to go home," I cut him off, not wanting to hear his apology anymore. With the blanket tucked under my arm, I head back to my car, hearing his muttered curse as he grabs his shirt and follows me.

The ride home is filled with angry silence. I stare out my window, fear overshadowing all else. I'm worried the damage is irreparable and we won't be able to fix this—that I will lose him forever.

Once we arrive at my house and climb out of the car, he turns to me, handing me my keys. I wait for him to say something, anything to fix this between us.

"Remember, if you need anything, go to Cooper."

I stare back at him, his eyes cold and distant; he's completely closed himself off to me. I can't believe that after everything we've been through together, that's all he's going to say.

It drives the final nail into my heart.

"I don't need a damn babysitter, I can take care of myself. Good-bye, Jaxson." I manage to hold in my sob until I'm safely in my house. As soon as I close the door behind me, I shatter, knowing I just lost the one person who will forever hold my heart.

Jaxson

I watch the one person who means the most to me in the entire fucking world run out of my life, and I don't stop her because I know in the end it's for the best.

Jesus, I can't believe I did this.

I love you, Jaxson.

It's the first time anyone has said those words to me, and it makes my chest hurt so fucking bad that I want to rip my heart out.

I fight the urge to go in after her and tell her how much she means to me because I know in the end it still won't change why we can't be together. I wish things were different, I wish I had different blood running through my veins.

I wish I were good enough.

After looking at the house one last time, I climb on my bike, my throat feeling so tight I can't swallow.

What the fuck is happening to me?

I haven't cried since I was seven years old, and I swore I never would again. But that's what Julia does to me—what she has always done to me—makes me feel shit I thought I was incapable of feeling. And I just fucked it up.

I lost the best thing that's ever happened to me.

Julia

The sound of my phone ringing pulls me from my deep slumber. Moaning, I crack an eye open and squint at the screen to see it's Kayla. *Oh god, what time is it?*

I glance at my bedside clock and see it's 7:40 a.m.

Shit! The ferry leaves in twenty minutes.

Dashing from my bed, I take a quick peek in the mirror and wince at the sight of my red, puffy eyes. Since I don't have time to make myself presentable, I toss my hair up in a messy bun, and throw a cardigan over my black tank and matching yoga shorts. On my way out of my room, I swipe my big sunglasses off my dresser to shield my bloodshot eyes and bound down the stairs.

As I'm putting my flip-flops on, Grams pokes her head out from the kitchen. "Julia, where are you going so early?"

"I don't have time to explain right now, Grams, but I need to see Jaxson before he leaves. I have to make things right." I feel bad running out the door when she calls my name, but time is of the essence right now.

My foot is heavy on the gas pedal as I speed through town, driving as fast as I dare without getting pulled over. I arrive five minutes later at the harbor and almost forget to shut the car door in my haste. There's a small crowd gathered on the dock, waiting to board the ferry. I spot Jaxson quickly, and see he's about to walk on.

"Jaxson!" Yelling his name, I start running faster than I ever thought possible. After the third time of calling out to him, he finally hears me; stopping, he turns around to see me charging at him. He's stunned for only a moment then drops his bag and strides toward me, meeting me halfway.

I throw myself at him, my arms wrapping around his neck and legs around his waist. "I'm so sorry, please forgive me," I cry. "It's okay that you don't love me back. I just need you in my life. Please don't leave hating me." Every word falls on a desperate plea as I try to make things right again.

He puts me down on my feet, cradling my wet cheeks between his hands. My tattered heart squeezes painfully when I see his eyes are brimmed red with unshed tears.

He rests his forehead on mine, giving me the intimacy I always crave to have with him. "I could never hate you, Jules. You mean more to me than anyone else in my life. If I had it in me to love someone, it would be you."

The crack in his voice sends my already emotional heart into a frenzy. I grab him, sobbing hysterically into his chest. "I love you, Jaxson, you will always be my best friend. Promise me you're not going to leave forever."

"I promise." He holds me close until the final boarding call is made. "I better get moving," he says against my hair.

"Okay," I whisper back but contradict my words by hugging him tighter.

Laughter rumbles in his chest, vibrating against my cheek. "Julia, you have to let go of me."

Sighing, I breathe him in one last time before stepping back. I frame his face between my hands and say one more thing before letting him leave. "I'm going to miss you. But I want you to know that when you come back, you will always have someone here waiting for you."

His jaw locks as he keeps his emotions reined in. "I'll miss you too, Jules. I'll text you when I get in, okay?"

I nod, my throat too tight to speak. He presses his kiss to my forehead, lingering longer than usual then picks up his bag, slinging it over his shoulder, and boards the ferry.

My feet remain planted, heart heavy as I watch the boat begin its journey. He turns back to me on the deck, giving me one last wave before walking inside where I can no longer see him.

Feeling lost and alone, I turn to walk back to my car, and find Kayla and Cooper waiting for me at the end of the dock. The sight of them brings me a small measure of peace, it's the familiarity I need right at this moment.

Kayla and I start toward one another, our feet bounding down the wooden dock as we run into each other's arms.

"How did you know I was here?" I ask, swiping at my wet cheeks as I step back.

"When Coop got home this morning there was a hole in the wall. I figured things didn't go well with Jaxson. Since you didn't answer your cell, I called the house and Grams told me. I'm so sorry, Julia, I shouldn't have pushed you into telling him."

I shake my head. "It isn't your fault. It was my decision, and I don't regret it; I'm glad he knows." My gaze moves to the ferry where it sails farther away, taking the one man I love most with it. "I miss him so much already."

She pulls me into her arms again, holding together my broken pieces.

Cooper eventually joins in, wrapping his arms around the both of us. "He'll come back, Julia. Trust me."

I wish I felt as confident as him.

"Come on, I'll take you girls out for breakfast," he says, throwing an arm around each of our shoulders.

I begin walking to what feels like a new life for me, one that doesn't seem whole—one without Jaxson.

7

Giving In To Temptation

Julia

Five Years Later

"**C**an I get you something to drink, miss?"

I glance up at the flight attendant as she puts her hand on my shoulder. She's been very attentive, and I'm sure it's because she can tell I'm a total wreck, even though I've been trying to hide it.

"Vodka on the rocks please," I respond quietly. Right now, any alcohol would be welcome. I need something to calm my rattled nerves.

Her smile is warm as she sets the small bottle and glass with ice on my tray. "Let me know if I can get you anything else."

"Thank you."

With a shaky hand, I pour the bottle into the glass and take a hefty sip, relishing in the burn that coats my throat. My head drops back on the headrest behind me, my eyes closing as I think back to my phone conversation with Kayla that happened less than ten hours ago...

My cell rings as I carry groceries in from my car. Placing the bags down on the table, I pull my phone out of my purse and smile at the picture of Kayla and me on the screen. I answer as I head back outside for the next load. "Hey, can I call you back in a few minutes? I'm just bringing groceries in."

A long moment of silence fills the line before she finally responds. "Julia."

I falter at the sound of tears in her voice. "Kayla? What is it, what's wrong?"

"It's Jaxson, something has happened."

My heart plummets straight to my stomach, my legs giving out beneath me as I drop to my knees. "No!" I whisper brokenly.

"Listen, he's alive, but he's been hurt really bad."

"What's happened? Where is he?"

"I don't know much, and Coop is going to kill me when he finds out I called you. The only reason I know is because I was with him when he got the phone call last night. He must be Jaxson's emergency contact. All Coop knew was that he was on a rescue mission that went bad. He's at a hospital in Germany. It sounds like he is in rough shape."

My world shatters with every devastating word she breathes.

"Cooper left early this morning to go see him. I'm sorry I didn't tell you sooner, but Jaxson wanted this kept from you and I had to make sure Coop was gone before I said anything. I think you have a right to know."

At the moment I can't even be hurt that he tried to keep this from me, all I can comprehend is that I need to go. I need to be with him. "I'm going. I don't care if he wants me there or not."

"I figured you were going to say that," she sighs. "I've already looked at flight options for you, and there's one that leaves in six hours. Do you think you can make that? The next one after that isn't for a few days."

"Yes, book it." I rush back into the house and begin packing.

"I'm doing it as we speak. I'll be there soon to help you pack, then I'll drive you to the airport."

"Thanks, Kayla," I whisper, valuing her loyalty and friendship more than ever. "I'll try to smooth things over with Cooper for you when I get there."

"Don't worry about Coop, I'll deal with him. He's going to be spittin' mad, but he'll forgive me, eventually. You deserve to know."

Damn right I do and if I wasn't so terrified for him I would be angry that he wanted it kept from me. Instead, I plead with God for him to be okay.

I'm pulled back to the present when the elderly gentleman next to me asks a question. "Are you going to Germany for business or pleasure, sugar?" He winks, giving me a flirtatious grin.

I try to return a smile but don't have much luck. "Neither, actually. I'm going to visit a friend who's in the hospital there."

His easy demeanor changes, expression sobering. "A soldier?" he asks, surprising me.

"Close, a Navy SEAL. How did you know?"

"I'm an ex-Marine. I've had to visit a few of my men in Germany a time or two," he tells me, his expression dark. "How bad is he?" He shakes his head before I'm able to respond. "Never mind, that was rude of me to ask."

"No. It's all right. Honestly, I'm really not sure. I haven't spoken to him, he doesn't even know I'm coming."

A low whistles hurdles past his lips as he tries lightening the moment. "If he's a SEAL he must have a pretty big ego." He chuckles, and this time I do smile back.

"Sometimes, but he's a really good guy, the best I've ever known," I answer, swallowing past the ache in my throat.

"It seems that this fellow may be more than a friend?"

"It's complicated."

"Love can be complicated, I agree with that."

Unsure of how to respond, I nod then lay my head back again, remembering Jaxson's graduation. I had found out about it only a few days before from Cooper. He wanted to go, but couldn't leave work. I was hurt that Jaxson never told me about it but there was no way I wasn't going to be there for him. So I had booked a flight to leave that Saturday morning and decided to stay the night in hopes Jaxson would be able to do something after.

It was a night that changed my life forever...

My nerves are a jumbled mess by the time I arrive at the training center. I'm hoping the soft purple maxi dress I'm wearing is appropriate. I have no idea how formal the ceremony is going to be. My fears are laid to rest when I walk in and see everyone else dressed in relatively the same manner.

They are all seated with their cameras, waiting proudly. It makes me sad to think if I hadn't found out about it then no one would have been here for Jaxson.

I choose a spot in the middle. I want him to see me, but not too easily. Cooper promised not to tell him I was coming.

When the graduates finally walk in, my breath locks in my chest at the sight of Jaxson. It has been six long months since I laid eyes on him and he looks incredibly sexy in his formal Navy uniform.

As he takes his seat, I see him laugh at something the guy next to him is saying. It's something that is rare for him to do and I can't stop from smiling with him. He looks so at ease, so... himself. Emotion wells inside of me when I realize this is what he was talking about when he said he didn't fit in back home. The only time I've ever saw him like this was when he's with Cooper or me. But in this moment, among all the other graduates, he looks like he is exactly where he's meant to be.

A senior officer makes his way to the podium and begins his speech. He congratulates the men on their hard work, and the importance of where their lives are headed. The speech is incredibly moving, and it's impossible not to respect all the men who are seated there, waiting to be awarded for their accomplishment.

When he finishes, each of the men are called up one at a time and given a certificate and medal. There are so many cheers and pictures being taken from loved ones that I make sure my camera and lungs are ready for Jaxson. He hasn't looked into the crowd once, thinking no one will be here for him. My heart pinches at the thought.

"Before I call out the next name, I want to give special recognition to this new SEAL," the senior officer says. "He's graduating top of this class, and may be one of the strongest men I've ever had come into this program. His dedication and hard work impressed not only myself, but many other senior officers and fellow SEALs. Every man sitting here has proven himself, but this officer made history by setting record times in his physical training. So with that being said, I'd like you all to congratulate Officer Jaxson Reid."

My jaw hits the floor as the crowd erupts in applause. The other graduates give a standing ovation while I stand there with my mouth hanging open. He told me he was doing well in training but I had no idea he set records. I am so proud of him and make sure I cheer loudly so I am heard over the others... It works.

Jaxson stops mid stride, his gaze whipping to the crowd. He spots me instantly, his ice blue eyes striking my very foundation. Complete and utter shock steals his expression. Time stands still, everyone else falling away in this moment but us.

Tears burn the back of my eyes but I push through them and grace him with a small smile before blowing him a kiss.

It knocks him from his shock. He shakes his head but rewards me with one of his sexy smirks, the same one that always makes my tummy flutter.

I snap a few pictures of him receiving his award, and can see he's uncomfortable with the recognition. It's typical Jaxson.

After the speeches and awards are done, the graduates join their families, hugging and smiling. I wander around looking for Jaxson, having lost sight of him in the crowd. When someone grabs me from behind, I yelp, startled, but relax quickly, recognizing whose hard body I'm up against.

"I guess I'm going to have to kill Cooper," Jaxson murmurs in my ear, his deep voice sending a delicious shiver down my spine. "What are you doing here, Jules?"

I pull myself together and spin around to face him. My heart tumbles as I look up into his ice-blue eyes. "If anyone has a right to be mad, Jaxson, it's me. How could you not tell me about this?"

"Because it's not a big deal and you have a lot going on with school. You just told me you had exams coming up this week. You should focus on that, not this."

It's exactly the answer I expected, but it still doesn't make me happy. "I disagree, I think it's a very big deal. I would have been heartbroken if I missed this. But..." I sigh dramatically. "If you don't want to see me I guess I'll be on my way then."

As I turn away he grabs my arm with a growl. "I never said I wasn't happy to see you, I'm just saying you didn't need to go to the trouble to be here."

I peer up at him, wishing he knew how important he is to me. "It's no trouble, I want to be here. I've really missed you."

"I've missed you too, Jules. So fucking much." He pulls me into his arms and holds me close, giving me the safe haven I've had to live without for over six months.

"I'm really proud of you, Jax," I whisper, my faced buried in his strong chest.

"Thanks." He shifts, uncomfortable with the praise.

Lightening the mood, I step back and grab the lapels of his uniform. "I must say, Officer Reid, you look very handsome in your uniform."

He doesn't smile like I expect him to, instead he stares down at me with his intense steel blue eyes that always take my breath away. "And you are still so fucking beautiful."

My heart skips a beat, his words melting my insides to goo.

Unfortunately, our moment gets interrupted. "Well, well, well, let me guess— Julia, in the flesh. I started to think maybe you weren't real, but looking at you now I can see you're very real."

My attention is drawn to the left where the deep booming voice came from. Two attractive men are walking toward us. The one who spoke has a cocky grin and looks me over with blatant appreciation. The other one is the opposite. He has a hard expression and doesn't look friendly at all.

"Come on, buddy, aren't you going to introduce us?" The cocky one asks as he slings an arm around Jaxson.

Jaxson glares at him but introduces us. "Jules, this nosey, annoying dickhead is Sawyer Evans."

I giggle at the introduction.

"And the less annoying one is Cade Walker, both are my roommates. We were also grouped together as a team during training."

Sawyer reminds me a little of a surfer with his shaggy, dirty blond hair, green eyes, and olive skin. He was the one Jaxson was laughing with when they first walked in. Where Jaxson and Sawyer are long and lean, Cade is a little bigger, more muscular, but they all stand close in height. His hair is a tad shorter than Sawyer's and darker like Jaxson's. He looks partially Hispanic with his warm skin tone and hazel eyes. I can tell he has a past; his eyes have the same haunted look in them as Jaxson's.

"Hi, it's nice to meet you guys." I wave shyly.

Cade nods his greeting, whereas Sawyer grabs my hand and raises it to his mouth "Believe me the pleasure is all mine."

Before he makes contact, Jaxson slaps him upside the head, and rips my hand from his.

"What? I'm just trying to be nice to your Jules."

I quirk a brow at Jaxson. "Your Jules?"

He shakes his head. "Never mind him, he's just being an idiot, as usual."

Sawyer chuckles, not the least bit offended. It's obvious they banter a lot. "All right, I'll knock it off... for now. Are we still hitting O'Rileys tonight to celebrate?"

Jaxson meets my gaze. "How long are you here for?"

"I leave in the morning," I tell him regretfully.

He turns back to Sawyer. "Count me out."

"No, Jax, it's okay. Go ahead and celebrate, you deserve it." Of course I'm only being half truthful. I really want to spend time with him, but I don't want to interrupt his celebration either.

"No, I'm staying with you." His tone brooks no further argument.

"Why don't you bring her along?" Sawyer asks.

"No."

I'm not sure if he doesn't want me there or if he wants to spend time alone. I'm hoping it's the latter.

Sawyer flashes him a cocky smirk. "What's wrong? Worried one of us sexier SEALs are going to steal her away?"

I can't help the small giggle that escapes. I don't know why Sawyer thinks Jaxson feels more for me than a friend. If he only knew the truth... "We can go for a bit if you want. I don't mind," I tell him.

He searches my gaze before finally relenting. "Fine, we'll go for a bit."

Sawyer claps him on the back. "That's what I'm talking about. See you in an hour?"

Jaxson agrees then they walk away, leaving us alone again. "You sure about this, Jules? Because just say the word and we won't go."

"It's fine, really." As long as I am with him, I don't care what we do.

"All right, we'll go for a bit, then we'll catch up, just the two us."

I can't stop the smile that takes over my face and as much as I don't mind hanging out with his friends, I can't wait until we are alone.

We walk into O'Rileys an hour later, an Irish pub that seems to be at capacity. Sawyer waves us over where he sits in the back with a group of other graduates, some who have girls seated on their laps that I assume are their girlfriends.

Jaxson guides me toward the table with his hand on my lower back, the small touch searing the patch of skin beneath my dress.

"Well hi again, Julia!" Sawyer greets me as I take the seat next to him. He moves to sling his arm around my shoulders but Jaxson catches him quick enough and throws it away.

"Knock it off, Evans. I mean it, you're pissing me off."

Most people would be intimidated by Jaxson, but not Sawyer, he only seems amused by it all. If he only knew that Jaxson wasn't jealous, just protective, I'm sure he would stop.

Once I'm settled at the table and introduced to everyone, Jaxson gets up to get us drinks. Most of the girls give me the cold shoulder but I just ignore them and chat with people who aren't rude.

Cade is quiet and stares into his drink, looking like he'd rather be anywhere but here.

"Hi again, Cade," I greet him quietly.

His head jerks up in surprise and it makes me wonder if everyone usually ignores him. The thought hurts my heart.

"Hey, Julia," he responds, his hard expression a little softer.

I smile, appreciating I got words back and not just a nod like last time.

His eyes tighten in confusion, as if assessing me, trying to figure me out.

Jaxson interrupts the exchange when he comes back with our drinks.

Conversation flows steadily as the night wears on. I get to hear a lot about their time in training, which was grueling by the sound of it. But it's also clear that Jaxson has made some very good friends, especially Sawyer and Cade. I am happy for him, really happy, but also a little jealous. Other than Cooper, I'm his best friend and I'm not quite sure where I fit into his life anymore.

When Jaxson gets up to use the bathroom, Sawyer leans over to me. "So, what is it with you two?"

"What do you mean?" I ask.

"I'm trying to figure you guys out. Are you friends or more? I've tried asking Jaxson, but he's tight-lipped when it comes to you."

"There's nothing to figure out, we're just friends. Actually, he's my best friend," I add softly.

"Really? I didn't know best friends carry pictures of each other in their wallets," he says with a smirk.

I rear back. "Jaxson has a picture of me?"

"You didn't know? I thought you gave it to him."

I shake my head.

Now it's Sawyer's turn to be surprised. "Unbelievable." He chuckles.

"Leave her the hell alone!" Cade fires, inserting himself into the conversation.

"What? I'm just asking about the picture. You're my best friend and I don't carry a picture of you."

Before any of us can say more, Jaxson returns, ending the conversation. However, it doesn't stop me from wondering what picture Sawyer is talking about. I'm completely floored to know he has one. It warms me and also eases a little bit of my earlier worry about where I stand with him.

About an hour later Jaxson asks if I am ready to leave. I don't want to sound too eager but I don't hold back either, because the truth is, I need to be with him. Just the two of us.

"Yeah," I respond with a smile.

"What hotel are you staying at?"

"The Delta. It's not far from where the ceremony was."

He nods. "I know which one."

We stand up and are saying our good-byes when a girl comes stumbling toward us, her blood shot eyes on Jaxson only.

I feel him stiffen as she approaches.

"Hi, Jaxson, I didn't know you were going to be here tonight. Lucky me," she croons, her finger running down his arm.

I feel like someone has punched me in the stomach.

"Kat. We were just leaving," he replies stiffly.

She moves her attention to me, her eyes narrowing. "Who's the whore?"

Before I'm able to tell the bitch where to go, Jaxson steps in front of me, getting *in her face. "Back off! You don't know anything about her. You got a problem with me, fine, but you fucking leave her out of it."*

It takes her down a notch. She shifts on her feet and takes a nervous swallow. "I'm sorry, Jax, I've just missed you."

Jax?

No one calls him that but me and it sends my already heated blood rising to a dangerous temperature. I hate that I'm caught up in this embarrassing scene and everyone is staring. But most of all, I'm mad that Jaxson is nothing more than a manwhore.

I decide it's time to leave before the situation gets more out of hand. But first, I turn to the table of guys and offer a quick wave, not wanting to be rude. "Well it's been fun, nice meeting y'all, and good luck with your new career."

I don't wait for their goodbyes before I get the hell out of there.

The moment I step outside into the fresh air, I inhale a deep breath and try to shove aside the angry hurt that is lodged in my throat.

Jaxson races out the door after me but I take off, walking in the opposite direction.

"Julia, wait!"

I ignore him and keep my pace, the fast clicking of my heels matching the angry rhythm of my heartbeat.

"Damn it, Julia. Get your sweet little ass back here."

If he thinks by calling my ass sweet that I'm going to come strolling back, he has another thing comin'.

He catches up to me, spinning me around to face him. "Where the hell are you going?"

"To my hotel!" I yank my arm back and continue on my way.

"You're not even going the right way."

Damn!

Stopping, I turn back around and start in the other direction.

"Why the hell are you mad at me?"

He is so oblivious it makes me want to slap the stupid out of him. Instead, I round on him, my angry eyes colliding with his. "Did you screw her?" The question flies out of my mouth before I'm able to stop it. I put my hand up at his stunned expression. "Never mind, don't answer that. I already know the answer, because you're a stupid manwhore! I'm glad to see how easy it's been for you to start a new life." I know that isn't fair to say, but I can't seem to stop. I'm so angry and hurt.

"What the fuck does that mean?"

"It means that all of you have moved on but me. For the longest time it was always the four of us—Kayla and Cooper, you and me. Kayla still has Cooper. You moved here and made new friends and started a new life so easily. I just had it thrown in my face that what happened between us six months ago means nothing to you. While back home I can't move on because I can't stop thinking about you and missing you. I know it's not your fault that you don't care for me the same way I care for you, but it still hurts damn it!" The last of my words fall on a sob.

"Jesus, Julia." His voice is gruff as he pulls me into his arms. "You're wrong. Yes, I've moved on in some ways, but don't think for one second that I've moved on from you. I think about you every damn day. That night with you on the beach fucking haunts me, and that bitch means nothing to me, just like the rest of them. I know you don't understand that but it's the truth."

"She called you Jax," I whisper.

"What?"

"She called you Jax. Only I call you that." I don't care how dumb it sounds. That is something between the two of us.

"I didn't even notice; she's someone I went home with months ago when I was drunker than shit, and she hasn't left me alone since. You know I don't repeat women. She means absolutely nothing to me, and she now knows to stay the fuck away from me."

"I'm so humiliated," I admit, hating that this is the first impression his friends have of me.

"The only one who should be embarrassed is her, not you, Julia," he says, pulling me into his arms.

It feels so good to be held by him that it is impossible to stay mad. "I'm sorry I called you stupid, Jaxson. You're not stupid; you're the smartest person I know," I apologize. "And I'm sorry I called you a manwhore, even if you are, I shouldn't have said it. I was just jealous."

Chuckling, he rubs his hands up and down my arms in a soothing gesture. "It's okay, Jules. Believe me, you have nothing to be jealous about, no one will ever mean more to me than you."

I wish he meant it the way I want him to, but I know he doesn't.

"I knew you liked me more than Cooper," I tease, hoping to lighten the mood.

He grunts. "Believe me, what I feel for you is completely different than what I feel for Coop." Before I have a chance to think about that, he puts his arm around me and kisses my forehead, just like old times. "Come on, let's get the hell out of here."

We make it back to my hotel fifteen minutes later. I head into the bathroom to freshen up and wash my tear-streaked face. I'm still a little upset about what happened at the bar, but I know I don't have a right to be angry with him. I decide to push it all aside and enjoy the rest of our time together. I'm hoping he will stay the night. I want to spend every second that I can with him.

My heart races at the thought of sleeping in his arms, but I tamp it down.

"Just friends, Julia, just friends," I remind myself. Hopefully one day my heart will believe it, too.

I change into my usual shorts and tank that I sleep in then step out of the bathroom. I switch the main light off but keep the lamp on, leaving the room in a soft glow. My steps falter when I see Jaxson pacing back and forth, looking edgy. "What's the matter?"

His head snaps up and he sucks in a sharp breath at the sight of me. "Why aren't you wearing any clothes?"

I stare back at him like he has two heads. "What are you talking about? These are my pajamas."

His eyes dart around the room warily, looking everywhere but at me. "Maybe we should go downstairs to the lounge to catch up."

"Why?" I ask, wondering what has changed.

He doesn't answer and remains rooted to his spot.

"Jaxson, I'm tired, let's just stay here and relax," I say, crawling on the bed.

His pained groan fills the room.

My head twists in his direction and I find his eyes glued to my ass. His expression is filled with sheer dominance and... restraint.

It's now that I finally realize what has him so uncomfortable. Rather than ignoring it like I've done every other time, I decide to call him out on it, asking the one question that has been burning inside of me since that night on the beach with him six months ago.

"You say that I mean more to you than any other girl, but then why do they get a part of you that I don't?" His eyes finally lift to mine, but before he can say anything, I continue, "It's no secret I'd give myself to you. I've wanted you for so long that some days I worry I'm going to die a virgin because you're the only one I want to be with. It's you who doesn't want me."

"Are you fucking crazy? I want you more than I want my next breath, but I can't do that to you. You ask about those other girls and it's because I don't give a shit about them, but with you, I care. I care too fucking much."

My heart squeezes painfully at his tortured admission. "I'm not better than you, I'm better with you."

I know if anything is ever going to change between us, now is the time to push. By the tormented look in his eyes I can see he wants me as badly as I do him. Who knows when the next time will be that I'll see him?

Gathering up all the courage I can muster, I stand from the bed and start toward him. He glances at the door nervously, as if considering running out. I don't give him the chance. My arms wrap around his waist as I reveal something to him that we both already know. "I want my first time to be with you, and I want it to happen tonight."

His eyes briefly close, jaw locking in restraint. "Julia, don't do this. You don't know what you're asking, and I only have so much control."

"I know exactly what I'm asking. I don't want to be a virgin anymore."

"What's wrong with being a virgin?" he asks gruffly.

I glare at him, irritated that he is denying us what we both want. "Fine." I unwind my arms from his waist, breaking the moment. "I'm not going to beg you. I guess when I get back, I'll just have to find the first willing guy to take me home," I say sweetly, knowing it will get under his skin.

When I head for the bed again he walks up behind me, his hands gripping my hips to yank me back against him.

I suck in a startled breath when I feel how hard he is against my bottom.

One of his arms locks around my chest and the other around my waist, keeping me close. "Be careful, Julia, you're playing with fire. I've tried hard for a long time to do the right thing, but you're about to make me throw it all away." His rough warning has a shiver dancing down my spine.

My breathing speeds up in anticipation for what is about to happen.

I turn back to face him, letting him see my truth. "I want it to be you, not someone else. I know you can't give me forever, but you can give me who I want it to be with."

A battle rages in his eyes, exposing all of his demons he always fights so hard against. I pray I know what I am getting us both into. My hands shake as I grab the hem of my tank top and pull it over my head, dropping it to the floor. His eyes melt into liquid fire as I stand before him in my lilac, lace bra. I fight through the urge to cover myself, ready to finally give myself freely to him, body and soul.

A curse pushes past his lips as he jerks me against him and claims my mouth in a ruthless kiss. The taste of him, mingled with beer, floods my senses and sends *my head reeling. I decide the next time someone asks me what I want to drink it will be a beer, the one I'm getting the luxury to taste now.*

Our kiss is desperate and consumes us from the beginning. I pry my fingers from his belt buckle and slide my hands under the hem of his shirt, gliding them over the smooth, hard plains of his stomach.

A whimper escapes me with the need to feel more of him, to feel his skin upon mine again. He severs our connection only long enough to get rid of his shirt, and the moment the material is shed from his body, I gasp, my heart stopping at the sight before me.

My hand moves to his chest, lifting the St. Michael pendant that is hanging around his neck. "You're wearing it," I whisper.

"I promised you I would."

He did, and I should have known he would never break that promise. Emotion clogs my throat, stopping me from speaking. Leaning in, I press a kiss to the pendant, then another right over his heart, feeling its fast beat against my lips. His breath quickens as my tongue slides along his chest, loving the salty taste of his skin. It's like an aphrodisiac, sparking the fire already burning inside me. When my teeth graze his nipple, he groans, the vibration powerful.

He cups my bottom in his large hands and effortlessly lifts me up. My legs hug his waist and my arms hook around his neck.

"Be sure about this, Julia," he says, his eyes holding mine. "Because once we start I don't think I'll be able to stop. I've been restraining myself for far too long, but I can't anymore. I know I don't deserve you, but the thought of someone else taking this from you makes me fucking insane."

I rest my forehead against his, forcing him to the see the truth. "I've never been more sure about anything in my life. I need it to be you, Jaxson. This is right... we are right."

Without further argument, he carries me over to the bed and lays me down before him. He stands above me, his eyes vulnerable. "I know you deserve all that romantic shit. Like flowers and candles, everything that I don't have right now, but I swear I'll be good to you, Julia. I'll take care of you."

"I don't need any of that stuff. I just need you." I offer him my hand to take, needing his trust in this moment.

He gives it to me and I pull him down, his hard body covering mine as his lips descend upon my skin, kissing the swell of my breasts. My body reacts to his touch like always, and goose bumps break out across my fevered skin.

Sighing, I thread my fingers through his hair, loving the feel of his soft, firm lips. He trails his mouth over my taut nipple and grazes it with his teeth through the lace of my bra.

A heated moan parts my lips and I arch up, begging for more.

His hand comes around my back and unhooks the clasp of my bra. The cups fall away and the way he looks down at my exposed body steals my breath, washing away any insecurity I felt earlier. "You make me feel beautiful when you look at me like this."

"Jesus, Julia, you have no idea," he breathes. "If you only knew how beautiful I think you are, you would never question it again."

A smile steals my lips, but it vanishes the moment he cups my breasts, kneading my soft flesh.

"Your tits are fucking perfect," he growls. "The memory of them torture me when I lie in bed at night, remembering how they filled my hands." He rolls my nipples between his fingers, feeding the hunger that burns within my blood. "And how good they felt against my tongue." He bends down, lashing the fiery tip before his lips close around it.

A harsh whimper spills past me, my body igniting like an inferno.

He slides down my body; trailing wet kisses across my stomach before grabbing the waistband of my shorts. I lift my hips as he pulls them down slowly, leaving me in only my matching lavender, hipster panties.

"I think purple is my new favorite color," he groans, tossing my discarded shorts behind him as he kneels on the floor between my opened legs. His lips place a hot, openmouthed kiss to my quivering stomach, leaving fire in its wake. "You know what my biggest regret is from that night, Julia?"

I tense, hating to hear the word regret from his mouth when it comes to the two of us. But my fear is laid to rest with what he says next.

"I regret not tasting you," he admits, his voice as rough as sandpaper. "I smelled your sweet scent on my fingers that entire night when I got home and hated myself for not taking the chance I had to taste this." His knuckles skim down the center of my wet lace, passing over the spot that has slight tremors traveling through my body. "Are you still bare, baby?"

My cheeks flame with his question, but it also turns me on. I nod; worrying my voice will betray my nervousness.

"I was hoping you were going to say that." He brings his nose against me and inhales a deep breath. "You smell even better than I remember," he growls. His lips brush the inside of my thigh before he slides my panties down, baring every inch of my body for his view.

My legs begin to close on their own accord, but Jaxson grabs my knees, keeping them apart. "Don't hide yourself from me, Julia. You are way too fucking pretty and I want to commit this to memory."

I do what he asks because I, too, never want him to forget a second of this moment.

I never want him to forget me.

Once he gets his fill, he leans in and begins trailing his tongue up the inside of my thigh. Heat licks up my skin as anticipation builds low in my belly, but I'm also nervous. Really nervous. I rise to my elbows and look down at him between my parted legs. "Jax, I'm not so sure about this."

He glances up at me, his lips poised over my most intimate part. "Trust me, you're going to like this, and so am I."

All of my thoughts and hesitations vanish when his tongue glides through my hot flesh.

"Oh!" I fall to my back, my hips involuntarily lifting to his mouth, greedily seeking a pleasure I have never known.

He drops an arm across my lower tummy, holding my hips in place, while his mouth devours me. "Jesus, you taste fucking incredible," he says, his voice husky.

I tangle my hands in his hair, begging for something I don't quite understand. My breath races as one sensation collides with the next. "Jaxson, I think I'm going to come," I whimper.

His groan vibrates against my clit, and sends me careening over the beautiful edge of destruction. Lights explode behind my eyes as sweet ecstasy soars through every nerve ending of my body. My cry of pleasure tears through the room, ricocheting off the walls but I'm too lost to care.

When I finally join reality again, I open my eyes and find Jaxson undoing his belt, muttering something to himself I can't quite catch. Embarrassment starts setting in when I realize how loud I was, my throat raw from the pleasure that ripped from me. "I hope the people next door didn't hear that," I mumble.

His heated gaze snaps to mine. "Christ, Julia, I'm pretty sure the whole fucking hotel heard you."

Covering my face with my hands, I groan from humiliation.

He grabs my wrists, pulling my hands away. "Don't. Don't be embarrassed, not with me. It was so damn hot I almost came in my fucking pants."

I give him an appreciative smile and reach up, tracing his lips with my fingertips. He circles my wrist with his fingers and turns my hand over, his lips brushing a kiss to the palm of my hand. Deep affection is laced amongst the stark hunger in his gaze and it makes me feel cherished.

I spot the condom in his hand and the reality of what we are about to do sets in. I begin to feel unsure. Not from giving myself to him, but of losing him.

Concern darkens his expression as he senses my hesitation. "What's wrong, baby? Did you change your mind?"

I shake my head and swallow past the knot in my throat. "Promise me, that after this, no matter what happens, you'll still be my friend." My voice cracks and I close my eyes, dread curling around my heart at the thought.

"Look at me, Julia."

My eyes snap open at his harsh demand, his fierce gaze pinning me with the truth of the moment.

"I may not be able to give you the forever you deserve, but I fucking promise you, I will never stop being your friend." He seals the promise with a kiss, obliterating my biggest fear. His lips trail across my cheek, stopping at my ear. "Are you ready, baby?"

"Yes," I reply softly but with certainty.

When he stands up I scoot back to the middle of the bed and suck in a startled breath at the sight of him sheathing himself with the condom.

Is that size normal?

I have never really seen one before, but that seems awfully big. I take a hard swallow, an entirely new brand of fear taking over me.

"Seeing your horrified expression while staring at my dick is not good for my ego," he says with a smirk.

My expression does nothing to his ego, he knows exactly what I'm thinking.

"I don't think this is going to work. I don't think you'll fit," I admit, heat invading my cheeks as I speak the words.

He leans over me, bracing himself on his elbows, and I feel his erection on the inside of my thigh. "It'll fit," he says with certainty. "I'll go slow, but you have to know, Julia, it's going to hurt."

I can tell it bothers him to know I will feel pain, and I don't want him to change his mind. With a shaky breath, I nod and give him what I hope is a reassuring smile. Then I hook a hand around his neck, and bring his mouth down on mine.

It's all I need. The last of my worry disappears at the first touch of his perfect lips against mine.

He reaches between us and wraps his hand around his erection, gently pushing the tip of himself inside of me.

I gasp and he groans at the first beautiful moment. Although it is tight and uncomfortable, it's not so bad; I can handle it. But then he pushes in further and the pain steals my breath. I hug him tightly, my face burying in his neck at the snug invasion.

"Breathe, baby, relax a bit, Julia," he gently urges, pushing my knees apart that have a tight grip on his hips.

I shake my head, not knowing what to do. It hurts much more than I thought it would.

"Do you trust me?" he asks, his body tense as he stares down at me.

"Yes." That one word falls from my lips without any hesitation. I trust no one more in the world than him.

"Hold onto me, baby, I'm going to get this over with before it kills us both."

I tighten my arms around his shoulders, and before I can ask what he is going to do, he pushes himself inside me with one fast thrust.

A cry of agony tears through me, a blinding white-hot pain exploding behind my eyes.

Jaxson groans in pleasure but all I feel is pain.

"God, Jaxson," I whisper.

"I'm sorry, baby, so fucking sorry," he chokes out, kissing my shoulder.

The guilt in his voice snaps me out of my pained state. "It's okay." I brush a kiss across his lips and wiggle my hips to reassure him. That's when I feel more discomfort than pain.

"You sure?" he asks through hard breaths.

"Yes, just go slow."

Straightening his arms, he rises above me and begins to rock slowly back and forth. The first few strokes are tender but the more he moves inside me, the better it feels, and I begin feeling a different sensation. I even begin lifting my hips to meet his thrusts.

"That's it, baby. Does it feel better?"

I nod, staring up into his ice-blue eyes that are filled with an emotion I can't quite name. One that makes me feel desired and cherished. "I love feeling you inside of me," I tell him.

His forehead drops on mine. "You feel fucking incredible, Julia, I've never felt anything more perfect than you."

We've always had a strong connection, one I've never shared with anyone else. But now it's so much more—deeper, because right in this moment, we are one. Our bodies were the only way we hadn't connected yet, and now that we have I know he will not only own my heart but also my soul.

"I want more of you," I whisper, wrapping one of my legs around him, bringing him deeper than I thought possible.

"Shit." His jaw flexes as he pushes back up on his arms and begins thrusting a little harder and faster.

My hands roam his hard flesh, anywhere I can reach, loving the way his strong body ripples as he moves inside me. His hand reaches between our sweat-slicked bodies, his finger finding my throbbing clit.

I whimper, my gaze snapping to his in surprise at the pleasure I'm feeling again, especially after the powerful orgasm I'd just had.

"I want you to come again, Julia, I need to feel you come around my cock, baby."

My breath races as his finger strokes faster, his hips pushing deeper, and it isn't long before he sends me once again hurtling over the edge, leading me into divine oblivion.

"Fuck yes, me too," he groans, then stills, spilling himself inside me. I love getting to see this side of him, what he looks like when he lets himself go. His walls are gone, all that is between us is a connection and pleasure that only we can create.

I hold him close as our breaths begin to even out, our hearts beating together as one.

"Thank you," I whisper, my lips brushing his ear, feeling the need to express to him what this just meant to me.

His head lifts, face hovering above mine. My heart pinches at the vulnerable expression on his handsome face. He stares down at me like he is about to say something monumental that will change our lives forever. I foolishly hold my breath waiting for words I long to hear.

"I'm really glad you came today, Jules."

My hope deflates quickly and I give him a simple smile back. It may not have been exactly what I wanted to hear but I know better and I'm not going back on my word to him. He gave me something tonight that I will cherish forever.

After pressing his lips to my forehead, he pulls out of me and I instantly miss the connection. As he makes his way to the bathroom, I pull my panties back on then grab his shirt from the floor, throwing it over my head.

Once the door closes, I bend down and grab his wallet out of his jeans, on a mission to find what Sawyer was talking about earlier tonight. The moment I flip it open, my breath catches. There, staring up at me, is a picture of myself that

I'd never seen before, but I remember the day. I had been waiting for Jaxson at our spot on the beach. My long, cream beach dress rested high on my thighs, my arms wrapped around my knees as the cool water rushed over my feet. My face was turned up to the sky, basking in the warmth of the sun, the long locks of my hair cascading down my back. The way the sun shone down on me gave me an ethereal glow.

I swallow thickly, amazed that the beautiful girl in this picture is me.

"If you needed money, Julia, you should have just asked."

I gasp, Jaxson's voice startling me out of the moment. I was so caught up in the picture that I never heard him come out. He doesn't seem all that mad, just... embarrassed maybe?

"How did you take this?" I ask, lifting the wallet.

He clears his throat. "With my phone."

"I look beautiful," I remark quietly, my eyes moving back to the photo.

"That's how you always look to me."

My gaze drifts back to him, his admission shocking me yet warming me at the same time. "I think you're beautiful," I whisper, my eyes roaming down his half naked body. He really is nothing short of perfection; the man looks like he's been carved from stone. The black ink that is woven up his cut arms only makes him sexier. He looks like heaven and sin wrapped in one package.

He grunts. "I am not beautiful, Julia. Attractive, sexy, good looking. You could even say hot, but not beautiful."

His grumbling has me smiling. Setting his wallet back down, I stand and ever so slowly start toward him. His eyes darken as I close the distance between us, devouring my body that is only covered by his shirt. Lifting to my tiptoes, I hook my arms around his neck. His hands mold to my bottom, pulling me flush against him.

"Mmm, you are sexy," I murmur, burying my nose in his neck to breathe in his delicious scent, "and beautiful." My lips slide up his throat and across his jaw, peppering soft kisses.

Growling, he hoists me up, his fingers digging into my soft flesh. "Keep that shit up, Julia, and I'll forget how sore you are and we'll go for round two," he threatens, walking us back to the bed.

"Promise?"

He swats my butt playfully. "Behave."

A laugh tumbles past my lips as he tosses me on the bed. He follows me down a moment later, stretching out and lying next to me, propped up on his elbow. His eyes hold mine, depicting something I can't quite decipher.

"What is it?" I ask.

"Nothing, I just… I love your laugh and I've really missed hearing it."

His words send my heart into a tailspin. Reaching up, I cup his jaw. "I've really missed you."

He drops a kiss on my forehead but not before I see the longing in his eyes, the same one I harbor deep inside of me.

I hug him close, wishing this night would never end. "Are you going to stay?"

My heart sinks when I feel him stiffen. He pulls back to look down at me. "Do you want me to?"

I contemplate lying to him, saying that I don't care either way. I don't want to sound needy, but I have never been a good liar and for just tonight, I want all of him. No holding back. "Yes. I want to sleep in your arms, all night."

I wait with bated breath as he stares down at me, his blue irises saying everything he would never voice. "Then, I'll stay," he says.

I relax, my imprisoned breath escaping me.

His brows pull into a frown. "What, did you think I would say no?"

"I wasn't sure. I hoped you'd say yes."

"Don't you know by now, Julia, I'd give you anything you wanted if I could?"

I wish I had the courage to confess that all I want is him, completely and in every way, but I'm too afraid after his rejection last time. Instead of saying that, I rise up and brush my lips against his. He reciprocates with another toe curling kiss that takes my breath away.

Eventually, we move beneath the covers and get situated for the night, his arms wrapping tight around me as I lie across his chest.

"I really enjoyed meeting your friends today. Sawyer and Cade both seem nice," I tell him.

"Yeah they're cool but Sawyer needs a good ass-kicking, which he's going to get when I'm back tomorrow."

I smile as I remember how much Sawyer ribbed him earlier, but it fades when I begin thinking about Cade. "What's Cade's story?"

"What do you mean?"

I shrug. "I don't know. He comes off intimidating, but he seems… vulnerable somehow."

He grunts, thinking I'm ridiculous.

"There's a pain in his eyes, Jaxson, the same one I see in yours sometimes. I can tell he has a past and I just wondered what it is."

He's quiet for a moment and I begin to feel bad for asking. Before I can offer *an apology he speaks. "I don't know much. He and Sawyer are best friends; they enlisted together. He had a sister who died when he was younger. I don't know the story. It's something he doesn't talk about. Sawyer says it was really bad and fucked him up good. I don't ask Cade about it because I know what it's like to not want to talk about shit."*

"That's horrible," I whisper, my heart breaking to hear that. "I feel bad for him. It seems like he's in the background a lot, and I'm sure it gets lonely."

"He's not lonely, Jules, trust me. He likes being on his own, and the three of us hang out on our free time."

I don't respond, because I disagree. Who would like being alone all of the time?

"I can tell he likes you too," he says, "and that's saying something because he doesn't like anybody."

I smile, glad to hear I make the exception. Contentment settles over me as I listen to Jaxson's steady heartbeat beneath my cheek while his fingers drag across my lower back. Being with him like this feels so... right. It's the most peace I've felt since my mother passed away, and I wish we could stay like this forever.

His hand stills a few minutes later, his breathing slow and even. I lift my cheek to look at him and see he's sound asleep. He looks so peaceful, something that is rare to see. I press a gentle kiss on his mouth, then whisper the words I didn't dare say when he was awake. "I love you."

My head rests back down on his chest, and as I drift off, a dream hits me fast, one where I swear he whispers the same words back to me.

I startle awake when the pilot announces our descent and realize I must have dozed off while thinking back to Jaxson's graduation. It had been the best night of my life. It was also the last time I saw Jaxson. We kept in touch with emails and phone calls but neither of us could get away to see each other. He was sent out on missions shortly after, and it seemed he's stayed gone since. Sometimes I think he's avoided me because, obviously, our relationship changed that night, no matter how much we hoped it wouldn't.

He calls me at least once or twice a month, and I send him packages of baked goods, which he says Sawyer and Cade also enjoy.

I smile, thinking how crazy it is, the three of them getting to be a part of the same SEAL team. Then my heart pinches, wondering if they're the other two who were with him. I feel like it's a safe bet to assume they were.

Please, God, let them all be okay.

As I'm walking off the plane, the elderly gentleman who was sitting next to me stops me with a hand on my shoulder. "Good luck with your friend, miss."

I offer him a smile. "Thank you."

After retrieving my luggage, I hail a taxi and direct the driver to take me straight to the hospital. I'm too anxious to wait any longer to see Jaxson; I need to know he's all right.

My stomach is one giant knot as I walk into the hospital and ask for Jaxson. I'm grateful to discover the nurses speak English.

"I'll have to check if he can have visitors. There are restrictions on his room. Please have a seat in the waiting area, miss…?"

"Julia. Julia Sinclair."

Nodding, she walks off.

I head into the waiting room and take a seat, my knee bouncing as I wait anxiously for her to come back. She doesn't. Instead, I'm met by an enraged Cooper, his long legs striding toward me. "I'm going to fucking kill my girlfriend!"

Anger begins overriding my fear. Standing, I advance on him, meeting him halfway. "I don't think so, Cooper," I seethe, poking my finger in his chest. "How dare you keep this from me, how dare both of you keep this from me!"

Toe to toe, we glare at each other but amongst the anger reflecting back at me, is fear and it has me taking a step back. With a shaky breath, I ask the question that's been haunting me since Kayla's phone call.

"Is he okay?" A terrified sob tumbles past my lips before I can stop it.

Cooper releases a heavy breath of his own, pinching the bridge of his nose, something he often does when he's stressed. "He's going to be okay, over time. He's really fucked up, Julia, you shouldn't have come."

"He's my best friend. How can you say that to me?"

He shakes his head. "Please don't make this harder than it has to be."

"How am I making it harder by wanting to be here for him?"

"Because he doesn't want you here."

I flinch, feeling like I've been slapped.

"Christ! He doesn't want you to see him like this. He needs time."

My temper flares, and I stand toe to toe with him again. I try to look intimidating, but that's pretty hard to do with someone the size of Coop. "You listen here, Cooper McKay, I'm seeing him one way or another, even if I have to physically go through you. So you tell him I'm here and that I'm not leaving until I see him."

He shakes his head again.

"Fine, have it your way." I storm past him but don't make it far before he grabs me from behind, his arms banding around my body so I can't get free. "Hey, what the hell do you think you're doing?"

The nurse behind the desk watches us anxiously as he carries me away, heading toward a side exit.

"Let go of me, Cooper, or I swear I'll scream," I warn, struggling to get free.

He grunts, unconcerned, and it only pisses me off further.

Panic grips me when he blows through the large double doors that lead outside, taking me farther away from Jaxson. Since reasoning hasn't worked with him, I turn my head and bite his shoulder.

"Ow, fuck!" He places me on my feet and grabs my shoulders, giving me a shake. "Goddamn it, Julia, listen to me! He knows you're here, and he's refusing to see you. No matter how hard you fight you're not going to see him. I'm sorry." The fierce determination in his eyes has fear slamming into my chest like a sledge hammer.

"Please, I've come all this way, Cooper, I need to see him," I plead, trying to hold onto my fragile composure as tears stream down my cheeks. "You of all people, know how much he means to me. Please don't do this."

A curse flees from him and he pulls me into his arms, holding me tight. "I'm sorry, but I respect his decision."

Stepping back, I look up to see his eyes dark with regret. "You tell him if he doesn't allow me to see him then he can forget about ever speaking to me again," I say, meaning it.

"Don't be foolish."

"Me be foolish! Are you kidding me?" I shriek. "I'm sick of this macho bullshit. I've gone through a lot to be here, and I haven't seen him in five fucking years, Cooper! I'm serious; if he sends me away after everything we've been through, then... I'm done."

"This isn't about macho bullshit!"

"The hell it isn't, you're allowed to see him."

"It's for the best, Julia, I know you don't understand that right now, but it is."

I stare back at him, unable to believe that Jaxson would do this to me. My heart has been split in two, and I know I can't do this anymore, I just can't. The realization that our friendship is over has a sob shattering my chest.

"Goddamn Kayla," he snaps furiously.

"No! Goddamn you! And goddamn Jaxson! Kayla's my only true friend."

I don't bother sticking around any longer, knowing it's useless. I storm off, ignoring Cooper when he tries calling me back and leave behind every beautiful memory I ever had with Jaxson.

Jaxson

At the sound of my door opening, I look over and brace myself, praying it isn't Julia. My body relaxes when I see it's only Coop.

"Well, that sucked."

"How bad was it?" I croak, pain slicing through me with just those few words.

The remorse in his eyes, says it all. "Pretty bad. Are you sure about this?"

My eyes narrow at the question. "Would you let Kayla see you like this?"

He shakes his head, his hard expression easing. "No, you're right. I just feel like shit, you didn't see her when she left."

"I'll make it up to her."

"I hope you do, man, because as mad as I am at my girlfriend right now, I know she's going to be way more pissed at me when Julia tells her I sent her away."

I'm pissed at myself but I can't let her see me like this. It will ruin what's left of me.

"I will, I just don't know when. After here, they're sending us to a rehabilitation clinic to make sure our heads get back on straight."

I'm dreading that the most. The last thing I want is some doctor trying to get into my fucking mind and push feelings out of me.

"I'm warning you now, Jaxson, it's not going to be easy. Not this time."

"I know." Julia is the most forgiving person I know, but I realize I'm going to have to work hard to make her understand.

Another wave of nausea suddenly hits me. Leaning over, I throw up into the small pan next to me, agony ripping through my broken body as I shake violently.

"I wish you wouldn't refuse the drugs," Cooper says, taking the bowl from me.

"Nothing else is getting pumped into my fucking body. Not ever again,"

He looks like he's about to argue, but thankfully he's smart enough to back off. "All right, I'll forget it. Do you want me to get you anything before I make my phone call to Kayla? It's going to be ugly, so it may take a while."

"No, but thanks, man… for everything."

He nods, heading toward the door. "By the way, I saw Sawyer not long ago. He told me to tell you that you're a pussy." It's obvious he enjoys delivering the message by the stupid grin on his face.

"I guess that means he's doing all right?"

He shrugs. "He looks like you. Both he and Cade are refusing the drugs, too."

"I figured they would." I take a deep breath before asking about the other person, "How about Anna?"

He clears his throat, his expression sobering at the thought of the battered fourteen year old girl. "They just reached her parents, and they're trying to get here as soon as they can. The nurse says she's been asking for you though; said she's scared and wants to stay close to you."

I have no idea why she would want to. It's not like I made it in time.

Guilt threatens to choke me at the thought. "Tell them she can see me if she needs to."

He nods then heads out the door.

Lying back, I close my eyes and think about Julia. For the last week, it was the memories I have of her that kept me alive. Every time one of those assholes came in to torture us, I would retreat into my mind and think about her. I'd think about our nights together on the beach. I'd remember the way her eyes lit up when she smiled, and the peace I always felt from just being around her. And most of all, I'd remember the sound of her laugh. I'd let the beautiful melody wash over me as I felt every lash that tore down on my skin.

There were times I thought I'd never see her again, and that was when I decided if I ever got out of there alive, I wouldn't stay away. Not anymore. I stayed away as long as I did because after knowing what it felt like to be inside of her, I couldn't trust myself not to do it again. It's going to be hell on my control, but I need her in my life. I've seen so much bad shit over the last few years; I need her to remind me of the good again.

Some Things Are Worth Fighting For

Jaxson

1 Year Later

I pull up to the small, southern-style house and look down at the address Cooper gave me, making sure that I'm at the right place. It's something I should know, but in all fairness, she moved here not that long ago and I've been away from civilization for a good long while. Something that I'm happy to be a part of again.

As I climb out of the truck, I take in my surroundings. It's a nice place, even with needing some fixing up, but I hate how secluded she is. Even though it's only a few minutes from town, her closest neighbor is a mile down the road. With so many trees you can't even see the house. If she were ever in trouble, no one would hear her call for help.

Don't go there, man, you have enough shit to worry about when it comes to her.

Shaking my head, I walk up the front porch and knock, my fist heavy on the door.

"Come in!"

My muscles tense and eyes narrow. *She has no idea who's here and she just yells at them to come in?*

Feeling pissed now, I let myself in and hear Julia moving around upstairs.

"I'm sorry, I must have gotten the time wrong. I thought you said seven. Go on into the kitchen and grab yourself something to drink. I just need a few minutes, I'll be right down."

Hearing the sound of her voice, after being gone so long, stirs up

emotions I haven't felt in a really long time. It's obvious she's expecting someone. I check the time and see it's just after six. I have less than an hour to
plead my case.

Walking straight ahead, I find the kitchen and see cookies on the counter.
They're still on the baking sheet, warm from the oven. Snatching one, I pop
the whole thing in my mouth and groan at how good it is.

Damn, Margaret taught her well.

Taking one more, I sit down at the kitchen table and wonder if it's Kayla
she's expecting. I'm about to shoot Coop a text when I hear Julia's soft steps
coming down the stairs. I take a deep breath and stand, bracing myself for
the shit-storm that's about to hit.

Julia

I can't believe I got the time wrong, I could have sworn he said seven.
Thankfully I started getting ready early. My steps are slow and cautious as
I descend the stairs, holding the massive vase of flowers he sent me earlier.
I'm hoping the outfit I have on is dressy enough. I figured the soft yellow,
strapless sundress would be perfect for the hot, humid night, but I guess it's
depending where he takes me.

Smiling, I round the bottom of the stairs and head into the kitchen.
"Thanks so much for the flowers, you—" I come to an abrupt halt, my breath
locking in my throat as I stare at the person leaning against my counter.

"Hey, Jules." Jaxson greets me with his arms crossed, looking arrogantly
determined. His eyes sweep down the length of me, lingering over certain
parts as I stare back dumbstruck.

"Jaxson?" I whisper, wondering if I'm hallucinating. The vase slips from
my shaking hands and shatters all over the floor by my feet, but I remain frozen, shock rooting me to my spot.

"Don't move," he orders and maneuvers around my kitchen, searching
my cabinets for something.

"What are you doing here?" I ask numbly, stepping toward him.

He moves quickly, picking me up around my waist. "Damn it! I said
don't move."

My arms hook around his neck as I look down to see glass crunching under his boots.

"Where's your broom?" he asks, setting me on the counter. When I don't answer, he grabs my bare calf and lifts my foot to examine it. "Are you okay? Did you step in any?"

My attention anchors on his hand, the warmth of his warm touch beginning to invade my shock.

Why is he here? Why now?

"Julia! Will you fucking answer me? Are you hurt?"

I shake my head and open my mouth to say something but then close it, not knowing where to start. So many emotions suffocate me right now. Relief, sadness, but most of all, anger as the painful memory from a year ago comes rushing back with a vengeance.

Clearing my throat, I try again, this time getting words out. "What are you doing here?"

"I came to see you."

I stare back into his ice-blue eyes, the same ones I haven't seen for six long years, and try to gauge any emotion from him. There's something in his gaze that wasn't there before, something harder. But I don't see anything else—no remorse, no apology, nothing.

Feeling irritated, I push him out of my space and hop off the counter, grabbing the broom from the pantry.

As I start sweeping up the glass, he crowds my back, his hand gripping the handle. "I'll do it."

Not letting go, I yank it back in my direction. "No! I'll do it!"

His eyes narrow but he backs off.

I redirect my attention to sweeping again. "Did Cooper not give you my message a year ago?" I ask, bending down to brush the glass into the dustpan.

"Yeah, he did," the reply flows easily past his lips, obviously not caring.

I brush past him to dump the glass in the trash and notice cookies missing off the baking sheet. It takes my annoyance up another level. Turning, I glare at him. "If you think I wasn't serious, Jaxson, then you're very mistaken."

"Come on, Julia," he says, as if I'm being irrational.

"No, you *come on*! How dare you think after what happened a year ago that you can waltz right into my house like nothing is wrong and eat *my cookies*." I point at the baking sheet, noting the two that are missing. "These are for someone else, not you!"

"I didn't just waltz into your house, you fucking invited me in, not even knowing who was at your door. What the hell is wrong with you? I could have been anyone."

"Obviously I thought you were someone else. Believe me, Jaxson, if I had known it was you, I wouldn't have invited you in." I toss him an extra hard glare, hoping to hide the lie.

"I don't give a shit if you were expecting someone or not, don't ever do that again," he commands, pointing his finger at me.

Oh the nerve! I slap his hand away but really want to slap the arrogance right off his sexy face. "Just who the hell do you think you are? You have no say in how I answer my door. You have no say in anything I do in my life. Not anymore. So you can take your self-righteous ass and get out of my house."

I brush past him to show him to the door but he grabs my arm and pulls me back, his hard face only inches from mine. "I don't think so, baby. We have unfinished business, and you're not going anywhere until you hear me out." His words are filled with determination, and I hate it when I catch myself drawn to his full lips.

I take a step back, not trusting myself to be this close to him. "Fine, you want to talk, let's talk. Let's talk about the fact that before Germany I hadn't seen you in five years. Five fucking years, Jaxson! I received short phone calls, but that's it. Then I spend almost all of my savings to come see you, and you refuse me. I went through a lot to be there for you, it's not like you were just in the next state!"

His angry expression softens. "I'll pay you back for—"

"This isn't about money," I scream, finding it harder by the second to hold on to my control. Taking a deep breath, I say the one thing that hurts most. "When I got that phone call from Kayla, telling me you were hurt, my whole world stopped because nothing mattered to me more than you. Even after you stayed away from me for so long, you still mattered to me. Do you have any idea what it felt like when you had Cooper get rid of me? It was a shitty way to find out I didn't mean anything to you anymore." My voice catches, but I will myself not to cry. I swore a year ago I would never shed another tear over him again.

"Julia." His voice is gruff as he starts toward me.

I hold up my hand, warding him off. If I let him touch me I'll give in, and I can't. Not this time. Not anymore. "Are you even sorry at all? Do you regret it?" I ask, fearing for his answer.

He drives a frustrated hand through his hair, my heart pinching at his tortured expression.

Stay strong, Julia.

"I'm sorry I hurt you, Jules, more than you will ever know. But I don't regret my decision to send you away."

I guess I'm not surprised, but it still hurts. My eyes fall to the floor, needing to focus anywhere else but him. "Then we have nothing more to say to each other."

"Goddamn it! Would you try to understand? I didn't want anyone to see me like that."

"Even me?" I yell back.

"Especially you! How can you not fucking understand that?"

Silence fills the air as we glare back at each other, hurt and anger swirling between us. Before either of us can say more, my front door swings opens.

"Julia, where are you?" Kayla yells, her voice panicked.

"In the kitchen," I call out, my eyes remaining on Jaxson.

"You are never going to believe who's ba—" She stops short, her gaze moving between Jaxson and me. "Uh, never mind, I guess you know."

I nod, appreciating she had my back once again.

"Everything okay in here, Jules?" she asks, her eyes narrowing on Jaxson.

He flicks her an annoyed glance. "Everything's fine, *Kayla.*"

"I wasn't asking you, I was asking Julia," she bites out.

Kayla can be pretty intimidating when she wants to be. Of course not to Jaxson, but I don't think anyone intimidates him.

"I'm okay," I reply softly, appreciating her concern.

"Are you sure? Because I'll fuck him up if you need me to," she offers, completely serious.

Jaxson grunts at this like it's ridiculous.

"What, you don't think I can? I'll have you know, Coop's been showing me some stuff. So I'd watch yourself, buddy."

My teeth sink into my lower lip as I suppress a smile. "Really, Kayla, everything is okay, but you'll be the first to know if I change my mind."

She finally swings her attention back to me, her eyes taking me in from head to toe. "Looking good, my friend. You ready for your hot date?"

My heart lodges in my throat, knowing exactly what she's trying to pull. I flick a nervous glance at Jaxson, his blue irises locked on me.

If he finds out who I'm going out with tonight, things are going to get way uglier than they are now.

"I will be once I'm left alone," I say quietly, hating to be rude but I need Jaxson out of here... now.

Thankfully, Kayla gets the hint and isn't the least bit offended. "Of course, I'm out of here." She pulls me in for a quick hug. "Don't come home early, if you know what I mean."

I bury my groan, not appreciating her not so subtle comments.

I'm rewarded with a wink before she drags her gaze over to Jaxson, flashing him a smug smile. "See you around, Jaxson."

He doesn't acknowledge her, his hard eyes remaining on me.

Her proud chuckle drifts through the air as she leaves the kitchen. The moment my front door closes, the silence becomes deafening.

Great, this is awkward.

"So that's who you thought I was, your date?" Jaxson asks easily, his tone a contradiction to his hard expression.

I nod. "He's going to be here soon, so you should go." Guilt settles over me, my heart squeezing painfully as soon as the words leave my mouth.

Stay strong, Julia, you have nothing to feel guilty about.

"We aren't done talking yet."

"There's nothing left to say, Jaxson."

"Bullshit! There's still a lot to say."

Great. It's obvious he's not going to leave easily. My eyes shift to the clock, seeing I only have five minutes. I have to get him out of here before Wyatt shows up.

"Who's your date? Is it someone I know?" he asks, suspicion coating his tone.

"What do you care?"

He shrugs. "I'm just curious."

"Are you shocked, Jaxson, that someone may actually want to date me?" As horrible as it is, I'm hoping the comment will piss him off enough to make him leave.

Of course I should have known better.

"Watch it, Julia, you don't want to play this game with me."

Glaring back at him, I give in. "Not that it's any of your business, but yes, you know who he is."

"Who is it?"

"I just said it's none of your damn business," I snap.

"Fine. Then I'll stay and see for myself."

"Oh no you won't, you're leaving right now." I grab his arm with the intention of dragging his butt to the door but he doesn't budge, no matter how hard I pull.

Ugh!

I stomp my foot childishly, then feel embarrassed.

A smirk plays at the corner of his ridiculously sexy mouth, knowing he has the upper hand. "Just tell me who it is and I'll leave," he says.

"You promise?"

His nod is halfhearted but I don't feel like I have much choice, it's my only hope.

Sighing, I take a step back, putting some distance between us. Really quietly, I mumble the name.

"What?"

I repeat the name again but still not loud enough, the power of my voice stuck in my throat.

"Speak up, I can't hear you."

"Wyatt." This time it's loud and clear.

He stares back at me with a calmness that scares the hell out of me. "That's not funny, Julia."

I swallow nervously. "I'm not kidding."

Before I can anticipate his move, he yanks me against him, his grip on my arm tight but not painful. My heart thumps wildly, echoing in my ears. His expression is filled with a rage I've never seen before, and I've seen him pretty damn mad.

"You fucking promised me. You promised me you would stay the hell away from him! What are you thinking?"

I rip my arm back, my own anger sparking again. "And I kept that promise. For five years he asked me out, and I always declined because of you... for you. But that promise went out the window a year ago when you threw me away."

I don't share with him that this is only the third and final date. The more time I spend with Wyatt, the more I realize I just don't have those kind of feelings for him. But I wanted to try one more time, just to see if there's something, anything, I can build on. He's asked me out for so long I feel bad.

"Jesus, Julia, I didn't throw you away. I'm sorry I hurt you, but don't do this, don't do this because you're mad at me."

"This has nothing to do with you, this has to do with me. I don't want to be alone for the rest of my life." I snap my mouth shut, regretting the words as soon as they're out.

"I'm not telling you to be alone for the rest of your life. I'm telling you to stay the hell away from him. He's dangerous. I thought you understood that."

"Listen, Jaxson, I don't know what went down with you guys all those years ago, but whatever you think of him, you're wrong."

"Have you fucked him?"

I flinch, his question a slap in the face. "None of your business," I seethe. "Actually, none of this is your business. I don't owe you any explanations."

He takes a menacing step forward, stealing my personal space. My back kisses the fridge as I retreat with nowhere else to go. His arms plant on either side of my head, caging me in. My traitorous heart skips a beat at his close proximity, the heat of his body warming me from the inside out. "You are my business and you always will be. Whether you like it or not."

I shake my head sadly. "Not anymore, Jaxson."

The sound of a car pulling up cuts through the silence.

Shit!

"Julia, you here?" Wyatt bellows, walking into my house without knocking.

Jaxson tenses over me, his hard body coiled tight. There's so much rage in his eyes that I consider calling Cooper before he can kill Wyatt.

"Please don't," I plead with a whisper.

"Julia!" Wyatt calls again, impatiently.

"I'm coming." I duck under Jaxson's arm and walk out to greet him.

"There you are, what's going on? Whose truck is that out front?" His eyes move over my shoulder, shock resonating on his face before fury quickly follows, and I know Jaxson has come out behind me. "What the fuck are you doing here?" His angry gaze swings back to me. "What the hell is going on, Julia?"

Before I can explain, Jaxson starts for him, each step calculating. "I should be asking you that question, Jennings. You don't listen very well. You must not value your life."

Oh god!

I step in front of Jaxson, my shaking hands pressing on his chest to keep him back.

"She's no longer your concern, Reid, she's mine now."

Wyatt's arrogant reply ticks me off. "Both of you stop, right now! Or I'll call Cooper and have him throw you both in jail. And, for the record, I am no one's concern but my own."

Wyatt grabs my arm, tugging me to stand beside him.

"Let go of her." Jaxson's voice is dangerously low.

I pull out of Wyatt's grasp to reassure him that I'm fine and insert myself between them. "Wyatt, please wait for me in the car, before this gets out of control. I'll be right out."

"I'm not leaving you alone with him."

"We both know I'm not the one she needs to fear," Jaxson says, his jaw tight.

"Wyatt, please, I'm asking you to do the right thing. Jaxson would never hurt me. I swear I'll be right out."

Thankfully he leaves but he's not happy about it. The door slams behind him, the crack echoing in my house.

My eyes fall closed and I place a shaky hand to my stomach, feeling sick with anxiety.

"Don't do this, Julia. Stay, let me explain." There's so much anguish and panic in those few words, it cracks my heart another fraction.

"I'm sorry, I'm not doing this to hurt you," I whisper, trying to hold back my sob. "Please, if you leave now I promise we will talk, all right? This is all so much for me right now. I need some time, Jaxson. I'm begging you, please don't cause a scene."

He invades my personal space once again, and surprises me by framing my face between his hands; his gentle touch a contradiction to the fury in his eyes. Leaning down, he presses a familiar kiss on my forehead. One that I feel through my whole body.

My breath catches and I close my eyes again, before he can see the tears.

"This isn't over. I'm not giving up." Without another word, he releases me and walks out.

My feet remain planted as I hear the door open behind me, my skin still warm from his lips.

I'm yanked from the beautiful feeling at the sound of Jaxson's angry voice. "I'm nowhere near done with you, Jennings. If you hurt her in any way tonight I will fucking kill you."

I hurry outside to find Jaxson climbing into his truck. He guns the gas, speeding out of my driveway, purposely spitting rocks at Wyatt's BMW.

"That son of a bitch!" Wyatt bellows, checking his car.

I get the familiar urge to stick up for Jaxson but I tamp it down. I've had enough arguing for one day.

Sighing tiredly, I lock up my house then meet Wyatt at his car. The last thing I want to do right now is go out but I continue to put one foot in front of the other, feeling Wyatt's angry eyes on me as I climb in. I flinch at the slam of his door.

"What was he doing here, Julia? I thought you guys weren't friends anymore," he questions, his tone accusing.

"I was just as surprised to see him as you were. I didn't know he was in town. I haven't spoken to him in a year."

"What did he want?"

"He said he wanted to talk about what happened between us, said he wanted to explain himself." I shrug tiredly. "We didn't talk much before you showed up."

Wyatt knows Jaxson turned me away when I went to see him in Germany but nothing else. It's not my place to say what happened. *I* don't even know the extent of what happened.

"I'm telling you now, Julia, I won't put up with it. If you're with me, then you won't be seeing him."

My eyes snap to his, anger beginning to override my exhaustion. "Don't, Wyatt. Don't make me choose, because if you do, it won't be you. I don't know what's going to happen with Jaxson, but no one tells me who I can be friends with."

There's a wild anger in his eyes that has a shiver of apprehension creeping up my spine. I've never seen him like this before. It's then that Jaxson's words invade me.

He's dangerous. I thought you understood that.

"Look, maybe this is a mistake," I say nervously, my hand reaching for the handle of the car. "Maybe we should do this another time."

He grabs my wrist, stopping me before I can open the door. "No, wait. Listen, I'm sorry. He just really gets under my skin. You know we have a past, but you're right, I shouldn't tell you who you can be friends with. I'll leave that up to you to decide. I just hope for your sake that you're smart about it. It's only a matter of time before he leaves again."

I'm well aware of that. I didn't need the sting of his words to remind me.

He takes my hand, his touch gentle. "Let's not let this ruin our night, okay? Let me take you for a drink. It will get your mind off your troubles."

I want to say no. All I feel like doing is going to bed and crying myself to sleep. However, in the end, I agree because I know deep down it will be the last one and I need to tell him that... later. "Yeah, okay," I respond, offering him a small smile.

I really do feel bad that I don't have feelings for him. He's attractive, charming and has a good career as a lawyer. It has always surprised me that he's wasted so much time asking me out when he could have his pick of women.

"Great." Lifting my hand to his mouth, he presses a soft kiss to my skin.

I wait for that spark. The one that I feel through my whole body, the one I get when...

Don't go there, Julia.

Damn, who am I kidding? I'm so screwed.

9

Jaxson

My truck roars through town, my muscles wound tight with a dangerous rage. I expected a lot of shit, but not this. What the hell is she thinking?

I don't want to be alone for the rest of my life.

Her painful admission causes my chest to tighten. I need to stop this before something happens to her; she doesn't know what she's getting herself into. The thought of that bastard putting his hands on her makes me sick to my stomach.

I come to a hard stop on Cooper's driveway and barely have my truck shut off before I'm running up his front steps. My fist pounds on the door, and I decide if it doesn't open in the next few seconds I'm going to kick it in.

"What the hell!" he bellows, flinging his door open.

I grab him by the shirt, catching him off guard, and throw him into the wall. "Why didn't you tell me?"

He shoves me back. "Get the fuck off me, man. What the hell is wrong with you?"

With anger hot in my veins, I spring for him. He meets me halfway, our bodies colliding hard as we land of the floor.

Chaos erupts around us, the sound of glass shattering filling the air.

"What are you two idiots doing? Stop!" Kayla yells, panic thick in her voice but it does nothing to break through our rage. We continue to roll around, trying to pin one another, our fists powering out.

"How could you let her date that piece of shit?" I grind out.

"What the hell are you talking about?"

I still, and it's a mistake because I get a powerful fist in the jaw.

Shit!

When I don't strike back he stops too. Eventually, we both sit up, our chests heaving as we catch our breaths.

Cooper's furious eyes narrow on me. "What the fuck is wrong with you, man?"

"She just left with Jennings," I reply, feeling sick.

"Who?"

"Julia!" It's obvious he has no clue what I'm talking about but I find myself asking anyway. "You didn't know?"

"No, damn it! I would have fucking told you if I did."

Guilt grips my chest for what an asshole I was. "I'm sorry, I thought you knew."

Both of our eyes shift to Kayla where she stands looking nervous as hell.

"Why didn't you tell me?" Cooper asks.

Her shoulders straighten and chin lifts, as if she's ready to take us both on. "Because it's none of your business. It's especially not his," she snaps, pointing her finger at me.

Pushing to my feet, I try to make her understand. "She isn't safe, Kayla, she's in danger with him."

"Just because you don't like him doesn't make him dangerous."

Cooper stands too and advances on her. "That's not what this is about. Jaxson and I know shit about him that you girls don't."

"Tell me where they went," I demand, not wanting to waste another precious second.

Her fiery eyes snap back to me. "As if I'm going to tell you. You think you can just roll back into town and dictate who she can date after what you did to her. Just who the hell do you think you are, Jaxson? If you're so worried about her then where the hell have you been for the last six years?"

I know I deserve the wrath but the first person to get an explanation from me will be Julia, not her.

"Easy, Kayla, you don't know the whole story," Cooper cuts in, defending me. It makes me feel like shit even more for what I just did to him. I should have known he had no idea. He's always had my back, no questions asked.

"I know enough. I was the one there for her when she cried her eyes out, because he fucked her then never saw her again."

I tense, the truth of her words slicing my chest deep.

"What? You think I didn't know?" she asks.

I guess I shouldn't be surprised. Girls talk about shit like that.

"I've made mistakes, Kayla, and I'm going to make it up to her, I swear. But you have to listen to me; Jennings is not right in the head. I'm serious when I say she's in danger."

She begins looking unsure but she's still too pissed to let it go. "What kind of danger are we talking about here? Danger as in having her heart broken? Because that's no different than what you've done to her."

"No, damn it!" I fire back, sick of the back and forth with her. "I'm talking about physical danger. Coop and I have seen the bruises he's left on girls. If you want to protect her, like you say you do, then you will stop picking a fight with me and tell me right now where the fuck they went!"

Her eyes flare, both in disbelief and fear. "He's never laid a hand on her, I'm sure of it. Julia would never allow someone to do that to her."

"How long has she been seeing him?" Cooper asks.

Fear clenches my gut as I wait for her answer.

"This is only their third date."

"Then it's probably because he hasn't gotten the chance yet."

Because they haven't slept together yet—thank christ for that.

"It's still three dates too many," I say, cutting back in. "We're wasting time, tell me where they went."

"Hold on, don't answer that yet," Cooper says, his eyes tracking back to me. "What are you going to do, Jaxson? I don't like this any more than you do, but you causing a scene isn't going to help. It's going to piss Julia off more and force me to arrest you. As pissed as I am for what you just pulled, I really don't want to have to do that."

"I'm just going to keep an eye on her. You can't expect me to sit here and do nothing, Cooper, we both know what he's capable of."

Silence consumes the room but his eyes say it all. He knows I'm right.

"Where did they go, baby?" he asks, his attention back on Kayla.

She sighs, finally relenting. "The Oceanfront Tavern."

Her words have barely registered by the time my feet are moving for the door.

"Hold up." Cooper grabs my arms. "I'll come with you."

"Me, too," Kayla pipes in.

Coop turns on her. "No, you stay here."

"No way. Julia's going to know I told you where she is. If shit goes down I need to be there for her," she says, grabbing her purse.

"Damn it, Kayla."

"Save it, Cooper, I'm going. So either I drive with you or I drive myself." Swiping her purse off the chair, she pushes out the screen door and turns back to us impatiently. "Are you two coming or not?"

I offer Cooper a sympathetic shrug then get my ass in gear, meeting her on the steps.

"The woman doesn't listen to shit." His grumble reaches my ears as he follows out after me.

10

Julia

I put my empty glass of beer down on the table and find myself feeling a little more relaxed. The Oceanfront Tavern is one of my favorite places to come in the summer. There are candle-lit ceramic tables scattered across the beach, tiki torches lit at dusk, and soft background music. It all comes together for a relaxing ambience. Tonight is quieter than usual, which I'm thankful for. I'm not in the mood for a big crowd.

"Another one?" Wyatt asks hopefully.

I really want to say no. I'm trying to be good company, but my thoughts are consumed with Jaxson. Over the last year I've worked hard at trying not to think about him. I went from thinking about him every second of the day to only once or twice in a twenty-four hour span.

Wyatt and I have only been here for thirty minutes, and I don't want to be rude so I relent with a nod. "Sure, maybe one more."

I'm hoping he catches on to the *one more* part.

He lifts my empty glass at the waitress, letting her know to bring another. "I have to say, Julia, I was surprised to find out you're a beer girl." There's nothing rude about his comment, but something about the way he says it seems like he disapproves.

If he only knew why I like it. It's a taste I acquired after that night six years ago. One I can't will myself to forget.

"Have you heard back about your interview yet?" he asks, stopping my traitorous thoughts before they can go any further.

"Not yet, but I'm hoping soon. Otherwise, I'll have to look into a different school. Which wouldn't be so bad, I just have my hopes set on Foothills.

I really enjoyed doing my practicum there, and I want to teach elementary level."

"I'll get my dad to talk to the principal for you," he says, tipping his glass of whisky to his lips.

"Oh no. That's not necessary, but thank you."

"Why not? He's in a position of power, Julia, let him use it."

I completely disagree with that statement, but I tread carefully, not wanting to offend him. "No, really, Wyatt, it's important to me that I get it on my own. I want them to hire me because they want me there, not because of your father."

"Fine, suit yourself." He shrugs easily, but his tone says something different.

I shift in my seat, feeling uncomfortable now and decide to change the subject to something I know he enjoys talking about. "So how has work been going for you?"

"Great! I just landed a big client from Charleston. There were three of us fighting for this company, and I received the call yesterday that I got it. I'm getting quite the reputation already," he says proudly.

He only recently started up his own private practice specializing in corporate law.

"That's great. Congratulations." I'm about to ask another question but the words get stuck in my throat when my gaze lands on the three people walking in: Jaxson, Cooper, and Kayla.

What the hell?

Noticing where my attention is drawn, Wyatt turns around. "You've got to be fucking kidding me."

Kayla shoots me an apologetic look as they take a seat at the bar. Jaxson sits with his back to it, his gaze burning into the side of my face. When our eyes meet, my heart skips a beat. I hate that after all this time he can still make me feel this way.

"You told him we were coming here?" Wyatt asks accusingly, breaking our exchange.

"No, I didn't."

Jaxson's and Wyatt's eyes meet next, glare to glare. You can feel the hatred roll off them in waves.

Dread grips my chest at the thought of what could happen if we don't leave. "Maybe we should go."

"Fuck that, we aren't going anywhere," Wyatt snaps. "If that asshole wants to watch, then let him. He's going to have to get used to it anyway."

His last remark has my stomach sinking further. I have to be upfront with him tonight. I feel awful, but I don't want to lead him on. He already thinks this is more serious than it is.

Kayla gets up from her chair and motions for me to follow her. "I'll be right back. I need to use the ladies' room."

He nods distractedly, his fingers typing furiously as he texts someone on his phone.

Standing, I trail behind Kayla, following her into the bathroom. Once the door closes behind us she turns to me, regret heavy in her eyes. "I'm so sorry, Julia."

"What's going on?" I ask, knowing something had to have happened. Not much can make her squeal, she's a tough one to crack.

"Listen, Jules, Jaxson went ape shit, like I mean crazy. He and Coop got into a fist fight over this."

Guilt plagues me, hating that I'm the cause of it.

"He demanded to know where you guys went. Of course I gave him a piece of my mind and told him to go to hell. But... both he and Coop say you're in danger. I know they've said it before, but this time was different." She pauses, preparing me for what she says next. "They told me that Wyatt physically abuses the girls he's with."

"What?" I shriek, thinking I misheard her.

"I know, I told them that he's never laid a hand on you, but they're both swearing it's only a matter of time. Please don't be mad at me, I didn't know what to do. I was worried about you."

My expression softens. "I'm not mad. I just don't know what to think. Wyatt has never attempted such a thing. It has to be a misunderstanding," I say, desperately wanting to believe that. He's always been fairly calm around me, besides tonight that is. But still, I can't see him physically hurting a woman.

"I don't know, Jules, if this was just Jaxson then maybe. But we both know Cooper is pretty reasonable most of the time. I don't know why they never told us before. Even now it seems like they're holding something back."

"Well, you guys don't need to worry about me because this is going to be the last date for us. I really tried to have feelings for him, Kayla, but they just aren't there," I admit, guilt building inside of me once again.

"Don't feel bad, you can't change what you feel for someone."

Isn't that the truth.

"Anyway, Cooper and I are here to make sure Jaxson doesn't cause trouble. He promised he wouldn't."

"Yeah right, him just being here causes trouble." I sigh tiredly. "I'm going to get Wyatt to take me home after our drink. The sooner the better."

"I'm really sorry again, Jules," she whispers.

I pull her in for a long hug. "Don't be, I understand. I would have done the same thing for you." I offer her an easy smile, showing her I mean it.

"Good. Now let's get back out there before all hell breaks loose." She opens the door, gesturing for me to go first.

As we head to our separate tables, I feel Jaxson's eyes on me the entire time, beckoning me to look but I choose to ignore it. If I don't, I will find myself in even more trouble tonight.

"Everything all right?" Wyatt asks as I take my seat. I don't miss the annoyed glance he tosses Kayla's way.

I nod. "Yes, everything is fine. Unfortunately, Kayla just got bullied into telling them where we went." Which isn't a lie… it's just not the whole truth.

"It's none of their fucking business." His angry words make me tense. Reaching across the table, he grabs my hand, lacing our fingers together. "I'm sorry, I shouldn't have said that. Can we just ignore him? I don't want this to ruin our night."

Flashing him an easy smile, I remove my hand and grab my beer. "Yes, of course."

I suck back big gulps, wanting desperately to finish it and get the hell out of here. Disappointment crushes me when I notice Wyatt's glass is still half full.

"Another?" he asks as I place down my empty glass.

"No, I better not. I'm getting up early to go visit Grams at the senior home tomorrow morning. They're having a pancake breakfast to celebrate her birthday."

It's actually more of a brunch so it's not that early, but he doesn't need to know that.

"How old is Margaret turning?"

"Seventy," I reply with a proud smile. One would never guess her age; she looks at least ten years younger.

Wyatt doesn't offer anything more. His eyes shift around the restaurant, as if he's searching for someone.

"Everything okay, Wyatt?"

My question startles him out of his distraction. "Yes, sorry... so I have some big news to share. My dad has decided to run for mayor," he tells me.

Mr. Jennings running for mayor scares me, especially after Wyatt's earlier comment about his position of power. But I keep that to myself and fake a smile. I'm getting good at those tonight. "That's great. Are you going to help with his campaign?"

"Of course."

As he shares with me what their plans are, something pulls my attention over to the others. My stomach tightens when I see none other than Melissa Carmichael rubbing herself against Jaxson like a dog in heat.

This night just keeps getting better and better.

The black cocktail dress she wears is a few sizes too small and her heels are so high she can barely stand in them. Melissa used to be very pretty in high school, but the last few years have not been kind to her. She's Jaxson's age, so two years older than me, but she looks ten years older. I've heard rumors that she has a drug problem, and the way she's gone downhill, it wouldn't surprise me.

I watch on with jealousy as she whispers suggestively in Jaxson's ear, something I have no business feeling. His disinterest should make me feel better, but it doesn't.

"Go figure, those two are made for each other," Wyatt grunts, annoying me with his comment.

I tear my eyes away, not wanting to witness him go home with her if that's what he chooses to do. Just the thought of them together makes me sick. However, my attention is reverted back to them when Melissa's whiny voice rises above the restaurant's noise. "Come on, Jaxson. Don't you remember how good we used to be?"

He shrugs her off his shoulder. "Give it a rest. I mean it. Go home and sleep it off."

"Come with me and I'll show you what you've been missing."

I roll my eyes at her arrogance; someone needs to put her in her place. The two beers I just had are making me think I should be that person.

Leave it alone, Julia, this isn't your problem.

"I'm serious, Melissa, leave. You're only embarrassing yourself."

His rejection infuriates her. She steps back, her arms crossing over her chest as she cocks a hip. "Heard you couldn't cut it in the Navy, Jaxson. I guess you're not as tough as you thought."

A gasp shoves past my lips, her hurtful comment striking my heart as if it was directed toward me.

That's it! This bitch is going down.

I push to my feet, determination burning in my veins.

"What the hell are you doing, Julia? Stay out of it!" Wyatt hisses furiously.

Ignoring him, I march over to them, inserting myself in front of Jaxson protectively. "Back off! He said he's not interested, so stop trying to whore yourself out and take a hint." My voice is low, not wanting to draw more attention to the situation.

Her dazed eyes narrow into angry slits and I notice there's a wet, white substance on the bottom of her nose, confirming the rumors I've heard. "Mind your own business, bitch." She shoves me hard, knocking me back into Jaxson.

So much for not drawing attention.

Jaxson rights me quickly, his hands holding my shoulders as he pushes to stand behind me. "Watch it, Melissa. Don't put your fucking hands on her again," his warning is calm but no less intimidating.

"Of course. We wouldn't want anything to happen to your *precious Jules*, would we now?" she spits, her glare shifting from Jaxson back to me. "Do you really think you're any different to him than the rest of us?" She leans in close, her smile taunting. "After we were done fucking, we used to laugh at how pathetic you were. Why do you think he left in the first place? He couldn't wait to get rid of you."

Before I can even register her hurtful words, Jaxson reaches over my shoulder and grabs her wrist. "You're a fucking liar and she knows it. We had one night together, one that I regret. Don't make it out to be more than what it was. Now get the fuck out of here before you're thrown out."

She yanks her arm back. "I think you forget where you come from, Jaxson. You think just because you joined the Navy you're a better person? You're still nothing but trash, you always have been and always will be."

My fists clench at my sides as I take a forceful step toward her. "The only trash here is you, so do everyone a favor and go back to whatever street corner you came from tonight. And while you're at it, wipe your nose." I pick up the napkin next to me and throw it at her.

Kayla coughs, trying to muffle her laugh.

Melissa touches the skin beneath her nose and realizes what's there.

Instead of being embarrassed, like most people would, she turns into more of a bitch. There's so much hatred in her expression that it causes a shiver to run down my spine.

I know things are about to get much worse.

"You think you're better than everyone else. You've fooled many with your innocent little act, but I've always known better. You're nothing more than a whore, just like your dead mother was."

I hear Kayla's gasp behind me, penetrating the blood rushing in my ears.

The comment is almost enough to bring me to my knees, a white hot pain striking my chest before a deep seated anger overrides it.

My fist pulls back then shoots forward like a sling shot, all of my fury in its power as I hit her square in the face. A sickening crack fills the air as her head snaps back. Gasps of alarm fill the air as blood sprays from her nose, pooling between her fingers where she cups it.

It's not enough.

I launch for her, fists swinging, but before I am able to make contact, Jaxson catches me midair. I fight against his hold, her comment still ripping apart my heart. "How dare you bring my mother into this, you bitch!" I cry, hating the tears streaming down my face.

She doesn't deserve them.

"I hate you!" she screams back. "Why does it always have to be you?" Her words make no sense but before she can spew more hateful garbage Wyatt grabs her arm and hauls her out of the restaurant.

Jaxson carries me to the opposite side of the parking lot from where she is. My kicking body ready to take another round out of her. "Easy, Julia, she's not worth it. Let it go, baby," he soothes in my ear.

"I can't believe she said that about my mother," I sob, pain replacing my anger once again.

"She knew it would hurt you. Don't let her win."

I close my eyes and breathe through the hurt trying to suffocate me. She does not deserve my pain and I know this, but it's hard. I've never hit anyone before but there are some boundaries you never cross and family is one of them.

Jaxson turns me to face him. His fingers curl under my chin as he tilts my head up, forcing my watery eyes to his. "When the hell did you turn into Mike Tyson?"

Laughter spills past my lips, lightening my heavy heart. "She deserved it," I tell him, my amusement vanishing when I think about her comment.

He nods, his own smile fading. "Yeah, she did."

Our eyes hold their connection, the last six years dancing between us for a fraction of a second before he pulls me into his arms. I return his embrace, breathing in his familiar scent that used to bring me so much comfort. *It still does.*

My arms hug him tight while I forget about our problems—just for a little while.

"You didn't have to come to my defense, Jules," he whispers against my hair.

"Yes, I did, she was way out of line. And it's not like you can hit her. Besides, I had two drinks, so I felt like it was my place," I admit, mumbling the words into his chest.

He chuckles as his hands continue to rub soothing circles on my back. It's exactly what I need for the moment.

"What the hell are you doing? Get your fucking hands off of her!" Wyatt's rage breaks up our moment.

I twist to the side, panic thrumming through my veins. "Wyatt, calm down."

Jaxson pushes me behind him and starts forward, heading straight for Wyatt. Thankfully, Cooper and Kayla come running over at that moment.

"Easy, Jaxson," Coop warns, standing between them with his hand on Jaxson's chest.

Kayla throws her arms around me. "Are you all right, Jules?"

"I'm fine." I hug her back, wondering where they've been this whole time. I imagine Cooper was trying to calm down some furious managers.

"I can't believe what that bitch said," Kayla seethes. "If you hadn't broken her nose, I sure the hell was going to."

I have no doubt that she would have, and she would've done much more damage than me.

"Let's go, Julia, we're leaving right now," Wyatt bellows the order at me.

Jaxson reaches over Cooper and shoves him. "Watch your tone, asshole!"

"It's okay, Jaxson," I say, wrapping my arms around myself to ward off the sudden chill. One that took over me when he stepped away. "I want to go home now anyway."

I move to walk around him but his large frame intercepts me. "You don't have to leave with him. Come home with us instead."

A part of me wants to do just that, especially with Wyatt being so angry. But I've already made myself too vulnerable with Jaxson, and I need to end whatever it is Wyatt thinks we have.

"I need to go with Wyatt, I'm sorry. We'll talk later though, I promise."

Kayla's hand grasps my shoulder, her eyes darting to Wyatt nervously. "Julia, are you sure?"

"I'll be fine," I reassure her, offering a weak smile.

I don't miss Wyatt's smug smirk at Jaxson as we start for his car. Once I'm seated in the passenger seat, I can't help but glance at Jaxson as we pull away, guilt crawling up my throat at the helpless expression on his face.

"What the hell were you thinking getting involved with that shit?" Wyatt snaps, yanking me from my torment. "You completely embarrassed me. I have an image to uphold, especially for my father."

I gape at him, complete and utter shock rolling through me. "I can't believe you're mad at me for standing up for myself. Did you not hear what she said about my mother?"

"She wouldn't have said anything if you would have minded your own damn business."

"I was standing up for my friend. She needed to be put in her place."

"Right. The same friend who threw you away a year ago."

My teeth grind in regret, hating that I shared anything with him when it came to Jaxson and me.

"You know, Melissa didn't say anything to him that was untrue. Jaxson is a fucking loser. I don't know why you can't see that."

"He is not a loser! Don't talk about him like that," I yell, tears beginning to burn the back of my eyes.

His hands grip the steering wheel, knuckles turning white as he shoots me a furious look, one that has fear leaping into my throat.

I sit back in my seat and remain silent the rest of the way, my fingers gripping the handle of the door. It isn't long before we arrive at my house. The moment the car rolls to a stop, I jump out, thankful to be away from him. Unfortunately, he gets out, too.

"What are you doing?" I ask, stepping further away as he rounds the vehicle.

"I'm coming in, we aren't done talking."

"I have nothing more to say to you. I don't want to see you again, Wyatt, so stay the hell away from me!" I turn my back on him to flee into my house but he grabs my arm in a painful grip and spins me back around to face him. Terror seizes my chest at the thunderous expression on his face.

I lick my lips, trying to remain calm. "Wyatt, let go of my arm."

My body shoots forward as he jerks me against him. "You aren't going to fucking do this to me. I've been patient for years while you have been nothing more than a cocktease. I'm not letting you go just because that asshole is back in town."

"This has nothing to do with Jaxson."

"Don't fucking lie to me," he bellows. "It has everything to do with him."

I shake my head, panic robbing me of breath. "No, it doesn't, I swear I was going to tell you tonight after our date. I don't have the same feelings for you that you do for me."

"You're wrong and I'm going to show you how good we can be together." His eyes drop to my mouth, filling my body with revulsion.

"No! Stop. I mean it. Let go of me!"

The squeal of tires suddenly fill the night, bright headlights blinding my eyes. As I pull harder to free myself, Wyatt releases me at the same time and it sends me flying backward. I land hard, the impact knocking the breath from my lungs as I slide across the gravel. My head smacks into a large rock and I fist my hair as agony pounds in my ears.

11

Jaxson

A white-hot fury pumps through my body when I see Julia hit the ground. I jump out of the truck before Cooper even comes to a stop. "I'm going to rip you apart, asshole. You're fucking dead!" My body slams into his at full speed, my fists striking out hard and fast.

"Enough, Jaxson!" Cooper reaches for me but I don't slow my blows. "Damn it! I said enough." He finally gets a good grip and rips me back.

"Julia, you're bleeding." Kayla's terrified voice penetrates my rage.

Looking over, I find her down on her knees next to Julia, trying to help her sit up. My boots slip as I kick off the gravel and rush over, dropping down next to her. "Let me see, baby." I tilt her face up to mine, fear burning in my gut at the sight of blood trickling from the corner of her forehead.

Kayla hands me the scarf from around her neck and I use it to compress the large gash.

"I'm okay," her assurance is weak and eyes disorientated.

"I want him arrested, McKay. I'm pressing charges," Wyatt yells as he stands, spitting blood from his mouth.

"No, don't," Julia cries, the sound making her flinch in pain.

"Shh, it's going to be okay." I scoop her up into my arms and head for the truck. "Let's move, Coop, she needs to see a doctor now." My swift feet falter and I spare a furious glance at Wyatt. "You *will* pay for this!"

"It was an accident. Julia, you know I would never hurt you, right? I love you."

What the fuck did he just say?

He starts forward, his eyes locked on her.

The guy has more balls than I thought.

Cooper stops him before he can come any closer. "Go home, Jennings. I'll pay you a visit later," he orders and ushers a crying Kayla into the truck ahead of him.

Climbing in the backseat, I hold Julia between my legs and cradle her head to my chest, making sure to keep pressure on the scarf.

"I'm so sorry, I should have listened to you," she whispers, her dazed eyes filled with regret.

Unable to find words at the moment, I lean down and carefully press a kiss to her forehead. Panic infiltrates my chest when her eyes begin to flutter close. "Hey, Jules, don't fall asleep. I need you to stay awake, okay? Come on, look at me."

"I'm so tired," she mumbles, her voice heavy.

"I know, baby, but not yet, you can sleep after the doctor sees you." I can tell she's trying but I'm not sure she's going to be able to hold off much longer. "Hurry up, Coop, what the fuck is taking so long?"

"We've only been driving for two minutes. We're almost there."

It takes less than that before we pull up to the entrance of the emergency room. Kayla swings open the door for me and I waste no time. The moment I breach the sliding glass doors a nurse spots me and hurries over with a bed. "What happened?"

"She fell and hit her head," Kayla explains as I reluctantly lay Julia down. My boots hit the hard floor as I follow the wheeling bed down the hall.

"Is she allergic to anything? Any medications?"

Is she? She never used to be... I don't think. Damn it! I should know this.

"No," Kayla answers again.

"Can you hear me, miss? What's your name?"

The loud questions have Julia moaning in pain.

"Jesus, lady, do you need to fucking yell like that, she has a headache."

"Easy, Jaxson, she's just trying to do her job," Cooper cuts in.

"Well she can do it quieter."

Once we reach the room, the nurse tries to prevent me from entering. "Sir, you can't come in, you have to wait out here."

"I don't think so, lady. I go where she goes."

"Sir, I'm sorry—"

"Please let him stay with me," Julia softly pleads, grabbing my hand.

My eyes narrow on the nurse, daring her to say no.

"All right, fine. But you better watch yourself or you're out," she warns, pointing her finger at me. "Sheriff, I want you in here in case I need him removed."

"I'll wait for you guys out here," Kayla whispers, tears staining her cheeks. "Just come tell me right away when I can see her."

Coop pulls her in for a kiss. "She's going to be okay, baby. Why don't you grab us some coffee from the cafeteria? Hopefully by the time you're back we'll have some answers."

I miss the rest of the conversation since I follow close behind the nurse, Julia still gripping my hand. She opens her eyes a little more when the lights are dimmed, the room falling to a soft glow.

"That better?" she asks softly.

Well at least she's stopped fucking yelling for the time being.

"Yes, a little. Thank you."

"On a scale from one to ten, what's your pain?"

"About an eight."

"Are you hurt anywhere else?"

"My ribs," she replies, pointing to her left side.

Shit, I didn't even think to check her for other injuries.

The nurse grabs a sheet to cover Julia's lower half, then lifts her dress, exposing her beautiful, toned stomach. A sharp inhale moves swiftly into my lungs at the sight of her ribs. They're already turning blue, road rash evident from her hip all the way up to where her bra is.

"Wow, what did you fall on, dear?"

"My driveway, well I more slid, I guess," she explains, her eyes drifting to mine anxiously.

I sit in the chair by her bed and bring her hand to my mouth, trying to control the violence threatening to consume me.

"The doctor will be here any minute. In the meantime, I'll go get you something for the pain."

Once the nurse leaves, Julia brings her attention back to me. "How did you know to come?"

"Kayla told me you were ending it with him. I knew it wouldn't go over well."

"I've made a mess of everything. I'm so sorry," she apologizes, touching my mouth that's cut from when Cooper and I got into it earlier.

I shake my head. "It's not your fault."

A knock on the door interrupts our conversation and in comes the doctor, one who looks really young.

"Hi, Julia." He greets her with a familiar smile.

"Hi, Dr. Carson."

"Call me Blake, remember?" he says, flashing her a wink.

Who the fuck is this asshole?

He glances down at Julia's hips where the sheet isn't covering. I rip it up, shielding half of her stomach and cast him a warning glare.

He loses some of his confidence. "And you are?"

"A friend," I tell him, my voice tight.

His eyes dart away nervously and back to Julia. "Nurse Debbie says you had quite the fall." He removes the scarf from her head. "This is going to need a few stitches."

He begins asking her simple questions, like her age and name. I decide if the prick asks for her phone number I'm going to lay him out.

Thankfully, he doesn't.

Next, he shines a light in her eyes, checking for a concussion, then starts probing around the cut with his fingers, making her gasp in pain.

"Watch it, asshole," I snap.

"Jesus, Jaxson, lay off. He's trying to help her," Cooper steps in.

Knowing he's right, I back off… slightly.

The nurse brings Julia the pain medication then the doctor starts on her stitches. She remains still and doesn't seem to be in much pain. Thankfully he finishes quickly.

"Well, Julia, you're all finished," he announces, stepping back. "Now you do have a minor concussion, so we have two options. Either you can stay here for the night, as you will need to be woken up every two hours, or if you have someone at home who can do this, then I can let you leave with them. I will also give you something for the pain to take with you. You'll probably need it for a day or two."

"I'll be taking care of her," I tell him before she has a chance to answer. No way is she staying here with the good doctor. Besides, she will rest better in her own bed.

"No. It's fine, Jaxson, I'll stay here. No need to keep you or anyone else up all night."

"Don't argue. I said I'd do it."

"Fine," she relents on a tired sigh.

The doctor turns to address me. "As I said, it's important to wake her every two hours. Ask her simple questions, like her name or her age. The drugs could make her drowsy and a little disoriented, so expect that. But she should be able to answer the easy questions. If she seems worse, bring her in, otherwise I expect a full recovery."

"Thank you, Blake," Julia whispers, making me tense at the use of his first name.

"No problem-o." He winks again at her.

What a jackass.

Noticing my look of disapproval, he clears his throat. "Nurse Debbie will bandage your ribs and show you how to care for the dressing. Take care, Miss Julia."

Once he's gone I look down at Julia, brushing aside a piece of her chestnut hair. "How are you feeling?"

"The pain has lessened. I'm just really tired," she admits. "Where's Kayla?"

"I'll get her now," Cooper answers, heading for the door.

The nurse enters as he leaves. "All right, dear. I'm going to put some ointment on your ribs and bandage you up. Keep this up for a couple of days; it will prevent infection. Cover it with saran wrap when you shower, okay? You will probably need some help with it."

"I'll help her," I assure her.

I watch and listen carefully to her instructions right up until she finishes.

"Okay, all set, you can leave when you're ready. Take your time."

"Thank you," Julia's voice is soft, her eyes heavy with exhaustion.

Kayla pushes through the door with Coop following close behind her, her eyes bloodshot from crying. "I'm so glad you're okay," she says, gently hugging Julia.

Cooper interrupts their exchange. "I need to know what happened tonight, Julia."

"Not now," I tell him firmly. "She's too tired. We can talk about it tomorrow."

He drives a frustrated hand through his hair. "Fine, but we can't leave it past then. I have a feeling I'll be having that dickhead's father on my ass, so I need to know details."

I can only imagine the shit he puts up with as the sheriff when dealing with arrogant pricks like the Jennings.

"Come on, Jules, let's get out of here," Kayla says, helping her out of bed.

"Whoa." Julia grabs on to her unsteadily as she loses her balance.

Bypassing Kayla, I scoop her up into my arms.

"I can walk, Jaxson, I just need a minute."

I ignore her protest and continue out of the room. By the time we reach the truck she's sound asleep. In the ten minutes it takes us to arrive at her house, I hold her close, my eyes drawn to her peaceful expression. My chest tightens when I realize just how much I've missed her.

Kayla and Cooper help me get into her house. "Her room is at the top of the stairs to the right," Kayla instructs quietly.

Nodding my thanks, I look to Cooper next. "I'll call you tomorrow when she wakes up."

"I'll be waiting."

I begin my climb up the long staircase when Kayla starts in on me again. "No funny business, Jaxson, or I will kick your ass."

My response is a grunt. Whatever Cooper has been showing her, he needs to tone it down. That's the second time she has threatened to cause me physical harm.

I enter into Julia's dark room, leaving the lights off for her benefit then lay her down on the bed. It isn't long before I'm left wondering what to do about her dress.

Shit!

I charge out of the room and down the stairs, hoping Kayla and Coop haven't left. The moment I burst through the front door, I catch the taillights on Coop's truck as they drive away.

Damn it!

I head back into Julia's room and stare down at her with indecision.

Just don't think about it and do it.

Turning her so she's lying on her uninjured side, I unzip her dress then roll her onto her back again. As I slide the soft material down her body, she moans. "Mmmm, Jaxson."

Every muscle in my body hardens. Looking closer, I see she's still sound asleep. With a heavy breath, I try to control the need pounding through my veins and continue my task, as fast as possible. Once her dress is all the way off I can't help but torture myself more, my eyes sweeping down the length of her beautiful body. One I remember so well.

I could never forget.

Her bra and panties match the dress she was wearing, the pale yellow complimenting her smooth olive skin.

Rage ignites inside of me once again at the sight of her bandaged ribs but I shove it aside for the time being and pull the blanket over her. I pick a spot on the floor by her bed and rest my head against the wall, watching her sleep. Minutes eventually turn into hours. When it's time, I move to sit next to her. "Jules."

She stirs, her face pinching in a frown.

My knuckles graze her soft cheek. "Come on, baby, I need you to wake up."

"No!" she mumbles and slaps my hand away.

"What's your name?" I ask, amused by her grumpiness. When I get no response, I give her a gentle nudge. "Come on, I need you to answer me."

A frustrated growl shoves past her delicate throat and she cracks an eye open. "My name is Julia, I'm twenty-four years old, and you are Jaxson… my *ex*-best friend. Now shut up and leave me alone." She rolls away from me and is out cold again.

Damn! She's pissy when she's tired.

I take my spot back on the floor once again. Clearly, by her *ex*-best friend comment, she's far from forgiving me. I will find a way to make this right. I would have made it up to her before now if I hadn't been holed up in that fucking rehabilitation clinic for all those months.

Stretching out my legs, I come into contact with something under her bed. I reach under to see what it is and am surprised when I pull out a framed picture of Julia and me from my graduation. All the memories from that day come flooding back. She looked incredible. I remember the shock I felt when I was called up and her beautiful unmistakable voice rose above the crowd of applause.

It was the best surprise I could have ever gotten and one of the reasons why I reciprocated, wanting to be there for hers. It had been three years since I'd last seen her. When I arrived back home I found out she had a boyfriend, someone more in her league, a med student. She had no idea I was there; I didn't want to fuck up her relationship. And if I was being honest, I didn't want her to realize just how different I was from that guy. How unworthy I was—even of her friendship.

From what Coop had gathered from Kayla, the guy was good to her. It drove me crazy thinking of anyone touching her, but all I cared about was her happiness. Obviously it never lasted, something I'm grateful for, otherwise it would be him here right now and not me.

I'm yanked out of my thoughts at the sound of Julia's soft moan. I look over to see her holding her head. Putting the picture back under her bed, I move back up to sit next to her. "Hey, what's wrong?" I ask.

Her eyes narrow in confusion. "Jaxson?"

"It's me, do you remember tonight?"

She looks around disoriented. "Some… I think. What time is it?"

"Two in the morning."

"My head really hurts," she confesses on a painful whisper.

"Here, take some more of these." I grab her pills and shake out two, handing them to her, with the glass of water I got earlier.

"Thanks," she mumbles as I help her sit up. I'm about to move back down on the floor when she grabs my arm, her eyes wild with panic. "Don't leave me."

"I'm not. I've been sitting right over there." I point over to my spot on the floor.

"Lay here with me."

Jesus! This is a different Julia than the one I woke up an hour ago. Can I control myself? I peer down at her pleading eyes and find I can't say no. I don't *want* to either.

When I make my move she opens the blankets to invite me in, clearing not realizing she's in nothing but her underwear. "Don't do that, baby." I tuck the quilt back around her again. "I'll lie on top of the blankets."

Once my shoulder meets the mattress, she rolls on her side to face me. Her eyes are dazed and glassy as she reaches over and lays her hand gently on the side of my face. "I've really missed you."

My chest tightens at her admission. Grabbing her warm hand, I bring it to my mouth, giving it a soft kiss. "Me too, baby," is all I manage to say.

She scoots in closer, her face burying in my chest. She's the only woman I've ever held. It's a foreign concept to me, but feels natural and so goddamn good with her. Her sweet scent envelops me, and I try really hard not to think about what she's wearing, or rather, not wearing, beneath the covers.

The tips of my fingers trail along the smooth skin of her back as she finds sleep once again. This time I decide to set my watch and follow along with her, feeling at peace for the first time since the night I was buried deep inside her.

12

Julia

As morning descends upon me, I wake up enveloped in the most amazing warmth. "Mmm," I moan, cocooning myself deeper in the comforting heat.

A loud growl penetrates the silence, a large hand gripping my hips to keep me in place. "Stay the fuck still!"

I stiffen, my heart in my throat as memories from last night plague me.

Oh god… Jaxson.

The mattress dips as he flies off the bed. "Shit." His palm meets the wall with a hard slap before he enters the bathroom and slams the door.

What the heck just happened? And why was he in my bed?

I try to remember anything after the hospital but can't, my memory is clouded. Lifting the blankets I see I'm only in my bra and underwear.

Oh sweet jesus!

Please don't tell me I tried to seduce him. Humiliation burns inside of me as I think of the way I just rubbed myself all over him. I'm no better than that two-bit whore Melissa.

Way to stay mad at him, Julia, he's really going to be sorry now.

The bathroom door opens a moment later. I sit up quickly, wincing from my bruised ribs, and pull the blankets up under my arms to cover myself as much as possible. Jaxson comes to stand in front of me, leaning against the wall, his fierce gaze penetrating, but I'm too embarrassed to look at him.

"Look, Jaxson, I'm really sorry," I start, deciding to get this over with. "I was out of it last night, I know it's no excuse, but I don't remember it."

"What the hell are you talking about?" he asks, confused.

Of course he's going to make me say it. "I'm sorry for trying to… have sex with you, all right!" My cheeks burn furiously as I wait for him to respond. When silence continues to fill the air I chance a look at him and find him watching me with an amused smirk.

"Let me get this straight. You wake up half naked with me in your bed. You don't remember shit, and you think it was you who seduced me?"

"Well, why else am I half naked?"

"Because I took your dress off while you were sleeping," he explains, as if I'm an idiot.

"Why did you do that?"

"Would you have rather slept in it?"

I think about what he just said, my foggy mind trying to catch up. "Wait, so I didn't try to have sex with you?"

Oh please let that be true.

"If you had tried to have sex with me, Julia, you would still be feeling me inside of you."

A current of heat sparks inside of me, his husky voice making my heart skip a beat. I glare at him, hoping to hide the effect and wait for a better answer.

"You passed out before we even got in the truck," he tells me. "I brought you up here, and Kayla left before I realized I would need help getting you out of your clothes. I stayed on the floor but then halfway through the night you asked me to lay down with you, so I did." The last of his words end on a happy note, clearly amused by my confusion.

"I'm glad you're finding this so funny."

"I don't understand why you wouldn't think I was the one who tried something."

"It never crossed my mind. I know you would never take advantage of me."

His amusement evaporates and he shakes his head.

"What?"

"Nothing," he says then changes the subject. "How's your head?"

"Not too bad, it's my ribs that hurt terribly this morning."

"We should probably change the dressing and put more of that ointment on. Do you want to shower first?"

I become uncomfortable as I think about him doing it. Then I remember Grams's brunch today. "Shit! What time is it?"

"Nine."

"Crap! I have to hurry, I need to be at the senior home in an hour."

"I don't think that's a good idea, Jules. You should stay home and rest."

"It's Grams's birthday. I'm not missing it, I'll be fine." I throw the blankets off then shriek, remembering I'm only in my underwear and yank the sheet back in place. "Do you mind?"

"Not at all," he replies, making no effort to leave.

I point at the door. "Out!"

"It's nothing I haven't seen before, Julia."

Our eyes lock, tension filling the room as we both remember that night. I look away, breaking the connection. "Yeah, well, that was a long time ago, things change."

We both know I'm not talking about my body anymore.

"Not everything changes," he replies softly.

I'm not ready to have this conversation yet so I ignore the comment. "I need to get in the shower so…" I gesture to the door again.

"You need to cover your bandage before you shower, remember?"

No, I don't.

"Where do you keep your plastic wrap?" he asks.

"In the pantry."

Once he leaves, I carefully climb out of bed and head into my closet, sliding on my silk robe. I'm in the midst of tying it when he walks back in, his large frame overpowering the confines of my room.

"Thanks," I say, reaching for the wrap.

He keeps it clutched firmly in his hand. "I'll do it."

His overbearingness really begins to grate on my nerves. "I can manage, Jaxson, now give it to me." I rip the box out of his hand and head into the bathroom. The task proves harder than I thought it would and I want to kick myself for letting my pride get the best of me. In the end, I manage to get it done and step into the shower, a blissful sigh escaping me as the hot water pours down my aching body. As much as I'd love to stay in here forever, I wash quickly, needing to get to Grams.

After drying off, I throw on a pair of panties and bra, then adorn my robe once again. When I exit the bathroom I come to a hard stop at the sight of Jaxson sitting on my freshly made bed. He has gauze, bandages, and ointment next to him.

"Can't a girl get some privacy?" I ask, annoyed.

"Quit your grumbling and get over here."

The last thing I want is for him to touch me, especially my bare skin. Dangerous things can happen from that. "I'll try and do it myself."

"No. I know what to do, you don't."

"You can't expect me to stand in front of you half naked."

"It's not a big deal, just come over here and we'll get it over with."

I remain where I am, not moving any closer to him.

"Now, Julia!" he demands.

With a frustrated huff, I start across the room, but glare at him, making sure he knows I'm not happy about it. I'm a pretty private person; only two people have ever seen me naked and Jaxson is one of them. Both were a long time ago.

Coming to stand in front of him, I turn to my injured side and try to figure out a way to let him see my ribs without having to fully open my robe. It doesn't work so well.

"I can't get to it like this. Take off the robe," he says, his voice gruffer than it was a moment ago.

"No!"

"Jesus, Julia, I won't look anywhere else but your ribs, okay? You're wasting time. Don't you need to get to Grams's soon?"

Damn it, he's right.

"Fine. But I mean it, Jaxson, don't look anywhere else."

I probably shouldn't be so paranoid. The guy has stayed away from me for the last six years, it's not like he's going to jump at the first opportunity to see me naked. Loosening the knot on my robe, the silk material has barely slipped aside before he opens his mouth. "Jesus, that's nice."

"That's it!" I clutch my robe closed and am about to storm off but he grabs my arm before I can escape, his laughter filling the air.

"I'm kidding, Jules."

"It's not funny."

"I'm sorry, I couldn't resist. I won't do it again," he promises but still has that stupid smirk on his face.

Fine, two can play at this game.

"You promise you won't do it again?" I ask.

He nods. "I promise."

I step between his opened legs, closing the gap between us. This time when I untie the robe, I allow it to slip down my arms and pool at my feet.

His sharp breath fills the tense air, as I stand before him in my black satin bra and panties.

My earlier irritation vanishes when the smirk he had moments ago is wiped off his smug face. He keeps his promise to me, his eyes remaining only on my stomach, jaw flexing in restraint.

Not so funny now, is it, buddy?

"Hello? Are you going to start anytime soon? I'm a little cold here," I snap impatiently, enjoying his torment.

Shaking his head, he begins the task of re-bandaging my ribs.

A painful gasp parts my lips when he begins to peel the bandage off. I grab onto his broad shoulders as the sticky tape holding the gauze pulls excruciatingly at my raw skin.

"I'm sorry, I'm trying to be careful," he apologizes.

My pain fades at the feel of his hot breath whispering across my bare skin. I suddenly become aware of how close my body is to his, and how strong his shoulders feel under my fingers. It takes every ounce of my willpower not to squeeze my legs together to stop the ache that's building between them.

"Do you want to take some more pain medication?"

His question snaps me back into myself. I clear my throat and try not to let my voice betray what I'm feeling. "Maybe after Grams's. I don't want to be drowsy during brunch."

Once he gets the bandage removed, he gently applies the ointment. The coolness is a welcome relief to my overheated body.

Jaxson's shoulders tense beneath my fingertips as he applies it. "I'm seriously going to kill that fucker."

"It was mostly an accident," I admit on a whisper. It's unfortunate but I yanked away at the same time Wyatt let go.

"It shouldn't have happened in the first place."

I don't respond because I don't want to talk about Wyatt right now, especially with him.

"Cooper is coming by today to talk to you about last night," he informs me.

"Okay, but it will have to wait until after Grams's brunch."

He nods in agreement.

After he finishes the last of the bandaging, he grabs my good hip and drags me in closer to him. It catches me off balance, and my fingers tighten on his shoulders to steady myself.

His heated eyes slowly move up my body, passing over every inch, until the blue irises lock with mine, stealing my breath. "Next time you pull something like that, Julia, sore ribs or not, I won't let you off the hook so easily."

Oh the man is infuriating! Sexy, but infuriating.

"Then next time, Jaxson, don't start something you won't finish," I say with more confidence than I feel.

His grip tightens on my hip, fingers digging into my flesh. "Oh, Julia, you know me better than that. I always finish what I start."

My breath is stolen when he leans in and presses a gentle kiss to my quivering stomach. His confident hands glide up the back of my legs, cupping my bottom. A traitorous moan breaches my lips, my fingers tightening on his shoulders to ensure I don't buckle from the need coursing through me.

Right when I think there's going to be no coming back, his phone rings, dragging me back to reality.

A frustrated growl rumbles from his chest, his forehead drops to my stomach. I shove against his shoulders, stepping out of the dangerous territory and try to regain control of my body.

"What?" He snaps the greeting into his phone. His eyes meet mine as he listens to whoever is on the other end, seeing much more than I want him to.

Breaking the connection, I head over to my walk-in closet, feeling his eyes burning into my back as I disappear. I close the door behind me and drop back against it, all the air pushing from my lungs.

What on earth am I thinking? Why did I have to challenge him like that? It's like dangling a piece of meat in front of a bear. I'm disgusted with myself for how easily I caved to him; the man still has so much control over me.

I overhear him talking to who I'm assuming is Cooper. "She's visiting Margaret this morning, we'll call you when we get back then you guys can come."

Since when are *we* going to Grams's, I think, annoyed.

"I don't give a fuck what he wants, I'll kill him if he comes near her again."

Not wanting to hear the rest of the conversation, I move away from the door and get dressed. I was going to wear shorts, but change my mind, not wanting anything snug against my sore hip. Instead I throw on a short, black, cotton baby-doll sundress. When I don't hear Jaxson on the phone anymore, I pull myself together, open the door, and march straight into the bathroom without looking in his direction.

I'm applying my makeup when he comes to stand at the bathroom door, his eyes penetrating me through the reflecting glass.

"Running scared, Julia?"

Ignoring him, I flick on my blow-dryer and drown out anything else he might say. He doesn't walk away like most people would do. Instead he stays exactly where he is, waiting patiently, or not so patiently, with a narrowed gaze.

Once my hair is dry, I part it over my stitches, thankfully able to cover most of them.

"Are you going to ignore me all day?" he asks.

"Nope. Because you're not going to be here all day," I inform him then make an effort to leave but his large frame remains blocking the door. "Do you mind?"

"We're going to have to talk about this sometime, Julia."

I sigh tiredly, and it's only 9:30 in the morning. "I know, but not right now."

"Fine," he relents but isn't happy about it. "We need to call Cooper when we get back from brunch."

"Why are you saying *we*?"

"Because I'm coming with you."

"No, you're not."

"I'm not leaving you, Julia, so forget about it!"

"You already did!"

Damn! Why the hell did I have to say that?

I look away from him, angry with myself for letting him know just how hurt I still am.

He collects two steps closer and takes my face in both of his hands, forcing my gaze to his. For the first time since seeing seen him again, I see remorse reflecting back at me. "I promise, I'll make this right."

"Maybe it's too late?"

"It's never too late, because I will never give up on you."

My throat urns with emotion, all the words I want to say to him lodged inside.

"Let me come with you to Grams, I'd really like to see her."

I know Grams would be over the moon to see him, too. It's that thought that has me caving. "Fine. But let's get one thing straight, Jaxson," I say, my finger poking into his hard chest. "I'm saying yes because I know she will be happy to see you. I'm doing this for her, not for you. This does not mean that I forgive you."

His lips curl in amusement, kicking my annoyance up another level.

"Lose the smirk and let's go." I storm past him, my shoulder knocking into his in the process.

His chuckle trails behind me, making me want to turn back and slap his sexy face.

On the way over to Grams's, we stop by Jaxson's hotel first, so he can quickly shower and change. After what happened back in my room I figured it was safer for me to wait in the car.

He emerges from the hotel a few minutes later, his strides as confident as the man himself. A white T-shirt stretches across his defined chest, and he's added an unbuttoned, long-sleeved, navy henley over it, the sleeves rolled up enough to see some of the tattoos on his arms. His dark-washed jeans hang just low enough on his hips to visually tease me.

I swear the man is a walking orgasm. It's completely unfair.

"Like what you see, Julia?" he asks, a cocky grin gracing his face as he climbs into my car.

Heat invades my cheeks when I realize I've been busted gawking at him like an idiot.

God, I'm pathetic.

"I'm surprised you aren't staying with Cooper," I comment, evading his question.

"He offered, but I didn't want to intrude, or hear him and Kayla fucking each other's brains out. I remember what it was like living with that shit before. Besides, with the way Kayla has been acting toward me it's probably safer. She might just kill me in my sleep if she gets the chance."

I giggle, knowing that's probably true.

The short drive to Sunny Acres is silent as the tension hangs heavy between us. There's so much that needs to be said, but they're words I'm scared to say and questions I'm terrified to know the answers to. Once we arrive, I quickly exit the car, anxious to breathe in the fresh ocean air and blossoming flowers of the gardens nearby where residents sit and sip their afternoon tea.

"When did Margaret move here?" Jaxson asks, climbing out after me.

"About two years ago. It was difficult for her to leave her home, but she knew she couldn't keep up with all the yard work. She seems to really love it here. There's always an event going on—bingo, dances, and even margarita nights."

He flashes me a knowing grin. "I'll bet she likes that."

I return his smile, the first genuine one I've had today. "That she does, the woman loves her margaritas."

We walk inside, heading directly to the dining area that's filled with seniors. I spot Grams at the back of the room, laughing with a few of her friends. One of them points me out, and she turns around with a beaming smile that dies quickly when she sees Jaxson. She brings a shaky hand to her throat, staring at him in shock.

My heart swells when I look over to see Jaxson with his hands in his pockets, looking unsure of himself.

Grams starts toward us, her stunned gaze frozen on the man next to me. "Jaxson?" she asks quietly.

He clears his throat and nods. "It's me, how are you doing, Miss Margaret?"

"Oh, Jaxson!" she sobs, wrapping her arms around his waist. "I'm so glad you're okay, honey."

Her emotion sparks my own, tears burn the back of my eyes as I watch her cry against his chest. She knows about Jaxson getting hurt and everything that happened when I went to Germany.

His body is stiff from the affection but he pats her back. "It's good to see you, too."

She looks up at him, her hands grabbing either side of his face to pull him down for a kiss. "You're even more handsome than I remember. How is that possible?"

I roll my eyes; the man doesn't need his ego boosted any more.

"This is the best birthday present I could have gotten," she gushes.

Really? I knew she would be happy to see him, but I didn't think she would let him off the hook so easily.

Once she finishes fawning all over him, she finally acknowledges me. "I told you he would come back, sweetheart."

"Grams," I scold under my breath.

She snickers at my embarrassment. "Come here, honey." She hugs me tight, thankfully on my good side, but gasps when she leans in to kiss my cheek, spotting my stitches. "Julia, what on earth happened to you?"

"I had a little fall last night, but I'm fine, it's nothing to worry about."

Jaxson grunts, making me look like a liar.

"Julia Sinclair. What aren't you telling me?"

I guess she's going to hear about it sooner or later. Nothing stays quiet in this town. "I had a minor altercation with Wyatt is all."

"Wyatt did this to you?" she asks in outrage. "I knew that boy was trouble, he has always rubbed me the wrong way, same with his father." She swings her angry eyes over at Jaxson. "Did you kick his ass?"

"Grams!" I scold her again; knowing Jaxson doesn't need any further encouragement.

"Damn straight, and I'm not done with him either."

"Good boy," she praises, patting his shoulder.

"I'll be right back. I need to use the ladies' room," I mumble and start away, needing a moment to collect myself.

This is going to be a long couple of hours.

Jaxson

I watch Julia walk away, knowing she's pissed that I made Margaret aware of what happened.

"Come on, honey, have a seat." Margaret leads me over to an empty table. The moment I take a seat she slaps me upside the head. "That's for hurting Julia, mister," she says, shaking her finger in my face.

I knew it wasn't going to be that easy with her but I try my best to explain my actions. "I'm sorry I hurt her, but trust me when I say it was for the best. She wouldn't have been able to handle seeing me like I was."

Her expression softens as she lays her hand over mine. "I've told you before, Jaxson, she's stronger than you think. You hurt her really badly when you sent her away like that. I worried she was never going to come out of it."

My chest constricts with guilt and I swallow thickly. "I'll make it up to her."

"I know you will, but I'm warning you, it's not going to be easy."

"I know, but I won't stop until she forgives me."

"Good." She pats the side of my face, a lot more gentle than the pat that was just delivered to my head. "And while you're asking for forgiveness, you may as well tell her you love her."

My eyes snap to hers, panic seizing my chest.

"Oh don't look at me like that. I've always known you love her, Jaxson. I've waited a long time for you to come to terms with it, but you're a little slow on the uptake," she snickers.

I shake my head. "She needs someone who can love her the way she deserves. I don't know how to, it's something I was never around."

"Jaxson, love isn't always something you learn, it's something that you feel. And I know you feel it, I can see it in your eyes every time you look at her."

"I'm really messed up, Margaret, even more so after what happened in Iraq." I'm uncomfortable admitting this to her, but I'm trying to make her understand.

"Oh, honey," she sighs, laying her worn hand on the side of my face. "If you'd let her, she could help you heal. I don't know anyone else who will love Julia or protect her more than you. Just look at what happened with that no-good scoundrel, Wyatt."

Anger swells in my veins at the reminder of last night. I'm pissed at myself, knowing if I had been here in the first place none of it would have happened. I always thought I was doing the right thing by staying away, but look at the mess it created.

"All I'm saying is, for once think with your heart instead of your head. See where that leads you."

We're interrupted when one of the staff walks over to us. A girl that looks to be around Julia's age. "Hi, Margaret, is this your grandson?" she asks, flashing me a flirtatious smile.

"No! He's Julia's man, now get outta here!" Margaret snaps, surprising the hell out of me. She glares at the girl's retreating back. "That girl is a hussy. You should see some of the stockings she wears with her uniform."

The lady amuses the shit out of me. My attention anchors to the left as Julia makes her way back over to us, that usual shift in my chest happening at the sight of her. She's so fucking beautiful it hurts just to look at her, mainly because I have to force my dick to stay down whenever I'm around her.

I can tell by the way she's walking that she's in pain but trying to hide it. When she takes the seat next to me, I lean over to whisper in her ear. "I brought your pain medication in case you needed to take some."

She shakes her head. "I'm okay, but thanks." Before I have a chance to argue with her, she hands Margaret the present she brought. "Happy birthday, Grams."

"Julia, I tell you every year not to get me anything."

"And every year I do, so stop your fussin' and open it."

Margaret does and pulls out a big black book from the gift bag. Opening it, she gasps, tears forming in her eyes. "Oh, Julia, this is so beautiful, thank you."

"You're welcome."

Once Margaret finishes leafing through the pages, she hands it to me to look at. The book is filled with pictures of her and her husband, along with Julia and her mom. I've seen photos of Julia's mom before and am always taken aback by her beauty. Julia is a spitting image of her.

"That's my pappi, right after he got out of the Navy," Julia explains, pointing to a picture of him.

"Wasn't he handsome?" Margaret asks me.

I nod awkwardly, feeling weird to agree but don't know what else to say.

Julia chuckles, amused by my discomfort.

"The man took my breath away whenever he walked into a room," she continues, sadness creeping into her voice. "No matter how long we were together, I never got tired of looking at him. I miss him dearly."

Julia reaches over and grabs her hand.

"He would have liked you, Jaxson. I told you this before and I meant it, you're a lot like him. I knew the moment I met you, you were right for my Julia."

Jesus, the woman doesn't hold back, does she?

Julia scoffs and releases her hand. "Give it a rest, Grams."

Before any of us can say more, two elderly ladies come and sit with us, both of them smiling and eyeing me with curiosity.

"Margaret, who is this boy and where have you been hiding him?"

"This is Julia's Jaxson," she replies happily.

"He is not my anything."

I chuckle at Julia's growl.

"Why not? He's handsome, Julia. You have to hold on tight to men like him," one says, winking at me.

Okay, that's a little uncomfortable.

Julia smiles, noticing my discomfort, and slings an arm around my shoulders. "Well, Gladys, looks like it's your lucky day, because it just so happens that Jaxson here is single."

I glare at her, wondering what the hell she's up to.

"Oh really?" Gladys replies, eyeing me like I'm a fucking treat or something.

"Yep, and I promise to bring him here more often for you. I should bring him on your dance nights; he loves to dance, Gladys."

Oh she's going to fucking pay for this. She damn well knows I hate to dance. I glance over at Margaret, hoping she will help me, but she just looks amused as hell.

"You like to dance?" Gladys asks excitedly.

"Uh, actually, no."

Her face falls, making me feel like a dick.

I never thought the day would come that I'd have to worry about hurting an old lady's feelings by shutting her down. "It's just that I'm not a very good dancer is all."

Her eyes light back up. "Oh, honey, don't you worry. I can dance well enough for the both of us."

Is this lady for real?

Julia grabs the side of my face. "Oh don't listen to him," she coos, "Jaxson's just being modest. Believe me, this guy has some killer moves."

That's it! Grabbing the back of her head, I kiss the fucking smirk right off her face.

"Attaboy, Jaxson," Margaret cheers.

Julia gasps the moment my mouth collides with hers. I swallow the breathy sound, feeling it rush through my veins like the sweetest drug. She remains frozen at first, making no move to reciprocate. That's until I lick the seam of her lips. Her mouth parts on a sexy moan and I plunge my tongue, becoming intoxicated with her taste.

Fuck me! She tastes even better than I remember.

"Oh my!" someone says at the table, reminding me we aren't alone.

I reluctantly pull back and stare into her heavy-lidded gaze. Shit! I only meant to press a hard kiss to her mouth, not maul her in front of everyone. Not that I regret it.

Her eyes flash with anger, but it doesn't hide the need I see in them. "What the hell are you doing?" she hisses, pushing me back.

"What? I was just demonstrating some of my *killer moves* you were telling them about."

Margaret's snicker fills the moment. "All right. Come on, you two, food's ready."

The three of them get up and start making their way to the buffet table. "I gotta tell you, I'd like to see what that guy is packing," Gladys says.

I tense, wondering if I just heard her right.

"Don't you ever do that again," Julia snaps, shaking her finger in my face.

Grabbing her wrist, I yank her in close. "Then next time, think twice before you play games with me. When you challenge me like that, Julia, all it does is make my dick hard. I thought you learned that in your room this morning."

"You are so infuriating."

"Admit it, you liked it, and you want more."

I know I shouldn't push her, but I can't resist.

Her eyes drop to my lap, staring at my now hard dick through my jeans. She looks back up at me, her brow quirked in amusement. "You seem to be the one affected, Jaxson."

"Don't tell me that if I shoved my hand up that dress of yours right now, I wouldn't find your panties soaked."

Heat sparks in her eyes but she tries to hide it behind her smirk. "I guess that's something you will never find out." She stands and adds, "Take your time to settle down before you come and get your food."

She strolls away, leaving me with the urge to haul her to the bathroom and show her just who's in control.

Damn it!

The woman is testing my limits, and I haven't even been around her for twenty-four hours. Clearly, it's going to be harder to restrain myself than I thought. I need to keep a clear head; I'm trying to fix the mess I made, not screw it up more.

I track her over to the table where she stands in line, helping Margaret with her plate. My gaze zeroes in on her sweet ass when she reaches for the punch.

I'm so fucked!

Julia

We leave shortly after eating because I needed to get away from Grams's knowing smile. I haven't been the same since that kiss from Jaxson. I shift in my seat, feeling restless, and cross my legs to stop the throbbing that's happening between them.

I'm pathetic.

It doesn't help that it's been a long time since I've been with anyone. Justin is the only person I have slept with other than Jaxson. That was almost two years ago, and for the man being a med student, he had absolutely no idea where a woman's clitoris was located. Or maybe he just didn't care. I dated him for nine months in hopes of getting over Jaxson. It didn't work, of course, but at least I wasn't alone and the company was nice.

Cooper's truck is already parked out front by the time we arrive at my house. He and Kayla climb out the same time we do, and I'm happy to see she came with him.

"Hey, how are you feeling?" she asks, greeting me with a gentle hug.

"Not too bad, my ribs are sore today but my head feels better."

"Good." She offers me a smile that doesn't quite reach her eyes.

I'm about to ask her if everything is okay but Cooper speaks first. "Mind if we talk about last night?"

"Sure, come in." Leading them into the house, I get everyone a drink before we all sit down together at my kitchen table.

"Okay, tell me what went down last night," Cooper starts. "Jennings is saying it was an accident, and he's demanding that I arrest Jaxson for assault."

Panic seizes my chest at the thought. "It was kind of an accident...or not." I shake my head. "I don't know, Cooper, I've never seen him like that before. I'm still trying to wrap my head around it. He was so angry when we left you guys."

I relay the rest of the events from that evening, up to when I told Wyatt I no longer wanted to see him. Jaxson tenses next to me when I tell them about Wyatt grabbing me and calling me a cocktease. "He said he was going to show me how good we could be together. I knew he was going to kiss me. I tried pulling away and that's when you guys showed up. He finally let me go, and I fell."

I glance over at Jaxson nervously and see him staring straight ahead, his expression hard as stone.

My attention reverts back to Cooper. "The thing is, I have no idea what he's talking about when he says I've been playing head games with him. I've barely had any contact with him. That was only the third date we've ever had. I've run into him here and there while I was going to school. He would ask me out and I'd always politely decline. It wasn't until recently that I ran into him again, and when he asked me again I said okay." I shrug, hating how wrong I was. I should have kept declining.

Kayla senses my thoughts and leans over to grab my hand. "Don't you dare blame yourself for any of this. This is his fault, not yours."

I can't help but feel partly responsible.

"Julia, you have grounds to press charges," Cooper says. "You wouldn't have fallen and gotten hurt if he hadn't forced you there to begin with."

I look over at Jaxson, my heart aching at the thought of him receiving any kind of punishment for this. His eyes narrow back at me, knowing exactly where my head is at.

"I'm not pressing charges," I whisper.

"Fuck that!" He slams his fist on the table, making me jump. "Yes, you are!"

"Don't yell at her like that!" Kayla snaps.

"Kayla, stay out of it." Cooper's tone is as angry as hers.

"Then you tell him too, this is Julia's decision, and hers alone. I will not let her be bullied into anything."

They glare at one another, the tension so thick you could cut it with a knife.

I drop my head in my hands, hating that everyone is fighting over this.

"Julia, I think you should reconsider," Cooper starts again.

"She doesn't want to press charges because of me. She thinks if she doesn't then he won't, but you're wrong." Jaxson's tone softens and he cups my cheek, turning my face toward his. "If he wants to press charges he will, no matter what you do. Don't let him get away with this, Julia."

"I don't want anything to happen to you because of this," I tell him thickly then look over at Cooper. "Couldn't you talk to him, Cooper? Tell Wyatt that I'll drop the charges against him if he drops his against Jaxson."

"No!"

I ignore Jaxson's protest and continue. "Trust me, he won't want me pressing charges, especially right now. He told me his dad is running for mayor. With the campaign starting up soon, he won't want bad publicity."

Surprise passes over Cooper's expression. "He said his old man is running for mayor?"

I nod.

"Fuck, that's the last thing we need. You're right though, it's leverage."

"Damn it, I said no! I don't give a shit what happens to me. She's pressing charges."

"Well I do care, and it's my decision," I argue back.

Jaxson stands, his chair slamming into the wall as he starts pacing angrily.

"Look, just calm down. Julia's right, it's something we can try." Cooper puts up his hand, silencing Jaxson's protest but his determined eyes remain on me. "But I think you need to consider putting a restraining order on him at the very least."

My eyes flare in surprise. "A restraining order?"

"The guy thinks he's in love with you, Julia. If you have had as little contact as you say you have, then that shit's not normal."

"I don't think that's necessary. I think putting a restraining order on him will just make the situation worse in the end."

"Listen, Julia. When I questioned him, the shit he said made me nervous. He's not right in the head, I'm telling you, you need this. I have no doubt he will not leave you alone unless you do."

"I'll fucking kill him if he goes anywhere near her." There's a terrifying calmness in Jaxson's voice, his words holding promise.

"Jesus, I did not just hear you say that," Cooper says, distressed.

I decide to relent, wanting this to be over. "I'll put a restraining order on him. But first I want you to try to get the charges dropped against Jaxson."

"For fuck's sake!" Jaxson's heated curse slices through the air but I ignore it.

Cooper nods his agreement then looks over at Jaxson. "You need to come to the station with me and do an official statement. We have a strong case to get the charges dropped either way, but we can use Julia's for leverage."

I feel much better after hearing that, but I can tell Jaxson is not happy about it.

"Julia shouldn't be alone right now. She's still healing," he says.

"I'll be fine on my own."

"I'll stay with her for a while," Kayla offers.

"You don't have to."

"I know, but I want to. We can catch up, maybe watch a movie while you rest."

I smile. "Sure, that sounds good."

"All right, let's go and get this over with," Cooper says, pushing to his feet.

The rest of us stand and Jaxson comes over to hand me my pain pills. "Take these, I know you're hurting."

I roll my eyes at his bossiness. "I'll be fine. I can take care of myself. Now go with Cooper and cooperate, or I'll be forced to call Gladys for your punishment," I tease, biting back a smile.

He grunts unamused. "You're such a smart-ass." His arm hooks around my waist, yanking me in close so he can plant a hard kiss right on my lips.

"I told you to stop doing that." I try to sound angry but it comes out breathless.

The arrogant ass just smirks, knowing his effect on me, and walks away.

"Who the fuck is Gladys?" Cooper asks as they walk out the door.

"Yeah, good-bye to you, too."

I look over at Kayla and see she's upset. "Is everything all right?"

"Yeah, Cooper and I have just been butting heads lately. That's all." She flashes me a reassuring smile that doesn't quite reach her eyes again.

"I hope it isn't because of Jaxson and me?"

"No." She waves away my concern. "Really, it's fine. Let's go pick a movie. Want to watch it in your room so you can rest in bed?"

"Sure." She heads for the living room but I grab her arm before she can leave. "You know I'm always here for you, right? You can call me day or night."

"Yeah, I know. Thanks, Jules." She hugs me tight, unfortunately it's on my injured side.

I suck in a sharp breath and wince.

"Shit, sorry. Are you going to take the medication?"

"No. I don't feel like I need them yet."

"All right. I won't push like Mr. Bossy," she teases.

"Thanks. I appreciate that."

After making some popcorn, we pick our favorite movie, *Dirty Dancing,* and go snuggle down in bed, becoming enraptured with Patrick Swayze like always.

Halfway through the movie, Kayla turns to me. "We should go out dancing one night, it's been a while. We can make it a girls' night and invite Grace, too."

"Sure, that would be fun. Let's do it soon. Grace could use a night off; she's been working herself into the ground. I saw her the other day and she looked ready to fall over."

"I know. I'm pretty sure it's because she needs the money."

I nod, agreeing.

Grace moved to Sunset Bay a little over a year ago. Kayla and I hit it off with her right away, and we all quickly became friends. There's still a lot we don't know about her, but we can tell something has happened to her. When she found out about my mom passing away, she opened up, telling us that she lost her mom too, but she never shared how. I didn't want to be rude and ask. As far as we know, Grace is alone with no other family. I'm hoping she will open up once she gets more comfortable with us.

"Depending on how you're feeling, what about next weekend?" Kayla asks.

"That works for me. I'm sure I'll be fine. I'm surprised how well I'm doing today, considering."

"I still can't believe we never knew about Wyatt. Why wouldn't Coop and Jaxson just tell us the reason from the start?"

I shrug, not having any idea and I don't try to figure it out either. It doesn't matter, not anymore.

"So fill me in on what's been happening with Jaxson. Your conversation looked pretty intense when I walked in yesterday."

"Yeah, and you didn't help by the way, talking about my 'hot date.'"

She chuckles. "Sorry, I couldn't resist. I wanted to make sure he knew you weren't just kickin' around waiting for his sorry ass. Believe me, I regretted it when he came storming over later like the Incredible Hulk."

We share a laugh, the nickname very fitting for Jaxson, but I sober quickly. "I don't know, Kayla. We haven't had much of a chance to talk about it. He says he's going to make things right, but he also said he doesn't regret sending me away. A part of me wants to forgive him, it feels so good to be around him again, but that's what scares me the most. He still affects me so strongly. I've worked really hard trying to get over him, and all of it just crumbled the moment I laid eyes on him again. What if I forgive him and he eventually leaves?"

"Well I guess that's what you need to find out. I don't know what the right thing is to tell you, Jules. I do believe that in his fucked-up head he thinks he did the right thing and believes he was protecting you. Listen to what he has to say about his future plans. If it's something that includes you, then maybe make him work at your friendship, don't let him off too easily."

We're interrupted when she gets a phone call. I hold my breath, praying it's news about Jaxson.

"Hello… What? I'm supposed to have today off, can't someone else take them?" It's obviously the massage clinic where Kayla works.

What's taking them so long?

"Fine, I'm on my way." Hanging up, she looks over at me regretfully. "I'm sorry, I gotta go. Someone called in sick and I need to take her appointments. It'll only be for a few hours."

"It's okay, thanks for staying as long as you did. Come on, I'll drive you over," I say, climbing out of bed.

"Are you sure? I can ask Coop to come get me?"

"No, it's fine. I need the fresh air."

After dropping her off, I decide to go visit my mom for a while. I sit and talk to her about Jaxson being back and ask her for guidance. Once my heart feels a little lighter, I leave and find myself pulling up to the beach.

I start across the warm sand, heading toward the one place I haven't been to in over a year—our spot. I used to come often, especially when I was missing Jaxson. But after Germany I tried to rid myself of any reminders of him, it was too painful.

Sitting down, I lean back against the log and take a deep breath of the ocean-filled air, letting the crash of the waves soothe me. I close my eyes, trying to clear my head, and the next thing I know I'm being startled awake.

"Where the fuck have you been?"

My eyes spring open and I sit up in a panic. Jaxson stands over me, looking like he's ready to commit murder. I lay a hand over my thundering heart. "You scared me to death." The sun has started to set and I notice it's visibly cooler out.

How long have I been here?

"I scared *you*?" he shouts in outrage. "Do you have any idea how long I've been looking for you?"

I shake my head, a little scared to ask.

"Almost two fucking hours, Julia! I checked here before and never saw you."

"I visited my mom for a bit then I came here. Geez, calm down."

"Are you kidding me? I find you sleeping on the beach and you tell me to calm down. What the hell is the matter with you?"

That's it! Grabbing my shoes, I push to my feet. "Screw you! I don't need to listen to this shit," I start across the beach without looking back.

His frustrated breath sounds behind me. "Shit! Julia, wait."

I ignore him and keep walking, my bare feet stomping through the sand.

He catches up to me, grabbing my arm before I can make it too far. "I'm sorry, okay? You scared the hell out of me when I couldn't find you. All of this shit with Wyatt has me going crazy. I thought something happened to you."

I soften when I realize how scared he is. "Why didn't you just call me? My number is still the same, although, I imagine you forgot it after all this time." I can't resist adding in that last part.

He looks at me like I've lost my mind. "Julia, I called it about a hundred fucking times."

"What?" Reaching into my purse, I grab my phone and see twenty-seven missed calls and eighteen voice mails, all from Jaxson. There's also a text from Kayla.

Kayla: *Hulk Alert! Jaxson's going crazy looking for you.*

Turning my phone to the side, I see it's on silent. *Oops!* "Sorry, it seems my ringer was off."

"Jesus!"

I clear my throat sheepishly. "So... how did it go at the station with Cooper?"

His expression is filled with disbelief, clearly not feeling the change of topic. He shakes his head, an exasperated chuckle leaving him. "Damn it, woman." He pulls me against his chest, wrapping me in his arms. His heart thumps against my cheek, proving just how scared he was. "You shouldn't have fallen asleep on the beach, Julia, it's dangerous. Promise me you won't do that again."

"I didn't mean to. I'm sorry I scared you." Stepping back, I look up at him and repeat the question that's been plaguing me since he left this morning. "Did everything work out with Cooper?"

He gestures over to our spot.

I trudge back through the sand and we sit next to each other, just like old times. It has me feeling a little panicked so I inch away, leaving a small gap between us.

"Well, you were right," he starts, his eyes focused on the ocean in front of us. "He dropped the charges when Cooper told him you were going to press them if he didn't."

"Good," I sigh in relief.

Annoyance flashes in his eyes. "I still don't agree with it, Julia, that bastard should have some consequence for what he did to you."

"I think you smashing his face in was consequence enough."

"No, it's not. You need to go in and get that restraining order."

I clear my throat, knowing he's not going to like what I say next. "You know, I was thinking about that and I really don't think it's necessary. I mean what if—"

"Julia," my name falls on a warning growl.

"All right, calm down, I'll go tomorrow."

"I'll pick you up in the morning and take you to get it done."

"That's okay. I can manage on my own," I mumble.

"I'm sure you can, but I told you, I'll take you."

I shake my head, too tired to argue with him.

Things fall quiet between us, the sound of the crashing waves filling the tense silence.

"Well, I should go," I say awkwardly.

He grabs my wrist before I can stand, his touch burning my skin. "Not so fast. No more stalling, it's time you hear me out."

Damn. I knew it.

"What's the point, Jaxson? You sending me away in Germany is not something we are ever going to agree on, no matter what you say to me."

"Why can't you just try to understand that I didn't want anyone to see me like that?"

"Cooper did!" I point out angrily.

"That's because he was my emergency contact; I didn't really have a choice. Believe me, if I could have prevented him from seeing me like that too, I would have. But I also knew he could handle it. You don't get just how fucked-up I was."

"Of course I don't, because you never gave me the chance to."

"I'm sorry, but it was for the best, trust me."

"Well that's a really shitty explanation. Did you come back thinking it was going to be that easy, Jaxson?"

"No. I know it's going to take time for you to forgive me, but I'm asking you to at least give me the chance to make it right."

"It's not just about Germany. Why did you stay away from me for so long?"

Guilt flashes in his eyes before he looks away. I wait for him to say something, to explain himself, but he doesn't. His casted armor firmly in place, preventing me from seeing anything.

"Was Melissa telling the truth last night?" I whisper.

That gets a reaction out of him. He whips his head in my direction. "What are you asking me?"

"Did you leave in the first place because of me?"

His expression hardens, jaw locking in anger. "You know better than that. Nothing that bitch said last night was true."

"Then answer my question! Why did you stay away from me for six years?"

"Because I didn't think I could keep my dick in my pants, all right?"

I rear back in surprise, not expecting that admission.

"Christ!" Shoving to his feet, he begins pacing angrily. "Let's face it, Julia, that night changed everything between us."

"Are you saying you regret it?" Just the thought makes me want to throw up.

"No, damn it! I probably should, but I don't. That was the best fucking night of my life." I can tell he immediately regrets letting that out.

"Mine, too," I admit quietly.

His hard expression softens, eyes holding mine and reflecting everything that I'm feeling.

"You promised me that night that you would stay my friend, and you broke that promise." I look away as tears form in my eyes.

Kneeling down, he cups my face in both of his hands, forcing my gaze to his. "I'm sorry I fucked up. I thought I was doing the right thing. Believe me, if I could go back and change the way I handled things I would."

Emotion clogs my throat as I try to keep my tears at bay. "Why do you feel differently now? What's changed?"

Something dark and heartbreaking steals his expression. "Because there was a point when I didn't think I'd ever see you again, and the thought fucking ripped me apart."

A sharp pain seizes my chest and captures my breath.

"I swore to myself that if I got out of there alive I'd fix the mess I made with you. I can't live without you, Julia. I'll fix this, even if it kills me trying."

His tortured admission breaks me. Sliding off the log onto my knees in front of him, I wrap my arms around his neck, sobs racking my body.

He lifts me to straddle him and holds me close as all the years of hurt pour out of me. I cry over our loss of years together. I cry for him, that someone hurt him. I cry until the energy to cry any more has been completely drained out of me. Eventually, my tears subside, leaving only the sound of my labored breathing.

"I'll get us back to what we had, Julia, I promise," he whispers, making me believe him.

"Okay."

He pulls back, framing my face again between his hands. "Okay?" he asks, unsure if he heard me right.

I nod, my throat too tight to speak.

A breath of relief leaves him. "Okay."

Pressing a soft kiss to my temple, he rests his forehead on mine. I close my eyes, savoring the intimate contact with him.

"Are you going to be okay?"

My eyes spring back open at the gruff sound of his voice and I become intimately aware of our position. My dress is hiked up to my hips with his warm hands resting high on my bare thighs. I shift a little, only to feel how hard he is beneath me. His jaw flexes and grip tightens. My labored breathing is for a whole other reason now. His eyes draw to my mouth when I lick my dry lips.

Groaning, he drops his head on my shoulder. "Jules, this is one of those times where my control is being tested, so I need you to get up before I rip your panties off."

My breath stalls in my chest. "What if I want you to rip them off?"

"Oh fuck, don't say that to me right now. I'm trying to do the right thing and fix my mistakes. Help me out, Jules."

He's right, as much as I want him, now is not the time. If we are ever intimate again, it will be his move and his alone.

I begin to stand but his grip tightens, holding me in place. "Answer my question first. Are you okay?"

"I will be, I'm just tired. It's been an eventful few days."

He nods. "I know. Come on, I'll drive you home."

"I drove here, remember?" I remind him as I stand to my feet.

"Don't worry about it. Coop and I will drive your car back later."

I'm grateful he offers, because I'm too tired to drive right now anyway.

"Thanks." My arms wrap around his one as we start back to his truck. "Whatever happened to your bike?" I ask curiously.

"I still have it, it's in storage." He cracks a sexy grin. "Why? Want to go for a ride?"

"Yeah, I do. I miss it. I haven't been on a bike since you left."

"Good," he grunts. "I'll take you out once you're better."

"I'd like that." As much as I love his bike I have to say his truck is very nice too. It's black with chrome trim and tinted windows, but it's way too tall.

My head cranes back as we approach it, wondering how the hell I'm going to get in. "Geez, Jaxson, your truck doesn't quite reach the streetlight. I think you need to jack it up some more. How the heck am I supposed to get in this thing?"

"Get over here, smart-ass, and I'll help you," he replies, opening the passenger door for me.

Giggling, I move in front of him. His hands span my hips, but before giving me the lift I need, he leans in close, his mouth brushing my ear. "When you're lippy like that, Julia, it makes me want to do things to that smart-ass mouth of yours."

Heat surges through my blood when I think of all the things he would do to my mouth. His knowing chuckle tickles my ear before he boosts me up into the truck, making sure to be mindful of my sore hip. Walking over to his side, he hops up gracefully, the height not being an issue for him.

Sexy jerk.

Smiling, I lean my head against the window, feeling lighter and happier than I have in a long time. My tired eyes flutter close, and the next thing I know I feel myself being lifted. I come awake with a gasp, my arms flailing around in a panic as I grab on to something solid.

"Shh, it's okay, it's just me. I've got you."

Releasing a breath, I wrap my arms around Jaxson's neck and rest my head on his shoulder, falling in and out of consciousness.

"Where are your keys?" he asks softly.

"The door's unlocked."

His body tenses, a growl escaping him. "Damn it, Julia."

I ignore his outburst, too tired to argue.

Once in the house, he makes the climb up my stairs, keeping me in his protective arms… ones I've missed so much. My body eventually meets the cool hard mattress and I snuggle in with a moan as he drapes the blankets over me.

"Jesus." I hear him breathe out.

What is his problem now?

He digs in my purse on the nightstand, fishing out my car keys. "Is your house key on here so I can lock the door behind me?"

"Mmm hmm," I mumble sleepily.

He chuckles. "I'll be back in the morning to take you to the station."

Before he can leave, I reach out and grab his wrist. He looks back at me, his blue eyes meeting mine in the shadows of my room. "Don't ever leave me again, because if you do I might not survive it." I hate admitting that to him, but I need him to understand. I can't have him do that to me again.

His expression softens. "I'm not going anywhere." He promises, his voice sure. Leaning down, he gives me one more kiss on the forehead. "Good night, Julia."

This time I let him go and fall into a blissful sleep.

14

Jaxson

I lock the door on my way out then hop in my truck and head to the station. The lust burning inside of me is hard to ignore but I remind myself to keep focus on what's important and fix the mess I've made with Julia. Not get into her panties, no matter how bad I want back in them.

When I arrive at the station, I park next to Coop's truck and head inside. The receptionist from this afternoon jumps to her feet, eye fucking me like she did earlier. "Hey, Jaxson, back so soon?" she purrs, leaning over to give me a view of her cleavage that comes from a great looking pair of fake tits.

"Uh yeah, is Coop around?"

"He's in his office, go right in."

"Thanks." I start forward but turn back around when she calls out to me.

"I'm off in an hour, wanna hook up?"

I consider it for all of three seconds. I haven't been with anyone since Iraq; it's been a really long year. But I know from experience that fucking any other girl won't do anything to satisfy my need for Julia.

"Maybe another time," I say noncommittally.

"Let me know."

Heading into Coop's office I see him bent over a file, looking pissed. There's a coffee and a half-eaten doughnut next to him.

Typical.

"Hard at work with your coffee and doughnuts, I see."

His head snaps up. "Jesus, I didn't even hear you come in."

That's one way of knowing he's upset about something. "What has you looking like you're ready to kill someone?"

He pinches the bridge of his nose, something he always does when he's stressed. "Nothing, just some shit I found on someone's past I wish I didn't know."

"Anyone I know?"

"No, but you will probably meet her. She's a friend of the girls. Now shut up and don't ask me any more questions, because I can't answer them."

"Is it something Julia can get hurt from?"

"No, lover boy, so calm down."

I glare at his 'lover boy' comment as I take a seat in the chair across from him.

"So what brings you back here? Don't tell me you're turning yourself in for murdering Jennings."

I grunt. "I wouldn't turn myself in, I know exactly what to do with that prick's body so he was never found."

"Jesus, Jaxson, don't say shit like that to me."

I chuckle, loving that I get a rise out of him. "I need you to help me get Julia's car home for her. I gave her a ride earlier."

He relaxes back into his chair, crossing his arms with a knowing smirk. "So you finally found her. I was right, wasn't I? She was hiding from you."

"No, asshole, she wasn't. I found her sleeping on the beach."

He sobers, all earlier amusement wiped from his face. "Seriously? What the hell is wrong with her?"

"Believe me, I asked the same thing…a little more pissed off, mind you. It didn't go over very well."

He grunts. "I bet not."

"Speaking of which, what have you been teaching your girlfriend?"

"What are you talking about?"

"She's been constantly threatening to kick my ass and seems to think she can do some serious damage to me. She says you have been *showing her stuff*. Whatever the hell you're doing, tone it down."

He shakes his head. "I showed her how to get out of a few holds if someone ever tried to attack her. She seems to think she's Rocky now or some shit."

"Yeah, well, I swear she's more pissed at me than Julia is."

"Ignore it. She's been pissed at me lately for something too, and I don't have a fucking clue why. I don't know what's going on in that head of hers."

I can tell he's bothered by it. "Everything okay?"

He shrugs. "It will be. Come on, I'll help you take Julia's car home."

"Thanks."

As we walk out of his office, the receptionist stands up again, shoving her tits out.

"I'm gone for the night, Jenny, you can transfer all calls to my cell."

"You betcha, darlin'. See you around, Jaxson." She tosses me a wink as we head out the door.

"Jesus, that's quite the receptionist you have there. Has Kayla met her yet? Maybe that's why she's pissed at you."

He grunts. "Yeah, she's met her all right. Kayla put the gears to her when she started and the girl barely made eye contact with me for the first month." He looks over at me. "Be careful with her, she's a persistent one. And she's been banged more times than a snooze button on a Monday morning."

A beat of silence stretches between us until we both crack into laughter.

Damn. It's good to be back.

15

Julia

I wake up the next morning feeling almost like myself again. My ribs look worse today but thankfully they feel better, which is most important.

After my shower, I throw on a pair of black capri leggings and an off-the-shoulder white shirt that's loose and comfortable, then throw my natural wavy hair into a high, messy bun. I have no idea what time Jaxson's coming, all he said was morning, so I don't want to take too long getting ready. My stomach does a little flip at the thought of getting to see him again so soon, but I shove the dangerous feeling aside and concentrate on making my morning smoothie. Just as the blender finishes its racket my doorbell rings. I expect it to be Jaxson, so I'm surprised when I open it to find Grace.

"Grace, this is a pleasant surprise."

"Hi, Julia." She steps in, giving me a gentle hug. "I heard what happened, are you okay?"

"You heard already?"

"Yeah, Kayla told me."

"Oh good, at least I know you got the right story then," I say with a chuckle. "Come in, I'm just making myself a smoothie, want one?"

"Sure." She follows me into the kitchen and sets a pie down on my counter. "I made this for you, it's fresh from this morning."

Grace is an amazing baker, her specialty is pies, but she can bake anything. She creates and names them all herself too.

"It's only nine in the morning and you already baked this for me?"

She shrugs like it's no big deal. "I had an itch to create something, and when Kayla told me what happened I created something with all of your favorites."

My heart warms. "That's really sweet, thank you. What did you call it?"

Her shoulders straighten and expression hardens. "I named it, Wyatt Is An Asshole Pie."

We burst into a fit of laughter, my heart lightening further.

"That's a great name," I tell her.

Her smile fades. "You know, Julia, I'm happy you ended things with him. After your guys' first date, he came into the diner, and the way he acted with me... Well, it scared me a bit," she admits nervously.

"Oh, Grace, why didn't you say something?"

"Well I didn't want to jump to conclusions, I thought maybe I took it wrong. You and Kayla grew up with him; I figured you knew him better. I'm sorry, I wish I would have said somethin' now."

"Don't be sorry, just know you can always tell me anything."

Our conversation is interrupted when my front door opens and slams. Jaxson storms into the kitchen, looking angry as hell.

Grace grabs my arm with a gasp, scared spit-less.

"What the hell did I tell you about locking that damn door!"

I cock my hip and glare at him. "Well good morning to you too, ya jerk. And why on earth would I lock it? I'm home for heaven's sake."

"That's why you should lock it."

I roll my eyes. "Give it a rest and watch your mouth. I have my friend here, and you're making a terrible first impression."

For the first time he looks at Grace. Her grip on me has loosened, realizing I know him. But I notice she's quite shaken up.

"Jaxson, this is my friend, Grace."

"Nice to meet you. Sorry about that, but the woman doesn't listen about locking her doors," he says as an explanation, glaring at me.

Grace's eyes roam down Jaxson, and I can't help but smile. I have a feeling I know exactly what she's thinking.

She gives him a nervous wave and clears her throat. "Um, hello. Ah, what was your name again?"

"Jaxson," we both reply at the same time.

Grace snaps her head in my direction. "Jaxson?" she asks in shock. Leaning in, she whispers, "*The* Jaxson?"

I guess Kayla left that part out this morning. Nodding, I give her a look, telling her I'll explain everything later. Thankfully, she gets the memo.

Jaxson interrupts the silent exchange. "Are you ready to go to the station or should I come back?"

Grace jumps in. "Oh no, I need to get to work, I just stopped in to check on Julia and give her this pie."

"Did you walk here or take a cab?" I ask, knowing it's one or the other because she doesn't own a car.

"I walked."

"You walked here?" Jaxson asks in exasperation.

"Um, yes?" she replies, looking unsure.

"Do you have any idea how dangerous that is?"

"Lay off, Jaxson. What are you, the safety police?"

"You live in the country and she's walking alone on a gravel road."

"It's not that far," Grace argues back defensively.

He shakes his head. "Whatever. I'll drive you back in and drop you off wherever it is you work."

Her back straightens and chin lifts. "No, that's all right. I enjoy walkin'."

I take pity on her, knowing it's a battle she won't win. "Trust me, Grace, the argument is pointless. Let us drive you back, we're headed that way anyway."

She nods but it's a bit stiff. "All right, thank you."

Grabbing two travel mugs, I fill them both with the smoothie then hand one to Grace.

"Thanks." She accepts it, smiling again.

As we head out of the kitchen she grabs my arm and leans in close to me. "Wow, Julia, you and Kayla weren't kiddin'. The man is sexy. A little scary and arrogant, but damn sexy."

A laugh tumbles past my lips. "I know."

Jaxson stands at the front door, impatiently waiting for us to follow. We quickly snap out of our giggling and get moving.

Once we arrive at the station, Jaxson comes over and helps me out of the truck. He seems to be in a better mood since I promised him on the way here that I would start locking my doors all the time.

I stare at the building in front of me, my stomach twisting anxiously for what I'm about to do. Jaxson laces his fingers with mine and gives them a re-assuring squeeze. I look up to see his gaze warm and understanding. "It'll be all right, Jules, you're doing the right thing."

I nod even though I feel unsure of that.

When we enter through the front doors, Jenny stands and gives Jaxson a flirtatious smile. "Hi, Jaxson, miss me already?"

I tense, jealousy heating my blood.

She looks down at our joined hands, her nose lifting in distaste. "Julia, what are you doing here?"

I don't get the chance to respond because Jaxson does. "That's none of your business. We're here to see Cooper."

I stand a little taller by the way he puts her in her place. She glares at me a second longer before pointing in the direction of Cooper's office. Jaxson gives my hand a tug, leading me across the station.

"Wow, you've been busy. First Gladys, now Jenny," I tease, unable to help myself.

He quirks a brow. "Jealous, Julia?"

I scoff. "Yeah, right…"

Deputy Wilkinson comes walking out of Coop's office. "Well hello, Miss Julia, you're looking lovely today."

Now it's Jaxson's turn to tense, and I can't help but rub it in just a little. "Why thank you, Trevor, you're not looking too bad yourself today either."

With a growl, Jaxson propels me forward.

"Jealous, Jaxson?" I mock, a smug smile tugging at my lips.

"You're pushing it, Julia."

I giggle as we enter Cooper's office.

"Hey," he greets us, looking exhausted.

"You look like shit," Jaxson points out rudely.

"Thanks, asshole."

Seeing Cooper like this reminds me of how sad Kayla was yesterday. I hope everything is all right between them.

"Hi, Coop. Thanks for driving my car home last night with Jaxson."

"No problem." He rises out of his chair and points for me to sit in it. When I do he places a pile of papers in front of me. "I need you to fill all of this out."

Picking up the pen, I hesitate and again try my best to get out of doing this but they won't hear it.

"Trust me, Julia, when I say this is necessary," Cooper says.

"I do trust you. I'm just scared this is going to make things worse, but if you think it's that important I'll do it."

Reluctantly, I fill out the paperwork, then hand them over to Cooper when I'm finished.

"It takes anywhere from twenty-four to forty-eight hours for this to process. I will speed it up as quickly as I can. You need to tell us right away if he tries to contact you. I mean it."

"I will."

We walk out of his office and a moment of panic strikes me when he hands the papers off to Jenny. "I need you to fax this to the number attached right away."

She glances down at them, before her shocked eyes lock on mine. "You're putting a restraining order on Wyatt Jennings? Aren't you dating him?"

My heart plummets at her outburst, embarrassment heating my cheeks.

"Jenny, you have no right to ask questions," Cooper snaps. "Do I need to remind you what your job is?"

She shifts nervously. "No, of course not. I understand."

Swallowing thickly, I storm out of the station.

Jaxson rushes out after me and tugs me against him. "Forget about her, Jules."

"Everybody is going to think what she just said," I mumble into his chest.

"Who gives a fuck what anyone else thinks? You did the right thing."

"Can you just take me home?" I ask.

"Yeah, come on." He slings an arm around my shoulder and leads me to his truck.

We arrive at my house a few minutes later. Jaxson leaves his truck running, the motor idling loudly as he climbs out to help me down. I try to ignore the way my skin tingles where his hands grip my waist.

"What are you doing tonight?" he asks, slamming the door behind me.

"Nothing at the moment."

"Want to go out and do something? Maybe grab supper?"

A smile dances across my lips at the way his feet shift. If I didn't know better I'd think he is nervous. "Yeah, I'd like that," I tell him.

"I'll pick you up at six, okay?"

I nod then clear my throat, feeling nervous for what I'm about to say next. "You know, Jaxson, you don't have to stay at the hotel, you could stay here with me if you want to." I notice his body visibly stiffen but before he can get the wrong idea I rush on to say, "I have more than enough room, I have three spare rooms."

I see the answer before he even responds. "I don't think that's a good idea, Jules."

My eyes fall to the ground where I kick at the gravel. "Okay," I reply quietly, then shrug, acting like it's no big deal. "Just thought I'd offer. I'll see you at six."

When I turn to leave, he wraps his arms around me from behind and pulls me back against him. A gasp parts my lips when I feel how hard he is against my bottom.

"I appreciate the offer, Julia, but the problem is, your bedroom door will do nothing to stop me from coming into your room at night and sinking into that sweet, hot pussy of yours."

Oh lord!

A current of heat explodes through my body like an inferno. Unable to stop myself, I push back against his erection, a fiery whimper breaching my lips at the contact.

A groan rumbles from his chest, his grip tightening on my hips. "Be a good girl, Julia, and go into the house before I lose control and fuck you right here on your driveway."

I try to move, I really do, but I'm completely rooted to my spot, need pounding through every nerve ending of my body.

Growling, Jaxson spins me around, his lips dropping a hard kiss on my forehead. "I'll be back at six." He walks off without another word.

Once he's in his truck again I manage to get my feet moving and hightail it into the house. Closing the door, I drop back against it.

Holy crap!

My breath races and senses reel. My back still burns hot from where he was pressed against me. I turn my head and look at the lock on my door, another smile curving my lips when I click it in place.

16

Julia

A s I'm folding laundry later that afternoon, there's a knock on the door. I glance at the clock wondering if it's Jaxson, but know it's too early. Bounding down the stairs, I open the door to see Kayla with tears streaming down her face. "Kayla, what's wrong?"

"You're never going to believe this," she chokes out on a sob, her arms wrapped around her stomach as if trying to keep warm.

I pull her in and usher her to my couch, forcing her to sit down. "What is it? You're scaring me to death."

She looks at me, her blue eyes filled with devastation. "I'm pretty sure Cooper is cheating on me."

"What?" I gasp. "No way, Kayla, he'd never do something like that to you, he loves you."

"I've suspected something for a couple of weeks now, but I shut the thought down because, just like you, I thought he would never do that to me." Her breath catches as she tries to compose herself enough to speak. "I caught him lying to me. The other night he called me at six and told me he was working late at the station. I decided to surprise him and bring him supper. When I got there he wasn't there, Jenny said he left at five. Julia, he didn't get home until ten that night."

I rub her back, trying to soothe her. "Did you ask him where he was?"

"Yeah, he said he got a call and had to meet with another officer at the department in Charleston. I could tell he was lying, but I dropped it because a small part of me hoped he was telling the truth." She shakes her head, a bitter laugh escaping her. "I've caught him a few times whispering into his phone, but as soon as I walk in he hangs up. Anytime I asked who it was he'd say it was the wrong number."

That does seem suspicious, but this is Cooper, he's one of the most honest men I know.

"Today the moment of truth came out," she continues. "His phone rang when he was in the shower. I didn't recognize the number but saw it was from Charleston. When I answered someone gasped then hung up. So I called it back a few minutes later from my cell, blocking my number, and a woman answered. When I didn't say anything, you know what she said?"

I shake my head, afraid to ask.

"She whispered, 'Cooper, is that you?' She whispered it, Julia! Like it was a secret."

"What did you say?"

"Nothing, I couldn't speak. I was frozen because my heart had just broken in two."

I wrap my arms around her as another sob shreds from her throat. "You have to talk to Cooper about this. There has to be some explanation."

"He's meeting her this Friday at a motel on I-90 between here and Charleston."

"No!"

She nods. "I scrolled through his text messages after and found the number. There wasn't much, except that she looked forward to seeing him and what room she would be in."

"Oh my god!" I can't believe this is happening, I never thought Cooper would do this in a million years. "Are you going to confront him?"

Her back straightens and eyes flash with anger. "Damn straight, this Friday at the motel when I bust him and his whore."

I suck in a sharp breath. "Oh, Kayla, I'm not sure that's a good idea."

"I have to. I need to see it with my own eyes. If I ask him, he'll just lie to me like he has been for weeks." Her hand rests on her stomach, looking like she might be sick. "I can't believe this is happening. I thought we were going to get married and have babies, Julia. We've been together for years. How could he do this to me?"

She breaks down again, and I can't stop my own tears from falling, her devastation shattering my heart. "I'm so sorry."

I think back to seeing Cooper this morning, remembering how awful he looked. Maybe the guilt is eating at him.

The bastard!

"I'll come with you on Friday."

She gives me a sad smile. "I was hoping you would say that."

"Of course, I'd never let you go through this alone."

"Thanks, Jules," she whispers, her voice sounding as sad as her eyes look. "Anyway, I better get going. I work evenings this week, and I need to make myself somewhat presentable."

"Maybe you should take a few days off?"

She shakes her head. "No, it's good for me, it will keep me busy and away from Cooper."

"Okay. Call me if you need anything. I mean it, Kayla."

"I will, I'll text you the details for Friday."

We give each other one last hug before she heads out the door. I drop down on my couch again, my mind reeling.

A few minutes later, another knock sounds on my door. I answer it, thinking it's Kayla again until I open it and see Wyatt. My heart sinks to the pit of my stomach. He looks terribly angry, his face black and blue from Jaxson's fists.

"You're putting a fucking restraining order on me?"

"Cooper thought it was necessary," I tell him anxiously, deciding it's best to leave Jaxson's name out of it.

"How could you fucking do this to me, after everything we've been through."

I gape at him, my mouth ajar. "This is why, Wyatt. We've had three dates and you act like what we had was serious."

It was the wrong thing to say.

His fists clench at his sides, as if he's going to hit something. I'm praying that something isn't me. "Don't give me that shit. We've been in love with each other for years. I waited patiently, because I know that son of a bitch brainwashed you to stay away from me."

Oh my god!

He's completely serious; he really believes this.

"You're going to drop the restraining order," he says firmly.

"No, I'm not. You need to leave, Wyatt, right now." I start to close my door but he shoves his foot inside. "Don't make me call Cooper," my threat is weak and shaky, shredding my brave facade.

His expression softens as he reaches up to touch my face and I flinch at the unwanted contact. "Don't be scared. I'd never hurt you."

"You already did," I choke out.

His jaw flexes in anger. "That was an accident."

I shake my head. "It doesn't matter."

"Don't throw away what we have for him, Julia. It will only be a matter of time before he leaves you again."

"This isn't about Jaxson."

"Bullshit!" he barks, making me jump. "It's always been about him."

A gasp flees me, panic thrashing through my veins as he grabs my arm in a painful grip.

"Have you spread your legs for him already? Have you let him have what's mine?" His expression is full of violence, but his eyes are glazed over, almost as if he's not there.

He's crazy. Absolutely certifiably crazy.

"Answer me now!" he bellows, giving my shoulders a shake.

I tread carefully, realizing that he's completely irrational. Tears stream down my face as I shake my head.

His expression eases again. "Good girl."

My body stiffens when he leans in closer, putting his mouth to my ear. "Wyatt, what are you doing?" I ask, stifling my sob.

"Shhh." He inhales deeply through his nose and groans, the sound has bile inching up my throat. His hand runs up my spine and grabs a fistful of my hair, yanking my head back. "Drop the restraining order or I will make your life hell."

I stumble back a step when he shoves away from me. The moment he turns his back and starts down my steps I slam the door and lock it. It isn't long before I hear his car peeling away.

An hour later my body is still trembling violently. I threw on sweats and a blanket, but can't seem to get warm. Icy terror has ruthlessly taken over me and won't let go. Fear leaps into my throat when there's another knock on the door. Standing, I approach slowly, my heart thundering, praying it's not him again. Peeking through the peephole, I see it's Jaxson. Unlocking the latch, I swing the door open.

"I'm glad to see the door is locked," he says with a smirk that vanishes the moment he sees me. "Jules?" He grabs my shoulders in concern. "What's wrong? What happened?"

I shove him off of me, anger bubbling up to the surface hot and fast and it overrides everything else. "I told you! I told you both that it was a mistake.

But you didn't listen to me and now everything is worse." My fists strike out, hitting him in the chest as I release my anger and fear on him. "Why didn't you listen to me?"

"Goddamn it, stop!" He spins me around, my back to his front, and locks his arms around me so I can't get loose.

My knees give out beneath me as a sob shatters my chest.

He falls with me, holding me tight. "Talk to me, baby, what happened?"

"He came here," I choke out.

He turns me to face him, his hands gripping my arms firmly. "What did he do? Did he fucking hurt you?"

I can't answer him, because I'm crying too hard.

"Answer me, are you hurt?"

I shake my head, my emotion robbing me of breath.

"God, Julia, breathe, baby, it's okay." He pulls me into his chest, trying to talk me through whatever is happening to me. Eventually, the deep baritone of his voice, and the comforting circles he's rubbing on my back begin to calm me enough that I'm able to catch my breath.

Leaning back, he takes my face between his hands, his expression lethal. "I'm going to fucking kill him."

I grab his shirt, panic seizing my chest at the thought. "No, you can't! Jaxson, you have to listen to me! He's crazy. Like I mean, seriously crazy. He thinks I'm his. He thinks we have been in love with each other for years, he thinks… Oh god." I start losing control of my breath again.

"Stop, just calm down."

He tries to stand but I cling to him. "No! Don't leave me."

"Fuck me!" Picking me up, he carries me into the kitchen with him and sets me on the counter. He fills a glass of water and hands it to me. "Drink this, just a little at a time."

I do as he says, the cool water a welcome relief to my raw throat.

Once I'm finished he takes it back and comes to stand between my legs, his hands cradling my face. "I need you to tell me exactly what happened and what he said." My mouth opens to blast him with the information but he cuts me off, his hand covering my mouth. "Calmly, everything is going to be okay."

Closing my eyes, I take a deep breath then relay everything that was said. A dangerous rage fills his expression when I tell him about Wyatt asking me if I spread my legs for him. "I told you this would happen," I say through a fresh wave of tears. "I'm dropping the restraining order."

"No, you're not! Julia, listen to me, he's trying to scare you."

I laugh bitterly. "Yeah, well it worked, I'm fucking scared. I'm serious, Jaxson. I'm dropping it and there's not a damn thing you or Cooper can do to stop me."

"Damn it! Listen to everything you just told me. Now more than ever, you should understand just how much you need that restraining order."

"No. If I drop it everything can go back to the way it was, and I'll just stay clear of him."

"Do you really think it will be that easy?"

"I don't have any other choice!"

"Yes, you do! You stand up to him. He's a rich asshole who's used to getting his way, by either paying people off or threatening them. Don't let him push you around."

"I'm scared" I whisper. "You didn't see him, he's crazy."

He wraps me in his arms, holding me close. "I won't let him hurt you. He might be crazy, but he's a fucking coward. It's why he came to you and not me."

I shake my head as tears stream down my face.

"What do you think he's going to do once you lift that restraining order? Do you really think he will just leave you alone? He's infatuated with you. Lifting it is only going to cause you more harm."

He's right. I know he is but it doesn't make it any easier. "How did he find out about it already? I thought Cooper said it would take a couple of days."

His jaw hardens. "I don't know, but I'm going to find out." Fishing his cell out of his pocket, he dials Coop's number. "Yeah, hold on a sec." He covers the phone to speak to me. "Go ahead and get your shoes on. I'll meet you at the door."

"I don't want to go out anymore."

"We're not, we're going to my hotel so I can get my things and check out."

"Why?"

"Because I'm staying here with you."

His explanation brings me a small measure of peace. I really don't want to stay by myself, especially tonight.

Hopping off the counter, I head to the bathroom first and wash my face, the cool water stinging my hot eyes. Afterward, I slip my shoes on and walk back into the kitchen to see Jaxson still on the phone with Cooper.

His tone is quiet but harsh. "Oh come on, we both know she told him."

I'm assuming he's talking about Jenny. I figured it was probably her, too.

"I don't fucking care! I'm telling you now, Cooper, if he comes near her again I won't tell you first, I'll deal with him my way." Icy disdain drips from his promise. "Fine, get back to me after you do." He hangs up and slips the phone back in his pocket. "Fuck!" His angry curse pierces the air as he braces his hands on my counter, head hanging in defeat.

My steps are slow as I approach him. His muscles tense as I lay my hand on his back before wrapping my arms around him, wanting to ease his fury.

A few beats pass before he turns to face me, reciprocating my hug. His heart thunders against my cheek, chest heaving in anger.

"I'll keep the restraining order," I tell him quietly.

His stiff muscles relax. "Thanks, baby. You just saved us from having a really big fight." The corner of my mouth lifts in a smile as he kisses the top of my head. "Come on, let's go. We'll pick up something to eat on the way home."

17

Jaxson

Later that evening, we're sitting on Julia's couch eating supper and watching a movie. All my stuff is piled in the guest room upstairs, right next to Julia's bedroom. From here on out, I will be getting no sleep, my hard dick will be keeping me up all night. I just hope I'm not plagued by any nightmares. I haven't had one for some time now, but every once in a while, one will sneak up on me.

Looking down at Julia, I notice she still hasn't touched her food. "Eat," I demand, pointing to her untouched burger.

"I'm not very hungry," she responds quietly. She's wrapped in a blanket, her face pale and eyes bright with fear. I want to kill that fucker. The only thing stopping me is I don't want to leave her, especially right now; she scared the hell out of me with her panic attack earlier. Cooper promised me he would deal with the asshole. It's his only shot. Then the bastard is mine.

"Eat, Julia!" I say again.

She rolls her eyes and takes a dramatic bite of her burger. "There, happy?"

I grunt. "I will be when it's gone."

She finishes most of it, so I let her be. Eventually she lies down, putting her feet across my lap while she watches the movie, some chick flick I haven't been paying attention to. My mind is too busy conjuring up images of beating Jennings to death. I knew the fucker wasn't all there, but even Cooper and I didn't realize it was this bad. The fact that Wyatt thinks Julia is his goes to show just how crazy he is. Everyone in this town has always known she's mine.

It makes me rethink my decision about this just friends bullshit. Clearly, we already have a hard time controlling our emotions. Staying here with her is only going to make it worse. But I know it's not fair to Julia; she deserves to have a life, a family. That's something she can never have with me, because no way in hell do I ever plan on having kids. My bloodline stops with me, the thought of fucking a kid up like my father did to me makes me sick.

Glancing back down at her, I see she's sound asleep. She looks so small and fragile like this that it makes me want to lock her in here forever so no one can hurt her.

I turn off the TV then pick her up effortlessly; she doesn't stir. Climbing the stairs, I carry her into her room and lay her down. Putting her to bed is seeming to become a ritual for the two of us, one I could definitely get used to, but one that's dangerous. I decide to leave her in her sweats, knowing I'll have a hard enough time sleeping tonight as it is.

After locking up, I head to bed and settle in for a long fucking night.

18

Julia

I wake up in my bed the next morning, still in my sweats with a blanket draped over me and realize I must have fallen asleep watching the movie last night. Stretching out my tired muscles, I think about yesterday's events and still can't believe how delusional I was about Wyatt.

How has he gone so long in this town without people realizing how crazy he is?

The thought is interrupted when my phone chimes with a text. Reaching over, I grab it off my nightstand to see it's from Kayla.

Kayla: *Be ready for 7 on Friday. Make sure you dress in dark clothes and wear a hat. We're going to bust this fucker.*

After everything that happened with Wyatt yesterday, I had forgotten all about her, which makes me feel terrible. I'm still reeling over the thought that Cooper could do this. I've thought about mentioning it to Jaxson but I know he won't keep it from Cooper.

The sound of the shower turning on down the hall in the guest bathroom alerts me Jaxson is awake. I get up and take one myself, but make it quick, wanting to cook him breakfast before he's done.

After changing into a pair of faded jean shorts and a soft pink tank, I head out into the hall and peek my head into his room when I see the door slightly ajar. "Hey, what do you want—" My words die in my throat and I suck in a sharp, painful breath at the sight before me.

Jaxson stands faced away from me without a shirt on, a massive tattoo covering his defined back. It's the most beautiful angel I've ever seen. Her detailing so distinctive you would swear she was real. There's a darkness that swirls around her, but it does nothing to take away from her beauty. The image is mostly black and shaded, except her eyes. They're a bright aquamarine—the same color as mine.

Although the tattoo is large, it does nothing to cover the horrendous scars that mark his skin. It looks like someone whipped him or cut him... I don't know which, and I'm not sure I want to.

My burning, watery eyes roam up his back and collide with his hard ones. Tears soak my cheeks as my heart swells painfully in my chest. I try to speak, to say something, but the words are lodged in my aching throat. They end up invading me a moment later. "I-I'm sorry, I didn't realize you were changing." Closing the door, I make my way downstairs and head into the kitchen, my blood rushing in my ears. I lean over the sink and put a shaking hand to my stomach, feeling like I'm going to be sick.

How could someone do that to him? To anyone? What does the tattoo mean?

I snap out of my thoughts when Jaxson walks in. Clearing my throat, I swipe my tears away and busy myself around the kitchen. "What do you want for breakfast? I can make eggs, pancakes—"

"Julia."

I continue to move about and talk over him. "I don't have any bacon but I can make French toast, or if you like we can go into town and eat at the diner."

"Julia, stop!" Reaching out, his fingers curl around my arm as he pulls me against him, his strong arms holding my shattered pieces together.

My sob breaks free, exploding past my lips. "What did they do to you?"

He lifts me off my feet and sets me on the counter, coming to stand between my legs. My arms hug his neck as I keep him close, wishing I had the power to heal what I just saw a moment ago.

"Don't cry for me, Jules," he says, his voice gruff as he rubs my back.

"I hate that someone hurt you."

"We made it out, that's all that matters."

When he says *we* it reminds me he wasn't the only one hurt. I lean back to look at him. "Were Sawyer and Cade the other ones with you?"

He confirms the question with a nod.

"Are they okay?" I ask on a painful breath.

He drops his forehead on mine. "Yeah, baby, they're okay. We all are. We're a little fucked-up maybe, but what else is new?" He grins, trying to make light of the moment, but there's nothing funny about it.

"Don't make jokes."

His expression sobers, a dark pain entering his eyes. "Do you understand now, Julia? Do you get why I sent you away. I see you hurt like this and it fucking kills me. Trust me when I say what you would have seen in that hospital was a hundred times worse than what you just saw."

I think about this for a moment then nod. "I understand, but it doesn't change that I wanted to be there for you. Yes, it would have hurt me to see you like that, but I wanted to help you. I wanted to make it better for you."

"After seeing the tattoo don't you understand that you did? The angel is you, Julia. You were always there with me in the darkness. Every time those fuckers came in to torture us, I went into my mind and thought about you."

My breath seizes in my lungs, his words stealing my breath.

"I would think about your smile and your eyes," he says, his thumb brushing my cheek. "Then I would think about the night I was buried inside your warm body, and I'd completely lose myself in you. It made everything I went through bearable, it made me fight to get the fuck out of there."

His beautiful words are my undoing. Grabbing his shirt, I seal his mouth over mine, but that's where my control ends. His fingers thread in my hair with a firm grip, tilting my head back, to deepen the kiss. All of our pent up desire unleashes, our mouths aligning in fevered hunger.

I suck in air as his lips move down my throat, scalding my sensitive skin. His hand presses on my chest, coaxing me to my back. He tugs down my tank top, freeing my breasts. The cool air whispers across my fevered flesh, my nipples pebbling beneath his heated gaze.

A low growl rumbles from his throat as he leans down and latches on to one aching point. Heat sweeps through my body like a desert storm, stealing my senses.

Moaning, I arch off the counter, my fingers threading in his still-damp hair. I thrust against his hard stomach, seeking friction for the throbbing between my legs.

Reaching between our bodies, Jaxson snaps open the button to my jean shorts, and shoves his hand in my panties. "Ah yeah, you're so fucking wet," he groans, gliding his fingers through my arousal before entering two of them deep inside of me.

A heated cry breaches my lips and I grab onto his biceps, my fingers getting lost in the grooves of his muscles.

"Jesus, I love seeing you burn for me, baby."

My fiery moans fill the air around us. I'm so lost in the pleasure that I don't hear the knock on the door until Jaxson tenses.

I still and listen again, praying it's not… yep, it's my door.

"Are you fucking serious?" he asks, exasperated.

Disappointment crushes me, tears leaking from my eyes at the need torturing my body. I gasp when Jaxson's fingers return to their delicious thrusting.

He peers down at me, a wicked grin curving his lips. "I won't leave you hangin', baby, but you only have a few seconds here, so try not to be too loud."

With a smile of my own, I pull his mouth down to mine and rock my hips to the rhythm of his fingers. My fast breaths tumble past my lips with the anticipation of my climax.

"That's it, baby. Let go and come all over my fingers."

My orgasm slams into me and I fall apart, a total shaking mess. He claims my lips, smothering my cries of pleasure.

Once I'm limp and sated, I notice the knocking has stopped. I yelp, startled at the vibration between my legs.

"It's just my phone," Jaxson chuckles.

He removes his hand from my shorts then shocks me by putting his fingers to his mouth, sucking my arousal off them, his eyes never leaving mine. A growl rumbles from him, his face savage. "Go to the bathroom and get decent; it's Cooper." Without another word, he leaves the kitchen.

Righting my shirt, I hurry into the bathroom, my legs feeling like jelly from the intense orgasm that just crashed through me. I splash water on my face, trying to rid my flushed skin tone.

Jaxson's and Cooper's voices carry from the kitchen. Exiting the bathroom, I head into the kitchen to find them in a heated discussion. I have a hard time looking Cooper in the eye. I'm sure he has a pretty good idea what was taking us so long to answer. It also doesn't help that I'm furious at him for what he's doing to Kayla, but I try to mask that, not wanting to give anything away.

"Hey, Julia."

"Cooper," I acknowledge with a tight nod, failing miserably at my attempt.

He frowns at my less-than-friendly greeting. "I came by to let you know that I served Jennings the restraining order today, and I also laid into him about coming over here last night. He shouldn't be bothering you again."

"Thank you," I reply, my words a little softer this time.

He nods. "I found out it was Jenny who told him about the restraining order. I fired her this morning."

"You didn't have to do that."

Jaxson grunts. "The bitch is lucky that's all she got."

"If Wyatt comes anywhere near you again I want you to call me right away. If you run into him somewhere by chance, he has to leave immediately, not the other way around."

"He must have been pretty mad, huh?" I ask, chewing my nail nervously.

He shrugs. "Doesn't matter. I think he was hoping he scared you enough yesterday that you would drop it. I'm glad you didn't. He knows now that you're serious, so I do believe he'll leave you alone. Either way, I think it's good Jaxson stays here for a while with you."

My attention anchors on Jaxson, his expression void of any emotion. His armor is back in place. I can tell we won't be picking up where we left off, much to my disappointment.

"Anyway, I better get back, but I wanted to come by and tell you in person that it has been taken care of."

My eyes narrow suspiciously. "Where are you going?"

"Back to work," he answers slowly.

"You sure about that?"

Ugh, shut up, Julia!

He looks at me like I've lost my mind. "Yeah, I'm sure. Why?"

"Just curious." I shrug easily, hoping to cover the lie. "Thanks for stopping by." Walking over to the sink I grab myself a glass of water. Out of the corner of my eye I see Cooper and Jaxson exchange a look.

Damn, I hope I didn't ruin anything and he's figured out that I know.

With a shake of his head, Cooper mumbles a good-bye then leaves.

I feel Jaxson's gaze burning me but I ignore it and pay close attention to the glass of water in my hand. "What was that all about?"

"What?" I feign ignorance.

"Your suspicious questions, that's what."

"I just wondered if he was going back to work."

"Where else would he be going?"

"I don't know, Jaxson, *do you?*"

Shit! Now I'm accusing him, too.

"What the fuck is with you?"

"Never mind, forget I said anything." I decide to change the subject to a topic that's no less easy to talk about. "So, are we going to talk about what just happened?"

He shrugs. "Nothing much to say. Heat of the moment, we got wrapped up in our emotions."

"Really, that's how we're going to play this?"

"What do you want me to say, Julia? Do I want to fuck you? Yeah, I do, but what do we do after that?"

"Why do we have to decide? Why can't we just see where it goes?"

"I don't know how to do that. I've never had a fucking girlfriend before."

"Well it's quite easy, Jaxson. You see, it would be exactly how we are now except we get to have sex, lots of sex. Sounds like a damn good deal to me."

He doesn't smile like I hope for him to. "And what do we do when our time is up? Because once we change our relationship there's no going back to just being friends."

"Why does there have to be a time limit?"

"Because one day you're going to want to get married and have kids, something I never plan to have."

Pain slices through my chest, my heart twisting at his words. "Yeah, well, as much as I really want kids one day it's never going to happen, because I can't have children." My words come out as raw and painful as the wound in my chest.

"What the hell are you talking about?"

"I have polycystic ovary syndrome," I tell him, my throat tight. "I found out after I came back from your graduation. I had a physical with my doctor after we... well you know, and it came up. I don't ovulate because I don't have regular menstrual cycles. It's why I am on the pill. The doctor told me my chances of ever having children are slim to none."

"Shit." His long legs eat up the distance between us, his arms banding around me. "I'm sorry, Jules, you would make a good mom."

I shrug and stay silent, not wanting to talk about the painful topic.

"Look, let's get back what we had before, then we'll go from there. I don't want to lose you again."

I peer up at him, his startling blue eyes striking me deeper. "You never lost me, Jaxson, you pushed me away. There's a difference." Slipping out from his grasp, I walk away.

He does nothing to stop me, but I didn't expect him to. I'm tired of being rejected, and I decide from here on out there will be no more attempts on my part. The rest is up to him.

19

Julia

A few days later I'm standing at my kitchen sink, cursing up a storm, as I try to pry up the handle on the tap but can't. The darn thing is stuck.

"What's wrong?" Jaxson asks, walking up behind me.

"The stupid tap is jammed. I should just buy a whole new sink, the damn thing is like a hundred years old anyway."

He nudges me to the side. "Watch out, I got this."

My eyes roll at his arrogance, but I step aside. At first he tries to pull it up firmly, but not too hard. When he has no luck with that, he gives up and really yanks on it. A loud pop pierces the air.

I gasp and jump out of the way as water sprays out, all over Jaxson.

"Fuck!" He tries screwing the handle back on while water soaks his chest and face. Finally, he manages to get it back on. "Shit," he mutters with a heavy breath, looking a little stunned.

I stand with my hand cupped over my mouth, my body shaking as I try to hold in my laughter.

He turns to face me, eyes narrowing. "Are you laughing?"

I shake my head but a snort escapes me, outing the lie.

"You think this is funny, Julia?" he asks with a gleam in his eye.

Uh-oh, I know that look. Shoving from the counter, I haul ass out of the kitchen. His heavy steps gain on me but I push myself harder, barreling up the stairs for my bedroom. Of course I'm nowhere near fast enough. Jaxson's arms snag my waist, holding me tight as he carries my flailing body up the remainder of the stairs, hauling me into the main bathroom.

"What are you doing?" I shriek, trying to kick free as he leans down to start the shower. "You wouldn't dare!"

"Yeah, I would."

I manage to break free for all of a second before he has me back against him. "Jaxson, don't you do it! I mean it, I will kick your ass."

He grunts, unconcerned by the threat, then lifts me into the shower, forcing me under the warm water.

"I hate you, I hate you, I hate you!" I grind out and give him my best glare.

He chuckles, proud of himself. "What are you going to do about it, Julia?"

The challenge fuels me. My eyes track down his body, his wet shirt showing every line and curve of his muscles. The perfect idea forms and I grace him with a smirk of my own. His smugness disappears as I saunter closer to him. "I can think of a few things to do," I say breathlessly, dragging a finger slowly down his chest to the waistband of his jeans.

"What are you doing?" he asks, voice gruff.

Reaching down I grab his hard length through his wet jeans, giving it a gentle squeeze.

"Shit," he breathes, dropping his head against the wall.

"You know, Jaxson, I owe you for the other day, and I'm thinking now would be a good time to repay you." I drop to my knees before him and unsnap his jeans.

"Ah fuck!" the curse flees him on a hiss, his muscles tense.

Even though I'm only messing with him, I can't help it when my own breathing speeds up, desire igniting in my blood. Unzipping him, I push open the flaps of his jeans then lean in and press a soft kiss to his hard length over his black boxer briefs.

A loud groan rumbles from him, and I can't deny that my clothes aren't the only things wet right now. I look up to see his jaw locked and eyes shut, waiting for me to take him in my mouth.

"Oh wait, what am I doing?"

His eyes snap open as I stand.

"I totally forgot… *friends only*," I give myself a tap on the head and let out a dramatic sigh. "Well, I guess I better go and change now." Giving him a pat on the chest, I move to step out of the shower when I'm yanked back.

"I don't fucking think so."

His mouth descends hard.

Claiming.

Branding.

Moaning, I kiss him back with the same passion, letting the taste of him settle deep into my bones.

His hands cup my bottom, hoisting me up. My legs hug his waist as he shoves me up against the shower wall. He pulls back, his eyes holding mine beneath the hood of his dark lashes. "It's time you learned just who is in control here, Julia."

He drives his hip against the apex of my thighs, dragging a fiery whimper from my throat.

Lord, he can be really sexy when he's arrogant.

His head dips, teeth grazing my stiff nipple through my thin, wet tank top.

"Oh god, Jaxson, please," I beg shamelessly, my nails digging into his shoulders.

"You want it so bad, don't you, baby?"

"Yes," I manage through short breaths.

"Not as bad as me." His hips push forward again, giving me more but it's still not enough.

My fingers grip his wet shirt, dragging it up his back, needing his skin upon mine.

I feel him tense and he stops his delicious assault.

"What?" I ask breathlessly.

Then I hear it… a knock on my door.

This is not happening.

"What the hell?" he asks in disbelief. "Are you expecting someone?"

I shake my head.

Someone bangs on the door again, and not all that gently.

"Ignore it," I say, taking his mouth again in a desperate attempt to make him forget he heard anything.

The insistent knocking finally stops but instead of leaving they ring the doorbell.

"Shit!" Jaxson pulls his mouth free, regret burning in his ice-blue eyes. "We should answer it, it might be Cooper."

If it is Cooper again, I'm gonna kill him. My body slides sinfully down Jaxson's as he releases me. I want to cling to it and beg him to never let go.

"Who's going to answer it?" I ask, looking down at our wet clothes.

His eyes lock on my plastered tank top. "Definitely not you. I'll answer it, you go change."

Giggling, I grab a towel and dash out of the bathroom and into my room. I dry my hair as best as I can then trade my wet tank top and capris for a light denim jean skirt and sage green, lace tank top that shows some cleavage. Hopefully, it will tempt Jaxson to finish what we started. I know I said he had to be the first to make the move from now on, but that doesn't mean I'm going to make it easy on him.

As I descend the stairs, I hear a couple of male voices that I don't recognize. Wondering whom it could be, I enter into the kitchen and come to an abrupt halt, gaping at the men before me. "Oh my gosh! Sawyer? Cade?" I ask, unsure if what I'm seeing is real.

"Holy shit, look who went and got even hotter," Sawyer boasts with that charming smile of his, one I've never forgotten. His arms open invitingly. "Get your pretty ass over here."

Smiling, I run into his outstretched arms, hugging him tight. Tears sting my eyes, relief filling my chest to know he's okay.

He places me back on my feet and grabs a lock of my damp hair. "Did you get nice and wet just for me, *Jules*?"

"Oh you!" I laugh, slapping him in the chest.

"Watch yourself, Evans!" Jaxson growls.

Sawyer chuckles, not the least bit intimidated. Turning, I face Cade. He hasn't changed a bit, his expression still cold and hard, maybe even harder but I know better.

"Hi, Julia." He nods the greeting.

"Oh, Cade." With a teary smile, I walk up to him and wrap my arms around his waist. His body stiffens but he pats my back awkwardly. "I'm so glad you're okay; I'm glad you're both okay," I blubber, my arm reaching to bring Sawyer in too.

"You want to get in on this group hug, Reid? I'll be nice and share Julia."

A giggle tumbles past my lips and I look over at Jaxson to find him glaring at Sawyer, clearly not finding it as funny as we do. Stepping back, I grab a tissue to wipe under my eyes. "What are y'all doing here?" I ask with a sniffle.

"We came to see you and figured while we're here we'd see what this jackass has been up to," Sawyer explains.

I shake my head, a knowing smile curving my lips.

"All right. We actually went to see Jaxson at the hotel we thought he was staying at, but they said he checked out. Then we ran into your sheriff, and he told us he's living with you now," he says, his green eyes filled with questions.

My attention shifts to Jaxson and I see him tight-lipped, still pouting.

Whatever!

"Jaxson is staying with me… in the guest bedroom, by his own choice," I add, feeling his disapproving gaze on me but I ignore it. "How long are y'all here for?"

Sawyer shrugs. "I don't know, we're playing it by ear, but so far I like it here. I may just stay a while," he admits, his lip kicking up in a dirty grin.

"Oh fuck off," Jaxson mumbles.

I toss him a silent warning before retracting my eyes back to Sawyer. "Well you both can stay here."

"No, they can't!" Jaxson barks.

"Yes, they can. I have more than enough spare rooms, and it's my house!"

"Yeah, it's her house," Sawyer steps in, backing me up. "And if there aren't enough rooms I'll just crawl in bed and sleep with her…since you aren't."

I burst into a fit of laughter, unable to stop myself.

"You're seriously pissing me off, Evans."

"Oh lighten up, Jaxson," I scold. "Are you boys hungry? I was going to see if Jaxson wanted to head to the diner in town for supper, want to come?"

"I could eat, I can always eat," Sawyer answers.

Cade shrugs, not caring either way.

I look over at Jaxson next. "Are you coming, grumpy, or are you going to stay here and pout?" I really shouldn't antagonize him, but it's annoying that he acts all territorial over me and then says we can only be friends.

"I'm coming, just let me change," he grumbles, walking out of the kitchen.

Sawyer flashes me another smirk. "This is going to be fun."

I shake my head, biting back a smile.

Jaxson comes down in record time, his scowl still in place. Sawyer slings an arm around my shoulders as we start for the door but Jaxson shoves it off of me. "You, asshole, can drive yourself. Julia and I will go in my truck."

Sawyer feigns offense. "Why don't I take Julia and you take Cade?"

"Why don't we all just drive together?" I suggest before Jaxson has the chance to throttle him.

"Sounds good to me," Sawyer agrees. "Julia can ride in the back with me. I'll be nice and give Cade shotgun."

Jaxson shakes his head, his jaw locked in annoyance.

I hold back a laugh, knowing it won't be appreciated. I have a feeling this is going to be a long night, but I couldn't be happier right now.

20

Julia

We arrive at the diner and are lucky to get a booth since the place is packed. I watch poor Grace running her butt off, looking flustered and realize they must be short-staffed, again.

Looking around the crowded diner, my eyes land on one person, one that has my stomach bottoming out.

Ray Jennings, Wyatt's dad.

He sits at the counter, his disapproving eyes on our booth. Jaxson senses my unease and follows my gaze. I feel him stiffen next to me but I don't look over at him. I can't. My attention is rooted on Mr. Jennings, my belly twisting anxiously.

Jaxson's warm hand cups my cheek and forces my eyes to his. "Forget about him. It's fine."

Nodding, I open my menu, chewing on my thumbnail.

"What is it?" Sawyer asks, glancing back at Ray.

"Later," Jaxson's tone is clipped, shutting down the conversation before it can even start.

Grace comes over at that moment, her head down as she tries to find her pad of paper. "Hi, y'all, sorry about the wait. What can I—" She looks up, finally noticing me. "Julia, hi," she greets me with a kind smile.

"Hi, Grace." I stand and give her a hug.

Her smile disappears and eyes widen when she takes in Sawyer and Cade.

"Grace, this is Sawyer and Cade," I introduce her. "They're friends of Jaxson's from the Navy. Guys, this is my good friend, Grace."

"Hi." She waves shyly, her cheeks pink.

Cade greets her with his usual nod, while Sawyer, of course, lays on the charm. "Well heya there, Grace, nice outfit," he compliments with a dashing smile.

She looks down at her uniform dress with a frown, her cheeks heating. "Thanks, I guess," she mumbles then brings her attention back to me, blatantly dismissing him. "What can I get y'all to drink?"

"Sweet tea for me please," I say, ordering my usual.

Once everyone else gives her their drink order, she walks away. Sawyer's eyes track her, his brows furrowed deep in thought.

Jaxson relaxes back into our seat, a smug grin on his face. "What's wrong, Evans, losing your touch?"

"I don't know, that's never happened to me before," he says, completely serious.

Jaxson grunts. "Well there's a first time for everything."

When Grace brings us our drinks and takes our order she doesn't glance at Sawyer once. I can tell it really bothers him.

This could get interesting…

Once she leaves us again, Sawyer snaps out of his mood and changes the subject. "So the admiral called me," he tells Jaxson, something flickering in his green eyes. "He's wondering why you aren't answering his calls?"

"What calls?" I ask.

"Not now, Sawyer." Jaxson's voice is tight as he refuses to discuss the topic.

Annoyance sparks inside of me and I can't help but feel a little hurt. It's obvious he doesn't want to talk about it in front of me.

Before I can give it too much thought a bigger problem forms when I catch sight of Ray Jennings making his way over to us.

My anxious fingers curl around Jaxson's wrist and I become terrified for the confrontation that's about to ensue.

Ray stops next to Jaxson, but his eyes are only on me. "Well, Miss Julia, I can't say I'm surprised. Disappointed maybe, but not surprised."

"Well, no one asked you, asshole, so get the fuck out of here," Jaxson says, his icy tone sending a chill through the air.

Ray ignores him and keeps his attention on me, the silent fury in his eyes making me more uncomfortable by the second. "I tried to tell my son you are who you hang out with, but he assured me you had enough class to be seen with him. I'm sad he had to learn the hard way."

Jaxson begins to stand up but I tighten my grip on his arm. "He's trying to goad you, don't take the bait."

Ray smirks, looking rather amused. "I remember your mother, Julia, she too was very pretty. I can only imagine the disappointment she feels from beyond the grave."

His hurtful words barely have time to register before Jaxson is out of the booth and has him by the lapels of his expensive suit. Sawyer and Cade both stand and flank him.

Oh lord!

"I told you to get the fuck out of here—"

"Jaxson, stop!" I insert myself between Sawyer and him, placing my shaking hand on his chest.

"Listen to her, son, you don't want to mess with me."

Jaxson leans in closer to Ray, fury hardening his expression. "Wrong, dickhead, you don't want to fuck with me. I'm trained to kill with my bare hands. I also know what to do with your body so no one would find you, so don't fucking tempt me. You and your crazy son better stay away from Julia, or you'll find out exactly what *trash* like me is capable of."

There's no denying the fear in Ray's eyes; he knows Jaxson not only means it but is capable of it.

"Julia, should I call Cooper?" Grace asks, her timid eyes moving from Ray to Jaxson.

"That isn't necessary, sweetheart," Ray says before I can answer. "I was just leaving."

I apply pressure to Jaxson's chest. "Come on, Jax. Let him go."

"I mean it, you leave her the fuck alone," his warning slices through the air as he steps back.

Ray straightens his suit, his jaw tight as he walks out the door.

"Jesus, who the fuck was that asshole?" Sawyer asks.

"Ray Jennings," I tell him quietly, my voice shaky. "He's on the town council. I had to put a restraining order on his son."

"Town council? The way that arrogant prick spoke you'd think he was President of the United States."

A laugh tumbles past my lips, my anxious heart a little lighter. Leave it to Sawyer to lighten the mood.

When we take our seats again, Jaxson turns to me, concern bright in his eyes. "You okay?"

I nod but my heart still beats a million miles a minute.

"You know what he said about your mom is bullshit, right?"

I smile. "Yeah. I do." My mother would never be disappointed of my friendship with Jaxson. Actually, if she were still alive, I know she'd love him just as much as Grams does.

"Good." He presses a hard kiss to my forehead, calming the storm of emotions that took over my body moments ago.

I really love it when he does that.

"All right, here's your food," Grace announces, laying the plates out in front of everyone. "Can I get y'all another drink?"

I shake my head. "I'm okay, thank you."

"I'd love another one," Sawyer says, tossing her another panty dropping smile, one Grace misses because she doesn't look at him.

Her very apparent dismissal seems to really bother him. In fact, he looks kind of pissed off, something I've never seen on him before. He's always so funny and happy.

Conversation flows throughout the rest of dinner, all the earlier tension evaporating, besides Sawyer and Grace that is. Once we finish our meals, the guys leave Grace a generous tip, one she tries refusing but eventually accepts due to Jaxson's demand.

I give her another hug before we leave and tell her I'll see her on Saturday. I'm hoping Kayla will still be up for it after tomorrow night. If not we can have a girls' night watching movies and veg out on junk food. Either way, I won't be leaving Kayla to sulk alone.

When we arrive back at my house, Cade and Sawyer start for their truck.

"Aren't you guys going to stay here?"

Sawyer smirks over at Jaxson, a silent challenge happening between them. "That's all right, Julia, but thanks for the offer. Cade and I are going to stay at the motel where Jaxson was. But I hope it's all right we come by and visit a lot while we're here?"

I glare over at Jaxson, knowing it's because of him they aren't staying. "Of course. Come over as much as you like. You're always welcome, and you can always change your minds, too."

"Great! Then I'll see you tomorrow." he swoops in, planting a kiss on my cheek until Jaxson shoves him back.

"Lips to yourself, asshole."

Laughing, Sawyer hops into his truck while Cade gives us a quick wave. Then they're driving away, leaving me with a grumpy Jaxson.

21

Jaxson

I climb out of the shower the next morning and hear familiar voices coming from downstairs.

Of course that fucker is already here this early. I'm sure he set his alarm just to piss me off.

Throwing on some clothes, I walk downstairs and into the kitchen to find Julia serving the asshole breakfast.

Sawyer turns to me with a grin. "Well good morning, sleepyhead."

"What the hell are you doing here already?"

"Boy, you're grumpy. What's wrong—didn't sleep well? I hope Julia and I didn't keep you up last night. I tried to keep her quiet—"

Julia gasps and slaps his shoulder. "Sawyer!" She scolds with a giggle.

The guy is going to get his ass kicked soon. "I'm not in the mood for your shit this morning, Evans, so lay off." I know he's only doing it to get a rise out of me, but the thought of him laying a hand on Julia drives me insane.

"Okay, you two, that's enough," Julia says. "Jaxson, what do you want? I have pancakes made, but I can make you something else if you'd like?" she offers, busying herself around the kitchen.

My eyes track her every move, my cock swelling in my jeans. Even this early in the morning she looks fucking good enough to eat. Her yoga pants and tank top fit her lithe body snugly, leaving nothing to the imagination. She has the best ass I've ever seen, and I want to punch the shit out of Sawyer when I see him staring at it as she bends down to grab something from the fridge. Instead I settle for a slap upside the head.

He chuckles, unashamed for being busted.

"Pancakes are good," I finally answer her and go grab a plate off the counter to dish my own food. "You didn't have to feed these assholes. Especially him." I jerk a thumb at Sawyer.

His cocky smirk spreads. "What can I say, she likes cooking me breakfast."

Shaking my head, I try to ignore the mouthy shit and load my plate with pancakes before I take a seat at the table.

"I don't mind, I like cooking breakfast… for *everyone*," she adds, smiling at Sawyer.

I don't want her to smile at him like that. It will give him ideas and fuel his obnoxiousness.

"Do you guys have a gym here?" Cade asks.

"Yeah, but I don't know what condition it's in though. They used to have a sparring ring and all," I tell him then glance back at Julia. "Does Big Mike still own it?"

"Yep, he does, but I know he's been thinking of selling. He told me he's getting too old. His son moved to Florida and has no interest in taking it over, much to Mike's disappointment."

"We can go by there later today if you want?" I tell Cade then look over at Sawyer. "I'd love to go a couple of rounds with you, asshole."

"I'm in for that. Wanna come, Julia? You can see me put your man to shame."

I can't wait to take his ass down.

"I think I'll pass," she declines with a smile, then swings her pretty eyes to me. "What do you have planned tonight?"

"Not sure, why?"

"I was just wondering because I'm going out with Kayla."

"I thought your girls' night is tomorrow night?"

"Girls' night?" Sawyer pipes back in. "Where? Is Grace going to be there?"

"It is, but Kayla and I have plans tonight, too," she tells me before looking over at Evans. "And yes, Sawyer, Grace is going to be with us."

"I'm in, I love girls' night. Where is it?"

"We're going out dancing. It's a *girls'* night which means you can't come if you have a penis."

He grunts. "If you're going to a club dancing, Julia, guys will be there."

Exactly! It's all I've thought about and it pisses me off.

"That I can't control." She shrugs.

No, but I can…

Sawyer, Cade, and I walk into Big Mike's gym later that afternoon. It looks the same as it did when I was here last, but more run-down. The place has a lot of potential, if he would put the money into it.

"Well I'll be damned, if it isn't Jaxson Reid!" Big Mike bellows, striding over to us. He, too, looks mostly the same but older—much older. By the tired lines around his eyes I can understand why he's looking at selling the place. He's got to be well into his sixties now.

Mike was a huge influence on me. When I was younger and got busted for fighting a lot, he brought me in here to train with him. He let me work my aggression out, something I had a lot of at that age.

"How are you doing, kid?" he asks, slapping me on the back.

"I'm good. It's great to see you again."

"You too. What are you doing here? You on leave?"

"I've been discharged." He has to know that after only being in the Navy for five years there's a reason why I've been discharged. Thankfully, he doesn't ask questions.

"You here to stay?"

I shrug. "Maybe."

"Well I'll bet Miss Julia is real happy about that."

Nodding, I end the topic there and gesture to the guys next to me. "These are some friends who are visiting. We were hoping to come work out and do some sparring."

"Of course. Come on in, the ring is free."

"Thanks."

"You bet, good to have you back." He claps me on the shoulder one more time before walking back to his office.

We head into the locker room to change and Sawyer wastes no time bringing up the admiral. "So why aren't you answering his calls?"

"Because I don't care what he has to say," I answer truthfully.

"Yeah, well, when you don't answer he comes for me next." He pauses, his eyes lifting to mine. "He wants us to do another mission, he put together a team and wants you to run it."

"Yeah, and how does he suppose that's going to work, since we're no longer in the Navy."

He shrugs. "He said he'd take care of it. Someone he knows specifically asked for the three of us."

"Why?"

There's a tense moment of silence and I can tell I'm not going to like this.

"Because it's a sex trafficking ring."

Disgust settles in my gut, heavy and hard. I drop down on the bench, feeling sick and glance over at Cade to see he looks much the same, his body tense and jaw locked. "What did you tell him?" I ask.

"I didn't tell him anything, I said I had to talk to you guys first." His eyes shift between Cade and me. "But we're done, right? I mean, I don't know about you guys, but I'm still fucked-up. And personally, after what the admiral tried to pull on us last time, he can go fuck himself for all I care."

I'm glad I'm not the only one still messed up.

"What are your thoughts?" I ask Cade.

"I don't care. I'll go if you guys want. I owe you at least that much."

His response is one I expected but it still pisses me off. "You don't owe us shit, man, how many times do we have to tell you that? It was our choice to follow you."

He remains quiet, his hard eyes on the floor.

"Have you spoken with Faith since the hospital?" I ask, treading carefully.

Pain darkens his expression and his jaw hardens. "No. It's for the best." He gets up, ending the conversation. "You guys discuss it and let me know. I'm going to hit the weights." He leaves without another word, leaving us with our demons brought to the surface. Although, his just might be worse than ours.

"Don't bother," Sawyer says, breaking the tense silence. "I've tried to talk to him about her, but he's an idiot, like you. Doesn't know what's right in front of him."

"You don't get it, Evans, it's not about us not knowing what's right in front of us. It's about trying to do the right thing. We don't come from the same family you do."

"Oh fuck that! I've had my issues too, man, life isn't perfect for anyone. You guys need to pull your heads out of your asses, because one day it might be too late. If I had someone that wanted me, like Julia does you, there would be no doubt I would take that shit, issues and all."

"Yeah, because you're an arrogant son of a bitch who thinks he's God's gift to women."

He grins, spreading his arms wide. "Hey, I can't help it that women find me irresistible."

I grunt. "Whatever. Let's go. I've been waiting since yesterday to pound the shit out of you." I stand, grabbing some gloves.

"Bring it," he counters, up for the challenge. "So what do I tell the admiral?"

I shake my head. "I don't know, let me think about it."

I want to help. The thought of another girl like Anna out there needing our help eats at me, the guilt almost unbearable. But the consequences this time could be even greater than the last.

22

Julia

At seven o'clock sharp, Kayla comes walking through my door, looking like a fierce, sexy spy all decked out in black. She has on dark leggings, thigh-high leather boots, and a black tank top. Her long, blonde hair is pulled into a low ponytail through the back of a black, military-style hat. She's also sporting a pair of aviator sunglasses, even though the sun has started to set.

"Wow, you look amazing," I tell her, glancing down at my own attire. I chose a dark pair of blue jeans with a black tank top and a similar hat with my hair pulled back in a ponytail.

"Thanks." She drops the backpack she brought with her and starts pulling stuff out. "I figured I may as well look good when I kick his ass, since this will be the last time the asshole sees me."

This fiercely pissed off woman is much better than the devastatingly sad one I saw a few days ago.

She hands me a walkie-talkie. "Here, I stole this from the top of our closet, turn it to channel nine."

"Why do we need these?"

"Just in case we get separated. Especially if I need you to be on the lookout while I try to bust the fucker."

I nod in understanding.

"You look great, too. Do you have a pair of sunglasses? I don't want him noticing us."

"Sure, I'll go get them." I dash upstairs into my room, snagging them off my nightstand. I also grab my boots from my closet and put them on since Kayla is wearing hers.

"Where's Jaxson?" she asks as I make my way back down the stairs.

"I don't know. He made himself scarce when I told him we were hang-ing out tonight. He's probably out with Sawyer and Cade."

"Did he suspect anything?"

"No, but I almost messed up when Coop was over here the other day." I tell her about how hard it was to keep my anger in check and act like noth-ing was wrong.

"Tell me about it. I've been trying to work as much as I can, taking other people's appointments then pretending to be asleep when he gets home. The other night he tried getting some and it took major self-control not to cut his dick off. In the end, I feigned being sick." She shrugs, sadness pinching her expression. "It sucked because I still wanted him, even after knowing what I do. I'll probably always want him," she whispers.

I pull her in for a hug, my own throat feeling tight. "You never know, Kayla, maybe we will find out tonight that we're wrong. There's still that possibility."

"I don't think so, Jules. I can feel it. All the lies he's told and her hanging up on me, there's no other explanation." Shaking her head, her back straight-ens, fierce determination brightening her eyes again. "Forget it. No more tears. Let's do this!"

There's a black SUV sitting out front as we step outside. "Whose is this?" I ask.

"A co-worker's, we switched vehicles. We're going to be parked right in front of the motel when he shows up. I had to take a vehicle he wouldn't rec-ognize, so that leaves out either of our cars."

I nod again in understanding, all of this feeling so surreal.

Twenty minutes later, we pull up to the motel, which is just off I-90. It's a seedy looking place, mainly where trucker's stop over for the night. The bar attached next door doesn't look much classier.

We end up parking at the gas station that's just across the street. Kayla shuts off the car and its lights, blanketing us in darkness except for the neon pink flashing sign. I'm feeling a little silly with my sunglasses on, but since Kayla is still wearing hers I keep mine in place.

"Right there," she says, pointing to a door across the way from us. "Room twenty-three is where the text said she would be."

We stare at it as if it's our lifeline.

"Shit! There's Cooper, get down," she hisses.

We hunker down in our seats as Cooper pulls into the lot across the way, his truck blocking half of our view of the door. I notice Kayla begin to shake so I grab her hand in silent comfort. Lifting our heads just enough to peek out the window, we both gasp when Cooper's passenger door opens first and Jaxson steps out.

"What the hell?" Kayla mumbles.

What on earth is he doing here?

Kayla and I exchange a confused look, before her eyes widen in shock. "Oh my god, do you think they're both fucking her?"

Pain strikes my chest and I instantly feel sick. After I give it some good thought, I come to my senses and shake my head.

"Yeah, you're right, that sounds a little too messed up. But what's he doing here then?"

I shrug, having no idea.

We watch Cooper as he exits the truck next. He waves at Jaxson as he makes his way over to the motel while Jaxson heads to the bar next door.

He's going to go drink while Cooper sleeps with her? How could he do something like this?

Kayla scoffs. "I really shouldn't be surprised."

Silence descends on us as Cooper knocks on the motel room door. We both wait with bated breath, waiting to see what happens. It swings open a moment later to reveal a beautiful brunette that looks close to our age. Dread sinks to the pit of my stomach when Cooper enters and closes the door behind him.

"Oh my god," Kayla whispers, sheer agony thick in her voice.

"I'm so sorry, Kayla."

"Did you get a good look at her? Do you recognize her?"

I shake my head.

"Me either," she spits, jaw tight. "Come on!" She climbs out of the SUV with purpose.

I follow suit and have to jog to catch up to her. "What are you going to do?"

"I want to get closer, hopefully I can see something in the window. Go stand by his truck and watch for Jaxson. Radio me if he comes out," she says, holding up her walkie-talkie.

"Okay, be careful." I take my spot by Coop's truck, making sure I have a good view of the bar door. "Anything?" I ask a moment later, whispering into the radio.

"Not really, but if I listen closely enough I can hear a little bit. The bitch is giggling a lot," she says, sounding pissed.

I'm so caught up in watching her that I miss Jaxson walking out of the bar. "Oh shit!" I duck behind Coop's truck, dropping to my hands and knees. I crawl around it, praying he didn't see me and bring the radio to my lips. "Kayla, get out now! Hurry, Jaxson is out."

"Julia?"

Shit!

I swing my head around and find Jaxson standing directly behind me.

"What the hell are you doing?" he asks, looking at me like I'm a complete loon.

Standing, I glance toward the motel room but don't see Kayla. Looking back at Jaxson my eyes narrow. "I can't believe you would do this, you should be ashamed of yourself!"

He rears back, *pretending* to be confused. "What the hell are you talking about?"

"Oh don't give me that. I know—" I gasp, my words dying in my throat when I hear glass shatter behind me. Running over to the other side of Cooper's truck, I find Kayla with a bat. She just smashed in the driver side window and now she's whacking the shit out of the door and side mirror.

Oh no!

"Holy shit, Kayla, what the fuck are you doing?" Jaxson's eyes are wide with shock, his hands on top of his head.

I remain frozen, not knowing what to do.

He reaches for the bat but jumps back when she raises it at him.

"Stay back, asshole, or you're next!" She walks around Coop's truck, smashing out his taillights and anything else she can hit.

"Damn it, Kayla! Stop!" Just when Jaxson starts for her again, Cooper hauls ass out of the motel room, the girl following close behind him.

Oh god, this is so bad.

"What the fuck?" Cooper bellows, his expression filled with disbelief. His quick feet stop at Kayla and he reaches for the bat but she turns around and swings at him, just missing his shoulder.

"You lying piece of shit!" she screams, taking another swing at him.

Cooper spins her around, his arms wrapping around her, trying to restrain her. The bat flails wildly behind her as she tries to strike him.

They get closer to me as they struggle but I'm unable to move. I'm completely frozen, watching their battle.

"Jesus christ!" Jaxson pulls me out of the way before I can get caught in the crossfire.

Cooper finally manages to pry the bat out of her hands and throws it across the parking lot. "What the hell do you think you're doing?"

"You lying, cheating bastard!" She continues to fight against him, tears streaming down her cheeks. Her anguish is completely devastating.

Spinning her around to face him, Cooper grips her upper arms firmly. "Stop!" He orders, giving her a hard shake.

I start toward them, scared for Kayla with seeing how mad he is, but Jaxson stops me. He also looks pretty pissed right now.

A bunch of people stand outside the bar, watching the scene unfold.

"How could you do this to me?" Kayla cries. "After everything we have been through!" Her foot strikes out, kicking him in the shin.

"That's enough. I'm not cheating on you!"

"You're seriously going to lie to me again, after I just busted your sorry ass?"

"You don't know anything, you have this all wrong!"

"Oh yeah, then who the fuck is this whore?" She points to the shocked looking brunette.

"This is Sarah Miller, my sister's friend. She's a jewelry designer. I'm here picking up your fucking engagement ring from her."

Shock slams into my chest like a sledgehammer.

Oh shit!

Kayla's entire body stills, her face paling. "My engagement ring?" she mumbles.

Cooper nods, his jaw locked so tight I'm surprised it doesn't snap.

"But the text, she hung up on me when I answered your phone, you told me you were working late when you weren't," Kayla rambles, trying to absorb what's happening.

"Yeah, I kind of wanted to keep it a fucking surprise and all," he bites out, shaking his head. "You really thought I was cheating on you?" His tone is furious, but you can see the hurt in his eyes. It makes me feel horrible, so I can only imagine what Kayla is feeling right now.

"I'm so sorry," she whispers.

He pushes away from her. "You're sorry? Look at my fucking truck!"

"I'll pay for it to get fixed—"

"Forget it! Go to the fucking car and wait for me."

"Cooper, please, will you just—"

"Now, Kayla!" He orders, pointing her away.

I tug on her arm. "Come on."

She stares at Cooper for a few more seconds then allows me to pull her away.

"Follow them," he tells Jaxson.

I link my arm with Kayla's, trying to comfort her as much as possible.

Jaxson steps in front of us, opening the back door of the SUV. "Get in. I'm going to help Cooper clean up the truck and let him know what vehicle you're in, since you aren't driving your own."

Kayla climbs in first. I glance at Jaxson to see him looking as mad as Cooper and decide it's best not to say anything and follow in behind Kayla.

Once the door slams, Kayla breaks down, gut wrenching sobs ripping from her chest. "Oh god, Julia, what have I done?"

My arm wraps around her shoulders. "Shh! It's going to be okay. You didn't know. The evidence was damning. I would have thought the same thing." I leave out that I probably wouldn't have beaten his truck in. I think she feels bad enough.

"He's so angry. He's never going to forgive me."

"Yes, he will. We'll explain it to him. We'll make him understand."

Minutes later, the driver's side door opens and Jaxson gets in. My eyes anchor on his furious ones in the rearview mirror while Cooper climbs in on the passenger side. He slams the door so hard both Kayla and I jump.

I grasp her hand as she continues to cry.

Angry silence fills the vehicle as Jaxson pulls away. I debate whether to say anything, but I'm scared. I've never seen Cooper this angry before, and I don't want to make it worse.

However, he ends up breaking the silence a moment later. "You know, girls, I just have to ask. What the fuck is with the outfits? Especially the sunglasses?"

Since Kayla is crying too hard I try my best to explain. "We didn't want you to notice us."

A bitter laugh barrels out of him. "Oh yeah, because I'm not going to notice two fucking chicks wearing goddamn sunglasses in the dark. Smart one, ladies."

My back straightens at his sarcasm. "You know, Cooper. I get that you're upset, but you don't need to be so rude. The evidence was pretty incriminating."

"So that makes it okay for you girls to dress up and play Charlie's fucking Angels for the night?"

I decide not to respond. He's too angry to understand where we were coming from.

When we arrive at their house, Cooper gets out and yanks open the back door that Kayla is leaning against. "Get in the fucking house."

"Don't talk to her like that!" I get out and meet Kayla around the other side. "Why don't you come sleep at my place tonight? Give him a chance to calm down," I suggest quietly, but not quiet enough because Cooper hears me.

"Stay out of this, Julia!"

"No, you're being irrational, Cooper. You're not even trying to understand where we're coming from—"

He advances on me, his expression hard as stone. "Just shut up, you have caused enough shit!"

Jaxson suddenly appears in front of me, his hand moving to Cooper's chest. "Watch it, Coop, I know you're mad and I don't blame you, but no one talks to her like that."

"Of course, this is where your loyalty lies."

"This isn't about loyalty, man—"

Cooper shoves him. "Whatever, you're so fucking pussy-whipped by her, and the worst part is she doesn't even give it up to you."

"Cooper!" Kayla gasps in horror.

Jaxson's fist slams into his face.

Oh god!

It's obvious that Cooper not only anticipated a fight but is also happy about it. He charges at Jaxson, primed and ready. They take each other down and roll around on the lawn, trying to pin each other.

"Both of you, stop, right now," I cry, my heart pounding in terror.

"Cooper, please, let's just go inside," Kayla pleads.

Finally, Jaxson gets the upper hand and manages to pin Cooper. "You need to stop picking a fight with me. Take your girlfriend into the house and figure out why the hell she thinks you're fucking cheating on her." He shoves himself off Cooper, getting to his feet.

Kayla runs into the house crying as Cooper stands. He glares back at Jaxson with so much anger I'm worried he's about to go after him again, but thankfully he has enough sense to walk away. He starts up the front steps, his fist smashing into the side of the house on the way in. The door slams behind him, the loud crack in the air leaving my blood cold.

"What do we do?" I cry, tears clogging my throat. "I can't leave her here with him while he's like this."

"Jesus, Julia, he's not going to hurt her. He's just majorly pissed off, with good fucking reason."

He's right. Cooper might be furious but he would never hurt her.

"Let's go," Jaxson says, climbing back into the SUV.

I follow hesitantly, guilt gripping my chest at the mistake we made.

The car ride home is silent, except for the sound of my tears. Jaxson doesn't spare me one glance until we finally walk into my house. "What the hell were you girls thinking? I mean christ, Julia, this is Cooper we're talking about here."

"I know, believe me, we feel terrible. This isn't something we just assumed over petty jealousy. The evidence was damning." I tell him about everything that happened and why we thought he was cheating.

"Okay, fine, but what about after you saw me there with him? I mean, didn't that clue you in?"

My eyes fall to the floor as I remember what our first thought was.

"Holy shit! You guys thought we were both fucking her, didn't you?"

I don't bother to confirm it, knowing my expression says it all.

A bitter laugh escapes him. "This is too fucked up, even for me. I'm going to bed." He starts up the stairs, leaving me without another word.

Locking up, I head up to bed and can't help worrying about Kayla. I send her a quick text telling her to call if she needs me, then I cry myself to sleep.

23

Jaxson

I don't know if it was from the fucked-up night with Kayla and Cooper, or from Sawyer bringing up what the admiral wants from us, but that night, a nightmare plagues me.

I'm back in that hellhole, the cold, damp cell reeking of blood and death. My wrists are chained above my head, as my broken body burns and aches from the pain I had endured earlier. A part of me almost wishes they would keep pumping those drugs into us that they did at the beginning, at least then I would be too fucked-up to feel all of this.

No. It's good they stopped; I need to keep a clear head if I'm going to get out of this. I peer over at Sawyer and Cade. If I look as bad as they do, then I know why those assholes think they don't have to worry about incapacitating us anymore.

Sawyer groans, his swollen battered face lifting to mine. "You look like shit."

I grunt, then immediately regret it when pain slices through me. "Yeah, well, you don't look too fucking pretty either."

I'm hoping Cade comes around soon. They really did a number on him after what he did to that sick bastard who was rubbing Faith in his face.

My head drops forward, too weak to remain up. Panic floods my system when I see my chest bare, the necklace Julia gave me gone. "Fuck!"

"What?" Sawyer mumbles.

"My chain, it's gone."

"They ripped it off of you," a quiet female voice says.

My head snaps to the cell on my left and there I find a girl chained to the bed. When the hell did she show up here?

"How long have you been here?" I ask.

"I'm not sure, a few hours, I think." Her voice trembles in fear and I realize she's American. She also sounds really young.

"How did you get here?"

"I don't know," she cries. "I'm traveling with my school. A friend and I snuck out at night to go to the beach. These boys were trying to take my friend home, she was drinking but something didn't seem right with her. I only had soda, but now I don't remember anything, and the next thing I know, I woke up in the back of a van, and I haven't seen my friend since."

"Your school traveled to Iraq?" Sawyer asks the question I was just thinking.

What school travels to a fucking war zone?

"Iraq? No, we're in Thailand."

Well shit. Knowing she was shipped here from Thailand confirms my original suspicion, that we're smack fucking dab in the middle of a human trafficking ring.

Her whimper cuts through the silence. "We, we aren't in Thailand?"

"No, you're in Iraq," I inform her regretfully.

"Oh my god, they're never going to find me. I'm never going to see my parents again." Her desperate sobs fill the bleak air.

My chest constricts at the sound of her agony, and something builds up in me that I haven't felt in a long time… protectiveness. "Listen, everything's going to be okay. What's your name?"

"A-Anna."

"I'm Jaxson and these are my buddies, Cade and Sawyer." I'm hoping she doesn't consider addressing Cade since he's still out of it. "We're Navy SEALs, do you know what that is?"

Her sobs begin to settle. "I think so, isn't that like soldiers?"

"Yeah, kind of."

"Except we're way more badass," Sawyer adds.

She giggles but soon quiets and I hear her crying again.

"How old are you?" I ask.

"Fourteen."

Jesus! "Well, Anna, we have every intention of getting out of here, and I promise we won't leave without you, okay?"

"O-okay."

"Where are you from?"

"South Carolina."

"No shit. So am I. What part?"

"Summerland."

"That's only a few hours from where I grew up."

She falls silent, and I think she's fallen asleep until she says, "It was the fat, smelly one."

"What's that?"

"The guy who ripped your necklace off. He's fat, smelly, and his teeth are disgusting. Do you know which one I'm talking about?"

"Yeah." The asshole whose nose I broke when he stole my picture of Julia and made the comment about fucking her.

"Was it special?" she asks quietly.

"Yeah."

"I'm sorry."

Me fucking, too.

"What are they going to do to me?" Her fearful question hits me like a blow to my chest.

"Nothing if I can help it."

A few minutes later, her exhaustion takes over and she falls asleep.

"You need to keep working on Irina," I whisper to Sawyer. "She's our only hope of getting the fuck out of here."

He nods. "I know."

We fall into a state of unconsciousness again and wake up some time later to a fearful scream. "No, don't touch me! Ow, stop!"

My head snaps up to see two guys grabbing Anna, one of them whose nose I broke. The bastard has her by the hair, dragging her from the bed. "Come on, bitch, we have a customer who can't wait to break you in."

Oh shit.

Anna's screams become louder. "No! Jaxson, help! Please, help me!"

I shoot awake, my body knifing up off the bed, drenched in sweat, my heart pounding so fucking loud it's all I can hear. I drop back down until I get my pulse under control.

Glancing at the clock, I see it's five a.m. and know I won't be going back to sleep. I get up and take a shower, hoping to wash away the fucking guilt that eats me alive every day.

24

Julia

The next morning, I roll over and look at my phone, hoping Kayla texted me back. She didn't. I send her another one asking her if she's all right, then get out of bed and throw on my robe before heading downstairs.

Jaxson is already up, sitting at the kitchen table with a cup of coffee and the paper. He doesn't acknowledge me as I walk in, and it makes me want to cry all over again.

Walking over to him, I take his face between my hands and force him to look at me. "Please don't be mad at me anymore."

He lets out a heavy breath and pulls me down on his lap.

I wrap my arms around him and bury my face in his neck. "We didn't know, Jaxson, all the evidence pointed to what we thought."

"I know, Jules." His hand slides under my robe, rubbing comforting circles on my upper thigh.

Lifting my face, I rest my forehead against his and gently touch the wound on his lip from his fight with Cooper. "This is my fault," I whisper, pressing a soft kiss to the corner of his mouth.

His eyes darken, fingers tightening on my skin. "No, it's not."

The doorbell rings, interrupting our moment.

"I'll answer it, you get yourself something to eat," he says, pressing a kiss to my forehead before letting me stand. The magic touch eases so much of my heavy heart.

I'm fixing myself some toast when Kayla comes in on a rush, still in her pajamas. Her eyes look the same as mine—red and puffy—but she has a huge smile on her face.

"Oh thank god!" I throw my arms around her, hugging her tight. "I've been so worried about you. Are you okay? How's Cooper?"

Cooper comes walking in at that moment with Jaxson trailing behind him. The sight of his busted lip hurts my heart as much as Jaxson's does. "Hey, Julia," he greets me with a nod.

"Hi, Coop." My greeting sounds as nervous as I feel.

I look back at Kayla who still has a huge smile on her face. "Everything's okay." She lifts her hand, showing me her finger.

Gasping, I grab her wrist and study the massive rock. "You're getting married?!"

She nods, her smile infectious.

"Oh my gosh, I'm so happy for you guys." I pull her in for another hug then look at Cooper, his easy smile telling me we're okay.

A sob builds in my throat as I walk over and wrap my arms around him. "I'm so sorry I thought you were a cheating bastard, Cooper," I apologize, blubbering into his chest.

He chuckles and hugs me back. "It's all right, Jules. Sorry I told you to shut the fuck up."

Cooper lifts his other arm for Kayla and pulls her in, too. "Don't you have something else to say, Cooper?" she says, sparing a glance at Jaxson.

"No."

"Coop, apologize to Jaxson, too," she orders quietly.

Jaxson smirks, enjoying Cooper's torment.

With a frustrated breath, he walks over and puts his hand out to Jaxson. "Sorry, asshole," he grumbles.

"Cooper!" Kayla scolds.

Jaxson accepts his hand smugly but remains silent.

"Jaxson, don't you have something to say back?" I urge.

"Why the fuck should I say sorry?"

"For punching him."

When he remains silent, Cooper cuts back in. "It's okay, Julia, I'm used to being the bigger man."

Jaxson puts him in a headlock, which he gets out of easily, and they start roughhousing.

Kayla and I roll our eyes at their barbaric way of apologizing. Her smile returns as she takes my hand. "Will you be my maid of honor?"

My heart melts into a giant puddle. "Of course I will. I'd be honored."

Unable to contain our excitement any longer, we start jumping up and down. "This is going to be so much fun!" I squeal excitedly.

"I know. I'm so fucking excited!"

"We can reschedule our girls' night if you want," I offer. "I understand if you want to celebrate with Cooper."

"No, he has to work for a bit tonight anyway. You, Grace, and I can celebrate. Katelyn told me about this great club that just opened in Charleston."

"Sounds good to me."

"How are you guys getting there?" Jaxson asks.

I shrug. "We'll take a cab."

"Coop said he will come get us after," Kayla adds, sending him a heart stopping smile.

"Perfect."

We make our plans and decide to get ready together here at my place.

"All right, let's go," Cooper says to Kayla. "I have plans for you for the rest of the day." He tosses her over his shoulder, making her squeal with laughter, and hauls her out of the house.

"See you later," I call out just before the door closes.

I turn back to Jaxson, my excitement close to bursting. "Oh my god, Jaxson, they're getting married!" I squeal enthusiastically, launching myself into his arms.

He catches me with a chuckle.

"Isn't this so amazing? I'm gonna call Grams and give her the news." Pushing out of his arms, I dash out of the kitchen and up to my room, happy that my terrible morning has turned around to be one of the best.

25

Julia

That evening, Kayla, Grace, and I are in my room getting ready. Kayla pulls a short, black cocktail dress out of her bag and slips it on. The strapless silk hugs her in all the right places. With her long, blonde hair flowing down her shoulders in big curls and smoky eye makeup, she looks like she just stepped out of a magazine.

"Wow," Grace and I say in unison.

"Why thank you," she says, her face glowing with happiness.

Grace looks over at me, her fingers fidgeting nervously. "Um, Julia, do you think I could borrow a dress from you? I don't really have anything nice enough for the club we're goin' to."

My heart pinches in guilt. Kayla and I should have thought about that and asked her earlier. Especially since we know she doesn't have the money to afford much.

"Of course, I have a couple you can pick from."

She ends up choosing my soft yellow, silk dress, which looks stunning against her golden skin. Grace is beautiful, but simple. Most of the time her long, blonde hair is tied back and her face free of makeup. One of her best features are her eyes. They're a unique, warm amber color, almost the same color as whiskey.

"Would you like Kayla and I to help with your hair and makeup?"

"Sure, but my makeup selection is kind of pathetic," she replies, embarrassed.

"Don't worry, we got you covered." Kayla pulls out her massive makeup bag. While she starts her foundation, I grab my curling wand and get to work on her hair.

"I still can't believe you're getting married, Kayla. I am so happy for you," Grace says, her excitement mirroring my own.

We told her earlier about our little escapade last night. We were all able to laugh about it, even though it wasn't very funny at the time.

"Thanks, Grace. I'd love for you to be a bridesmaid. It would mean a lot to me to have you and Julia by my side."

"Oh my gosh, really?"

Kayla nods at her with a smile.

"Oh I would love to. Thank you for askin' me." I pull the wand back as she hugs Kayla.

"I want to have a celebration supper for you and Cooper," I tell her. "Are you guys free two weeks from now?"

"That works for me. I'll make sure Coop takes it off."

"Me too," Grace says. "I'll make sure to book the entire day off so I can help you prepare."

"That'd be great. Thanks."

My doorbell chimes, interrupting our conversation. Both girls look at me in question.

"It's probably Sawyer and Cade. They're coming to hang out with Jaxson tonight."

"Ah, the famous SEAL boys I have yet to meet," Kayla muses. "Glad I'll finally get the chance. They're all I've heard about the entire week from clients who have spotted them around town."

"Oh they're somethin' all right," Grace mutters under her breath.

I smile, remembering the way Sawyer acted at the diner with her. "I think Sawyer has a crush on you, Grace."

She scoffs but her cheeks turn pink. "I think Sawyer is the type to have a crush on anythin' with boobs."

I laugh but don't deny her impression. He does seem that way, but there's something about the way he looked at Grace. It bothered him that she didn't melt into a puddle like every other girl does when he's near.

"Anyway, I'm not his type, at least not anymore," she says, her voice soft.

Kayla and I exchange a look. "Why would you say that?" I ask, treading carefully.

She shrugs. "I can just tell. He's a confident guy, which means he's into confident girls. Girls who know what they want and aren't afraid to go after it. Not girls who are… damaged." She pauses and clears her throat. "There's a lot I haven't told y'all."

"You can tell us anything, Grace," Kayla says. "You can trust us."

"Absolutely." Putting the curling wand down, I move to sit next to her. Kayla does the same, sitting on the other side and we take her hand, waiting patiently for her to continue.

"I told y'all that I lost my mother when I was seventeen, but I didn't tell you how. She was…raped and murdered."

Kayla and I suck in a sharp breath but remain silent, not wanting to interrupt her.

"We were really close, and she was all I had. I came home when it happened; they almost killed me, too."

My heart swells painfully at the devastation in her voice. "I'm so sorry, Grace. I know what it's like to lose someone you love so much."

She gives me a sad smile. "I know you do." Taking a breath, she continues. "The man who hurt her, hurt us, is in prison back in Florida; that's where I'm originally from. I came here to find my father; I've never met him. He lives in Charleston but I haven't had the courage to contact him yet. He's kind of a big deal… he's the lieutenant governor," she confesses quietly.

"Holy shit! Your father is John Weston, Jr.?" Kayla asks in shock.

She nods. "That's why I'm nervous. He knows about me, but has never contacted me. He has a family—a wife and two daughters. I'm scared of what his reaction will be if I reach out to him."

I give her hand a gentle squeeze. "He's lucky to have a daughter like you, Grace."

"Damn straight," Kayla adds.

She smiles but it's sad. "Thanks, I'm really glad I met y'all. You both have come to mean an awful lot to me."

"We feel the same way," I confess past the lump that has formed in my throat.

Kayla and I wrap our arms around her, offering comfort.

"Oh darn, we need to stop this," she says with a sniffle. "I didn't mean to put a damper on our girls' night. I'm sorry."

"You didn't. We're glad you opened up to us. I know there's more you probably haven't told us." Her expression confirms my suspicion. "Just know we're always here for you. You can trust us with anything."

"Thanks," she whispers.

"All right, let me fix your makeup before we take you to a mirror," Kayla says, standing once again.

I touch mine up too, since my cheeks are blotchy from the few tears that escaped.

After we finish, we take Grace into the bathroom with Kayla covering her eyes. When she removes her hands for the reveal Grace gasps. "Oh my gosh, I look... pretty," she says, sounding surprised.

"Of course you do, you always look beautiful, Grace."

"Thanks, Julia." She offers me a smile but I can tell she doesn't believe me and it breaks my heart further.

Heading out of the bathroom, I grab my dress hanging at the top of my door. It's almost identical to the one Grace borrowed, but hot pink. I haven't had a chance to wear it yet, so I'm excited to break it in. After slipping on my strappy, silver heels, I walk back into the bathroom.

The three of us stand in front of the mirror, taking in our appearances. "We look fucking hot, ladies!" Kayla comments, slinging her arms over our shoulders.

I have to agree. We clean up nice.

Kayla smirks, her eyes meeting mine in the reflecting glass. "How much do you want to bet we're going to see the Hulk come out when we go downstairs?"

"Probably, he's been pouting all day," I mumble. But I can't deny how eager I am for Jaxson to see me. I like it when he gets territorial, and tonight I'm ready to test his control again.

"Well then, let's get this show on the road. I love irritating that guy," Kayla says, rubbing her hands together in glee.

This shall be interesting.

26

Jaxson

awyer, Cade, and I are at the table having a beer. I'm trying to be social, but I'm in a pissy mood about Julia going out tonight. Why can't their girls' night consist of staying in the house and watching a movie? Do they really need to go to the club? It pisses me off to think about all the guys who will be sniffing around her all night.

It doesn't help that it's been a long fucking week. Being around her constantly and not burying myself inside her like I want to has been hell. I haven't jerked off this much since I was fourteen years old. I'm not sure how much longer I can hold back.

"Ho-ly shit!" Sawyer's outburst and gaping expression has lead settling in my gut as his attention becomes riveted on something behind me.

Turning around, I see the girls walk into the kitchen. My gaze zeroes in on Julia, and I suck in a sharp breath at the sight of her. My dick rages along with my temper. "What the fuck are you wearing?"

She cocks a sassy hip. "It's called a dress, haven't you ever seen one before?"

"You're not leaving looking like that."

Shit, I didn't mean it to come out quite like that.

Her eyes narrow, but before she can say anything Kayla cuts in. "Easy there, Hulk, we don't want things going smash."

The girls giggle, like it's some private joke.

Sawyer joins in too, acting like her comment is the funniest thing in the world. "Well, I personally think you girls look incredible."

"Thank you." Julia smiles, soaking in his attention.

He's such an asshole.

She gestures to Kayla. "Sawyer and Cade, I'd like you to meet my friend Kayla, Cooper's fiancée," she adds.

"Ah, yes, the famous fiancée," Sawyer says. "I heard you girls had quite the evening last night."

Both Kayla and Julia groan, knowing they won't ever live that down. Julia points to Grace next. "And y'all remember Grace."

Cade nods and Sawyer tries laying on the charm. "Of course, I never forget a beautiful woman. How are you doing, Grace?"

"Fine, thank you," she responds without making eye contact, which only seems to piss him off again.

His torment slightly eases my shitty mood… until I look over at Julia again.

"Will you stop glaring at me?" she snaps, making me glare harder. "Whatever," she mumbles, moving her attention to Kayla. "Want to go wait outside? The cab should be here soon."

I tense. "I told you I'd drive you."

"And I said, no thank you."

"Why the hell not?"

Kayla answers before she can. "Because if you take us they won't let us in after the scene you'll cause." She follows up her comment with a shitty impersonation. "Hulk like Julia. Hulk smash anyone who look at Julia."

Everyone bursts into laughter, Sawyer being the loudest of them all. "I fucking love this girl," he says, trying to catch his breath.

Dickhead!

"See ya later, boys, have a good night!" Julia blows me a kiss over her shoulder as she walks out.

I consider hauling her sweet ass upstairs and fucking the sass right out of her. Throwing my chair into the wall, I start pacing, wondering what the hell I'm going to do.

"You bring this shit on yourself, you know that, right?" Sawyer says, opening his big mouth.

"It's not that simple, Evans. I care more about her than I do about fucking her."

"Actually, it is that simple, take both. It doesn't have to be one or the other, you idiot."

"Lay off him, I get it," Cade says, stepping in to defend me.

Sawyer grunts. "Of course you get it because you're an idiot, too. I tell you boys, if I had women like Faith and Julia after me I wouldn't be fucking it up like you dumb asses," he says, giving us a smirk. "I'd be fucking them all night long."

Both Cade and I nail him in the shoulder. It only makes him laugh harder.

Eventually he gets control of himself, his expression sobering. "I'm telling you, Jaxson, somebody is going to fill that position sooner than later. You can't expect her to be alone for the rest of her life. So if I were you, I'd pull your head out of your ass and lay your claim before it's too late."

He's right. I can't expect her to be alone forever, and the thought of anyone else having her makes me sick. I stare back at him, watching a knowing smirk morph on his face.

"We're going, aren't we?" he asks, already knowing the answer.

"Yeah, we're going, just let me change."

"All right, busting up girls' night!" he cheers.

I send Cooper a quick text, telling him to meet us at the club rather than come here first. The time I spend getting ready I pray I know what the hell I'm doing.

27

Julia

"This place is awesome!" Kayla yells to be heard over the loud music. It is pretty great. Thankfully, Katelyn's name got us in quickly. The line outside is long, and it's packed in here.

We head right up to the bar to order a shot, and the handsome bartender welcomes us with a charming smile. "What can I get you ladies?"

Kayla leans over the counter and orders for us all. "Three lemon drops please."

I'm just about to ask her what that is but Grace beats me to it. "What's in that?"

"Trust me, you're going to love it," she says, giving no further explanations.

The bartender comes back with three shots and lemon wedges with sugar on them. Or is that salt?

Kayla grabs hers first and raises it. "Bottoms up, ladies."

"Wait!" I stop her before she can down it and raise my drink to make a toast. "To the future Mrs. McKay."

"Oh, yours is much better," she agrees with a smile.

Clinking our glasses, we throw back the clear liquid.

Yuck!

Grace and I both cough in disgust then grab our lemon wedge and suck them clean like Kayla. The citrus actually brings a nice flavor to the after taste and I find myself licking my lips for more.

"See, it's good, right?" Kayla says, as if hearing my thoughts. "Come on, ladies, let's dance."

We follow her out to the dance floor and for the next hour we drink and dance our asses off. After four shots and two drinks I'm quite tipsy, and it feels fantastic, freeing even. It's rare I ever get out like this and let loose. We're all having a blast, especially Grace, and it makes me so happy to see a genuine smile on her face. I laugh when a group of guys come up to dance with us and Kayla flashes her hand in front of their faces, making them back off respectfully.

Guys have been lining up to dance with Grace, some she has accepted, others not. I don't mind anyone dancing with me, as long as they don't grab inappropriately. There's nothing more annoying than being treated like a piece of meat.

The next song that plays is Kesha's "Die Young" it sends our bodies moving and hearts soaring. The guy behind me grabs my hips, and it's then that a feeling of awareness skitters down my spine. Even before I turn around I know exactly who is the cause of it.

Oh, this is going to be fun.

Jaxson

"Jesus, this place is insane," Cooper yells next to me, as we make our way through the club.

"No shit!"

After waiting in line outside for almost forty minutes, a friend of Kayla and Julia's spotted Cooper outside and got us in. If she hadn't we would have waited at least another hour.

It's just the three of us, Sawyer, Cooper, and me. Cade decided to bail and go to the gym. Sawyer said he's been spending most of his time there lately, putting his energy into working out. I have a feeling I know *who* he's trying to work out of his system.

My gaze searches for Julia as we weave in and out of people, making our way across the crowded bar. Some chick purposefully rubs her tits into my chest as she passes by.

"Sorry." She giggles annoyingly.

I ignore her and keep walking. We line up along the bar and order a round of beers.

"Holy shit, there are some grabby skanks in here; my junk has been grabbed twice already," Sawyer says, acting as if it bothers him to be assaulted.

"Like you care." The guy has fucked more than I have, which is saying something.

"Hey, I do. I have standards you know."

I grunt, and I'm just about to say something when the breath gets knocked out of my lungs at the sight of Julia on the dance floor, looking like every guy's wet dream. A new song starts that her and the girls go crazy over.

I become enraptured, watching her dance. Her arms are thrown over her head as her hips move in rhythm to the beat. There's a group of guys not far from them and when one comes up behind her, grabbing her hips, anger spikes in my veins.

The fucker is dead.

I slam my beer down and am about to storm over there but Cooper stops me with a hand to my chest. "Hold up, don't go getting us all kicked out now."

My pulse hammers, blood pumping with fury from seeing someone touch what's mine. As if feeling my furious gaze on her, Julia stills and turns around. There's a second of surprise in her eyes before her pretty lips curve into a sassy smile. She knows exactly what it's doing to me to see this guy with his hands on her.

I shake my head, warning her what will happen if the asshole doesn't back away. Turning around, she says something to the guy that has him making eye contact with me. He raises his hands in surrender and moves to the next girl.

Julia starts for me, her hips keeping rhythm with the beat. Heat explodes through my body, coiling low in my stomach, and everyone falls away as I watch her dance her way over, my cock hardening at every dip of her hips.

Once she reaches me, she turns around, shoving her tight fuckable ass against me. I grab her hips firmly, my fingers digging into her soft flesh. She tosses me a smile over her shoulder, feeling how hard my cock is for her. One of her arms lifts, curling around my neck and bringing my mouth down close to her ear. Her scent penetrates my senses; the smell of lemons mixed in with her usual, sweet scent, races through my blood like a fucking drug.

I nip her pierced earlobe, and she lets out the sexiest fucking moan. My mouth continues down her slender throat, feeling the rapid beat of her pulse against my lips. I suck and lick her delicate skin, wanting to brand her so every fucker in the place will know she's mine.

Her fiery whimper reaches my ears and she grinds against me, her sweet body eager for more. I'm so fucking turned on, it's taking every bit of control I have not to slip into her from behind and fuck her senseless right here.

When the song comes to an end, she turns to face me and wraps her arms around my neck. Her eyes flash with surprise when I pull her flush against my body.

"What are you doing at my girls' night? I thought I said no penises allowed."

A growl erupts from my throat before I can stop it. "What about the prick who just had his hands on you? He has a dick."

Smiling, she lifts a perfectly arched brow. "Why, yes, he does. What are you going to do about it, Jaxson?"

My blood pressure spikes along with my dick at her challenge. I lean in close to her ear so she can hear me over the thundering music. "I'm going to take you home and bury myself so deep inside that sweet pussy of yours. My scent will cling to every part of you. Then every fucking guy in the world will know you're mine."

I've barely registered her gasp before my mouth descends, finally taking what I've been denying myself for far too long. She whimpers against my lips, giving me the access I crave. My tongue slides in, seeking.

Tasting.

Her flavor explodes in my mouth and settles deep in my chest. It's time to get her out of here. This night has been coming for a long time, and I can't wait anymore. Pulling back, I stare into her glazed eyes that are burning with questions.

"Is that what I am, Jaxson, yours?" she asks, her voice hesitant.

"You've always been mine, in every way that matters." My chest tightens at the uncertainty in her eyes. She doesn't believe me, and I don't blame her. "I don't know what the future holds for us, Jules, but I think this week has proven we can't go back to what we had before."

Her slender fingers wrap around my wrist as she turns her face to the side, pressing her lips to my palm. "Then we'll make a new us."

I nod and tamp down the panic threatening to choke me.

Please don't let me fuck this up.

"Let's go home," I say, my arm hooking around her waist to bring her in closer. "I can't wait anymore."

Her eyes search mine for a solid two breaths before giving the answer I want to hear. "All right, let me go say good-bye first."

I press a hard kiss to her mouth then release her. Looking over at Sawyer, I see his hard eyes glued to the dance floor, glaring at the guy dancing with Grace. "I'm taking off. You okay to catch a ride with Coop?"

"Yeah." He waves me away, not once sparing me a glance.

After saying good-bye to Cooper, I start for Julia and see the asshole who had his hands on her earlier, eyeing her with eagerness, thinking she's come back for him. His hope deflates fast when he sees me charging at them. With quick strides I grab her from behind.

"What the hell are you doing?" she shrieks as I lift her up off her feet.

"Time's up, Julia, say good-bye to your friends."

She sputters in protest as I turn and head for the exit.

"It's about damn time," Kayla yells at my retreating back.

"Put me down right now, Jaxson! You're embarrassing me."

I ignore her and continue on. The cool night air hits us as I push open the doors and head over to my truck. Opening the passenger door, I toss her inside, her hair tangling around her pissed off face.

"Ugh! You are such a Neanderthal, what the hell—"

I claim her mouth, silencing her protest and her response is instant. Her hands fist in my shirt, yanking me closer and I swallow every sexy moan that falls past her lips. My hand slides under her dress, cupping the sweet spot between her legs.

A groan rips from my chest at the damp feel of her silk panties. "I'm done waiting, Julia, I need to get you home and sink into your hot pussy before I lose all control."

She arches against my touch, her eyes hooded with lust. "Oh, okay then."

I chuckle at her breathless response and drop one more kiss on her parted lips then remove my hand and slam the door.

Sweet, hot anticipation fills the truck most of the drive home, every second passing is torture on my control and dick.

Feeling her eyes on me, I glance over and find her staring at me with a knowing smile. "Wanna know something?"

"What, baby?"

"I'm just a wee bit drunk," she admits with a giggle, holding her thumb and finger up with a small gap between them.

I grunt. "Tell me something I don't know."

I feel her shift next to me. "Does it make you want to take advantage of me, Jaxson?"

My eyes retract their path back, the seductive tone of her voice beckoning me to look.

Oh jesus!

Her body is angled toward me, her back leaning against the door. One leg is propped on the seat, bent at the knee, giving me the perfect view of her sweet pussy hidden behind a pair of black silk panties. Air becomes trapped in my lungs when she trails a single finger up the inside of her thigh.

My jaw locks, not finding her cute anymore. "Stop that shit, Julia. I mean it. Turn around and sit properly until we get home."

She bursts into laughter, finding herself fucking hilarious.

Thankfully, it's not long before we pull up to her house. I come to a hard stop and barely have the truck shut off before I jump out. My feet eat up the gravel as I move for her, a dark primal need hammering through my veins.

It's time to finally claim what I have so foolishly kept from the both of us.

Julia's still trying to climb down out of the truck when I grab her around the waist. Slamming the door, I pin her against it and take her mouth, inhaling everything that belongs to me.

God, I fucking love the taste of her. I could kiss this girl for the rest of my life and it still wouldn't be long enough.

My hands slip under her dress and mold to the soft flesh of her ass. A fiery moan purges from her and I inhale the beautiful sound. When her teeth sink into my lip, it awakens the beast within me.

Growling, my hips drive forward, my aching cock begging to be released from its confines. "You want it, rough, baby?" I pull down the top of her strapless dress, revealing her black bra. My head dips, lips skimming across the swells of her tits as I descend to one tight nipple beneath the fabric and give a sharp nip.

"Jaxson!" My name falls on a heated cry, her nails digging into my shoulder.

I love the way she comes apart for me.

Unable to wait a second longer, I head to the door, keeping her in my arms as I dig in my pocket for the keys. Her lips kiss along my jaw while I try to unlock the door, but the goddamn thing is nothing but a hassle.

"See, Jaxson, this is why we shouldn't bother locking the stupid door."

My efforts cease and my eyes find hers, the sassy challenge reflecting back at me driving my need higher. Reaching up, I grab a fistful of her long silky hair, gently tugging her head back to stare into her seductive eyes. Eyes that are screaming for me to fuck her. "What did I tell you about that smart-ass mouth of yours, Julia?"

"Maybe you should shove something in it then to shut me up."

The breathless taunt sparks something dark and rich inside of me, calling it to the surface. I'm assuming my facial expression is comical by the way she laughs her ass off again. It fades the moment my fingers tighten in her hair. "Is that what you want, baby, my dick in your mouth?"

"God, yes."

Her needy response makes me whimper, fucking whimper like a pussy. I focus on the door again and finally get the damn thing unlocked. Once inside, I kick it shut and haul her sexy ass up the stairs to her room.

I slide her down my body until her feet touch the floor, then I collect a step back. "Take off your dress."

She raises an eyebrow at my command but does as I ask. Before she unzips the dress though, she bends down to take her shoes off.

"Leave them on."

Her head snaps up, a smile curving her pretty pink lips. "Mmm, bossy, bossy, you're lucky I like you like that."

She wants to see bossy, I'll fucking show her bossy.

Her eyes never leave mine as she unzips her dress, letting it pool at her feet. My cock jerks at the sight of her body, minimally covered by black satin and silver, fuck-me heels.

A low growl erupts from my throat. "Damn, woman, you're fucking sexy." I reach out to pull her to me, but she steps back before I can make contact.

"Uh-uh." She tsks, shaking her finger at me. "Not one step closer until you take some clothes off, too."

Reaching behind my shoulders, I pull my shirt off and stalk toward her but her sharp inhale halts me in my tracks.

"Oh my god, Jaxson," she breathes, her eyes locking on my chest.

I'm thinking her shock is from the scars. They're not as bad as my back, but it's still not a pretty sight. Until she grabs the beat-up, worn pendant that's hanging around my neck.

"I had to get a new chain for it, it got a little beat-up," I tell her, hating to think why it needed a new one to begin with.

She gives me a sad smile, her throat bobbing in emotion. "I guess it didn't do much good, huh?"

I shrug. "I don't know about that. I'm still here, aren't I?" I say that for her benefit because the truth is, I don't believe in that shit, but the thought of Julia losing her faith bothers me. She doesn't need to know how cruel the world really is.

"Yeah, you are, and thank God for that because I would die without you." Her choked words send a sharp pain through my chest, making it hard to breathe. No one has ever cared for me the way she does, and as good as it feels, it also scares the living shit out of me.

My abdominal muscles twitch as she lays her warm hand on my stomach. "Let me touch you, Jaxson. I want to know your body," she says, her eyes pleading.

Control is something I never give up, but for Julia, for a few moments, I will give it up for her.

At my nod, she glides her smooth palm across my chest as she walks around to my back. I feel her delicate fingers trace the angel before they are replaced with her lips, kissing all of my scars, as if trying to erase them from my body. She wraps her arms around me from behind, her breasts pressing against my back. A beat of a second passes before my skin becomes wet with her tears and it makes me feel as if someone just punched me in the fucking throat.

Even though it's hard for me to do, I let her hold me because I know she needs this, and well... maybe I do, too.

Eventually, she makes her way back in front of me, tracing the scars on my chest. Her warm lips press to every single one, her shoulders trembling with her sadness and it rips me apart.

My fingers thread through her hair and I bring her pained gaze to mine. "Please don't cry, Jules."

"I wish I could take them away."

"You do." It's the honest truth, no one calms the darkness inside of me but her. She's always been able to do that for me.

My mouth descends, closing the remaining distance between us as I pull her in my arms again. I consume every salty tear that falls, taking it as my own until there is nothing left but us and the dark desire claiming us.

Her hand trails down my stomach and she makes quick work of my belt and pants. My head drops back on my shoulders, a tortured groan vibrating in my throat when she reaches in and grabs my painfully stiff cock.

She strokes me firmly from base to tip, her soft thumb running over the smooth tip. "I want to taste you." She drops to her knees before me and it's the sweetest sight I've ever seen. Freeing my cock, she leans in and presses a soft kiss to my shaft. "I like knowing I affect you like this," she confesses with a smile, her warm breath hitting my flesh and making it jerk against her lips.

"Baby, my dick is in this state whenever you're in the same room as me."

"Well then, you should have let me take care of you long before now." With that smart-ass remark, she licks me from base to tip then closes her warm, wet mouth around my cock, knocking the breath from my lungs.

"Fuck me!"

She takes me as far down as she can before sucking her way back to the top, swirling her tongue around the tip, her fist pumping where her mouth can't reach.

Grinding my teeth, I try not to think about how she got to be good at this; the thought makes me see red.

Her eyes find mine beneath the hood of her thick dark lashes as she continues to drive me insane. I've pictured this countless times, but none of them came close to the pretty sight that's before me now.

Wrapping her long, thick locks around my fist, I begin controlling her rhythm, pumping my hips into her mouth with fast, steady strokes. "You have no idea what it does to me to see you on your knees, sucking my dick."

She moans, the vibration enough to make me come and I'm far from ready for that.

"Stop!" I tug her hair, pulling her mouth away, then haul her up against me.

"What is it, what's—"

Spinning her around, I lift her up and pin her against the wall, stealing her mouth in a ruthless kiss. I flick open the clasp of her strapless bra, letting it fall away from her body.

A groan rumbles from deep within my chest at the feel of her soft tits against my skin. I swoop down and take a soft, pink nipple into my mouth, grazing the tight tip with my teeth.

"Oh god, that feels so good," she whimpers, her wet panties sliding against my stomach as she tries to find release. A disappointed moan spills from her when I move away from her efforts. "Please, Jaxson."

"Easy, baby."

I carry her over to the bed, laying her out in front of me. Her brown hair fans out around her, high, firm breasts flushed and red from my mouth, begging for me.

"Jesus, you're a fucking sight." Dropping down in front of her, my face aligns directly in line with her pussy. I kiss her soft, toned stomach just above her panty line, a smirk pulling at my mouth when she tries pushing my head down. My eyes lift to hers. "What do you want, Jules?"

She moans in frustration. "You know what I want."

"Maybe, but I want to hear you say it."

She looks down at me, her teeth sinking into her bottom lip shyly. "I want you to kiss me."

"Where?"

She slides a shaking hand to the black satin. "Here."

I lean in and press a kiss to the wet material, her scent penetrating my senses.

She shakes her head. "I need more."

"Then tell me exactly what you want, Julia. I want to hear you say it… all of it."

Her cheeks flush a brighter shade of pink. "I want you to lick my… pussy."

Growling, I grab the side of her panties and rip the thin silk from her body. Her gasp of surprise turns into a pleasure-filled moan when I bury my tongue in her hot, wet flesh, the sweet taste of her exploding on my tongue.

"Oh god, yes!"

I fucking love how loud she is.

I groan in approval when she lets her knees fall open, giving me complete access. Her back arches, fingers roughly pulling my hair as I fuck her with my tongue. Her cries of pleasure and needy moans are enough to make me come. I can feel she's close, the small nub growing firmer with every fiery lick. My lips close around the bundle of nerves and it sends her flying.

She cries out my name, her body trembling as I drink every bit of pleasure that spills from her. She's still gasping for breath when I pull my mouth away and kiss my way up her body. I try to regain some measure of control before I humiliate myself and blow my load all over her stomach. However, she makes it extremely fucking difficult by moving restlessly under me.

"Easy, baby, we have all night," I murmur, tasting the delicate skin of her neck.

She grabs my face between her hands, angling me to look at her. "No! Listen, Jaxson. I don't want you to go slow. I want you to fuck me right now—hard and fast."

Well fuck me!

My control snaps. Rising up, I grab under her knees, positioning myself at her entrance. "Do I need to wear a condom, Julia?" I've always worn one, but knowing she can't get pregnant, I want to have nothing between us as I take her.

"No, I want nothing—" She loses her breath as I drive myself right into fucking heaven, a heated cry escaping her.

I still, worried I hurt her. "Are you okay, baby?"

"God, yes! Don't stop!"

She doesn't have to tell me twice.

I pound into her relentlessly, my dick surrounded in the hottest perfection I've ever felt. She wraps her legs around my waist, her heels digging into my back. I grind my teeth, the sting of pain sending heat to lick down my spine.

Our gazes remain locked as I completely lose myself to her. Reaching up, she touches my lips, something painful passing over her expression.

I still deep inside of her and rest my forehead against hers. "Talk to me, baby, what's wrong?"

"I just can't believe this is happening. I've waited so long to feel you inside of me again."

Her words strike me deep, my buried guilt rising to the surface. "I'll never stay away again, Julia, I can't. I need you as much as I need my next fucking breath, so get used to feeling me, because you're mine." I resume my pace, thrusting into her possessively with slow, hard strokes.

"Yes, yours. Always yours."

Damn fucking straight.

I take her lips, savoring her taste before descending down her delicate throat. Her nails rake along my back and her mouth finds my shoulder. When her teeth sink into my flesh, I come unglued and begin fucking her with a desperation I've never felt. The bed pounds against the wall with each hard, frantic thrust.

"Oh god, Jaxson, I'm coming," she screams, her pussy locking down on me.

"Fuck yeah, you are!" Feeling her spasm around my bare flesh is like nothing I've ever experienced. I fuck her through her orgasm, stealing every cry of pleasure from her until there's no more left. Then I let go, and take my own pleasure, losing the only part of myself I had left. She now owns all of me.

I drop down on top of her, trying to catch my breath as we lie in a sweaty, tangled mess.

"That was... wow," she says, her breath racing against my shoulder.

"That's the biggest fucking understatement ever."

I never want to move from this spot, I want to stay inside of her for the rest of my life.

I'm in serious shit.

"Jaxson?" she whispers.

"Yeah?"

"I can't breathe very well."

"Shit! Sorry." Rising up on my arms, I pull out of her, the disconnection making me want to cry like a pussy.

Like I said, I'm in serious shit.

After we clean up, we lie together in comfortable silence. Julia's sweet, soft body is draped over my chest while she traces the tattoo that runs from my arm to my shoulder. My hand does its own exploring along her lower back and soft curve of her ass.

"Jax?"

My hand stills in surprise. It's the first time she's called me that since I've been back, and I didn't realize how much I missed it until now. "Yeah, baby?"

"Can I ask you something?"

Trepidation sweeps over me, wondering where this conversation is about to go. "Yeah, Jules, you can ask me anything."

"What scares you the most about doing this with me?"

I frown in confusion. "What do you mean?"

She releases a nervous breath. "I mean, what scares you the most about us changing our relationship? Is it... is it not to have the freedom to be with anyone else?"

She barely finishes her sentence before I have her flat on her back under me, the quick action making her gasp. Frustration pumps through my blood but it fades quickly when I see the vulnerability in her eyes and realize she's serious.

"Is that what you really think?"

She shrugs. "I'm just asking. You can't really be that surprised I would think it. I've only been with one other person and—"

I cut her off with a hand over her mouth. "First off, Julia, don't ever mention you and your ex again. I know I wasn't around, but I don't want to fucking hear about it... ever. Got me? Secondly, I thought you understood you were different to me than everyone else. I mean christ, I have you fucking tattooed on my damn back."

She rips my hand away, her eyes narrowed in anger. *"First off, Jaxson,"* she mimics back to me with sass. "I do know that I mean more to you than your fuck buddies. That's not what I was asking. I can tell you're scared to do this with me, and let's be real, it's no secret how much you like women, or your freedom to do what you want with them. Secondly, buddy."

Buddy? Did she just fucking call me buddy?

"You're right, you weren't here for *six years*. So don't you dare tell me that I can't mention my ex, Justin is his name to be exact, and—"

That's it.

I claim her mouth, silencing whatever else is about to come out of her sassy mouth. The kiss is angry, desperate, and fucking soul crushing. "I told you I don't want to hear about him," I grind out, and reach between us for my hardening cock. "I'm going to fuck him right out of your mind. By the time I'm done with you, you won't even remember his fucking name."

Aligning myself, I push forward with one hard thrust, her hungry pussy accepting me eagerly. I take her without abandon, fucking her harder than I have ever anyone in my entire life.

"Oh god!" Her cry of pleasure pierces the air, her hands clawing at my shoulders, desperately trying to keep their grip. I feel her muscles contract around me, loving every frantic thrust I deliver.

"Look at me, Julia." Her eyes snap open at the command. "You feel this? Do you feel how perfect this is? This is the only pussy I want to feel around my dick—the only one. I could be the last man on the fucking planet having my pick, and I would always, only, pick you." I stare down at her, willing her to see the truth.

A smile takes over her face, and it's the biggest one I've ever seen on her. "Well, you certainly know how to make a girl feel special."

A laugh barrels out of me but it trails into a groan. "Jesus, woman, you drive me crazy."

"Good," she says, her smile still in place. "Now finish the statement you were making."

"I fucking plan on it." Grabbing her legs, I place them over my shoulders, driving myself in deeper.

By the time I'm finished with her, there's no way she remembers Dr. Med student whatever the hell his name was.

28

Julia

The next morning my phone chimes with a text message, pulling me from my blessed sleep. I moan at the painful throbbing behind my eyes. *Too much to drink.*

When it blares a second time, sounding way louder than it usually does, I grab my pillow and throw it over my head. The sound of a muffled chuckle meets my ears.

Pulling the pillow away, I squint against the powerful sunlight and am met with the sexiest sight of my life. Jaxson stands at the end of my bed, freshly showered, wearing only a pair of kick-ass jeans that hang low on his hips. The top button has been left undone, probably for my torture.

I ogle his naked chest, remembering how every taut muscle felt beneath my hands and lips. Then I remember where I had my mouth and have to squeeze my legs together. There's a glorious tenderness, muscles aching that haven't been used in a long time, especially as well used as last night.

My eyes lift to his ridiculously handsome face, and I find a cocky grin lifting his lips. I glare at him and his sexiness. "What are you doing looking so sexy and chipper this early in the morning?"

His grin spreads to a full-fledged smile.

God, the man is beautiful.

"Jules, it's noon."

"What!" I sit up with a gasp then instantly regret it when the room spins. Groaning, I grab my head, praying I don't humiliate myself and throw up the entire contents of my stomach.

"Easy, Jules," Jaxson soothes, sitting next to me. "Here, take this." He hands me a glass of water and two aspirin that I never even noticed he had. Probably because I was too busy looking at other places.

"Thanks." I toss back the white pills and drink half the glass of water, the cool liquid refreshing my parched throat.

When he takes the glass from me, I drop back down on another groan and close my eyes. At the sound of his chuckle, I peek up at him and can't help but smile.

"Hi," I whisper, reaching up to touch his face.

His warm fingers circle my wrist and he turns his face, kissing the inside of my wrist. "Hey, baby." He yanks the sheet from my body and sees me covered in his button-down shirt that he wore last night. A low growl erupts from his chest. "You look fucking sexy in my clothes."

I'm pretty sure I don't look any kind of sexy at all this morning.

Leaning down, he buries his face in my neck, nipping and tasting my skin. "Mmm." I thread my fingers in his freshly damp hair and breathe him in, loving the clean scent of his shampoo. He aligns his mouth to mine, but I slap my hand over it before he can make contact and shake my head. "Morning breath," I mumble.

His eyes narrow and he rips my hand away. "I don't give a shit about morning breath."

He tries to descend again, but I turn my head away. "No! I care—"

Grasping my chin, he forces my face back to him and swoops in for the kill. I keep my lips tightly shut, but he presses down on my chin to give him the access he needs. Once his tongue slips in, I'm lost in his world and I succumb to it completely. It's a a crazy whirlwind of a world that I would gladly live in for the rest of my life.

"Morning breath, my ass. You taste amazing," he mumbles, making me giggle. His forehead rests on mine, thumb stroking my cheek as he smiles down at me with an easiness that I haven't seen since he's come back. "What are your plans today?"

I'm just about to respond when my phone beeps with another text. Reaching over, I grab it and see six messages from a group text with Kayla and Grace. They want to meet up at the diner for brunch. A laugh tumbles out of me when I read the last text from Kayla.

Kayla: *Damn, Julia, tell that man to take his dick out of you already. You can make up for lost time after. I'm fucking hungry!*

I glance up at Jaxson to find him watching me in question. "It's just Kayla and Grace, they want to meet me for lunch at the diner."

"What's so funny about that?"

I clear my throat. "Nothing."

He rips the phone out of my hand and stands.

"Hey, give it back!" I jump from the bed and try to get it back but he holds it above his head to read.

The man is a freaking giant.

His arm curls around my waist, stopping my pathetic attempt of retrieval. "Jesus, that girl has a mouth on her," he says.

I scoff. "Coming from the guy who swears like a sailor." Realizing what I just said, I laugh at the irony of my comment.

That sexy grin of his steals his lips. "Maybe that's why I made such a damn good one."

"Mmm, maybe." I push up on my tiptoes to wrap my arms around his neck. "Or maybe it's because you're really smart, strong, and honorable." My lips pave a path across his shaven jaw, stopping at his ear. "Can I have my phone back now?" I ask, grazing the tender flesh with my teeth.

Growling, he hoists me up and pins me against the wall, his erection hitting me between the legs. The fire that burns in his eyes ignites in my own body. "You tell Kayla that I'll let you go for now, but don't plan on being gone too long. My dick and I have plans for you later." He follows up his dirty words with a pump of his hips.

"Okay, I'll pass the message on," I tell him, my voice breathless.

Chuckling, he sets me down on my feet, hands me back my phone, then presses a soft kiss to my forehead. By the time I open my eyes, he's gone, leaving me with a silly smile on my face.

An hour later, Kayla, Grace, and I are all seated in a booth waiting for our lunch. The diner is steady but not overly busy. It's nice to sit with Grace in here and have her eat with us rather than serve us.

"I still can't believe after all these years, Jaxson has finally pulled his head out of his ass," Kayla says, sipping on her sweet tea. "Okay, give us the details. How was it? I mean obviously it was good, given the

I-was-just-amazingly-fucked look on your face, but was it sweet and romantic or hot and desperate? My guess is hot and desperate. Grace, what do you think?"

"Um, I'm gonna say sweet and romantic," she guesses. "Jaxson doesn't seem like the sweet kinda guy, but you can tell he and Julia have somethin' special."

My heart warms at her insightful comment. "Actually, you're both right. It was all of the above, it was… perfect," I sigh, probably looking as dreamy as I feel.

Kayla drops back against her seat with a smile. "Damn, girl, I'm so happy for you. Okay, next question, how many times did you come?"

Grace gasps at the personal question.

"Oh as if you weren't wondering, too."

"Okay, you're right, I was," she admits with a giggle.

They both look at me expectantly, waiting for an answer.

"Four," I confess, feeling my cheeks heat.

"No way," Grace says, her eyes wide with disbelief.

I laugh. "Yes way."

Kayla nods in approval. "Not bad."

"You're serious?" Grace asks again.

"Yes."

"Wow."

"Why?" Kayla asks her. "How many times have you in one night?"

Her face turns the shade of a tomato. "Um, well, uh… never actually."

"What?" Kayla and I both shriek at the same time, drawing customers' attention to our table.

Oops.

"What do you mean, never?" Kayla hisses, leaning in close. "Are you telling us that you have never had an orgasm, Grace? Are you a virgin?"

She shifts, clearly uncomfortable, and it makes me feel horrible.

"It's okay, Grace, you don't have to tell us."

"The hell she doesn't!" Kayla says. "You can't tell us you've never had an orgasm and that's just the end of the conversation."

"I don't mind telling you guys," she says, biting her lip nervously. "I'm not a virgin, but I'm not real experienced either. I've only been with one person and although it wasn't horrible I wondered what all the fuss was about. I love romance novels, and I've heard other women talk about it like you and Julia do, but my experiences certainly weren't anything like what y'all talk about."

"Well no shit. If you've never come, then yeah, it isn't all that great," Kayla says. "Either he didn't know what the hell he was doing or he was too selfish to care."

"Or maybe it's me? Maybe there's something wrong with me?" she muses quietly.

"I doubt it. But have you tried to give yourself one?" Kayla is so blatant about the question that she may as well have just asked Grace what her favorite color was.

The girl has no shame.

Grace shifts uncomfortably. "Uh, no, I haven't."

"This is fucking insane!" Kayla mumbles, still not believing Grace's unfortunate circumstance.

"Well how many have you had in a night?" Grace asks.

"Six," she replies proudly. "And that was the night I smashed Coop's truck in. I'm considering doing it again sometime soon."

We bust into laughter, drawing everyone's attention over to us again.

Kayla leans in close. "We need to get this rectified, Grace, and fast. And I know just the person." A smile takes over her face as we wait with anticipation for who she's going to name. "Sawyer Evans."

"No way!" Grace rejects the idea quickly, shaking her head vehemently.

"Why not?" I ask, agreeing with Kayla.

"Because he is the most arrogant man I've ever met."

"Exactly," Kayla counters back. "He's arrogant for a reason, Grace. I mean, look at him. Don't get me wrong, I think Coop is sexy as hell but I'm not dead, and you can tell Sawyer is the kind of guy who can back up that mouth of his. I'll just bet that cocky mouth could do all sorts of things to you."

"Oh god, stop!" Grace groans, covering her ears.

"And look what happened last night? I'll bet he would be more than happy to help you out with your little problem."

I frown in confusion. "What happened last night?"

"After you left, Sawyer got all sorts of possessive and cranky when some guy got a little too touchy with Grace," Kayla explains with a smirk. "He wouldn't lay off when she told him to. Sawyer almost came to blows with the guy while defending Grace's honor."

Grace scoffs. "Yeah, but then he was all moody at me like it was my fault, which really ticked me off, by the way. It's not like I knew the guy was gonna try to have sex with me right on the dance floor, for cryin' out loud! I'm tellin' you, no way. Sawyer is out of the question, that man drives me crazy."

I smile as I recall Jaxson's words to me last night.

Jesus, woman, you drive me crazy.

I have a feeling Sawyer isn't all that out of the question.

29

Julia

Anticipation hums through my body as I head back home to Jaxson. Even though I enjoyed my time with Grace and Kayla, I missed him like crazy. I love that when I get home I don't have to hold my feelings in anymore. That I can freely walk up to him, wrap my arms around him and plant a deep kiss on his sexy face.

I never thought this day would come, but as happy as I am, I'm also scared. Because I know if something happens to end this—to end *us*—there will be no going back to being just friends. And the thought of not having him in my life again is unbearable to even think about.

As I pull up to my house, my gaze becomes riveted on the sleek black motorcycle parked out front. Excitement takes hold of me as I exit the car and race up my porch steps. "Jax?" I call, bolting through my front door.

He appears in the kitchen entry with a lopsided grin, wearing jeans, a T-shirt, and his riding boots. I run for him, launching myself into his arms. He catches me with a grunted chuckle that dies when I attack his mouth, showing him just how much I missed him.

My hands frame his face as I pull back to look at him. "Are you taking me riding?" I ask, hopefully.

"I was going to until you just did that. Now I'm thinking I should just take you upstairs for a ride instead."

"How about bike first, then bed?"

"Deal," he agrees with a smirk. "Do you still have your helmet?"

I nod.

"Bring it to me, I bought a Bluetooth for it."

"We can talk to each other now?"

"Yep, so run grab it for me and I'll install it while you get dressed," he says, placing me on my feet.

I clap my hands in excitement then run and grab him the pink helmet with the black face shield he bought me for my seventeenth birthday. After passing it off to him, I bound up the stairs and into my room.

Hmmm, what am I going to wear?

I dig through my fall clothes and decide on a pair of dark skinny jeans, a white tank top, and my thigh-high black boots. Grabbing my black leather bomber jacket, I throw it on over my tank then secure my hair in a ponytail at the nape of my neck so it won't interfere with my helmet. A few minutes later, I'm bounding back into the kitchen where Jaxson sits at the table bent over my helmet.

"I'm ready. Let's go."

He looks up at me with a smirk that vanishes the moment his eyes land on me, the light blue irises darkening as they sweep down my body from head to toe.

Leaning against the wall, I quirk a brow at him. "Like what you see, Jaxson?" I ask, throwing back the words he always says to me when I'm busted ogling him.

Silence fills the air as he pushes to his feet and starts toward me, his determined strides reminding me of an animal stalking its prey.

My heart thumps wildly in my chest, a familiar ache building between my legs. His arms come around me, his hands cupping my bottom to bring me flush against him. I bite back a moan at the feel of his erection pressing into my stomach.

"I always like what I see, Jules, but fuck me. Right now you look like every biker's fantasy. I want nothing more than to fuck you right now with nothing on but these boots you're wearing." He seals his words with a toe curling kiss.

My fingers grip in his disheveled hair as I succumb to the sensations this man instills in me. All too soon, he's breaking contact. We gaze back at one another, our breaths mingling in the air between us.

"Let's get the hell out of here before I change my mind and fuck you right up against this wall." He places me back on my feet, grabs my helmet, then takes my hand and drags me out of the house behind him.

Once we reach his bike he props the helmet over my head and makes sure the strap is secure. Even though I can fully manage to do this myself, I let him, because sometimes I really like it when he takes care of me.

After putting his own helmet on, he straddles the bike, looking as badass as I know he is. Since both of our visors are still up I'm totally busted for my appreciation. "Stop looking at me like that and get your pretty ass on the bike."

Giggling, I flick my shield down and climb on behind him. My feet land on the pegs as I wrap my arms around him, crushing the front of my body against his back.

His hard abs flex beneath my hands. "Christ, this is going to be a long fucking ride."

I smile when I hear his mumble through the Bluetooth. The loud roar of the bike starting up sends a long forgotten rush of adrenaline through me. The dull ache I had moments ago from his kiss in the kitchen comes pulsing to life from the vibration between my legs.

Jaxson's right, this is going to be a long ride.

The bike creeps forward and we keep a slower pace as he turns out of my driveway and onto the gravel road. Once we hit the interstate, Jaxson drops the throttle and the bike kicks forward on a rush.

I squeal in laughter and tighten my arms around his waist as we speed down the long stretch. The feeling of freedom washes over me, the one I've always gotten when I'm on the back of this bike with him. The thing I love most about riding, besides being so close to Jaxson, is how the whole world feels different. The fresh air feels cleaner, the sun feels warmer, and everything just seems more… peaceful. You get a whole new appreciation for the everyday things around you.

We drive for so long that my cheeks begin to ache from smiling so much. Eventually we leave the interstate and head up a curved road, the ocean below us getting further away as we weave up the steep hill.

"Where are we going?"

"You'll see." Is the only response I get.

A few minutes later, a lighthouse comes into view, sparking another rush of excitement through me. "Are you for real right now? Are we going there?"

His chuckle meets my ears through the bluetooth and my question is answered when he pulls into an opening off the road that leads to the stunning lighthouse.

I jump off the bike before he even has it turned off and remove my helmet as I walk closer to the edge of the cliff. The view is absolutely breathtaking, I've never seen anything like it.

I turn back to Jaxson, who's still sitting on the bike, holding his helmet on his lap, his signature sexy smirk curving his lips. "How on earth did you find this place?" Ever since I moved here, I've wanted to visit a lighthouse. You would think with us being so close to the ocean there would be a lot around us, but there's not.

"Coop told me about it. He discovered it coming back from a party he had to break up just a few miles up the road from here."

"I can't believe this has been here the whole time and we never knew about it." I look up, my head craning all the way back as I take in the tall, white lighthouse with black trim. The sun has started to set, making the beam of light at the top more prominent.

Jaxson comes up beside me and takes my hand. "Come on." He pulls me toward the entrance and we start making our way up a long flight of stairs.

I slow every time we near a window and try to get a peek of the view, but Jaxson tugs on my hand, not giving me the chance. "Patience, we're almost there."

Sure enough, a few more steps and we reach the top. My legs and lungs burn from our lengthy climb, but I don't let it slow me down. I run through the small opening at the top and gasp at the view before me. The Atlantic Ocean stretches out before us, the crystal blue water seeming to go on forever. Orange and pink hues dance across the glowing sky as the sun descends beyond the horizon.

Wanting to soak up everything about this incredible moment, I take off my leather jacket and lean forward against the railing with my arms out at my sides. My eyes fall closed as I take in a deep breath. Even from this high up, I can hear the crash of the waves as the warm ocean breeze blows gently across my face. I have never felt anything so warm and peaceful in my entire life, and for one fleeting moment, I think about my mother, and hope this is what she sees and feels wherever she is, every single day.

Right when I think this moment can't get any better, I feel Jaxson's strong arms come around me, proving me wrong. His body heat seeps into my back and his scent mingles with the salty ocean air. He slips my ponytail loose, freeing my waves from their confines and sweeps my blowing strands to the side so his lips can claim their place on my throat.

Reaching up, I curl my arm around his neck as his warm hands slip underneath the bottom of my tank and glide up on either side of my stomach. Goose bumps break out across my skin even though his touch brings only warmth.

"You're so beautiful, Jules," he whispers, his soft breath hitting the shell of my ear.

Smiling, I turn to face him and wrap my arms around his neck while his lock around my waist. The way he looks down at me makes me feel like the most beautiful woman in the world.

At this moment I desperately want to tell him how much I love him. Tell him that I never stopped, and I never will, because it's the god's honest truth. I will love this man until the day I die, but I know he isn't ready to hear that, not yet. So, instead, I swallow past the lump in my throat and try to put into words what I'm feeling. "I love that I am living out another beautiful moment of my life with you. Thank you for bringing me here."

"You deserve a lifetime of these moments." His head dips as he places his lips on mine, giving me a soul touching kiss.

Soon, we're shredding each other's clothes off and making love under the warmth of the sunset. He makes love to me with a tenderness I have never known, and I know in this moment, with every fiber of my being, that Jaxson Reid loves me as much as I love him.

30

Julia

Three weeks later, I'm in the kitchen starting the preparations for Kayla and Coop's engagement supper. I pushed the date back a week since Grace had a hard time getting off work. I didn't want her coming here drained after a long day at the diner.

As I'm peeling the potatoes, my phone rings, the screen flashing an unknown number. I answer it politely, even though I'm not expecting an answer.

This past week I've been getting a hang-up call at least once a day. Sure enough, the same thing happens again. Annoyed, I hang up and move back to my spot at the counter. At first I thought it was a wrong number or kids, but now I realize that's probably unlikely. I know it's something I should mention to Jaxson, but things have been amazing between us the last few weeks, and I really don't want anything to strain it.

Bending down, I grab a baking sheet from underneath the oven when something big and hard crowds me from behind, startling me. I reach up and grab onto the counter to balance myself.

"You can't stick this pretty ass in the air, Julia, and expect me not to do something about it." Jaxson's husky voice sends a delicious shiver through my body.

Unable to stop myself, I push back against his erection. He groans, his fingers digging into my hips.

Smiling, I force his hands away and turn around. "Behave. Kayla and Grace will be here soon."

Ignoring me, he spans my waist and lifts me on the counter, coming to stand between my legs. "Then I guess we better make it quick."

My giggle trails into a fiery moan when his tongue laves at the sensitive skin of my neck, leaving a path of heat in its wake. He gently squeezes my breast through my thin tank top, my nipple straining against his touch. I arch against his heated palm and slide my hands under his shirt, scoring my nails across his toned stomach.

Growling, he tugs the top of my tank down with my bra, freeing my breasts, and sucks an aching nipple into his mouth.

A harsh cry breaches my lips and warmth gathers between my thighs. I wrap my legs around his hips to reel him in closer. Just when I reach for his belt, the doorbell rings.

Of course.

"For fuck's sake." Jaxson's heated curse slices through the air, his frustration mirroring my own. He captures my mouth in one more fiery kiss, which is interrupted again when someone begins pounding on the door. Another growl rips from his throat as he pulls back. "We are fucking moving, Julia, and we aren't telling anyone where we live."

Chuckling, I right my top and trail behind him as he storms to the door. He swings it open aggressively, forcing Grace a step back, but not Kayla.

She cocks a hip and returns his glare. "You know, Jaxson, you and this door locking business is starting to piss me off. There was a time where I could just walk into my best friend's house when I showed up. I didn't have to knock."

"Well, Kayla, sorry to inconvenience you, but my door locking business is to keep your best friend's ass safe. Don't tell me Coop doesn't make you lock your damn door."

She tilts her head. "Wow, you're grouchy today. Is the Hulk going to be gracing us with his presence the whole time?" She walks past him, giving him a quick pat on the chest. "Coop's waiting for you in the truck to head to the liquor store whenever you decide to get over your tantrum."

Covering our mouths, Grace and I burst into muffled giggles.

Jaxson mutters to himself as he puts his shoes on, then walks over and gives me a quick, peck on the lips. "You need to find new friends."

"Ha!" Kayla fires back. "You would still have to put up with me because I'm marrying your best friend. Sorry, big guy, but you're stuck with me."

He shakes his head, but I don't miss the twitch of his lips before he heads out the door.

They secretly love each other.

I swing my attention over to Kayla to find her looking rather amused. "I love screwing with that guy."

Our laughter fills the air as we make our way into the kitchen. Grace places a tote bag on my counter and pulls out three freshly baked pies that look absolutely divine.

"Wow, these look great, Grace. Thanks for bringing them."

"No problem, they're nothin' fancy. I made an apple, a raspberry, and a blueberry."

"I'm sure they'll be delicious, as always."

"Have you heard from Katelyn?" Kayla asks. "Is she able to come tonight?"

"Yeah, she's coming. Between her, Sawyer, Cade, and Grams we will have a full house."

"I'm so glad Grams could make it. I haven't seen her in a while."

"You know Grams, she's always in the mood to celebrate, especially if there are margaritas."

Kayla snickers. "We'll make them nice and strong for her tonight."

We start to set up, pushing together tables and adding chairs. My back screams every time I lift anything. Since my fall from Wyatt it hasn't been the same, and it wasn't great to begin with.

"You all right, Jules?" Kayla asks, when I twist my body to relieve pressure.

"Yeah, it's just my back. It's a mess."

"I thought yoga was helping?"

"It was, but since my fall it hasn't been doing well. I've been meaning to come see you, but I've just been caught up in stuff."

"More like someone has been caught up in you," she mumbles. "Come on, I'll give you a quick fix to hold you over."

"Oh no, that's okay. I'll be fine. I'll make sure to come see you next week."

She gives me the *look*, the one that brooks no argument. "I'll be quick, come to the living room."

"All right, thanks." I follow her into the other room where she makes up a little spot on the floor with the throw blankets and pillows.

"Take off your tank and lie face down. Grace, I'm going to get you to hold certain points on her lower back while I work on her top. Between the both of us it won't take long."

Removing my shirt, I do as she instructs, making myself comfortable. As soon as she puts her hands on me, sweet oblivion claims me.

Jaxson

"Who's Katelyn?" I ask Cooper on our way back to the house.

"She's the girls' hairdresser. And... waxer," he adds, looking over at me with a smirk.

"Waxer? What kind of waxing are we talking about?" Sawyer asks from the backseat. He and Cade had pulled up just before we left to the liquor store.

"None of your damn business."

I'm not letting that shithead know anything about Julia's waxing.

"Oh, so it's that kind of waxing. Nice."

I turn back and glare at him, daring him to say more.

"She's the one who spotted us outside the club that night and got us in," Coop explains further. "She's nice, but dates some real douche bags. Especially this most recent one. He owns that club, which is how she got us all in. I met him at Big Mike's one day when I was there sparring with a deputy. I never wanted to kick someone's ass as much as I did his."

"Speaking of Big Mike," Sawyer cuts in. "He approached Cade and me the other day, and asked us if we wanted to buy his gym."

"What?" I ask, the information rocking me to my core.

"No bullshit. Actually, he said he wants the three of us to buy it. I'm considering it."

"You want to move here?" I couldn't be more surprised right now if the guy told me he had a pussy.

"Why not, I'm kind of digging this town. And with a little money we could do some pretty cool shit with that place."

I look over at Cade. "What about you?"

He shrugs. "I'm not sure I want to settle in one place, but I agree with Evans. We could do a lot with the place."

"It doesn't surprise me he asked you guys," Cooper says. "He's been wanting to sell it, but only to the right person." His eyes shift to me. "I think it's something you should consider."

I haven't thought much about what I'm going to do. I've only been thinking about Julia and fixing shit with her, but I have to admit, as shocked as I am about Big Mike's approach, the thought does appeal to me.

The conversation ends when we pull back up to the house. As we climb up the front steps, Sawyer looks down at the margarita mix I'm carrying and smirks. "In the mood for pussy drinks tonight?"

"It's for Julia's Grams, you asshole. She loves margaritas."

He chuckles. "Sure, sure, I'll just bet…" His words trail off when we walk into the house and hear a pleasure-filled moan.

It's a moan I'd know anywhere.

What the fuck?

"Oh yeah, right there, that's the spot," Julia says, her voice soft and seductive.

I'm about to storm through the place like a fucking tornado but Sawyer grabs my arm, stopping me. He puts a finger to his mouth, telling me to be quiet.

"Damn, Julia, you're tight. Grace, move over so I can get better access."

Sawyer's green eyes light up like it's fucking Christmas. "Ho-ly shit!" Shoving against my chest he heads for the living room.

I charge after him with Coop and Cade on my heels and yank him back. I don't know what the hell is going on, but I don't want anyone to see Julia moaning about anything.

All of us shove at each other to get through the entrance of the living room but freeze mid-struggle when we get a look at the sight before us. Julia lies face down on blankets, wearing no shirt. Kayla is on one side of her and Grace on the other with their hands on her back. The side swell of her perfect breast is visible and rage pumps through me, knowing everyone else can see it, too.

"Hey," Julia greets me with a smile, acting as if it's perfectly normal to be lying on the floor half naked for everyone to see.

"What the hell are you doing?"

Her eyes narrow at my harsh tone. "I'm getting a massage, what does it look like I'm doing?"

Sawyer's laughter pierces the air. Turning around, I shove him back a step. "Get the hell out of here. And you…" I point over at Julia. "Get your clothes back on."

She bristles at the order and awkward silence falls over the room.

Kayla fastens up her bra then stands and glares at me. "Come on, Grace, let's go finish setting up."

She storms past me with Grace and everyone else following behind her.

"You can be a real asshole, you know that?" Julia hisses, throwing her top back on. "What the hell is your problem?"

"You want to know what my problem is? I don't like coming home with a bunch of friends to see my girlfriend half fucking naked and moaning on the living room floor for everyone to see."

She crosses her arms, pushing her perfect tits up for my viewing. "Oh please, Jaxson, I was getting a massage. You act like what we were doing was inappropriate."

"It sure the hell sounded like that when we walked through the door."

"So that gives you the right to yell and embarrass me in front of everyone?" She turns away, but not before I see the hurt in her eyes.

Well shit!

Releasing a guilt-stricken breath, I walk over and pull her in my arms. "I'm sorry, you're right. I'm an asshole. I shouldn't have reacted like that. I was caught off guard when I walked in and heard shit that's only for me to hear."

She looks up at me, her cheeks pink. "Did it really sound that bad?"

"Baby, if I wasn't certain Kayla and Grace were in here with you, there would have been major destruction left in my path."

"Oh lord," she groans, hiding her face in my chest.

Grasping her chin, I bring her gaze back to mine. "I am really sorry. We good?"

She nods. "Yeah."

"Good." I drop a kiss on her forehead then release her.

"But just so we're clear, Jaxson, the next time you talk to me like that you'll be finding yourself a new place to sleep, and the moans I'll be making won't be coming from you. Got it?" She doesn't wait for a response before she sashays her sweet ass out of the room.

31

Julia

Kayla, Grace, and I are in the kitchen mixing the salads and getting things ready when the doorbell rings. Leaving my task, I go open the door and let Grams in.

"Hello, my sweet girl," she greets me, reaching up to kiss my cheek.

"Hi, Grams, come on in. Everyone's out back. We're just waiting on Katelyn."

I link her arm with mine and escort her into the kitchen. Grace and Kayla drop what they are doing and greet her with a big hug. Grams kisses and fusses over them, as always, then she grabs Kayla's hand to admire her ring. "I'm so happy for you, sweetheart. And I want you to know, I heard about what happened at the motel."

Kayla groans. "I'm never going to live that down, am I?"

"Now don't you be getting all embarrassed," Grams gently scolds, shaking a finger at her. "Desperate times call for desperate measures. It's important to show your man you will fight for him."

We share a laugh before I lead her out back where the guys are barbecuing. I take her over to Sawyer and Cade first. "Grams, this is Sawyer and Cade. They're friends of Jaxson's from the Navy."

"Well my goodness, aren't y'all both so handsome," she coos, kissing their cheeks. Cade tenses at her affection but tries to hide it and nods politely, but Sawyer soaks it up, loving every bit of the attention.

She turns to Jaxson next who stands over at the barbecue. "There's my favorite boy, come here, honey, and give me some love," she says, opening her arms.

It melts my heart when he accepts her affection comfortably and hugs her back.

Grams takes his face between her worn hands, making him have to bend down. "Miss Gladys wants me to give you a kiss for her, but I told her only on the cheek because you're Julia's now."

A laugh spills past my lips and it earns me a glare from him.

Next, she makes her way over to Cooper. "Cooper, you handsome devil. I'm so proud of you for making an honest woman out of Kayla," she praises, kissing his cheek. "Now I have something I need to tell you, honey. Something happened to me on the way over here."

I frown and start over to her. "Grams, what's wrong? Are you okay?"

She cuts a hand through the air, waving away my concern. "Now don't worry, I'm all right, but a man was blaring his horn at me, and driving like a maniac in his fancy-schmancy car. When we pulled up to a red light he rolled down his window and started yelling at me, told me I was driving too slow and to get off the effin' road."

I gasp, not liking to hear someone spoke to her like that.

Cooper doesn't like it either. "Did you get a good look at the guy?" he asks.

"Actually, I did one better, I wrote down his license plate number for you. I told him that I knew the sheriff personally and that he was going to get into some major trouble. He laughed and started yelling more profanities at me. So then I pulled out the big guns, I told him my grandson was a Navy SEAL, and he was going to kick his ass."

A small smile cracks my lips as I picture Grams threatening someone with Jaxson. But Jaxson doesn't find it funny. In fact, he looks down right pissed.

"There was a girl in the passenger seat," she continues. "I couldn't see her well, but she was yelling at him to stop. Whoever the poor girl is, I feel bad for her, being with someone like that can't be all that fun."

Cooper takes the paper from Grams. "No, I bet not. You did a good job writing down the license plate number, Miss Margaret. I'll look into this first thing tomorrow."

Grams pats his shoulder. "I know you will, honey."

I help Grams into her seat and offer her a drink. "Can I get you a margarita?"

"That would be lovely, thank you, dear."

I head back inside and fill Kayla and Grace in on what Grams just told us while I mix her drink.

"Oh my gosh, that's terrible," Grace says, sounding as upset as I feel.

Kayla's reaction is the opposite. She's furious. "What an asshole! I can't wait for Cooper to find his sorry ass."

Before either of us can say more the doorbell rings. The three of us go answer it and open the door to find Katelyn, and some guy who I'm assuming is her new boyfriend.

"Hey, Katelyn, come on in," I greet her with a smile but it fades when I notice her eyes are red and glassy. It looks as if she's been crying.

She steps inside, hugging Grace and Kayla before coming to me. "Hey, Jules. Um, so it turns out that Vince didn't have to work tonight. I hope it's okay that I brought him along?"

Something in her voice gives me the impression she didn't necessarily want to bring him but I don't want to make things awkward, so I paste a smile on my face and nod. "Of course, no problem. Hi, Vince, it's nice to meet you. I'm Julia, and this is Grace and Kayla."

His eyes sweep down my body, slowly and deliberately, blatantly checking me out. When his gaze finally makes it to my face he gives me a sleazy smile. "Hi."

Kayla, Grace, and I exchange a look.

So much for things not being awkward.

Katelyn clears her throat. "Can I use your bathroom?"

"Sure, follow me. I'll show you where it is. Kayla and Grace, can you guys get Vince a drink and take him out back?"

"Sure, right this way, Vince." Kayla leads him into the kitchen as I walk Katelyn down the hall toward the bathroom.

"Oh god, Julia, I'm so sorry," her choked whisper stops me in my tracks.

I turn around to see tears streaming down her face. "Are you okay?"

She shakes her head. "He is such a jerk. We had this huge fight on the way here. I'm seeing a side of him I didn't know he had. I tried to get rid of him, but he wouldn't listen. In the end I figured it was easier just to bring him and then deal with him later."

Just as I open my mouth to respond we hear a commotion out in the backyard. Katelyn and I rush outside to find Grams yelling and pointing at Vince. "That's him, Cooper! That's the guy who was yelling and cussing at me. I told you I knew the sheriff. You're in big trouble now, mister!"

"Oh no," Katelyn cries.

"You have got to be fucking kidding me," Vince mutters, annoyed.

"So you're the one who was harassing Miss Margaret." Cooper gets up from his chair, his eyes furious. I spot Jaxson across the yard with Sawyer and Cade and see them coming toward us.

"The bitch shouldn't be behind the wheel. She can't drive worth a shit."

I tense at Vince's cruel words and round on him. "Don't you talk about my Grams like that!"

He steps into my personal space and leans in close, his eyes wild and angry. "Listen, bitch. She—"

I'm yanked back and Vince vanishes before my eyes. Big hands grip my shoulders to steady me. Looking over my shoulder, I find Cade behind me. "Thanks," I say, my voice shaky.

Turning back around, I see Vince pinned against the house by a very pissed off Jaxson, his beer bottle shattered at their feet. "I don't know who the hell you are, but if you don't get off this property in ten seconds I will kick your fucking teeth through the back of your skull."

Vince's angry eyes take in the lot of us, considering his options. He's a big guy and I'm sure he can handle himself, but he's no match for Jaxson.

It's obvious he realizes this and raises his hands in surrender. "No problem, man, just let me get my girl and we're out of here."

Jaxson releases him but stays close.

"Let's go!" he barks at Katelyn, starting toward her.

I step next to her and reach for her hand. "No! She's staying here."

Katelyn gives my fingers a grateful squeeze.

"I don't think so, bitch. You better—"

Jaxson brings his knee up into Vince's gut, making him double over. "Time's up, asshole."

"I'm not leaving without my girl," Vince wheezes through painful breaths.

Cooper comes to stand in front of Katelyn. "Do you want to leave with him?"

She shakes her head. "No, I don't. Leave, Vince and don't ever contact me again."

"That's all I needed to hear." Cooper turns his back on us and helps Jaxson drag him out.

Tears slip down Katelyn's cheeks when she walks over to Grams. "I'm so sorry, Miss Margaret. I tried to tell him to stop. I feel even more terrible knowing it was you."

Grams pulls her in for a hug. "It's all right, dear, you have nothing to be sorry about. He's responsible for his own actions."

Katelyn turns to me next. "I'm sorry, Julia, I didn't mean to ruin anyone's night."

"You didn't. I'm glad you stayed."

"Me, too," Kayla says, giving her a hug.

"And me." Grace follows Kayla's lead and joins in on their hug.

"And me," Sawyer adds, enveloping all three girls in his arms, making all of us chuckle.

Leave it to Sawyer to lighten the heavy moment.

Feeling someone's eyes on me, my attention shifts to the back door and I find Jaxson leaning against it, watching me. I give him a small smile, appreciating what he just did for Katelyn. He returns it with one of his own and the beauty of it makes my heart skip a beat.

Our silent exchange needed no words. With just a look and a smile, the words we have yet said to each other were spoken.

Later that evening, when Sawyer and Cade are the only ones left, I decide to call it a night. I walk over to Jaxson where he sits at the kitchen table and wrap my arms around his neck. "I'm going to bed, y'all need anything before I head up?"

His hand strokes the inside of my bare leg, eliciting goose bumps across my skin. It's a touch of promise for what's to come later. "Nah, we're good. I'll be up after this," he says, lifting his beer.

"That's fine, take your time." After giving him a kiss, I move to Sawyer and Cade next and give them both a hug. "Good night, boys. Take that leftover pie."

Sawyer sneaks a kiss on my cheek. "Night, Jules, thanks for having us."

Jaxson kicks the bottom of his chair. "Lips to yourself, asshole."

Giggling, I shake my head and make my way upstairs. As I'm getting changed, I realize I left my cell down in the kitchen and I want to check in on Katelyn. Grabbing my thin sweater, I throw it over my tank top and make my way back down the stairs. Just as I reach the bottom I catch a glimpse of the guys' conversation.

"I can't hold the admiral off anymore, Jaxson. We need to make a decision and we need to make one now, are we going to help with this mission or not?"

I come to a hard stop, dread sinking into the pit of my stomach.

"I don't know. Instinct is telling me yes, we need to go help, but after what happened and the way things ended… I don't know if we are the right ones for this. Cade, what do you want to do?"

"Like I said, I'll do whatever you guys want."

Unable to listen to another word, I charge into the kitchen, shaking with hurt and anger. "How can any of you even consider this?"

All their eyes snap to me in surprise.

"Shit," Jaxson mumbles, shaking his head.

I stomp closer to him. "What are you thinking? Haven't you been through enough? Haven't you all been through enough?"

He reaches for me, but I step back. "Calm down, baby, come here. We haven't decided anything."

"Calm down? How could you keep this from me? What else are you hiding?"

"Damn it, Julia, nothing. You're overreacting."

"The hell I am! You promised. You promised you wouldn't leave again. You lied to me!"

Before I completely lose it in front of them all, I run back upstairs and into my room. Slamming the door, I crawl in bed and curl into a ball. The thought of Jaxson leaving again—and possibly getting hurt or worse—breaks something inside of me, something I may never get back.

32

Jaxson

"S hit!" I jump to my feet, my chair slamming into the wall behind me.

"I told you to tell her, man."

I glare over at Sawyer, not appreciating his two fucking cents at the moment. "I didn't want to say anything until we made a decision."

"Yeah, and because of that she just got blindsided. Listen, Jaxson, you need to think hard about this. Is this something that's worth hurting her over? I feel the same way as you do—I want to help. But let's face it, if we don't go, someone else will. It isn't like the mission will fail if we say no. If we were still in the Navy then this wouldn't even be a question, we would haul our asses out there and do what we needed to do. But we aren't anymore; and for a damn good reason too, if you ask me."

I run my hand through my hair, angry at myself because he's right. I should have told her, but things have been so good lately I didn't want to fuck it up.

Sawyer stands and claps me on the shoulder. "Think about it. You know we'll go along with whatever you want to do. Just remember what I said—someone else will do it if we say no."

Cade nods his agreement, then they both bid me goodbye before walking out the door.

I lock up behind them and head upstairs, wondering what the hell I'm going to encounter once I walk into the room. Bracing myself at the door, I open it and am met with darkness. Through the shadows of the room, I see Julia curled up on her side of the bed with her back to me. If it weren't for the quiet sniffles, I would think she was asleep. I switch on the lamp, bringing the room to a soft glow.

"Jules?" I call softly, my steps slow. When she doesn't answer, I kneel on the floor next to her. A tissue is clutched in her hand as she buries her face in the pillow, her shoulders trembling with her pain.

It rips me apart to see her like this, especially knowing I'm the cause of it. "Please don't cry, Jules. Everything's going to be okay."

She shakes her head. "No, it's not. It's not going to be okay, Jaxson. You lied to me. You promised you wouldn't leave me again."

"I'm sorry, I should've told you. But you need to know, if we decide to do this, if I leave, it won't be forever. I'll come back to you."

Her head snaps up and she fists my shirt with a strength that shocks the hell out of me. "Don't make promises you can't keep! You can't promise you will come back to me. Something could happen to you. Look what happened last time." Her anger quickly turns to agony. She drops back down, her shattered sobs slicing me right down the middle. "I've never asked anything from you. I've supported you in everything you've chosen to do, even if I didn't like it. But I'm begging you now, please don't do this, please don't leave again. I won't survive if something happens to you."

Her agonized plea destroys me, but also brings clarity. Leaning over, I cover the top half of her body with my own and trail my lips across her wet cheek, bringing my mouth to her ear. "Okay."

She falls completely still under me. "What?"

"Okay, I won't go. I'll do anything to not have you hurt like this."

It's the damn truth, nothing or no one matters to me more than her.

She lifts her chin, her devastating eyes wide with surprise. "Really? You won't leave me?"

I shake my head. "Never."

Her breath catches, a small sob of relief escaping her. She reaches up, her fingers fanning my jaw as she gazes back at me with an emotion I'm too scared to name. But I don't need to, because she breathes the words a moment later and they rock me to my fucking core just like they did six years ago. "I love you, Jaxson."

My heart swells so fucking much it hurts, emotion gripping the hollow organ in a tight vise. They're words I've longed to hear yet feared at the same time.

Her hand covers my mouth before I can respond. "Don't say anything.

I don't want you to say anything back. I just... I need you to know that I still love you. I never stopped and I never will."

She deserves to hear those same words, but they remain stuck in my throat. I'm too much of a pussy to say them because the last woman I said them to left and never came back.

"I don't deserve you." The truthful words sound gruff even to my own ears.

She sits up on the edge of the bed, her legs dangling on either side of me. "Yes, you do. You deserve all of me, including my heart." She grabs the bottom of her tank top and pulls it over her head, baring me to the most beautiful sight of my life.

Since I can't say the words I feel, I show her, my hands gliding up her smooth, toned stomach and cup the full weight of her breasts.

"Jaxson." My name breaches her lips on a fiery whimper as she leans back on straight arms, arching into my touch.

"You're so fucking pretty, Julia. Every perfect inch of you." I take a taut nipple into my mouth, licking and sucking the velvet tip.

With a harsh gasp, her hand curls in my hair, fingers gripping. The sting shoots straight to my cock and sends lust roaring through my veins. Her hips rise off the bed, her hot, covered center grinding against my stomach as she tugs at my shirt with urgent hands.

Leaning back, I get rid of the material quickly then lift her off the bed. Her arms cling to me, skin warming mine as I reverse our positions. I fall back onto the bed, my shoulders meeting the mattress as I bring her down on top of me.

A low growl shreds my throat when she takes the opportunity to grind her hot pussy down on my stiff cock. Spanning her hips, I inch her further up my stomach until she's sitting on my chest. Then, I fist the side of her tiny shorts and shred them from her body.

She sucks in a sharp breath, and grabs onto my shoulders to steady herself, her bare pussy only inches from my face.

My mouth waters at the sweet smell of her, the urge to taste her overwhelming. "Come here, baby, and grab onto the headboard."

"What are you going to do?" she asks, uncertainty shining in her eyes.

I smirk up at her. "You're going to ride my face while I fuck your pussy with my mouth."

Her cheeks flame, but there's no denying the need in her eyes, it's the same one raging in my blood. Tentatively, she grabs onto the headboard. I slide down a little more, bringing her soft, warm thighs on either side of my head, my mouth coming in direct line with what I crave most. Rising up, I burrow my mouth into her hot, wet flesh and groan when the taste of her explodes on my tongue.

"Oh shit!" Her cry of pleasure tears through the room. It fuels my efforts—challenging me. Her trepidation forgotten, she tangles one hand in my hair and fucks my mouth with greedy thrusts of her hips.

Groaning, I apply more pressure, my tongue working her clit, the nub getting harder and firmer. Her breath quickens and her movements become more frantic. Knowing she's close, I bring my hand up behind her and coat my fingers with her arousal before slipping two fingers inside her, and that's all it takes.

She sobs out her orgasm, trembling against my mouth and I drink every last fucking drop from her. Her legs begin to shake as she fights to hold herself up. My hands span her hips but before I can lift her, she grabs my wrists, stopping me. Our eyes meet between her legs and a seductive smile curves her lips. "Stay right where you are."

Slowly, she moves down my body, and I kiss every inch of golden skin that passes. When her perfect tits come in line with my mouth, I nip at one tight bud, dragging a heated moan from her throat.

Her lips meet the skin on my chest, tongue dipping and tasting the hard lines of my body. Need coils low in my stomach, my cock aching for release.

"Baby, as much as I love your mouth on my body, if you don't speed this up we're going to be in serious trouble."

She giggles, but thankfully moves with more urgency. Sitting on my thighs, she works the button on my jeans and lowers them enough to free my cock. Her fingers wrap around the thick base, stroking me with a firm grip.

"Fuck me!" My hips jerk off the bed as I pump myself into her hand, my dick charged and ready. "Julia, now!" I order.

She aligns herself over me and slowly begins to sink down on me. I grind my teeth, my fingers digging into the soft flesh of her hips. "So hot, so tight."

Her heat surrounds me, my whole body going warm, especially the spot in my chest. With her hands braced on my stomach, she begins riding me, her movement slow and unsure. But she's a fucking sight to behold.

Long brown hair tumbles past her slender shoulders, framing her perfect tits while a light sheen of sweat covers her skin, giving it a glowing affect.

With her eyes closed and face tilted up, her expression soft and sweet, she looks like a goddamn angel.

My angel.

"God, I love how you fill me up," she moans.

My teeth grind so hard with restraint that my jaw begins to ache. Reaching up, I cup both of her tits and she arches into my touch, her rhythm picking up.

"That's it, baby, fucking ride me." I jerk my hips up into her, burying myself so deep I'm not sure I'll ever find my way out.

"Oh!" She gasps, lips parting.

"You like that?" I repeat the motion but even harder, giving her more.

She whimpers. "I love it. I love everything I do with you. I... I love you."

My chest tightens with a mix of pleasure and pain. I still can't believe that I was lucky enough to meet this girl, to have her become my best friend, and then to become... mine.

She deserves better; she deserves more.

Wanting to silence the stupid, but truthful, voice in my head, I sit up and wrap an arm around her slender body. My hand anchors in the back of her hair as I bring her lips to mine, selfishly taking everything she has to give me.

This is my favorite place to be in the world, surrounded by Julia—her taste, her scent, to be inside of her. I constantly ache for her, body and soul. I have no idea how I went so many years without this, but I know I never will again.

I'd die without her.

"You own me, Julia, every fucking part of me." I look up at her, letting her see what I so cowardly can't say.

She gives me one of her beautiful smiles. A smile that always tightens my chest and proves to me that the world can be a good place. "I know," she whispers, before pressing a soft kiss against my forehead, just like the one I always give her. Then she drops one at the corner of my eye, my cheek... she doesn't stop and continues to heal all the broken parts of me with just a brush of her lips.

I bury my face in her soft skin, my throat burning like a motherfucker. Our bodies stop moving, my cock seated deep inside of her as we hold each other. As if sensing my internal battle, she leans down, bringing her mouth to my ear. "This is right, Jaxson, this has always been right. Something that feels this good could never be wrong."

Her words of truth destroy me and it all becomes too much. Needing to move on, my lips meet her warm skin as I coast them across the swell of her breasts, brushing them across her stiff nipple before sucking it into my mouth.

"Yes," she moans, her hips finding rhythm again.

I lie back down and keep one hand on her breast and the other on her hip, helping guide her. My hips pump up inside of her, driving my cock deeper.

"Oh god!" She braces her hands on my chest, further leaning over me, her full tits swaying inches from my mouth. "More, I want more."

My fucking pleasure.

Giving her what she wants, I drive up inside of her again and again, her inner muscles gripping my cock. "Your pussy is so greedy, baby. I fucking love it."

She whimpers, her teeth sinking into her bottom lip. I reach up and tug at the tender flesh. Her tongue darts out, curling around my thumb before she sucks it into her mouth.

It shreds the last of my control.

I fuck her hard, like I've been dying to. Her screams fill the air, nails digging into my flesh as she takes every hard, frantic thrust. Within seconds, she's shattering above me.

Her head falls back on a cry as ecstasy washes over her face. It's the most beautiful sight I've ever seen. Fire spreads through my body as I follow along with her, losing a little more of myself as I do.

It takes us a good few minutes before we're able to move and clean up. Julia walks out of the bathroom, looking rumpled and sexy as hell in my shirt. A soft smile curls her lips as she approaches the bed.

Reaching out, I catch her off guard and haul her on top of me. She squeals in laughter and accidentally kicks something off her nightstand.

"Oh crap!" Scrambling off of me she reaches over to pick up a framed picture of her and her mom on a Ferris wheel at some fair. Her expression is soft as she lies down on top of me, holding the picture up so we can both look at it. "Wasn't she beautiful, Jax?"

"Yeah, baby," I agree, holding her a little tighter. "Just like you."

She makes a fist on my chest, resting her chin on it, and smiles up at me. "She would have loved you."

I grunt. "I'll just bet she would've loved the guy that fantasized about all the ways to screw her daughter from the moment he laid eyes on her."

Giggling, she presses a kiss to my chest then stares up at me somberly. "She would have loved my best friend. The guy who helped take my pain away and made me smile again. The one who watched out for me, protected me." She reaches up, her fingers grazing the side of my face. "I've always believed she sent you to me that night in the graveyard."

My muscles tense, rage igniting in my blood as the memory of that fateful night resurfaces.

"It was the first time I had prayed since my mother died. I was so scared, thinking of what they were going to do to me, not knowing if they were going to kill me after. I was sad for Grams, thinking she was going to lose the last family she had left. So I prayed to my mom for help. I prayed so hard for something, anything, to stop what was happening. Then you showed up and saved my life, in more ways than one."

Little does she know it was her who saved me that night, not the other way around.

"I'll always protect you, Julia." I may not be able to give her everything she deserves, but I'm more than capable of giving her that.

"I know." She reaches up and drags her fingers along my lips, her expression sobering. "Are you going to resent me later for asking you not to go?"

I shake my head. "No. It's not something I have to do, and I wasn't sure I was going to do it. That's why I never told you, but seeing you hurt like that…" I shrug. "It just made the decision that I was struggling with easier. I'm surprised the admiral even asked us; the three of us aren't his favorite people."

"Why?"

"Because we went against his order," I tell her.

Pain enters her eyes, knowing it was that order that lead me to a week of hell. "How did it happen? How were you guys held for so long? Didn't they know where you were?"

With a heavy breath, I focus on the ceiling and think about how much to share with her. "We had just finished a mission that we were sent to do in Iraq. We were there for two weeks, learning the territory that we needed to cover and coming up with our plan of action. During that time, Cade would leave in the evenings. Wherever he was going had him tied up in knots when he came back. Some nights he came back, I don't know… relaxed? Then other times he was moody and restless. Sawyer and I didn't have a clue what the fuck was going on with him."

"He met someone, didn't he?" she asks.

I look down at her in surprise. "Yeah. How did you know?"

"Because he's a lot like you," she says, smiling up at me.

Huh, well if that isn't a little true.

"Anyway, moving on, Miss Know-It-All."

She chuckles.

"The day before we were supposed to come home, Cade was moodier than usual. Something went down the night before in his room. That's when Sawyer and I realized he was seeing someone, which was a big deal because the guy never sees the same girl twice."

After I say that, it strikes me again how similar he and I really are.

"Sawyer and I took him to the local bar we had gone to a few times, and tried to talk to him. In the middle of our beers a kid came running in, crying. He was yelling at Cade, half in English, the other half in Arabic—*'He took her, he took her.'* Cade understood more than we did and seemed to know the kid from somewhere. He went crazy. I've never seen him like that. Don't get me wrong, the guy is lethal but always in control."

I pause, remembering that day so vividly and what followed after.

"It turned out the girl he was seeing was an American. She was there on a mission trip with her church. Cade got into it the week before with some local asshole who was harassing her. As it turns out, that asshole was part of some pretty serious shit. He took her to punish him."

"Oh no," she whispers, but can't begin to understand just how bad it was. No one could, not unless you were there to hear the screams and the pain that was inflicted.

"Cade took off half-cocked and ready to shed blood," I continue, my voice harder—darker. "I held him back and told him we would go to the admiral to get backup. He agreed. But the admiral said no, told us that it wasn't our problem and we were to have our asses ready to ship out. Sawyer and I knew Cade wasn't going to leave her there, and we sure as hell weren't going to bail on him. So we loaded up with what weapons we could, and the kid said he would take us to her. But it was a fucking setup, he led us right into an ambush."

"Why would he do that?" she asks, her question thick with tears.

"He didn't have a choice, he was forced to do it. He was the son of one of our captors." My stomach churns when I think about what ended up happening to that poor kid.

"So in the end the Navy finally found you guys?"

A bitter laugh escapes me. "No, we got out on our own. With help from someone on the inside. The only reason we were honorably discharged was because we made our team look good. They didn't want it revealed that we were ordered not to help another American, so disclosures were signed and the three of us walked away with a big settlement."

"Did you guys get the girl out?" she asks softly.

My chest tightens as I think about more than one American girl. "Yeah, but not before she was hurt."

"Why isn't Cade with her now?"

"I don't know. He doesn't like to talk about it."

A moment of silence settles between us before she speaks again. "Jax?"

"Yeah."

"The men... the ones who hurt you, are they dead?"

"Most of them."

"Good," she says firmly, hugging me tighter.

I hold her close as she drifts off into a deep slumber. Meanwhile, sleep evades me and instead I'm left with the sound of tortured screams and the smell of death.

Julia

"Julia."

I moan from Jaxson's urgent whisper. "Again? Lord, man, don't you ever sleep?" I mumble, teasing.

"Julia, get up now."

My eyes spring open at the harsh tone of his voice, realizing something's wrong. Sitting up, I see he's out of bed, throwing on his jeans.

I glance at the clock and see it's only three a.m. "What is it, what's wrong?"

"Someone's in the house."

"What?" I screech.

He claps a hand over my mouth. "Listen, baby, everything's going to be all right, but you need to be quiet, okay?"

I nod.

Removing his hand, he reaches under the bed and pulls out a gun.

"Oh my god, you have a gun? In my house?" I whisper harshly.

He looks at me like I'm stupid. "Of course I have a gun."

I guess I shouldn't be surprised, but I deserve to know if I'm sleeping over top of one for goodness' sake. I climb out of bed quietly and follow Jaxson to my bedroom window that looks out over the front yard.

A loud clanging noise sounds from downstairs, startling me. I gasp and grab his arm, fear gripping my chest.

He hands me his cell phone. "Call Cooper, tell him what's going on and to bring backup."

"Where are you going?"

"I'm going down to find out who the fuck is in here."

"No! Jaxson, please just stay here with me. We have no idea who's down there or how many there are."

"I can handle myself, Julia, I promise. But I need you to be strong right now and do what I ask, okay?"

I resist the urge to argue and nod, tears lodging in my throat.

He hands me the gun but I step back and throw my hands up. "No way! I have no idea how to use that. I hate guns."

"Listen to me!" he snaps. "The safety is off, all you do is point and pull the trigger. You probably won't need it, but just in case."

The cold steel is placed in my hand as he forces me to take it.

"You stay right here. Don't fucking move from this spot. If anyone comes through that door you shoot first and ask questions later, got it?" he says, pulling another gun from behind him.

When the hell did he put that there?

"What if it's you?" I ask.

"I'll make sure you know it's me."

The sound of the front door slamming comes from downstairs. Jaxson's head snaps to the window. "Fuck! Call Cooper now!" he orders, charging out of the room.

Looking out the window, I watch someone dressed all in black running across my yard and disappearing into the woods. A second later Jaxson bolts out of the house, barefoot with no shirt on, gaining on the person quickly.

With my hands shaking and tears building behind my eyes, I struggle to dial Cooper.

He picks up after the second ring. "Do you have any idea what time it is, asshole?"

"Cooper?" His name trembles past my lips on a sob.

"Julia? What's wrong?"

"You need to come quick. Someone broke into my house and Jaxson took off running after him. He has a gun and—"

"Okay, calm down. I'm on my way, stay on the phone with me, all right?"

Tears stream down my face as I nod my head.

"Julia, you still there?"

"Yes, sorry, I'm here. Just please hurry. I'm scared for Jaxson."

"I'm heading to my truck now, I'll be there in a few minutes, can you..."

His voice fades out when I hear another noise come from downstairs.

"Shhh!" I tell him to be quiet and listen more closely. Slowly, I walk to my bedroom door, the sound getting more profound. "There's a noise coming from downstairs, it sounds like whimpering."

"Julia, just stay where you are. I'm almost there."

"What if someone is hurt?"

"I'll deal with it when I get there. I mean it, don't move!"

I know I should heed the warning but my instincts have me pushing forward, my steps slow and quiet as I descend the stairs.

"Damn it, Julia, are you fucking listening to me?"

"I'll keep you on the phone," I promise.

I ignore his heated curse, and pay close attention to my surroundings, the gun still firmly in my hand. Once I reach the bottom of the stairs, I'm able to pinpoint where it's coming from. "It's in the kitchen," I whisper and now realize that it isn't a whimper but a squeaking sound.

My heart is pounding so loud I'm surprised I can hear anything else besides its thundering beat. On shaking legs, I enter the kitchen, and what I see has my blood running cold and bile rising in my throat.

The phone slips from my hand as a scream shatters my chest.

Jaxson

Gun in hand, I charge down the stairs and out of the house to see the guy running into the woods. My bare feet pound the earth, gravel biting into the bottoms as I push forward, keeping him in sight.

"Jennings, is that you, you motherfucker?"

At first, I thought maybe it was that asshole Vince from tonight. But this guy isn't big enough to be him. My heart pumps faster, lungs working harder, as I gain on him.

You're mine, you son of a bitch.

A piercing scream rips through the night, stopping me in my tracks. I look back toward the house, realizing it's Julia. Fear grips hold of me and I start back the way I came, running faster than I thought myself possible.

"Julia?" I call out, barreling through the door. I move for the stairs at break neck speed but stop when I hear her in the kitchen. Dread curls its icy fingers around my heart as I enter inside and find her on the ground, retching and crying. I drop down next to her, my hand pushing aside her hair. "Julia, what's wrong? What happened?"

Before she has a chance to answer, my attention draws to the left and I see a gutted coyote hanging from the ceiling, a chain wrapped around its neck as it sways above the table.

"Jesus!"

Half of the kitchen is a fucking bloodbath from its insides, including the large window where blood spells out: *You're next, whore.*

Rage pumps through my blood with unrelenting fury. The sound of Julia's cries yank my attention back to her. "It's okay, I got you." Scooping her up in my arms, I carry her into the living room and that's when Cooper bolts through the door, almost throwing it off its hinges.

"Is she all right? Damn it, Julia. You scared the shit out of me. What happened?"

I jerk my head toward the kitchen, indicating for him to see for himself and take a seat on the couch. Julia curls into me, my arms vibrating from her trembling body.

Cooper walks back out of the kitchen, his jaw locked and eyes tight. "I guess you didn't catch the son of a bitch."

I shake my head. "I almost had him, but then I heard her scream and left him in the woods to run back here."

A couple of deputies come running in shortly after. "Sheriff?"

Coop orders them outside. "Get out in the woods across the way and search for him. He's probably gone by now, but look for anything that can link us to him." His eyes shift back to me. "What was he wearing?"

"All black with a hood over his head, medium build, about six feet tall. He's armed with at least a knife," I tell him, thinking about the gutted animal in the kitchen.

Once the deputies leave, I force Julia to look at me, hating the pain and fear that are in her eyes. "Why did you come down here? I told you to stay put."

"I'm sorry. I thought someone was hurt. I didn't know it was… that." She covers her ears, trying to block the sound of the swinging chain. "God, please make that sound stop!"

"I'm sorry, Julia, but we can't touch anything in here until the forensics team comes in," Cooper says regretfully.

I pull her into my chest and kiss the top of her head. "Let's go pack a bag and stay somewhere in town for tonight."

"You guys come stay at my place," Cooper says. "I need to call Kayla anyway, she was out of her mind when I flew out of the house."

Before I can accept his offer, Cade and Sawyer burst through the open front door.

"What the hell are you guys doing here?" Cooper asks.

"Kayla just called me freaking out," Sawyer explains. "She asked if I was with you guys. She wanted to know if Julia was okay."

"Jesus, that woman is fucking impatient," Cooper growls. Pulling out his phone, he steps out to call her.

"What the hell happened?" Sawyer asks, taking in the sight of Julia in my arms.

I nod toward the kitchen.

He and Cade both go check it out for themselves. By the time they walk back out, they look as angry as me, their expressions hard.

"Who?" Sawyer asks.

Just one word but it was the most important one.

"Meet us at Cooper's," I tell them.

They give me a tight nod then head out the door.

Standing with Julia in my arms, I start for the stairs. Vengeance burns in my blood, promising retribution.

The son of a bitch will pay for this.

34

Julia

I walk into Kayla and Cooper's house, feeling cold and detached from my body.

Kayla takes my bag from me and pulls me in for a hug, one I cannot feel. "Come on, let's take this into the spare room," she says, ushering me with an arm around my shoulders.

Jaxson trails behind us, his anger silent yet deafening at the same time.

As we bypass the kitchen, I see Sawyer and Cade sitting at the table, looking as furious as Jaxson. They both greet me with a tight nod. I smile in return, or at least I try to but it's weak at best.

Once we enter the spare room, Kayla drops my bag on the bed and turns to me, concern bright in her eyes. "Can I get you something? Some tea maybe?"

"Yeah, that would be great, thanks."

The guys' heated conversation drops as we enter back into the kitchen.

"Come here, baby." Jaxson opens his arms for me and I don't hesitate, walking into them, my body curling into his as I settle on his lap. His strong arms bring me the warmth and security I crave.

The front door slams and Cooper comes walking in a moment later, looking tired and stressed. "Forensics are going through things now," he says, his eyes moving from Jaxson to me. "Julia, who has a key to your house?"

"Just Kayla. Why?"

"Are you sure about that?"

"Yes, I'm positive. Not even Grams has one."

His attention moves to Kayla next. "Go check your keys to see if it's still there."

"What's this about, Coop?" Jaxson asks.

"No one broke into that house. They got into it with a key, there's no way they even picked the lock."

What?

Kayla comes back a moment later with her keys in her hand. "Yeah, it's still here."

Silence and tension consumes the kitchen while everyone ponders their thoughts.

"Do you think it was that prick from earlier tonight?" Sawyer asks.

"Vince?" Kayla and I ask at the same time.

He shrugs. "Why not? The guy was pissed about getting tossed out, plus it gave him an opportunity to swipe a key from somewhere."

"It wasn't him," Jaxson says, his tone filled with certainty. "The guy I ran after wasn't big enough. Besides, I already know who it was."

Wyatt!

A chill races up my spine at the thought. When Kayla hands me my tea, I wrap both of my hands around the steaming mug, trying to soak in its warmth.

"I don't know, Jaxson," Cooper says, doubtful. "Things have been quiet for weeks. Nothing out of the ordinary has happened. Why start trouble now?"

It's at this very moment that I remember the phone calls. "Well, something out of the ordinary has been going on," I tell them quietly.

Jaxson tenses, and everyone's eyes snap to me.

Regret plagues me as I focus only on Jaxson. "I'm sorry, I should have told you sooner."

"Tell me what?"

"I've been getting phone calls all week."

"Jesus, Julia! All fucking week and you're just now telling me?"

"Well, at first I just thought it was the wrong number, or kids playing a prank. No one said anything, they would just hang up. But the last two times I could hear someone breathing and—"

"For fuck's sake!"

"How many did you get?" Cooper asks.

"About one a day, all on my landline, not cell phone."

"I'll go question him tomorrow."

"Come on, Cooper," Jaxson snaps, his voice harsh. "It's not like the asshole is going to admit to it. He went too far this time, I'm dealing with him myself."

"No, you're not! I'm serious. Don't you do something stupid and make me have to arrest my best fucking friend."

Tense silence fills the air as they glare back at each other.

I rest my forehead on Jaxson's, my hand moving to his hard jaw. "He's right, Jax, please just let him handle it."

He remains silent, too angry right now to listen to reason.

A tired sigh escapes me and I press a soft kiss to his lips. "I'm going to go to bed." I climb off him and walk over to Cooper to hug him. "Thanks, Cooper, for everything."

"You're welcome but next time, you listen to me when I tell you to stay where you are."

"I will. I'm sorry." I turn and offer Sawyer and Cade a wave before heading out of the kitchen with Kayla following behind me.

"Do you want company?" she asks.

"Sure, I'd love some."

With a smile she follows me into bed. We both curl up on our sides and face each other.

"Are you going to be all right?" she asks quietly.

"Yeah, I just wish I could erase the image I have in my head. It was terrible, Kayla."

She reaches for my hand, her fingers folding around mine. "Don't worry, Jules. Coop will make the son of a bitch pay."

I hope she's right because if not, the next time it might not be an animal hanging from the ceiling. It could very well be me.

Jaxson

Cooper and I argue for a long while before I finally give in and let him handle things—for now. The fury that pumped through my body earlier has now settled in a low simmer, always there but controllable.

"Call us if you need help. You know we have your back," Sawyer says as he and Cade stand from the table.

I climb to my feet also and decide now is a good time to tell them about my decision about the Admiral. "I'm turning down the mission, especially now. I'm not leaving Julia."

Sawyer nods. "It's a good decision. I'll deal with the admiral."

"Thanks." I head out of the kitchen and stop short at the entrance to the spare room, a grin tugging at my mouth from the sight before me. "Hey, Coop, come get your woman out of my spot."

All three guys approach the doorway and peek in to see Kayla and Julia curled on their sides facing one another, their hands linked between their bodies as they soundly sleep.

"Aw, and look, they're both wearing your shirts. Someone take a picture," Sawyer chuckles.

Cooper walks over and lifts Kayla in his arms. "No, Coop, not with Jaxson and Julia here," she mumbles.

The three of us burst into muffled chuckles.

Grinning, he turns back to us and shrugs. "What can I say, I'm always on her mind."

Once he walks out, I close the door behind me and start removing my clothes.

"Jax?" Julia whispers, stirring awake.

"Yeah, baby."

"Did you and Cooper work everything out?"

"Yeah." I crawl into bed and pull her to me, needing to feel her warmth.

She buries her face in my neck, her lips planting heated kisses. Lust begins to stir in my blood, mixing with the deep seated rage. Groaning, I palm her ass in both of my hands, bringing her closer.

She sits up in a flash, straddling my hips and swiftly pulls my shirt off her body, bringing my dick to life with a jolt.

"I need you. I need to feel you right now." Her voice is frantic and hands urgent. "I can't get the image of that poor animal out of my head, and—"

I flip her over, cutting her off before she can fall into hysterics. "I've got you, baby." I pull her against me, her back to my front then lift her top leg and bring it back over mine. Grabbing her hip, my fingers curl in the silk fabric of her panties and I shred them from her body.

A harsh moan parts her lips. "As hot as that is, you really need to stop doing it or I'm not going to have any panties left."

"It's faster, and right now I don't have the patience to take them off of you any other way." I slide my hand between her legs, our groans mingling in the air when I feel her soaked and ready. "Always so wet and ready for me," I whisper, trailing my lips along her shoulder.

"Always for you."

I pull my underwear down just enough to free my cock, then enter her in one hard thrust.

She gasps, her head falling back on my shoulder. "God, yes. I need you."

"You have me." My lips brush the shell of her ear, teeth grazing as I pump into her warm body. Sweat builds between our skin, my hands palming her breasts as I fuck her hard and deep. "Feel me, baby. Only me."

"I do. It's all I feel," she whimpers, pushing back greedily with each thrust.

Reaching in front of her, I slide my finger through her wet slit, finding her swollen nub.

"Jaxson." My name is the only warning I get before her orgasm claims her. Her pussy locks down on me, gripping my cock like a tight vise and sucking it greedily into its hot depth.

"Good girl, come all over my cock." The dirty words drag another moan from her throat. Once I know I've claimed every bit of pleasure she has to give me, I allow myself my own release.

Afterward, I hold her close, my arms banded tight around her. "I'll take care of this, Julia, I promise."

I'll give Cooper his time, but after that, the motherfucker is mine.

Lifting my hand, she brings it to her mouth, her lips pressing a soft kiss to my palm. "I love you, Jaxson." The words are only a soft murmur in the dark but have the power to heal and destroy at the same time.

I drop a kiss on the back of her neck, a burning ache taking up residence in my chest. Once again I hate myself for not saying it back.

35

Julia

A week later I'm in the very place I thought I'd never be able to step foot in again—my kitchen. Jaxson took care of making sure it was thoroughly cleaned; he even bought me a new table. I can even still smell the fresh paint on the walls and I shudder when I think about why it needed a paint job to begin with.

Things have been strained between us lately, to say the least. Ever since we found out from Cooper that Wyatt had an airtight alibi for that night, Jaxson has been on edge. There's a quiet rage about him now that wasn't there before. He's always on guard, not letting me go anywhere by myself, and gets angry if I even suggest it.

He's been having nightmares, too, but anytime I try to talk about it with him, he says he's fine and closes himself off from me. Before all of this, things were so amazing for us. I could feel him opening up to me, letting me in more than he ever has before, but since that night he's completely shut me out and it breaks my heart. To make matters worse, I've been feeling terrible lately. The stress is really starting to get to me.

My phone rings, pulling me out of my depressing thoughts. Before I can answer it Jaxson comes charging in, throwing his hand up at me, to stay put and let him answer it.

"Hello." He snaps the greeting into the phone, his icy tone annoying me.

What if it's my grams?

"Who's this? Yeah, hold on."

He hands me the phone. "Some Don Thomson from Foothills Elementary."

Gasping, I rip the phone from him and pray this is the call I've been waiting for. "Hello, Mr. Thomson?"

A huge smile takes over my face as Don tells me I got the job. I start dancing around silently, fist pumping the air. He tells me I'll be subbing until Christmas, but after that my position will become full-time, and I'll be teaching second grade. I thank him for the opportunity and hang up.

I look up at Jaxson to see him leaning against the counter, watching me with a smile. "I got the job! I got the job! I got the job!" I cheer, launching myself into his arms.

His chuckle rumbles against my ear as he holds me tight. "Congratulations, Jules, you're going to be a great teacher."

It's the first time in a week I've heard his tone soft and genuine. It warms my heart and makes my throat tight. I rest my forehead against his and bring my lips to his, showing him how much I've missed him. When I pull back, there's a fire in his eyes that I haven't seen since we came back. He leans in for another taste but I push away from him, my stomach suddenly rebelling.

"Oh no!" Covering my mouth, I run to the bathroom and slam the door behind me. I barely make it to the toilet before emptying the contents of my stomach. Moaning, I lean my head against the side of the toilet, the cold porcelain bringing me a small measure of relief.

I startle when a wet cloth touches my forehead. My eyes spring open and I see Jaxson staring back at me in concern.

"Oh god, did you really just watch me throw up?" I groan. "That's so not hot."

He chuckles, finding my distress amusing. "There's nothing you could do that would make you '*not hot.*'" His hand cups my clammy cheek, his expression sobering though. "How long has this been going on?"

I shrug. "Not long. I think it's just the stress running me down."

"Make an appointment for the doctor, Jules."

"I'm fine, it's just the flu or something."

"I still want you to book an appointment, just in case, all right?"

"Okay." I relent with a sigh.

"Can I get you anything?"

I smile, my heart warming at his kindness. "No, I'm okay but thank you. I'm going to call Grams and tell her my good news."

He helps me to my feet and stays close while I rinse my mouth and splash cold water on my face. Once I feel a little more refreshed, I head upstairs and call Grams. She shares in my excitement and makes plans for next week to take both Jaxson and I out for supper to celebrate.

After my phone call with her, I go online to check my bank account. I had a decent amount in savings but without a steady paycheck until after Christmas, I may need to look into a part-time job. When I click on my balance, my eyes widen in shock, bugging out of my head at the number before me. "What on earth? This can't be right." Going through my history, I see there's no mistake, someone deposited ten thousand dollars into my account.

Who would do that? Grams? No, she would have told me, wouldn't she?

Logging off, I head down into the kitchen and grab a Coke from the fridge. I lean against the counter and think about why Grams would deposit money and not say something.

"What's wrong?" Jaxson asks from the kitchen table.

"Someone deposited ten thousand dollars in my account. It could only be Grams, but why would she not—"

"It was me."

I tense, a frown pulling between my brows. "What? Why would you do that?"

"Because I told you I would pay you back for Germany."

My eyes narrow, anger igniting in my blood. "First off, Jaxson, it was nowhere near ten thousand dollars. And secondly, I told you I didn't want your damn money."

He shrugs easily. "Don't worry about."

His blatant attitude only angers me further. I slam my drink down on the counter. "Are you listening to me? I am not taking it, so you can forget about it."

"Yes, you are."

My teeth grind at the order. "No. I'm not. I'm going to the bank tomorrow, withdrawing that money, and giving it back."

"What's your problem? Just take the damn money."

"No! I am not your whore."

He shoots to his feet, knocking the chair over in his haste. "What the fuck are you talking about?"

"Just because you're screwing me, it doesn't give you the right to deposit money into my account. Who the hell do you think you are? How could you…" I trail off and grab onto the counter for support, suddenly feeling lightheaded.

"Will you calm down?" He starts over to me in concern but I throw my hand up, holding him back.

Once the dizziness passes, I straighten and push away from the counter. "I'm giving the money back and that's final." Without another word, I head upstairs to my room and slam the door.

An hour later when I'm still too angry to face him, I decide to run a bubble bath, hoping it will help calm me. Throwing my hair up in a messy bun, I turn on my iPod for music and climb into the hot, sudsy water. It isn't long before my tight muscles begin to ease and I feel slightly more relaxed. The big, claw foot tub is my favorite place in the house, and when I say big, I mean massive. I could stretch out at the bottom of it and my feet still wouldn't hit the end.

Resting against the pink bath pillow, I close my eyes and hum softly to the song playing, Pink's duet with Nate Russ, "Just Give Me A Reason".

A moment later, I hear the click of the door and the air around me becomes hotter, awareness seeping into my body when I feel someone's gaze on me. Already knowing who it is, I open my eyes and find Jaxson leaning against the closed bathroom door, watching me; his fierce expression making my heart skip a beat.

"Are you still mad at me?"

"Yeah," I answer truthfully but softly.

His lips twitch with a smile before he starts toward me, his strides slow and confident as he peels his shirt off, revealing absolute perfection. His body is hard and strong, capable of both pleasure and pain.

My pulse races as I wait for him to take off his pants and join me, but he doesn't. Instead, he kneels on the floor beside the tub then leans over and cups the side of my neck, his thumb stroking over my thrumming pulse. The simple touch is electrifying; goose bumps break out over my body, even though I'm surrounded by hot water.

"Please take the money, Jules." His soft tone contradicts the fire that's in his eyes.

My gaze narrows. "No! And don't think for one second that I don't know what you're up to."

"I don't know what you're talking about," he says, leaning in to kiss my neck.

I hold him back. "Yes, you do. Now get your sexy lips away from me."

Chuckling, he pulls my hand away, holding it captive as he presses his lips to the base of my throat. His skillful tongue tastes and teeth nip the sensitive skin.

Oh god!

Heat surges through my blood, desire flooding every part of my body.

He trails warm kisses up my neck, moving for my lips. I try to turn my head to the side but he grasps my chin firmly between his thumb and finger, holding me in place, while his lips descend upon mine. My mouth remains soft and slack, as I try not to give in to the temptation but oh god, it's difficult.

"Come on, baby, kiss me, I know you want to."

"Uh-uh."

He continues his teasing assault, swiping his tongue across my top lip then grabbing my bottom between his teeth. And it's the little sting that breaks me. Moaning, I wrap my arms around his neck and kiss the ever-loving heck out of him.

A feral growl erupts from him, my lips tingling from the vibration of it. One hand dips into the water, grabbing my hip, then slides up my stomach to my breast. He circles my nipple with his finger, teasing but never touching.

When I pull away to take in air, he moves to my throat. "Come in here with me," I plead breathlessly, gripping his bare shoulders.

"I'm not much of a bath guy, Jules, but fuck do you make me wish I was." He sinks both hands in the water and spans my hips. "Sit up a bit, baby." He helps me move into a higher position, bringing my breasts out of the water, bubbles lightly surrounding them. "Seeing you all hot and wet like this…" A rough sound erupts from the back of his throat as he bends down, and sucks a stiff nipple into his mouth with heated force.

A heated cry spills from me, my clit swelling from the almost too much pain. He blows on the aching tip, soothing the sting before moving on to the next one, giving it the same greedy attention it thrives for.

"Please, Jaxson," I whimper, needing more.

"What do you want, baby?"

"Touch me."

"I am touching you."

"No, here." I shamelessly bring his hand between my legs, my hips lifting.

"My fucking pleasure." His fingers delve, immediately finding the spot that craves his attention.

A heated whimper shoves from my throat, my knees falling open to give him more access. "Touch yourself, Jules."

I tense at the rough command, my eyes lifting to his. "What?"

He grabs one of my hands and places it on my breast. "Touch yourself. Show me how you like it." Heat invades my cheeks at the thought and he senses my hesitation. "Don't be embarrassed, baby, it's just me."

As apprehensive as I am, I can't deny the way my body burns with the need to give him this. Closing my eyes, I let the sensation of his fingers take over my body, focusing on the pleasure. My hand begins kneading my breast, my sensitive nipple feeling like silk against my palm. A fiery moan leaves my lips as Jaxson's finger strokes a little harder and faster. I slide my other hand up and cup the other breast, freely giving into the pleasure I can bring myself.

"That's it, baby. Fuck, that's sexy." The rough arousal in his voice empowers me, and I completely abandon myself to my touch. I feel his eyes upon me, his hot gaze heating the air around us. "Have you touched yourself before, Jules?" He follows up the question by inserting a single finger inside of me.

I gasp and arch into his touch. "Yes," I answer breathlessly, "and I always thought of you when I did. Always imagined it was your hands on me."

"Jesus."

I cry out as he pushes a second finger inside of me. Pleasure soars through my body, and I vaguely hear Jaxson undoing his belt. My eyes snap open to see him stroking himself, and it's the most erotic thing I've ever seen. When pre-cum spills over the flushed tip I lick my lips, wishing it was in my mouth.

"Do you like watching me, Julia?" he asks, his fingers stroking that hidden spot deep inside of me.

"Yes," I moan, thrusting against his hand.

"Since the day I've laid eyes on you, you're all I thought about every time I stroked my cock. I'd imagine what you'd look like over me, under me, on your hands and knees in front of me," he growls. "And you're even fucking better than I imagined."

"Jaxson," I whimper, feeling myself teeter on the edge of destruction. He brings the heel of his hand against my clit and it's exactly what I need. A harsh cry flees from me, the intense orgasm crashing through my body and stealing the breath from my lungs.

"That's it, baby, come all over my fingers." He keeps his rhythm, dragging out the pleasure until I'm soft and limp.

I look down at his fist, as he pumps himself faster. Sitting up, I lean over the tub and stop his efforts. "I want to finish you with my mouth."

He stands in a flash, dropping his jeans a little more to fully free his cock. Before he can even guide it to my mouth I'm on him, sucking him as deep as I can possibly go, making sure my hand strokes where I can't reach. I glance up to see him watching me, his jaw clenched and eyes wild with lust.

His throaty groans spur me on as I slowly suck back to the head and give him a show, swirling my tongue around the swollen tip.

"That's it, baby, suck my dick, just like that." He pulls my hair from its hold on the top of my head and tightly wraps my loose strands around his fist, creating a delicious sting on my scalp. He controls my rhythm, pumping his hips, filling my mouth. When he hits the back of my throat, I hold him there and swallow.

"Shit!" He tries to pull my head back but I fight against it. "Julia, I'm going to come any second, so if you don't want to swallow, you better move your mouth."

I moan, letting him know I want it, and quicken my pace, sucking him harder and faster.

"Fuck!" His head falls back on a roar as his cock pulses, spilling a hot stream of semen down my throat. I keep my efforts strong and drink every bit of pleasure that spills from him.

"Jesus." He falls to his knees and gives me a mind numbing kiss before resting his forehead against mine, his hand cupping the side of my neck.

No words are spoken but none need to be. The love and devotion in his eyes says it all.

36

Jaxson

T hat night, another nightmare plagues me and it's the mother of all nightmares—the night I finally got out of hell, but not before others paid the price…

I pull against the chains with all the strength I have left, my wrists feeling close to snapping. Little bits of gravel from the wall crumble around me, and I'm shocked to discover I still have this much strength left. Cade and Sawyer struggle as hard as I do, all of us fighting for Faith and Anna's sake.

Please let one of us make progress. The memory of Anna's screams fuel me with adrenaline and strength I didn't know I still possessed.

The sound of our cell being unlocked has me stopping my attempts; Sawyer and Cade immediately follow and go slack. Irina walks in, the wife of one of our captors, and the mother of the boy who set us up. She holds a finger to her lips, her gaze darting around nervously, tears streaking down her face. "Okay, I'll help you," she says, whispering to Sawyer.

My aching muscles tense, suspicion rearing inside of me. "Why now?"

We've been asking for her help all week, and each time she coldly refused; she also helped inject that shit into us in the beginning.

"Because they just killed my boy," she sobs, throwing her hand over her mouth.

"Shit!" Cade hisses. Even though the kid helped with the ambush, you could see he had a soft spot for him.

"Listen, I don't have much time. Something's going down in about an hour. I don't know how much I can help once they're in here, but if you guys can over-power them, I'll help get you out. There's only going to be six of them on the whole

compound tonight. The rest are picking up a shipment at a location hours from here, and they're not due back until tomorrow."

"Where's the American girl, Anna?" I ask. When her eyes dart away, panic surges through my veins. "Where the fuck is she?"

She swallows nervously. "She's in one of the rooms at the other end of the building. Same floor as you. She's set to have a customer in less than an hour."

Dread sinks into my gut, heavy and hard. "You need to get her out of there, I won't make it in time."

She shakes her head. "I can't help her. They will kill me and then I will be no good to you guys."

"She's right, Jaxson," Sawyer cuts in. "Listen, we need to come up with a plan, then once we overpower the fuckers, we'll go get her. We have no other choice."

I grit my teeth, not liking that option.

"I will try to stall the customer," she says, trying to make me feel better, but it doesn't.

Not one damn bit.

"Can you tell us what's happening? What their plan is?" Sawyer asks.

"I honestly don't know, but they're bringing his woman down with them," she says, pointing to Cade.

Cade's head snaps up, his eyes hard.

"They said they're going to test your loyalty and honor."

Well that doesn't sound good at all.

Someone barks out Irina's name, making her jump in fear. "Listen, I have to go, I will do what I can."

"Irina," Sawyer calls out before she can leave. "We'll take you with us. We can get you out of here."

She shakes her head, a sob tearing from her. "I don't care if I live or die anymore, I only lived for my boy. He wanted you guys out of here, that's why I'm going to help you." She closes the door, leaving us in silence with our thoughts.

"They're going to try turning us against each other," I say quietly.

"Yeah, and they're going to use Faith to do it," Cade grits through clenched teeth. "I'm going to kill them, every last one of them. We don't leave here until they're all fucking dead." His rage ignites a fire and fuels my own.

"What's most important is getting Anna and Faith out of here. That comes even before killing them. And we need to take Irina, too," Sawyer says, being the sensible one as always.

Less than an hour later, heavy boot-falls make their way down the hall to us. In the last week, anytime we heard this sound, pain and torture always followed.

Not this time.

A calmness settles over me, one that leaves me cold and detached from my body. One where I don't feel human… but like a machine.

"Where are you taking me?" A female voice cuts through the air, thick with tears but filled with strength.

Only four out of the six guys enter our cell. Two of them on either side of a slender woman that's dressed in a long, black silk nightgown. Bruises mar every inch of bare skin that's exposed, including her face.

"Cade? Oh god, oh no!" She rips free of her captors and runs to Cade, sinking to her knees in front of him. She wraps her arms around his neck and sobs into his shoulder. "I'm so sorry. I'm so sorry, Cade!"

Why the hell is she sorry?

I watch Cade's head dip, murmuring something in her ear.

"Not so fast, bitch." One of the assholes who brought her in grabs her by the hair, dragging her away.

"Let go of me!" she screams, kicking and fighting. The guy flips around and backhands her across the face, knocking her to the ground.

An enraged roar rips from Cade, ricocheting off the walls. "I'm going to fucking kill you, every single one of you motherfuckers are dead!"

Shit!

"Is that so, soldier?" The one whose nose I broke walks closer to him, getting into his face. "Wait until you see what I have in store for you. I'm going to fucking break you."

Cade peers back at him, a lethal smile lifting his lips. "You can't break something that's already broken."

His response has another sob spilling from Faith.

"We're not soldiers, you fucking idiot, how many times do we have to tell you assholes that? We're N-a-v-y S-E-A-L-s," Sawyer taunts, trying to deflect the attention off Cade.

The guard walks over to him and sends a blow to the center of his chest with his baton, the spikes at the end of it ripping the flesh from his body. Other than the slight flinch and his lungs fighting to pull in a breath, he makes no sound.

"Navy SEALs…soldiers," he spits the words. "They're all the same, you all live and breathe your honor. Well, boys, we're going to see just what it will take for you to break your so-called honor." He turns to the men behind him. "Set her up."

Two of the men grab Faith again, setting her to her knees. The guy walks up to her, leaning down to get in her face. Faith glares back at him, defiance raging in her eyes.

Glad to see the fuckers haven't broken her completely.

"We're going to have some fun with this man you seem so smitten with. Maybe you can show him some of the new tricks we have taught you." He straightens, looking over at Cade. "Did you know, soldier, that many of us fucked her?"

Oh shit!

"Tied her to a bed and fucked her while she begged us not to. And after we finished, she got to choke on our dicks."

Faith sobs, her head hanging in shame as their laughter fills the cell.

Hate boils in my blood, merging with the deep seated anger. I can only imagine what Cade's feeling right now.

"Akram! Get the soldier ready."

The one referred to as Akram walks nervously over to Cade.

Please let him keep his cool.

He keeps Cade's wrists chained but unlocks them from the steel in the wall and drags him over to the other end of the cell. He sets him up the same way Faith is, forcing him on his knees. Then taking his makeshift weapon, he starts beating the shit out of him, his flesh and blood tearing from his body and spilling across the cell.

"No, stop! Please stop!" Faith's desperate pleas echo through the stale air that rains with rage, fear, and death. Finally, the fucker tires out, and other than Cade heaving for breaths, he remains calm and still.

The one barking orders walks over, relieving a guard from Faith's side, and takes up his position before pointing to me. "Grab that one first. The one who broke my nose." He smirks at me. "I told you, you would pay for that."

I'm unlocked the same way Cade was, my wrists chained in front of me. I make it difficult for him to drag me, letting him think I'm weaker than I am. My body may be weak, but my vengeance is stronger.

The guard positions me in front of Cade so I'm standing over him.

"Tell me, soldier, would you ever turn on a fellow brother?" The one whose nose I broke asks.

I remain silent, trying to figure out what his plan is when I'm delivered a painful blow to my spine, making my legs crumble beneath me. My teeth grind as I breathe through the pain.

"Get up!" The guard yanks me back to my feet. "Now answer Allah."

Allah? He calls himself God?

"No," I croak out my answer.

"No?" He laughs. "There's nothing that would make you kill this man in front of you? What if it was to save this woman here—his woman?"

I shake my head.

"Give him the knife," he orders Akram.

Faith whimpers in fear as Akram hands me the dagger.

Sawyer's right, they're fucking idiots.

"Don't get too excited and fill that head of yours with any ideas." The leader who calls himself Allah pulls a knife and holds it to Faith's throat. "Now, let's just see how loyal and honorable you are. I want you to end this so-called broken soldier's life. If you don't we will fuck this woman in front of you and make you all watch her beg until the moment I end her life."

"Oh God, please, no!" The desperate sob that escapes Faith has fire burning my chest.

"Shut up, bitch!" he yells, backhanding her.

Cade's jaw locks, fury like I've never seen raging in his eyes. "Do it! Just fucking do it!"

Not yet.

"No! Don't," Faith screams. "Please don't hurt him. I don't care what they do to me. Don't hurt him!"

The bastard laughs. "He's even telling you it's okay. You must choose soldier—this bitch's dignity or your honor to your brother?"

I raise the knife over my head, the blade pointing down at Cade.

He nods, his eyes hard.

Not yet, wait for it.

"No! Stop, please don't!" she pleads again.

"Bitch, if you don't shut the—"

Now.

It happens so fast, my dagger going right in the center of their leader's forehead. The knife he was holding to Faith's neck goes slack and falls from his hand. Before the others have time to react, Cade and I are on them.

I turn on the bastard behind me; my chains going around his throat, pulling tight until his neck snaps.

Grabbing the keys from his pocket, I run to Sawyer, knowing we will need him when the others come. I hear Faith scream and Cade's roar behind me.

Quickly freeing Sawyer and myself, I spin around, charged and ready for battle, except I find nothing but a bloodbath.

Ho-ly shit!

Every single guard is massacred. Most of their insides lie on the cold cement floor, including the leader who I had already killed with the dagger. Their blood soaks Cade's body where he holds a hysterical Faith in his arms.

Irina comes running in, unaffected by the gory scene. "This way," she orders, waving us along.

"The girl—Anna—where is she?" I ask.

She shakes her head. "You don't have time. There are two other guards who are going to come in here any—"

I grab her arm and yank her to me. "Listen, bitch, I'm not leaving here without her, so tell me where the fuck she is."

She lifts a stubborn chin. "Down that hall and to the left, then it's the third door on your right. But you will not make it out of here in time if you do this."

My eyes shift to Sawyer and Cade. "Go. You guys get Faith out of here. I'll get Anna and meet up with you."

"I'm not leaving you," Sawyer says.

"I'll be fine." I toss him one of the guns I grabbed from the guards. "You cover Cade. I'll be right behind you guys."

Without another word, I haul ass, running faster than I thought possible in my condition. My thoughts only on Anna.

Please let me make it in time.

Her desperate screams assault my ears as I near the end of the hallway. "Anna," I bellow, my hand turning the locked door knob. Backing up I kick the door in, and what I see will forever be ingrained into memory.

I was too late.

The bastard on top of her turns around, making eye contact with me. "Wait your turn, asshole."

A white-hot fury fuels a rage so deep inside of me it coils around every part of my body like a snake, and I completely lose control. Pushing forward, I pull the son of a bitch off her, and land blow after blow to his face. His bones shatter under my fist as I pummel him hard and fast, unleashing a violence inside of me I've never felt.

"J-Jaxson?" Anna's panicked voice snaps me out of my rage, and I look down to realize I'm beating a dead guy. I drop him to the floor and turn around to find her huddled in the corner, a bloody sheet pulled around her naked body. Her face is swollen and bruised, tears mixing with blood.

Her innocence stolen.

I swallow past the guilt in my throat and push aside my emotions. "Where are your clothes?"

"They took them from me," she cries.

"Can you walk?"

"I don't think so. The fat guy hit my ankle with his baton and I think it's broken." She covers her face as a sob of defeat explodes from her.

"It's going to be okay." I say but know it isn't true. The damage has been done. I look back to the asshole I just beat to death and find his gun not far from him. Picking it up, I make my way over to her. "Let's go, we're getting out of here, kid."

She launches herself at me, keeping the sheet against her. "Thank you," she cries. "Thank you for not leaving without me."

I hug her back, pain searing my chest. "Tie the sheet around you, I'm going to carry you out." Once she does I hand her the gun, and she takes it without question. "Have you shot one before?"

She shakes her head.

"The safety is off. You're going to have to wrap your legs around my waist for me to carry you out. It's the only way I can cover what's in front of me. I need you to keep this trained behind me. If you see anyone, you aim and pull the trigger. Do you understand?"

Tears continue to spill from her, but she nods and does what I ask.

"Wait!" she says when I begin to lift her. She reaches under her pillow and pulls out my pendant. "I got it back from that guy. I saw it hanging out of his pocket when he was dragging me, so I grabbed it. He thought I was trying to take his keys, that's why he hit me."

I stare down at the tarnished medal in her hand, pain restricting my chest at the sacrifice she made for me. "Thank you," I choke out.

"You're welcome." She closes it in her fist then wraps her arms around my neck again. "Okay, I'm ready."

Picking her up, I get us the fuck out of there. I head the way Irina told me to. My limbs are heavy, the strain of my broken body fighting against me but I clench my teeth and push through it.

I will not stop now.

A scream of terror erupts from Anna and I feel her tense in my arms. Instinct has me turning around and pulling the trigger. A guard drops, my bullet hitting him in the head. Twisting back around, I push myself harder, faster.

"I'm sorry," she sobs. "I panicked."

I don't respond, not wanting to waste any energy I have left. Finally, I hit the *side door and push through it into the night. It takes my eyes a moment to adjust to the darkness.*

"Jaxson, straight ahead," Sawyer yells from a distance.

My feet pummel the earth as I try to keep a steady pace. Out of nowhere Irina comes running up to me. "Over here, you have to—"

Thwack!

She falls right in front of me, a bullet hitting her in the chest.

"Fuck!" I drop to the ground on top of Anna, not knowing what direction it came from.

Sawyer charges out of the bushes, his gun shooting wildly over top of me. He leans down to pick up Irina.

"Leave me," she chokes out, blood sputtering from her mouth.

"No!" He scoops her up in his arms. "Come on, man, we have no choice, we have to make a run for it."

Somehow I find the strength to get Anna and myself both up. With heavy limbs, I follow Sawyer into the bush, only to hear another shot go off.

I bolt upright in bed, my body covered in a cold sweat and heart pounding wildly.

"Jax?" Julia sits up beside me, her hand going to my shoulder.

"I'm fine. I just need a minute." Getting up, I head to the bathroom, needing the privacy. The last thing I want is for her to see just how fucked-up I really am.

Julia

I jump at the slam of the bathroom door and hate that he's shutting me out again. A heavy sigh leaves me as I lie back down. This nightmare was by far the worst one yet. I glance at the bedside clock to see it's four in the morning.

Do I go to him?

At the sound of the shower turning on, I make my decision. Throwing the covers off with purpose, I climb out of bed. All I can do is try, if he shuts me out then I'll try again next time. I'll keep trying until he lets me in.

Entering the bathroom, I close the door behind me and watch Jaxson through the shower glass door. His hands are braced on the wall in front of him and head hanging low in defeat as water pours down his strong body.

My trepidation vanishes when I see how much he's hurting. I pull his shirt from my body and slide off my panties. Opening the shower door, I step in behind him, the thick steam enveloping me.

He's fully aware of my presence, yet he still tenses when I wrap my arms around him. My lips press to the wet mangled skin of his back as I try to ease his pain. Kissing the angel and his scars.

"Not a good idea, Julia. I don't have a lot of control right now." The pain that laces his words has me coming around to stand in front of him. He keeps his head down and under the spray, avoiding my gaze.

"Look at me, Jaxson," I order softly.

When he shakes his head, I step closer and frame his face between my hands, forcing his tortured eyes to mine. What I see staring back at me shatters my heart—despair, guilt, and most of all, self-loathing. His eyes are brimmed red with tears that desperately need to be shed, but he won't allow them to.

"Talk to me. Please, don't shut me out." Water drips from his dark hair and thick lashes, falling onto my face; his pain heavy in the humid air. "It's me, Jax. Let me in. Let me help you," I plead.

"I tried to get to her in time," he grinds out, his jaw flexing. "I tried so fucking hard, but I didn't make it. I was too late." Every word that spills from him is gruff with agony, completely breaking my heart.

"Who? Cade's girl?"

He shakes his head. "Anna," he chokes out, as if I should know who this person is. "She was only fourteen."

Oh god!

I swallow past the bile rising in my throat. "Did she die?"

He shakes his head. "No, but they took her innocence, they robbed her of something she will never get back. I almost made it in time; if I could have gotten there ten minutes sooner I would have made it... Fuck!" he breathes out the curse; his chest heaving rapidly from holding in the pain that desperately needs to be let out.

"Jaxson. Cry. It's okay to cry. You're hurting yourself by keeping it in."

Panic flashes in his gaze and he quickly shakes his head, his eyes squeezing shut.

I'm about to lose him.

"Did you get her out in the end?" I ask, hoping to keep him from shutting down.

When his eyes open, I know it's too late. I've lost him. The pain and emotion that were in them, now masked.

"Yeah, I got her out," he answers.

"Then that's what matters. I know I don't know the whole story, and I probably couldn't even begin to understand if I tried. But you need to understand, you're only human. You can't control other people's actions. You did the best you could, and in the end it turned out to be enough because you saved her life."

He shakes his head, not believing me.

"Yes. You have to work through this or it's going to kill you." I wrap my arms around his body, my breasts pressing against his hard chest as I hold him close, wishing I could take his pain away.

My lips press against his chest, right over his steady heart as hot water rains down on us, my tongue catching the rivulets that run down his body.

His cock swells against my stomach as his arms come around me, bringing me in closer. "I need you," he rasps in my ear. "I need you to remind me of the good."

He picks me up, my legs wrapping around his waist as he pins me against the wall. We gaze at each other, steam billowing around us. It's as if we are in our own world and no one else can enter but us.

My hand moves to the side of his face. "All you need to do is look in the mirror and you'll be reminded of the good this world has to offer." He closes his eyes, wanting to shut me out, but I don't let him. I kiss across his jaw, bringing my lips to his ear. "You're the best man I've ever known, Jaxson. You're strong, honorable, and loyal. The best thing that ever happened to that little girl was having you in the wrong place at the right time. Just like me."

"Stop," he croaks, not wanting to hear my words. With his hand gripping the back of my hair, he tilts my head back and seals his mouth over mine.

It's devastating and beautiful all at the same time.

He arranges my legs so they hang in the crook of his arms, then in one smooth motion he enters me—completing me.

I sob against his lips at the perfection our bodies make. "You're so good. Perfect—perfect for me." I cry into his mouth as he thrusts deep inside of me. My arms cling to him as I let him use my body as an outlet for his pain. Water and tears mix down my face as I feel my orgasm begin to build.

Jaxson groans. "That's it, baby. I can feel it. You're close. So close." He speeds up his pace, slamming into me faster and deeper, hitting the exact spot that I need him to.

My orgasm washes over me, pleasure exploding through every cell in my body.

I open my eyes and collide with Jaxson's tortured ones, his expression soft with sorrow and vulnerability. I drop my forehead on his. "I love you, every amazing part of you." His breathing kicks up, his fingers imprinting into my wet skin. "Let go, Jax. I want to feel you come inside of me." Taking his bottom lip between my teeth, I nip the soft flesh sharply, knowing it's all he needs.

He burrows his face into my neck, groaning through the intensity of his pleasure.

We stay in our position, soaking in a state of bliss.

I feel myself starting to slip so I begin to unwind my legs from his waist, but he grips me tighter. "Don't leave me," he rasps, the desperate plea tugging at my heart.

I hug him close. "I'll never leave you. I'll stay for as long as you'll have me."

"Forever," he mumbles in my neck.

"Forever," I repeat the word, my heart filling with peace.

37

Julia

"**W**ell, Julia, I am happy to tell you that you're completely healthy," Dr. Bayer says, looking through my paperwork. "So it's just stress then?"

"Actually, no. You're pregnant."

Shock slams into me like a freight train, my senses reeling. "Excuse me?" I choke out, swearing I misheard her.

She smiles. "You're pregnant."

"But… but that's impossible. You told me I couldn't get pregnant."

"No. I said your chances of getting pregnant were slim, but I didn't say it was impossible."

"But I'm on the pill."

Her expression sobers. "Yes, which is most likely how you got pregnant, it regulated your cycles, helping you to ovulate. This is very unusual, but I have heard of it happening before. However, you have to stop taking them now."

I'm pregnant.

My hand moves to my stomach, warmth spreading through my body.

"The last time we spoke you were not sexually active. Obviously that's changed?"

"Yes. It's very new, but he's someone I've known for a long time. Someone I've been in love with for a long time," I add softly.

Her smile returns. "Good to hear. I know how much it hurt when I told you about your diagnosis. We'll schedule you for an ultrasound so we can determine the due date." She writes something on a piece of paper and hands it to me. "This is the name of some prenatal vitamins you can pick up." She puts a gentle hand on my shoulder. "I'm happy this happened for you, Julia."

Emotion clogs my throat. "Me, too."

For as long as I can remember I've wanted to be a mother, and when I thought it would never happen for me, my heart broke into a million pieces. Finding out I am going to have the baby I've always wanted, and for it to also be Jaxson's...

Oh god, Jaxson.

Jaxson

I walk into Big Mike's gym to meet up with Cade and Sawyer. We set up a meeting with Mike to talk business. The more I've thought about buying into this gym, the more I want to do it.

Sawyer, Cade, and I have come up with some pretty cool ideas that we want to do with the place. And if I'm being honest, I like the idea of them sticking around. Yeah, Sawyer can drive me fucking crazy, especially when it comes to Julia. But other than Cooper, these guys are like the brothers I never had. We have been to hell and back together...literally. There are no other people I'd rather work side by side with than them.

"Hey, where's Julia?" Sawyer asks, he and Cade standing by the sparring ring.

"She has a doctor's appointment, then she's meeting with Kayla to talk wedding shit. Cooper said he'd bring her home after."

"How's she doing?" Cade asks.

I shrug. "Better, I guess. She found out the other day she got the job at the elementary school, so that has helped keep her mind off things."

"Are we going to deal with this fucker or what?" Sawyer asks.

I nod. "Yeah, we are. I just need to decide how I want to handle him. I don't want to make things hard for Coop."

"Just let us know when you have it figured out," Cade says.

"I will."

Big Mike pokes his head out of his office, a big grin eating up his face. "Come on in, boys, let's talk business."

Two hours later, agreements are made and things are set in motion for us to take over the gym. Normally, the thought of a commitment like this would have me freaking the hell out, but it actually feels good. Real good. And I can't wait to tell Julia.

Julia

Anxiety surges through my veins, my heart beating rapidly the entire drive home.

"Everything all right, Julia? You seem quiet," Cooper asks as he turns down the gravel road that leads to my house.

Kayla grabs my hand, giving it a sympathetic squeeze. I wanted to tell Jaxson before anyone else, but Kayla knew right away something was wrong. So I cracked and told her, and I'm thankful I did. She was extremely happy for me and shared in my excitement, but I know she's also nervous about Jaxson's reaction.

We both are.

I try to paste a reassuring smile on my face. "Yeah, I'm fine. Just tired is all."

He doesn't buy it, but thankfully, lets it go.

Maybe I'm worrying over nothing. I know Jaxson said having kids was something he never wanted, but a lot has changed since then. And there's been a new peace over us since the night of his nightmare; the night he finally opened up to me. He told me he wanted me forever, surely that has to mean something.

My thoughts come to a halt when Cooper pulls into my driveway. "Thanks for the ride, Coop."

"No problem."

I give Kayla a hug. "I'll see you tomorrow morning, I can't wait to go dress shopping."

"Me, too," she says, then lowers her voice. "Call me if you need me."

I nod.

As I climb out of the truck, Jaxson walks out of the house to greet me, waving at Cooper as he pulls away.

"Hey, baby." He pulls me against him, his hands cupping my behind as he gives me one of his toe curling kisses.

My arms wrap around his neck and his scent envelops me, easing my anxiety. "Well, hello to you, too," I whisper against his lips.

"How was your appointment? What did the doctor say?"

My nerves come rushing back.

He picks up on it immediately. "Jules, baby, everything okay?"

I take a deep breath. "Yeah, but can we go inside and talk?"

He nods, his expression concerned.

Our hands link as we walk into the house and I lead him over to the couch in the living room. I turn to face him, my knee bouncing incessantly as I nervously chew on my thumbnail.

He pulls my hand away from my mouth. "Jules, you're freaking me out. What's going on? Did the doctor give you bad news? Are you sick?"

I shake my head. "No, it's nothing like that. Um… well…um…" I blow out a breath and steel myself. "I'm pregnant."

He doesn't move, doesn't even blink. He just stares at me, his eyes going flat.

Uh-oh.

"What did you just say?" he chokes out.

My heart thunders so hard I swear it's trying to crawl its way out of my throat. "I'm pregnant," I whisper.

He jumps to his feet, immediately pacing a hole in the floor. "How the fuck did this happen?" I assume it's a rhetorical question, so I don't answer. "I thought you couldn't get pregnant."

"I did, too. It turns out that my case is very unusual, but it has happened, and I'm one of the lucky ones."

His swift feet falter and he stops in his tracks, staring at me in outrage. "Lucky? Julia, there's nothing lucky about this. Fuck!" he bellows, storming into the kitchen.

I get up and follow after him. His arms are braced on the counter with his head down, his body vibrating with… well, I'm not sure what. Anger? Fear? Probably both.

Tentatively, I lay a hand on his back. "I know this is a shock, Jax. It was for me too, but everything will be okay. You'll see."

He throws my hand off him and spins around to face me. My heart drops into my stomach at the anger in his eyes. If I didn't know better, I'd swear he hates me right now. I try to push aside my emotions, knowing he's scared.

"None of this is okay, Julia. Not for you, not for me, and especially not for the fucking kid. Do you not remember who my father is?"

It suddenly becomes achingly clear what he fears most. "I know all about your father, and I'm glad I never had to meet him. But he has nothing to do with this. You're nothing like him, Jax." I reach for his hand but he pulls away from me.

"What the fuck are you talking about? I'm exactly like him, because that's all I knew growing up. Why do you think I said I never fucking wanted kids? What part did you not understand?"

My blood heats in anger, mixing with the hurt. "You're acting as if I did this on purpose for god's sake."

"Did you?"

My eyes narrow and I grind my teeth against the pain staking my chest. "Be careful, Jaxson, some things you can't take back once they're said. I am not manipulative or a liar, and you know it."

His jaw flexes.

With a deep breath, I try a different tactic. "Listen, I know you're in shock and probably a little scared." He scoffs but I continue, not letting him interrupt me. "So am I, but I'm also really happy. I didn't think this would ever happen to me. I thought I'd never get a chance to be a mother, and the best part of all, to me, is that it's yours. We love each other. We—"

"Don't put words into my mouth, Julia."

I flinch, his words slashing my heart like a cruel blade. Unable to hold them back any longer, the first of many tears spill down my cheeks. "Are you saying you don't love me, Jaxson? Huh? Is that what you're saying?"

"I'm telling you I don't want the fucking baby! But you're not listening to me, goddamn it!" He loses control. His fist slams into the fridge repeatedly before moving to grab my crystal vase full of flowers and throwing it to smash against the wall.

I cover my ears at the sound of glass shattering, my knees weakening in fear. "Stop it! You're scaring me!"

He grabs my upper arms firmly, but I keep my hands over my ears, trying to quiet his rage. "Good, it's about fucking time!"

I close my eyes, sobbing through his violence.

"I've told you for a long time that you should have stayed the fuck away, but you didn't listen, you kept trying to make yourself believe that—" His words die abruptly.

I take the chance at opening my eyes and what I see staring back at me makes me cry harder—fear, panic, and regret.

"Jesus, I'm so sorry," he says, pushing away from me. "I have to get the fuck out of here."

"No, Jaxson, don't leave," I beg, but it's too late. Within seconds the front door slams with his departure. I remain frozen, trying to absorb what just happened. When the pain is too much I crumble to my knees, his words ringing repeatedly in my head.

I don't want the fucking baby.

Time comes to a standstill as I cry amidst the broken glass around me. When my front door swings open I look up, thinking it's Jaxson, but see it's Sawyer and Cade.

Sawyer takes in the mess and hurries over to me. "Jesus, Julia, what the hell happened? Are you okay?"

I shake my head. I'm not all right, not with all of us hurting so much. Especially Jaxson.

"Will you please tell me what the fuck is going on? Jaxson called us to come here. As soon as we showed up, he tore out of here, without any explanation."

"He doesn't want the baby." Saying the words out loud is torture. "I'm pregnant, Sawyer, but he doesn't want us," I tell him, agony ripping through my already tattered heart.

His eyes widen for a fraction of a second before he expels a loud breath and takes me into his arms. "That dumbass motherfuckin' asshole."

"I thought he loved me," I sob.

"Don't think for one second that he doesn't. He's just an idiot who's fucked in the head. But trust me, Julia, he does."

"It's true, he does," Cade adds, speaking up for the first time.

I shake my head, not knowing what to believe anymore. I was so certain that he did, but after what just happened, I'm not sure anymore. Or maybe the sad truth is, it doesn't matter if he does, because maybe love isn't enough.

"Take her upstairs. I'll clean this up," Cade says.

"Come on." Sawyer helps me to my feet, keeping his arm around me as he walks me upstairs to my room. "Do you want me to call someone? Kayla maybe?"

"No, thank you. I'm just going to try and get some sleep. I need to be up early."

He nods but hesitates to leave, his eyes concerned.

"I'm sorry you guys got roped into staying here with me," I say, feeling guilty.

"I don't mind being here, Julia. I'm just sorry he's being such an ass right now."

I shrug. "I know he's scared. I just…" I pause, feeling another sob build in my throat. "I love him so much, Sawyer, that it hurts. I don't want to lose him."

He wraps his arms around me again, offering me the comfort I so desperately need right now. "Just give him some time. Let him get his head back on straight. But if I were you, I'd make the prick grovel his ass off when he does come back. And I know he will, sooner rather than later."

I can only pray he's right, because the thought of living without Jaxson completely destroys me.

39

Jaxson

After driving through part of the night, I stopped at a motel just outside of my destination to catch a few hours of sleep, or at least, I tried to. But sleep proved impossible, because any time I closed my eyes, all I could see was her beautiful, tear-streaked face, pale with fear and twisted with agony; her body shaking while her hands covered her ears to quiet my violence.

I swallow past the knot in my throat, my teeth grinding against the ache in my chest. The one thing that matters most to me in the whole damn world, and I go and fuck it up. Who knew I could hate myself any more than I already did.

Now it's the crack of dawn, and I'm parked outside the one place I've been debating to visit since leaving the clinic—Anna's. The last time I saw her was in the hospital. She had asked me to come visit her. I'm not sure why last night, of all nights, I decided to finally come, but after I left the house, I drove for hours in a daze and this is where it took me.

She lives in a high-end neighborhood with big houses and vehicles that cost more than I ever came close to making in a year. Not surprising, since her father is a surgeon. I met her parents at the hospital. They seemed like really good people—good parents—which wasn't surprising considering the daughter they raised.

Glancing at the clock, I decide to wait another hour before knocking, not wanting to wake anyone up. I turn off the truck and drop my head against the headrest, trying not to think about the previous night, but it's impossible.

I'm pregnant.

Panic infiltrates my chest as the words float through my head. How the hell am I supposed to be a dad when my role model was an alcoholic who hated kids, especially his own. I doubt I'd be half as fucked-up if my mom had stuck around, but nope, she left because she was better off without my worthless father. I assume she thought she was better off without me too, since she didn't take me with her. I fight off the additional wave of pain that thought brings on.

Julia is the one person who's always been there for me whenever I needed her. And what did I do when she needed me? I threw a fucking tantrum and bailed on her. I hate myself so much right now I want to punch my own self in the face.

I'm yanked from my turmoil when Anna's mother steps out of the house in her robe to grab the paper.

Here goes nothing.

I climb out of the truck and make my way over to her. Once she notices me, she straightens, clutching the top of her robe. Her gaze darts around nervously before recognition dawns on her. "Jaxson?" she says, surprise clear in her voice.

"Hi, Susan. Sorry to drop by unexpectedly like this. I was hoping to see Anna."

"Of course. She will be thrilled to see you." She smiles, taking my hand. "Come on. She's just getting ready for church."

As I follow her into the house, Bill comes walking out of the kitchen in a suit.

"Look who came by to see Anna," Susan says, putting her hand on my arm as I awkwardly stand at the front door.

It takes him a moment before he recognizes me. "Well I'll be, how are you doing, Jaxson?" he asks, giving me a firm handshake.

"I'm doing good, sir. Sorry to stop by unannounced."

Susan waves away my apology. "Nonsense, you're always welcome in our home."

Bill nods. "Absolutely."

"Mom, who are you talking to?"

My chest seizes at the sound of Anna's voice from upstairs.

"Why don't you come down and see for yourself?" Susan says with a smile in her voice.

I stand in the entryway, directly at the bottom of the staircase and hear Anna's soft footsteps above us seconds before I see her. My breath stalls in my lungs, the wind getting knocked out of me. She looks beautiful. Innocent, and youthful. Not at all the damaged girl I saw a year ago.

She comes to an abrupt stop at the top, her brown eyes widening in shock. Seconds later, a big smile breaks out across her face. "Oh my god, Jaxson?" She bolts down the stairs, her excitement triggering a smile of my own.

My arms open for her and I catch her as she launches herself from the bottom step. "How are you doing, kid?" I whisper in her hair.

Her body trembles against me, quiet sobs racking her body.

My throat and eyes burn like a motherfucker as I hold her close.

"I'm so glad you came," she cries.

"Me, too."

"Honey, why don't you and Jaxson go catch up in the kitchen while your father and I get ready for church."

Bill is obviously ready, but he follows his wife upstairs, giving us privacy.

Placing Anna back on her feet, she looks up at me with a watery smile, and I can't stop myself from wiping the tears from her cheeks.

"Come on." She grabs my hand and drags me into the kitchen. "You want something to drink? Looks like my mom has coffee made."

I shake my head and take a seat at the table. "Nah, thanks anyway."

"About time you came and visited me," she says, sitting in the chair next to me.

"I only just got out of rehabilitation a couple of months ago."

"You look different," she muses softly. "You're kind of cute without all the blood and bruises."

I cock a brow at her. "Kind of?"

She giggles. "Oh whatever, you're hot and you know it. If I didn't love you like a big brother I would have a crush on you myself."

My chest tightens at her words. "Big brother, huh?"

She shrugs. "Yeah, well, I always wanted a sibling, and if I could choose a big brother he would be exactly like you." Her smile fades, expression sobering. "I think about you often," she whispers. "I've missed you."

"Me too, kid," I admit. "You look good. How have things been for you since coming home?"

A genuine smile transforms her face. "Really good. I'm in counseling and have joined a support group where there are other girls who went through what I did. It's helped a lot. I'm almost feeling like my old self again."

I let out a relieved breath, her words lifting some of the guilt that's been weighing heavily on me.

"I even have a boyfriend," she adds, blushing.

"Boyfriend?" I repeat, my tone harsher than I intend for it to be.

She nods, a shy smile curving her mouth. "He's amazing. Treats me well, and he's really cute, too," she says with a giggle.

I grunt. "What does your dad think about him?"

She groans. "Don't ask. You know what he said to Logan, when he came to pick me up on our first date?"

I smirk, waiting for her to tell me. By the look on her face I'm assuming it was pretty bad.

Coming to stand in front of me, she puts her hand on my shoulder. "He said, 'Just so you know, son,'" she mimics in a deep voice, "'whatever you do to my daughter tonight, I do to you later.'"

A throaty laugh barrels out of me.

That's a good one.

She groans again, but smiles. "Do not laugh. It was one of the most humiliating experiences of my life, I was furious. Thankfully Logan is not easily intimidated. My dad isn't a big fan; especially since he drives a motorcycle."

Shit! The kid drives a motorcycle?

Her voice drops to a whisper. "It's been real hard on my dad, everything that's happened to me."

I'll bet. It kills me so I can only imagine what it does to Bill.

"But he's trying for me, because he knows I really like him."

"Well as long as the kid is good to you, then that's what matters."

"He is, real good to me. You'll get to meet him; he should be here soon. He's joining us for church," she tells me, a giggle escaping her. "I don't think he's ever stepped foot in a church, but he's coming because he knows it will help my dad lighten up."

"Good. I'm glad I'll get to meet him."

Her eyes drop to my chest and she reaches out, fingering the pendant that's hanging around my neck. "Got a new chain for it, I see."

I nod, remembering what she did to get it back for me.

"Did you ever make things right with Julia?"

I told her about Julia in the hospital, it was hard not to when she was around me so much. "Yeah, I did. Actually, I just found out last night that she's pregnant, with my baby." Saying the words out loud brings on a fresh wave of panic.

Anna beams another smile, as if she also thinks this is great fucking news. "Jaxson, that's fantastic, congratulations," she says, hugging me. "Wow, your kid is so lucky."

I grunt. "How do you figure that?"

"Are you kidding me? From what you told me about Julia, she's going to be a rockin' mom. But having you for a father? Well, no one will love and protect that kid like you. If someone ever tried to mess with your child, I'd feel real sorry for the poor bugger. If I didn't love my dad so much, I'd totally pick you. Hence, naming you the big brother instead," she adds with a wink.

Her words hit me like a ton of bricks, the realization striking me to my core. She's right, I'd love that kid so fucking much, and I'd kick anyone's ass who tried to hurt him… or her.

I stare back at her, dumbstruck by the epiphany. "You're kind of smart for being a kid, you know that?"

"You're just figuring that out now?"

Chuckling, I stand and pull her into my arms. "Nah, I knew that a year ago when I met you."

She hugs me back, squeezing me harder than she looks capable of. "I'm really glad I met you, Jaxson. Even though it was under such awful circumstances."

Pain settles over me as I think about that fateful week. I clear my throat but my words still come out gruff. "I'm sorry, Anna. I wish I would have made it to you in time. You have no idea how much I regret that I didn't."

Her watery eyes lift to mine and she shakes her head. "Please don't. The last thing you should ever feel when it comes to me is guilt. If it weren't for you, I wouldn't even be alive right now, or God knows where I would be. Even if it was the most awful experience of my life, I'm not letting it define me and you shouldn't either. I've taken my life back, and it's all thanks to you."

Her words pull the guilt right out of my chest. She's right. She is okay—more than okay. I kept picturing the damaged girl I found a year ago, but that's not who she is at all. Instead, she's a smart, vibrant teenager who's living her life the way she deserves.

"You're one strong girl, Anna," I tell her, slinging an arm around her shoulders as we walk out of the kitchen.

"Yeah well, I could be stronger if you showed me how to fight like you."

She starts punching the air, her tiny fists the least threatening things I've ever seen.

A chuckle escapes me, but it dies quickly when I think about what she just said. "You know, that's not a bad idea. I actually just bought a gym in my hometown. You should come down one weekend and visit. I could teach you how to kick some aaa—butt."

"Oh my gosh, really?" She gasps, excitedly. "Yes! I'd love that."

"Cool, we'll work something out with your parents."

Susan and Bill come walking down the stairs the same time the doorbell rings.

"That's probably Logan," Anna says, blushing again.

I notice Bill tense and I bite back a smile, thinking about what Anna told me he said to the kid on their first date.

"Hi, come in," she greets shyly, stepping aside for him to enter.

My first thought when I get a look at him isn't a good one. He stands tall, looking a little older than Anna. Wearing a black leather riding jacket, jeans, and a black T-shirt, he reminds me exactly of myself at that age. And if his brain is thinking the same things I was, I want to beat the shit out of him.

He throws a possessive arm around Anna's shoulders, his eyes narrowing at me, sizing me up.

Yep, just like me.

Anna stands next to him with a nervous smile, looking at me for approval. "Logan, this is Jaxson. He's the Navy SEAL I told you about who saved my life."

His tight expression eases and he extends his hand. "Hey, nice to meet you. Anna's told me a lot about you."

I accept his gesture with a firm shake. "Nice to meet you, Logan, Anna has said good things about you too." I grip his hand tighter and yank him closer to me. "Make sure it stays that way."

"Jaxson!" Anna scolds under her breath, then looks up at Logan. "He's just kidding."

"No, I'm not."

I hear Bill chuckle behind me.

Logan rips his hand away, not seeming fazed in the least. "Yeah, well, that's not something you need to worry about."

Huh, the kid has some balls. Okay, maybe he'll be all right.

"Good. Make sure that it's not and we'll get along just fine."

Anna groans. "Come on, I'll walk you out."

I wave good-bye to Bill and Susan as she tugs on my arm.

"Glad you came, Jaxson. Come by anytime," Bill shouts, a big grin plastered across his face that I see just before the door closes.

"I can't believe you just did that," Anna hisses under her breath.

"What? I was just looking out for you. That's what big brothers do."

Her expression softens, her smile returning. "All right, really, what did you think?" She chews her nails nervously, my answer clearly meaning a lot to her.

"Honestly, the kid reminds me of myself. So if he wasn't dating you I'd think he's pretty cool, but since he is… I hate him."

She throws herself at me with a laugh. "Well, personally, I think I could do a whole lot worse. And if he turns out anything like you, I'd say I'm a pretty lucky girl."

I hug her tight. "Nah, he's the lucky one."

"Thanks, Jaxson," she whispers, hugging me for a long moment before stepping back. "I better get back inside, god knows what Dad is saying to him."

"All right, go on. We'll talk soon and set up a time for you to come and visit me."

"I can't wait. I'd love to meet Julia."

A flash of pain strikes me, thinking about the mess I've made. "I'd like that, too."

If she ever forgives me.

Logan steps out of the house and waits on the porch for Anna. With a smile, she starts toward him, tossing me a final wave over her shoulder. "See you soon, Jaxson."

"Yeah, see you soon, kid."

Logan grabs her around the waist and pulls her to him. The way he looks down at her… it makes me want to beat the shit out of him.

Shaking my head, I climb into my truck, knowing what I need to do. I just pray I didn't fuck things up beyond repair.

Julia

I wake up the next morning, and know before I even walk downstairs that Jaxson didn't come home last night.

Where could he be?

Sawyer and Cade are sitting at the table, arguing under harsh tones, as I enter the kitchen, their conversation stops abruptly when they catch sight of me.

"Hey, Julia." Sawyer stands, greeting me.

"Morning. Have you heard from him?"

They both shake their heads, confirming what I already expected.

"Me either."

"I'm sure you will hear something today," Sawyer says.

I wish I felt as confident as him.

The sound of my front door being unlocked, sends hope to fill my chest but it deflates when Kayla walks into the kitchen. She comes to an abrupt stop. "Uh, hey. I used the key because I didn't want to wake Jaxson up." Her gaze takes us all in before she notices my teary eyes. "He's not here?"

I shake my head, my throat too tight to speak.

"Well that son of a bitch. What did he do? I'm going to kick his ass."

Sawyer grunts. "Get in line."

She pulls me in for a hug. "You should have called, Julia. I would have come over and stayed with you."

"It's all right. Sawyer and Cade stayed with me, and we have a big day ahead of us. I didn't want you to be tired for it."

She steps back, her eyes sympathetic. "We don't need to go today. We can reschedule and just hang here."

I shake my head, rejecting the idea fast. "No. I'm looking forward to this. We are not going to let this ruin today. Besides, it will be good for me, help me keep my mind off him."

Yeah, right.

"If you're sure…"

"I am. Just give me a second." I grab a banana and an oatmeal bar to eat on the way then walk over and hug Sawyer. "Thank you for everything last night."

"No problem. You have my cell number, right? If you need anything today, make sure you call. Otherwise, if that dickhead isn't back when you get home, we will be."

"I have it. Thank you," I reply quietly, hoping that won't be the case. I move to Cade next and he surprises me by taking me in his arms, returning my embrace. Once we break apart, I look up at them both. "Will you guys try finding him today? Just check in and make sure he's all right?"

"We will," Cade promises.

"Thanks." With a heavy heart, I follow Kayla out of the house, and pray that when I get back, Jaxson will be here waiting for me.

The car is filled with silence as we turn onto I-90, heading toward Charleston; I find it eerily odd that the highway is completely deserted. "Is it me or does it feel like we're the only ones alive on this planet right now?" I joke, trying to lighten the mood.

"It's Sunday, everyone's at church. I have to say though, it's nice driving with no other traffic."

It is nice, the sun is shining and we have Kayla's sunroof open. The warmth beams down on us along with a mixture of fresh air, bringing a little peace to my aching heart.

"Well damn, looks like we spoke too soon," Kayla says.

I look back and see a silver truck coming up behind us. Turning around, I rest my head against the window, getting lost in my troubled thoughts.

"Are you sure you're going to be okay, Julia?"

"Yeah, I…" My words trail off on a gasp when my head jerks forward.

"What the hell?" Kayla shrieks in panic, her hands tightening on the steering wheel as she tries to maintain control of the car. "What is he doing?"

I twist around again and realize the silver truck just rear-ended us, and he's not easing up, he keeps right on our ass. Kayla pulls into the other lane to let him pass but he follows us, tailing close behind.

"What is his problem?" I ask, my voice trembling.

Kayla glances in the rearview mirror. "Do you recognize him? I can't tell."

"No, he's wearing a hat and sunglasses. I don't recognize the truck either."

He pulls up along Kayla's side next and turns the wheel sharply, side-swiping us.

We both scream as the car swerves.

"Julia, grab my cell and call 9-1-1. Hurry!"

Reaching into the console, I grab her phone where it's plugged into the charger. My fingers shake uncontrollably, barely able to dial the three numbers I need.

The asshole rams us again as I'm dialing.

"Son of a bitch," Kayla grits out in fury, stepping on the gas.

"9-1-1, what's your emergency?"

"We need help. My friend and I are on I-90, heading west to Charleston, there's a silver truck trying to run us off the road."

"Okay, ma'am, just stay calm and…"

That was the last I heard before he hit us again, this time causing the car to spin out of control.

Everything falls into slow motion around me, our screams fill the air, sounding distant even to my own ears, as the car tumbles into the ditch. We roll several times, glass shattering around us, nicking the delicate skin on my face.

The baby.

The quick thought has me throwing my arms around my mid-section, hoping to offer some protection. My seat belt bites into my hips, painfully restraining me in the seat. Finally, the car comes to a stop and we land upright in the ditch.

I sit, stunned, and try to get my bearings. Looking over at Kayla, I see her slumped forward on the steering wheel, blood trickling down her forehead.

"Oh god, Kayla?" I sob. "Kayla, wake up!" I shake her shoulder then remember I shouldn't touch her. With trembling hands, I undo my seat belt and look for her phone. Realizing I still have my purse around my shoulder, I dig through it to find my cell when my door flies open, startling me. I turn with a yelp to see Wyatt.

"Wyatt?" I scan my surroundings and realize he was driving the truck. "What the hell are you doing?" I yell. "Are you fucking crazy?"

He doesn't answer. His rough hands grab me, pulling me out of the car.

"Let go of me!" I scream at the top of my lungs and kick out at him repeatedly, trying to escape his strong grip. My body hits the ground with a hard thud, the impact knocking the breath out of my lungs.

Before I'm able to recover from it, he grabs a fist full of my hair and starts dragging me toward his truck.

"Ow! Stop it! Get off me, you son of a bitch!" I continue to struggle, feeling my hair being ripped from my scalp. "Kayla, wake up!" I cry out, willing her to wake up; terrified she's never going to.

Wyatt twists our positions so he's standing over top of me, his grip still strong in my hair. He whips his sunglasses off, his eyes filled with a wild rage I've never seen before. "Shut the fuck up, you dirty whore!" His fist smashes into my face, turning my world black.

11

Jaxson

S awyer sent me a text not long after I left Anna's telling me to meet him at the gym. I had wanted to see Julia first, but he reminded me that she and Kayla were gone dress shopping today.

Cade, Sawyer, and Cooper are all standing by the ring looking pissed when I walk in. I can already tell this is going to be messy.

Sawyer starts toward me, meeting me halfway. His posture is relaxed, but his eyes are hard. Before I can fully register his anger, he catches me off guard by throwing a left hook to the side of my jaw.

My head snaps back and I fall on my ass, not expecting the blow.

"You son of a bitch!" He moves for me again but this time I'm ready for him. Pushing to my feet, I block his next blow and throw a shot of my own.

"Take it easy, both of you," Cooper bellows and yanks me back while Cade grabs Sawyer.

Rage threatens to consume me but I keep it locked up because I know I deserved it. "Is she all right?" I ask quietly.

"No! She's not. What the hell is wrong with you? I walk in and find your woman on the floor, surrounded by broken glass. Crying her fucking eyes out that you don't love her or want the damn baby you knocked her up with."

I shake my head, a sharp ache seizing my chest. "I messed up."

"You're damn right you did. And I hope she cans your sorry ass."

My eyes narrow, my control slipping. "I'll bet you fucking do. I'm sure you loved being there for her last night, trying to console her."

"Fuck you! I have more respect for both of you than that. But I'll tell you something—it would have served your ass right. Have someone else step in and take care of her since you sure as hell can't."

Everything he says is the truth but I'll make it right. I'll do whatever I have to.

Cooper's radio goes off at his hip, interrupting the heated moment. "Sheriff?"

Keeping a hand on my chest he reaches down, grabbing his radio. "Yeah, what is it?"

"I'm sorry, sir, but you need to get over to the hospital right away. Kayla's been in a bad accident."

We all share a look; dread consuming the air around us.

Our fight forgotten, we scramble out the door and hop into Cooper's cruiser, hauling ass to the hospital.

The moment we enter through the emergency doors we can hear Kayla's pleading cry. "Please, you're wasting time. You need to find her!"

We follow the sound, charging into her room. A bandage is wrapped around her head, her face cut and swollen where she sits on the bed. Grace is beside her, holding her hand and crying, but doesn't look hurt.

"Where's Julia?" I ask, my gaze searching for her.

Cooper shoves me aside and rushes over to her. "Jesus, baby, are you all right? What happened?"

"Oh god, Cooper, you need to help Julia."

"Where the fuck is she?" I ask again, louder this time.

"He took her," Kayla cries, sending icy terror through my veins. "He fucking took her."

"Who damn it?"

"Wyatt! He ran us off the road. I passed out but I woke up to her scream-ing my name. He was dragging her by her hair to his truck, then he hit her." She starts sobbing uncontrollably. "Oh god, Cooper, he hit her so hard that she stopped screaming, he knocked her out."

Panic crawls up my throat, my knees threatening to buckle beneath me, until an overpowering fury consumes me, exploding through every cell in my body. "He's dead! I'm going to fucking kill him."

"Jaxson, man, take it easy. We'll find her." Sawyer's voice is distant to my ears as my fists strike out, destroying everything in my path.

A force knocks into me from behind, taking me to the ground. "Get con-trol of yourself," Cade grits out, his face inches from mine. "You're trained for shit like this, Jaxson. Keep your head together or you're not going to be able to help her."

My chest heaves with fury as I fight to find my control, knowing he's right.

"You good?" he asks, through an exerted breath.

I nod.

He climbs off me then extends his hand, helping me to my feet. I take in our surroundings, seeing the damage I caused. A chair is splintered in a million pieces, a table and tray flipped on its side, its medical tools scattered all over the place.

I drive a hand through my hair, panic thick in my veins. "Shit, I'm sorry."

Grace nods at my apology, looking ghost white.

"Cooper, please," Kayla cries. "You guys need to go find her."

I kneel before her. "Kayla, did you hear anything else? Did he say anything about where he was taking her?"

She shakes her head, a sob escaping her.

One of the deputies come walking in. "Sheriff, we have the 9-1-1 recording Miss Julia made during the accident. The operator stayed on the line while the crash happened, we have her being taken on tape."

Cooper nods, then turns to Kayla. "Jesus, I don't want to fucking leave you right now."

"You have to," she says, taking his face in her hands. "I'm going to be fine. Julia needs you now more than I do. You're the best. Please go find her."

"I'll stay with her," Grace offers quietly.

Cooper drops his forehead on hers, his jaw locked in turmoil. "I love you."

His three simple words strike a chord deep inside me. I never said them to Julia, all because I was too scared. Now she's god knows where, terrified and alone, thinking I don't love her or our baby...

The baby!

The thought sends another bolt of urgency through me.

"Let's go," I bark at Cade and Sawyer, leaving the room and sprinting down the hall.

"Jaxson, hold up," Cooper calls, but I don't stop.

Time's running out.

"Goddamn it, I said hold up."

When he grabs my arm, I throw him into the wall and get into his face. "I don't have time to hold up. I need to find her now."

"And you're going to do it without me?" he asks, betrayal thick in his voice.

"I have no choice, Coop. Right now the law means nothing to me, and it's not going to. That son of a bitch took my girl and my baby; he's fucking dead."

"Listen, I get where you're coming from, I do. I want to kill the bastard myself. But right now you need the law on your side. I have resources that you don't. Working together is only going to find her faster."

"He's right, Jaxson," Sawyer says, cutting in. "Think about Julia and the baby, they need you when this is over."

My eyes remain locked with Cooper's. "Do you understand what I'm telling you? The only thing that matters to me is getting Julia and my baby back alive, and I will stop at nothing to do it, even if it means breaking the law. Are you prepared for that?"

"Do you really think my first priority isn't the same as yours? She means a lot to me too, Jaxson."

I step back, knowing he's right. "All right, let's go, time's wasting."

"Sheriff?" a deputy calls out, running out of Kayla's room. "I just got word from Reynolds that Wyatt's home has been searched and cleared, no sign of either him or Miss Julia."

"I want all property records pulled under Jennings, that includes his old man. Also, bring Ray in for questioning, we'll meet you there."

"Yes, sir."

The four of us hop in Cooper's police cruiser and head to the station. The entire drive over I have only one thought in mind... vengeance.

42

Julia

I awake shivering, my body cold and aching; it feels like someone took a sledgehammer to me. Moaning, I try bringing my hand to my head but can't.

What the heck?

It takes only a moment for my memories to come flooding back.

Wyatt.

My eyes shoot open, a small whimper escaping me when I take in my surroundings. I'm in a cold, dark room lying on a cot, my hands chained to a wrought iron headboard. My mouth is gagged, making it difficult for me to pull in the deep breaths my lungs are desperately trying to inhale.

Looking down, I see I've been stripped down to my underwear.

Oh god!

I try to remain calm and find a way out of this, for both my baby's sake and mine.

Please let my baby be okay.

A loud noise has my head snapping to the right and I instantly regret it when pain radiates behind my eyes, making my stomach rebel.

Wyatt paces back and forth, his cell phone to his ear. "Come on, you bitch. Pick up!"

What I see beyond him has my panic escalating—candles are lit, highlighting an entire wall filled with pictures of me. Images of me walking around town, in my car, in my house, and worst of all, some are of me sleeping in bed. He was in my house while I was sleeping and I never knew.

"Well, look who's awake."

My attention snaps to him, his silhouette blurry from the tears streaking down my face. He walks over and sits next to me on the bed, trailing a finger from my cheek, down between my breasts.

I whimper behind the gag, trying to wiggle away from his unwanted touch. It only infuriates him. He backhands me so hard that my cheek splits on the inside, blood pooling in my mouth. Darkness dances in my vision, threatening to take me under again.

"You'll let that fucking trash touch you, but not me?"

I choke on my sob, the gag making it difficult to breathe.

Wyatt fingers the tie at my mouth. "If I remove this you're going to be good, right? Not that anyone will hear you scream, but it will get on my nerves. And right now my patience is thin when it comes to you, do you understand?" His voice is soft again, contradicting the wild rage that's in his eyes. "Answer me!" he snaps, his hand squeezing one of my breasts painfully.

A painful cry shoves past my throat and I quickly nod.

"Good girl."

When he removes the gag, I take in lungfuls of sobbing breaths. "Wyatt, please don't do this."

He cups my face, his touch gentle. "I hate that it had to come to this. I really do. You have no idea how much this pains me, I've loved you for so long…" His crazy words trail off as he gets a faraway look in his eyes.

I decide to try my own crazy. "I know that now. I'm so sorry. You were right, we had something special, and I should have given us more of a chance."

He stares down at me, searching for the truth. Whatever he finds isn't what he was looking for. Fury twists his expression, his jaw locking. "It's too late. You let that son of a bitch take you from me. You ruined my reputation with that fucking restraining order. Now you're both going to pay."

His hand tightens on my cheeks, making blood trickle down my mouth. He sucks in a sharp breath, his eyes filling with lust. A growl erupts from him and he crushes his mouth to mine with brutal force, thrusting his tongue past my lips.

It takes everything in me not to choke from the bile rising in my throat.

He pulls back, licking the smeared blood from his mouth. "Fucking beautiful. We're going to have some long, overdue fun, Julia. I'm finally going to have you. First though, we are going to teach that bastard a lesson for taking you from me."

Oh no, Jaxson.

43

Jaxson

Ow! Stop it! Get off me, you son of a bitch! Kayla, wake up!

Listening to Julia scream and struggle from the 9-1-1 recording is almost too much to bear.

Shut the fuck up, you dirty whore!

Then everything falls silent.

"Motherfucker!" Cade seethes.

I close my eyes and swallow past the burn in my throat, my body shaking with a violent rage, waiting to be unleashed.

Cade, Sawyer, and I turn back at the two-way mirror, looking into the interrogation room where Cooper questions Ray Jennings.

"I'm tellin' you, you're wrong. There's no way my son took Miss Julia." Ray lifts his hand, pointing a finger at Cooper. "If I were you, I would look at Jaxson Reid, Wyatt warned her—"

Cooper's fist slams down on the table, silencing whatever other bullshit he was about to spew. "I have a 9-1-1 recording that says Wyatt kidnapped her, not Jaxson. You arguing is wasting valuable time that could spare Julia her life. So I am going to ask you again, do you have any idea where he could have taken her? What other properties do you own?"

Ray's eyes narrow. "I don't believe you. I want my lawyer... now."

Cooper storms out of the room and joins us on the other side. "Wright!" he shouts out the open door. "What the fuck is taking so long on the list of properties?"

"I should be getting them anytime now, sir."

I rake a frustrated hand through my hair. "We don't have time for this shit."

"I'm with Jaxson, maybe we should split up, and some of us can at least start patrolling. We can backtrack from where the accident happened."

I'm about to agree with Sawyer when my cell starts ringing. Pulling it out of my pocket I look at the call display, and my heart stops when I see the screen. "It's Julia's number."

"Put it on speaker," Cooper orders, slamming the door.

I hit the intercom. "Julia, baby, you there?"

"Oh, she's here all right."

White-hot fury ignites through my blood at the sound of Wyatt's taunting voice. "Where are you hiding, motherfucker?"

"Tsk, tsk, it isn't very smart, Reid, to be calling someone names when that person has something that means a whole lot to you."

"I'm telling you now, Jennings, I will find you, and if you have hurt any part of her, I will fucking gut you alive and feed you your own insides."

The son of a bitch laughs. "Oh, Jaxson, I plan to hurt her all right. And you are finally going to know what it's like to have her taken away from you. I'm just deciding though, do I record me fucking her, or would you rather I just keep you on the phone so you can listen to her beg?"

My violence reaches a whole new level, pumping through my body like hot lava.

Before I lose control, Cooper speaks up. "Wyatt, it's Cooper. It's not too late to change things around. Think hard, is it worth losing everything over this?"

He grunts. "Of course you're already with the good sheriff. Sorry about your woman there, Sheriff, nothing personal, she just happened to be in the way. I'm assuming she's okay though, if you already knew Julia was with me."

"This is between you and me, Jennings," I say, cutting back in. "It always has been, so leave Julia out of it, and we can deal with it one-on-one."

His cool façade shatters. "This has everything to do with her, you son of a bitch! She was mine and you took her from me. For years you kept her from me."

"You're fucking crazy. Julia has always been mine, and everyone in this town knows it, including you."

"No! You're wrong. Tell him, you bitch, tell him right now that you were mine, that *you are mine.*"

Shuffling fills the line before Julia's voice comes on. "Jaxson?"

Agony rips through my chest at the sound of her sobs. "Julia, baby, I'm here. Hang in there, okay? I'm coming for you."

A loud crack has her screaming out in pain.

"Tell him right fucking now!"

"Jaxson," she whimpers. "I-I love you."

"You whore!" The second blow he sends to her is louder than the first, her cry of agony tearing through me, shredding my insides.

A growl rips from me, my fist connecting with the wall. "Jennings, I swear to God, I'm going to kill you!"

"You are going to do nothing because you will never find me. I'm finally going to have her, and when I'm done, I'm going to light the place on fire. By the time you find her, she will be nothing but fucking rubble. Have a nice life, you son of a bitch!"

I hear the click but still call out his name. "Jennings! Jennings!" I drop the phone on the table. "Fuck!" My fist crashes in the two-way mirror repeatedly, the glass cracking. When I look through it at Ray, I lose all control.

"Shit! Grab him!" Cooper orders.

I escape the arms that reach for me, and in a flash I'm in the room next door. Grabbing Ray, I throw him down on the table, my hands wrapping around his throat. "Tell us where she is!"

His hands slap at me, his face turning purple, but I don't let up.

"Jaxson, stop! Come on, man, you're going to kill him," Sawyer tries reasoning with me, but my rage fuels a strength that makes it impossible for all the arms to rip me off him.

"If anything happens to her because you didn't cooperate, I will make you watch while I gut your son like a fucking fish." Hoping this got through to him, I let go, allowing myself to be pulled back.

"Are you crazy?" Ray chokes and sputters, his hands soothing his throat.

Cooper bends down, getting in his face. "We just got a call from your son saying he's going to kill Julia. She's pregnant, and her life is depending on you. So tell us where they are or I will leave Jaxson in this room with you and lock the door on my way out."

Ray shakes his head. "I have no idea where they are. I swear, I never thought he would do something like this."

"Properties, give us properties that you own," Cooper presses.

Before he can answer, a deputy comes barreling in. "Sir, Melissa Carmichael is here saying she has information on Miss Julia's whereabouts."

I bolt out the door with everyone following close behind me. Melissa stands nervously by the front desk, sporting a black eye. Suspicion quickly rears its ugly head.

I should have known.

She backs into the counter, looking scared shitless when she sees me charging toward her. "I'm sorry. We were only supposed to scare her—"

I grab her arms, yanking her to me. "What the fuck have you done? Where is she?"

Sobs begin to pour from her but I feel no sympathy. "Wyatt's holding her at some fishing cabin that's twenty minutes from here. He's expecting me to pick him up in an hour to take him to the airport. His private plane is waiting for him. I swear I didn't know it would escalate to this."

"Why would you help him? She's never done a damn thing to you!"

Anger flashes in her gaze, masking some of the fear. "She took everything from me. From the moment she moved here everyone flocked to her, especially you."

All this over fucking jealousy?

"You make me sick." I shove her back. "If anything happens to her, or my baby, I will make you fucking pay."

She pales. "I didn't know she was pregnant. We were only supposed to scare her. I didn't think he would take it this far."

"Directions, now!" Cooper orders, slamming down a pen and paper on the desk.

With a shaking hand she gives us what we want.

"Take her into custody," Cooper orders, snatching the paper from her. "And keep Ray here too, don't allow him any phone calls."

Chaos explodes around us, a flurry of activity ensuing as the four of us rush out the door to save the only girl I've ever loved.

Primed and ready, I keep my fury locked up until the exact moment I will unleash it, making the son of a bitch pay for what he's done.

11

Julia

"Goddamn it, Melissa, pick up your phone. Listen, the cops already know I have her. It's only going to be a matter of time before they find the cabin. Get here, now!"

Wyatt's agitated voice brings me out of unconsciousness and I start coming around again. I'm not sure how many times I've faded in and out since he beat me with my phone repeatedly, shattering it against my face.

A strong smell penetrates my senses, burning my nostrils. Opening my eyes, I fight against the wave of pain it brings and look over to see Wyatt dousing the walls with gasoline.

So he was telling Jaxson the truth, he's going to burn me alive. I have begged, pleaded, and fought with everything I have left in me, but it has only ended with cruel taunts, inappropriate fondling, and severe beatings. I've come to accept that I'm not getting out of here, at least not alive. My broken body is already close to death, I can feel it.

Grief suffocates me, knowing that I couldn't protect the beautiful, little life inside of me. Knowing I'll never get to meet, hold, or kiss my baby. I knew I had taken a serious risk telling Jaxson I loved him in front of Wyatt. But I needed him to hear those words from me, needed him to know that despite everything that has happened, I still love him.

My heart aches, knowing I will never again feel his touch, see his ice-blue eyes, or his sexy smirk. And most of all, I ache knowing that this is going to kill him, because even though he acted the way he did about the baby, I know, with every fiber of my being, that he loves me.

"Ah, you're awake again. About time. It's no fun for me if you're asleep."

Instead of fear, Wyatt's taunting voice only fuels the anger inside of me. I hate him for doing this to me, for taking away everything I've always wanted.

He drops the gasoline can down and stalks over to me, pulling his shirt off in the process. "Unfortunately, I'm not going to be able to take my time with you, Julia. Plans have changed so we are going to have to make this quick," he says, flashing me a taunting smile. "But I promise it will still be good." He rubs the erection that strains the front of his jeans.

I turn my head away, not wanting to watch what comes next, and pray for the darkness dancing along the edge of my vision to take me under again. It's close; one more hit would probably do it.

I feel him crawl on top of me, his hot breath hitting the side of my face. I close my eyes and try to keep the numbness in place, not wanting to feel his naked chest on mine, or the erection that settles between my thighs. "Look at me, bitch!"

I ignore his demand, keeping my eyes tightly shut.

"I said, look at me!" He slaps my battered face.

My teeth clench from the pain, black spots dancing behind my eyes, but unfortunately, it doesn't pull me under.

Feeling a cold, sharp object along the curve of my breasts has my eyes springing open. Wyatt stares down at me with a cruel smile, dragging a large knife across my chest. I keep my face void of expression, knowing any fear I show will only give him satisfaction.

He slips the cruel blade under one of my bra straps and stills. "Tell me you want me," he pants heavily, his eyes raging with hunger.

"No." My response is quiet but firm. I will not let my last words be anything that will satisfy him and I'm hoping he will get mad enough to just end my life quickly.

He chuckles, enjoying my defiance. "Wrong answer, sweetheart." His hand wraps around my throat firmly, allowing only a small bit of oxygen through, then the sharp blade slices through my bra strap. "Tell me you're mine!" he seethes through clenched teeth, grinding his erection against me.

His pressure eases so I can speak, and I know the next words I choke out will be my last. "I hope when Jaxson finds you, he makes you die a slow and painful death."

My words have the effect I expected; a wild rage twists his face savagely. "You bitch!" He lands two more solid blows to my face.

Darkness taunts me cruelly, almost pulling me under. My eyes close again, but not because I'm forcing them to.

"I'm going to fuck you until my cock goes limp, then I'm going to light you on fire and watch you burn until there's nothing left of you but ash." His hand squeezes around my throat, cutting off all oxygen as I feel him fumble with his pants.

Darkness finally begins to close in on me, and I blessedly welcome it. Right when I am about to fade into nothing, an enraged roar rips through the room. "Motherfucker!"

Wyatt suddenly vanishes, his weight no longer crushing me into the mattress. I gasp and sputter from the released pressure on my throat. A loud crash sends a wave of heat exploding around me. I try to open my eyes and see what's happening, but can't.

Shouts and enraged curses fill the air, mixing in with the sound of crackling flames. I quickly realize that the candles have been knocked over, starting the fire.

A sickening crack fills the air then everything falls silent.

Hands scour my body, but it's a touch I welcome, one I thought I would never feel again—Jaxson's.

He made it.

My relief soon morphs into sadness when, no matter how hard I try, I can't open my eyes. I fight against the darkness that only a few minutes ago I wanted so desperately to consume me.

"Julia, baby, can you hear me?"

"Jaxson," I sob out weakly, not even sure if he heard me through my tender throat.

"It's me. I'm here, I'm going to get you out, just hang on." I feel him pull on my chains. "Fuck! Where's the key?"

I whimper when the heat starts feeling too close for comfort. My lungs begin to burn from thick smoke, making it impossible to breathe.

I feel him struggle harder to free me, my heart breaking because I know he'll die here with me if he waits too long.

"Leave me," I whisper.

"No! Don't say that. We're both getting out of here."

His words become distant as I feel myself drifting, my body giving up. I fight against it, just long enough to mumble what I want my last words to be. "I love you."

It's then the darkness finally takes me, sucking me into a sweet oblivion of nothing.

Jaxson

"Julia!" I shake her, fear squeezing my chest when I get no response. "Fuck!"

My eyes search frantically for anything to use to break through the chains, but the heavy, black smoke makes it impossible to see much. Knowing I'm running short on time, I lean back on my elbows and kick the shit out of the metal bed frame, particularly close to the pole that the chains are wrapped around. I put all my weight behind it, my heavy boot rattling the entire frame. Finally, it snaps.

A loud crash sounds in the distance. "Jaxson?" Cade yells, his voice barely penetrating over the roaring flames.

"Over here!"

I rip the broken pole out from the smashed bed frame then take Julia's chained wrists and throw them over my neck. Picking her up, I try not to think about how still her broken body is. "Hold on, baby, we're almost out," I whisper in her hair.

Cade, Sawyer, and Cooper come charging around the corner, emerging through the thick smoke. Cade holds an axe that would have fucking come in handy a minute ago.

"Where the hell have you guys been?" I snap. I had shot out of the cruiser before we even came to a stop, not wanting to waste another precious second, and thank God I did. Because a second longer would have been too late.

"We had to find another way in, the entrance burst into flames right after you ran through it," Sawyer explains. "We made a small opening in one of the rooms."

I watch Cooper's eyes fall to Wyatt's lifeless body on the ground, his head twisted awkwardly from where I broke his neck.

Another crash happens behind me, the heat at my back feeling a hell of a lot closer.

"We need to move, now," Cooper bellows, pointing behind me. "We probably have a minute before these flames reach the gas tank."

I follow Cade through the billowing black smoke, cradling Julia close to my chest. He leads me to a bedroom with a hole in the wall that's barely big enough to fit through. All of them make way to let me out first.

Once the fresh air hits me, I haul ass to get as far away as I can from the house before the explosion comes. I make it a good distance across the grassy field before the fierce blast happens, but the force of it still knocks me off my feet. I keep her close to me, twisting with just enough time to land on my back, taking the brunt of our fall.

Quickly, I roll her beneath me, covering her from any falling debris. Once we're in the clear, I sit up and look at her; really look at her. And what I see has my heart shattering in a million fucking pieces.

"Julia, baby, wake up!" My hands run along her battered body, noticing every bruise that marks her skin. "Julia! Wake up!"

She remains lifeless.

Pure terror grips my chest when I don't find a pulse, sending icy dread surging through my veins. "No, no, no!" Picking her up, I cradle her body against my chest, gently rocking her back and forth.

My eyes burn as bad as my throat, big ugly tears falling from my face and soaking her hair. For the first time since I was seven years old, I cry, the most excruciating grief ripping from my chest. "Please don't leave me, I'm so sorry, so fucking sorry. I love you so much. Please, Julia, wake up!"

I thought I had already experienced the most heart-wrenching pain that I'd ever feel in my life, but I was wrong. What I'm feeling now exceeds it by a thousand times more than anything I've ever felt. My heart fucking aches so bad I'm surprised it's still beating.

Seconds later, Cooper leans down, putting his hand on my shoulder. "Jaxson, man, paramedics are here, let them help her."

I lay her down, but remain close.

The paramedics drop down beside me. "Back away, sir. We need room to assess her injuries," one of them says.

I shake my head, refusing to let her go.

"Come on, man, give them space so they can help her," Cooper says, grabbing my shoulder again.

"Be careful with her, she's pregnant," I croak out, stepping back.

Sawyer and Cade come to stand on either side of me, but I don't look at them, my eyes never leaving Julia. I watch helplessly, my dread growing stronger with every second. "She's so still."

I ignore the one female paramedic's sympathetic glance.

Sawyer grips my shoulder. "She'll be all right, man, I know it. Have faith."

Faith.

Something I've never had, but Julia always did.

Bracing my hands behind my head, I start pacing back and forth and for the first time in my life, I pray.

"We have a pulse." The paramedic's shouted observation snaps me out of my silent plea.

"Holy shit!" I breathe, hope filling my chest.

Sawyer grins, clapping me on the back. "See? What the fuck did I tell you?"

"Let's move!" A paramedic orders as they lift the stretcher.

"I'm coming with her," I say, following them toward the ambulance.

I get a nod of approval and briefly notice the chaos of fire trucks and police cars before crawling into the ambulance.

"We'll meet you over there," Cooper says, just before they close the door.

I grab Julia's cold hand and bring it to my mouth. "Everything's going to be okay, Jules, just hang on."

45

Julia

"Why isn't she waking up?"

I cling to Jaxson's voice, wanting to hold onto it but am surrounded by darkness, one that's constantly sucking me in. I try to fight it off, wanting to see him but can't. I'm too tired.

"Her mind has shut down so her body can heal. I know it's difficult, but be patient, Mr. Reid, she and your baby need rest."

My baby.

Relief swamps me right before I slip into oblivion once again.

The next time I come around, I'm frustrated to be surrounded by the dark again. This time I not only hear Jaxson but can feel him too, the warmth of his hand wrapped around mine.

"I know what you're thinking, so why not just get it over with and ask me." I hear him say to someone.

"Because I'm not sure I want to know the answer, and to be honest, I don't really care either way."

Cooper.

I fight off my exhaustion, wanting to know what they're talking about.

"Yeah, well, for the record, I didn't run in and murder the son of a bitch. We were struggling, it was self-defense. But I'm also not sorry, I'd kill him again in a heartbeat."

"Can't say I blame you."

Wyatt's dead.

All I feel from hearing that is sweet relief. To know I will never have to face him again brings on a peace that I let sweep over me.

This time, I fully awake. I'm groggy and still tired, but feel attached to my body. I know if I want to open my eyes I can. But I keep them closed for the time being, because right now I'm feeling peaceful and I'm not sure what awaits me when I open them.

A warm gentle pressure weighs on my tummy. It doesn't take me long to realize it's Jaxson's hand. "I'm going to let you know now, kid, I'm probably going to fuck up, a lot." I hear him whisper. "I had a real shitty father growing up so I never learned how to be a good dad. Thankfully, you have an amazing mom, so hopefully she overshadows all of the mistakes I'll make."

I force my eyes open and am grateful the room is relatively dark, only a soft glow from the bathroom light illuminating Jaxson. He's bent over the side of my bed, his chin resting low on his forearm while he looks at his other hand that's rubbing gentle circles on my stomach. His gentleness warms my heart, but the exhaustion and sorrow on his face makes me ache for him.

"I promise though," he continues quietly, "I'll try really hard to make those mistakes few and far between. I promise I'll always love you, and I'll always protect you. I'll kick anyone's ass if they try to hurt you, even if it's just your feelings."

I stifle a chuckle, not wanting to interrupt his moment.

He drops his head in his arms with a groan. "See, I'm already fucking up. Listen to how much I'm swearing. Your first word is probably going to be shit."

My giggle breaks free. "Actually, it'll probably be fuck," I try to say teasingly, but my voice comes out raw and hoarse, not sounding like me at all.

Jaxson's entire body stiffens before his head snaps up in surprise. "Holy shit!" He jumps up, moving to sit beside me on the bed. "Jules, you're awake." He takes my face between his hands, making sure to be gentle, and rains kisses all over it. "Jesus, I've been waiting for what seems like forever for you to wake up."

Tears streak down my face when I didn't even realize I was crying. With my reflexes sluggish, I bring my hand up to Jaxson's jaw, needing to touch him. Shock washes over me when I realize the tears aren't my own, but his.

He buries his face in the crook of my neck, his shoulders trembling. He makes no sound, his silent tears soaking my skin. I hold him close, rubbing his shoulders, his back, any part of him I can reach, and let my own emotion free.

Eventually, he lifts his face, gently resting his forehead on mine.

"You're crying," I say sadly, still stunned by the simple act.

"I know," he chokes out. "I started when I didn't think you were going to wake up and now I can't seem to stop. I've turned into a real fucking pussy, Jules."

Another giggle escapes me, but it trails off into a sob. I wrap my arms around his neck, hugging him close. "I didn't think I was ever going to see you again," I cry, my lips softly brush his ear. "He was awful, Jaxson, and I was so sure he was going to finish what he started."

"It's going to be okay now, all of it. The baby is all right and..." He pauses. "He's dead, Jules, he can never hurt you again."

"I know. I heard you talking to Cooper... at least I think I did," I add, feeling a little unsure now.

Maybe I dreamed it?

"You were awake then?"

I nod. "I could hear you but I couldn't open my eyes. This was the first time where I came awake and felt in control of my body."

"I'm glad you finally did."

"How long have I been out for?" I ask, a little frightened to know the answer.

"Two days. And it has been the longest two fucking days of my life." He runs his hands through his hair and expels a heavy breath. "I have so much I need to say to you. So much to say I'm sorry for—for the things I said and did that night."

I shake my head, not wanting to think about it. It hurts too much.

Jaxson cups the side of my face, his thumb stroking my cheek. "Please, just hear me out."

I swallow thickly and nod.

"I was so scared, Julia. The only reason I've never wanted kids is because I'm fucking terrified I'll turn out to be just like him." He doesn't have to say his dad, because we both know who *he* is. "Let's be real, we both know I have one hot temper, and where do you think I get that from?" I'm about to argue but he places his fingers gently on my lip. "Just wait, let me finish."

I remain silent and let him get out what he needs to.

"After the way I snapped like that..." He pauses and shakes his head. "I didn't think I could hate myself any more than I already did, but I was wrong. After I left that night, I never hated myself more. Because the truth is, Jules, I do love you. I've probably loved you longer than you've loved me; you're just the one who said it first. I wanted to tell you so many times. But I was too scared because the last person I ever said those words to left me, and she never fucking came back."

Tears begin to stream down my face again, my heart breaking at every single agonizing word that falls from his lips. It's the first time he has ever talked about his mom with me.

"It really messed me up when she left, but it didn't destroy me. But the thought of you leaving me… it would completely fucking break me." His voice cracks, making my heart shatter into a million pieces.

I pull him to me, holding him close.

"Please forgive me, I swear I'll make it up to you."

My breath hitches as I try to hold in my emotion. "Where did you go that night? I was so scared you were never going to come back."

"I'm sorry I left you like that, but it's also good that I did, because I went and dealt with something I should have dealt with a long time ago."

My curiosity piques.

"I went and saw Anna."

I gasp. "The girl you saved?"

He nods. "She lives just a few hours away in Summerland. Before we left the hospital she had asked me to come visit her, but I couldn't bring myself to. I didn't want to be reminded of how I failed her."

It kills me to hear the guilt in his voice.

"But I'm glad I did. She looked real good, Jules. She was beautiful and happy, exactly how a fifteen-year-old girl should be."

Smiling, I lay my hand on the side of his face. "It's all because of you that she had this chance to heal and be happy again."

Encircling my wrist, he turns his face, kissing the marks on my wrist from where the chains rubbed raw. "I know that now. I walked away with a whole new perspective on things, most of all myself."

He pauses and I wait patiently, knowing it's hard for him to open up.

"The thing is, I never felt like I was even good enough to be your friend, let alone love you. And honestly, I still think that. I know I'm not, but I also know that no one will love you and protect you like I will. If you give me another chance, I'll work every day at trying to be the person you and our baby deserve." His hand moves to my tummy now. "I'm still fucking terrified about being a father, but I promise I will love and protect our baby with everything I am. I already do love him… her—whatever it is."

I chuckle, my heart close to bursting.

His fingers gently wipe away my flowing tears. "Please forgive me."

"I do. I've loved you since I was seventeen years old, and I will love you for the rest of my life. But for us to work, I need you to trust me with your heart and your feelings. When you're scared or angry, talk to me about it, don't run away."

"I promise, Jules, I'll never leave you, or lose control like that again. I'll try really hard to tell you what I'm always feeling, just be patient with me, it's not something I'm good at."

"I will. And I'll make sure to tell you how I'm feeling too, because the truth is, I'm a little scared myself about having this baby."

"Yeah?" he asks, surprised.

"Of course I am. I mean, I love our baby so much already, but I have no clue what to do. What diapers are best to use, what formula is better, when should they start food? All of it. It's something I have to learn, but we'll learn it together."

"Jesus. See I didn't even think about any of that shit. Knowing me, I'd probably forget to fucking feed it."

I burst into laughter, my throat raw and scratchy. "No, you won't, but these are all things we'll learn together. And if we fail, well, we always have Grams. She will definitely know what to do."

He grins. "Yeah, she will." His hand moves to my cheek in a gentle caress. "But I have no doubt, Jules, you will be the best mom in the world."

"And you will be the best father," I tell him, tears thick in my voice. "You are so much better than you know, Jaxson, you're perfect, and I hope our baby turns out to be just like you."

A nurse walks in, interrupting our moment. She smiles to see me awake and does a quick check, taking my vitals and topping up my pain medication. After she leaves I notice how exhausted Jaxson looks.

"Have you been home at all to sleep?"

He shakes his head. "I'm not going back until you do."

"Come here," I say softly, patting the bed next to me. "I want to feel you beside me."

"Jules, baby, I want to be next to you too, but I'm a little big for that bed, and you need room to rest and get better."

"All I need to get better is to have you beside me." I tell him, making room next to me.

It's obvious he still doesn't think it's a good idea but he gives in, taking the open spot beside me.

Carefully, I turn on my side to face him and he drapes an arm over me. We lie in the dark, silently watching one another.

"How bad do I look?" I ask, knowing it's probably pretty bad since my face feels about three times its usual size.

"You're still the most beautiful woman I've ever seen. Nothing else matters, Julia, the rest will fade over time," he says, pressing his lips to my forehead. "Sleep, baby."

I bury my face in his chest and run a hand up his shirt, feeling his warm bare flesh. "I love you."

"I love you, too," I hear him whisper just before I fall into a blissful sleep.

Julia

"Good morning, Julia, it's nice to finally see you awake. I'm Dr. Gordon, and I've been the one overseeing you the last few days. How are you feeling this morning?"

Dr. Gordon stands just inside the room, his hand resting on a machine that he rolled in with him. He must be new to the hospital, because I have never seen him before, and in a small town, you know everyone. He's an older man with a kind smile, and I instantly feel comfortable with him.

"I'm feeling all right. My throat is tender and raw, especially when I speak, but as long as the nurse keeps giving me what she has been, then I feel quite lovely actually."

He chuckles. "Yes, good old morphine always tends to make people feel that way, although, unfortunately, we will be changing your pain medication to something different soon. I'm sure the nurse told you though, that everything we are giving you is in smaller amounts, and is okay for your baby."

"Yes, sir. It was the first thing I asked."

"Ah, yes, the same as your young man here. Although, his approach was a little, shall we say… protective?" He chuckles.

My attention shifts to Jaxson and I shoot him a questioning look.

He shrugs, looking unregretful.

The poor nurses, I can only imagine what he was like.

"Anyway, I brought a little something in with me today that I think will brighten your morning," Dr. Gordon continues. "This machine is a portable ultrasound. Although the baby seems to be doing well after your injuries, I'd like to take a look, and thought you would, too."

Excitement barrels through me at the thought. "I'd love to."

"Will it hurt her?" Jaxson asks in concern.

"No, Jax, it's just a camera they put on my stomach so we can see the baby on that screen," I explain, pointing to the monitor.

"That's right," Dr. Gordon says, backing me up. "However, since you're in the very early stages of pregnancy this will be done internally. Are you okay with that?"

"Oh sure, no problem."

"Whoa, wait, hold the fuck up." Jaxson straightens, flipping his hand up. "What do you mean *internally*?"

"Jax, it's all right. This is normal."

"Yes it is," Dr. Gordon begins to explain it to him. "During pregnancy she will be having many things happen internally. This is still not going to hurt her and once she's further along, then the camera will be placed on her stomach."

"It'll be okay. You'll see," I assure him, taking his hand.

It's clear he doesn't like it but he accepts it. "Just be careful with her."

"I promise, she's in great hands." Dr. Gordon hits the button on the bed to lay me down before getting into position. Then he reaches under the blanket and inserts the camera.

Jaxson glares at him, looking ready to rip his head off any moment. I grab the side of his face, bringing his gaze to mine. "It's all right, Jax, I'm fine."

The sound of static and a fast thumping beat have both of us snapping our attention to the monitor.

"Let's have a look." Dr. Gordon hits a bunch of buttons and points to the screen at a small looking bean that flickers in rhythm.

"Holy shit, Jules, that's our baby," Jaxson says in awe.

Dr. Gordon chuckles. "Yes, it is, the flickering you see is the baby's heartbeat. It's nice and strong."

Tears fill my eyes, my smile big. "Isn't this so cool, Jax?"

"Yeah, baby, real cool," he says, bringing my hand to his for a kiss.

We both watch the screen with fascination and excitement as Dr. Gordon explains everything to us, measuring the baby at around six weeks.

"When are we able to find out the sex?" I ask.

"Around the eighteen week mark, which is when your next ultrasound will probably be scheduled for. Dr. Bayer is your physician, correct?"

I nod.

"Then I'll make sure she gets these results. Everything looks great though, your baby is strong and healthy."

I look over at Jaxson, and smile. "See. Just like you."

A storm of emotions pass over his expression before he drops his head in my lap. I run my fingers through his hair and don't say anything else and neither does the doctor. As he packs up his stuff, I thank him for everything, and then he's gone, leaving the two of us alone.

Jaxson moves up beside me and pulls me into his arms. "Our baby is going to be really fucking cool, Jules."

I snuggle in closer to him, my heart content. "Yeah, it will be."

17

Julia

A week later, I'm thankful to be getting out of the hospital and going home. My discharge papers have just been signed and Jaxson is packing up the rest of my stuff.

I look around at all the flowers and balloons that fill my room and feel so blessed to have the friends that I do. This whole week I've had constant visitors. Grace and Kayla even set up a little celebration party with everyone in my room to congratulate Jaxson and me on the baby.

Jaxson, Sawyer, and Cade also shared the news about them buying the gym. I thought it was a great thing for Jax, but most of all I'm happy that Cade and Sawyer are going to move here. They have become like brothers to me, the same way Cooper is. We're all like one big family; even Jaxson and Kayla called a truce. Well mostly, Kayla still loves messing with him, and to be honest, I can't ever see her stopping.

Jaxson stayed with me most of the time, only the last few days did he step out for a bit. He made sure someone was with me every time he did. Sawyer, Cooper, and Cade always went with him. I know he is up to something, but I have no idea what.

"Okay, I think that's it," Jaxson says, walking out of the bathroom, looking his usual sexy self. "Cade and Sawyer are going to come by later and grab all the flowers and balloons for us." He drops my bag by the door and looks over to see me watching him.

His eyes close, jaw locking. "Stop looking at me like that."

"Like what?" I ask innocently, sitting on the side of my hospital bed, with my feet dangling close to the ground. My white, baby-doll sundress rests against my upper thighs. I'm still covered in bruises, but thankfully they have begun to fade.

Jaxson moves for me, coming to stand between my legs and braces his hands on either side of my hips, his lips only a breath from mine. "Like you want me to do things to you that I can't do, especially right now."

"There is something you can do," I whisper breathlessly.

"What's that?"

"Kiss me." Fisting his shirt, I close the small gap between us, moaning at the beautiful contact of his mouth against mine.

A growl escapes him but he keeps his pressure gentle, like he has been with me all week. As much as I love this side of him, I want his other side back, the aggressive one. We haven't spoken much about what happened with Wyatt; it's just as difficult for me to talk about it as it is for him to hear.

I've had an overwhelming desire to be with him, for him to be inside of me and erase the ugly memories of Wyatt's unwanted hands.

"Uh, knock, knock." Cooper's voice breaks up our kiss.

Jaxson pulls back, his eyes dark with the same need claiming me. He turns to face Cooper. "What are you doing here?"

Cooper doesn't look at him, he only addresses me. "Um, Jules, there's someone here who's been wanting to talk to you. Is it okay?"

"Sure, who is it?" I ask, wondering why he seems so nervous.

"Well…"

"Me," Ray Jennings says, walking in behind Cooper.

Fear snakes down my spine, my heart beating wildly.

Jaxson moves for him in a flash. "What the fuck are you doing here?"

Cooper grabs him before he can reach Ray. "Easy, man, he just wants to talk to her. He's not here to start problems. I wouldn't have brought him otherwise."

"I don't give a shit, he's not welcome anywhere near her."

"It's all right, Jaxson." I don't know why on earth he wants to talk to me, but I know Cooper wouldn't have brought him here if it were to start trouble.

"No, it's not. You don't have to listen to anything he has to say. You owe him nothing."

Ray ignores Jaxson and keeps his gaze on me. "He's right, you don't owe me anything, but I feel like I owe you. And I'd really like it if you would hear me out, Miss Julia."

I take in Ray's appearance and for the first time, the wealthy, powerful man looks unkempt. He has dark circles under his eyes from exhaustion, and his clothes are wrinkled, looking as if he's slept in them. He looks… sad.

I nod. "All right, go ahead."

He clears his throat. "Well, first off, I just want to say I'm sorry. Real sorry for what my son did to you. I knew he was quite taken with you, but I did not think he was obsessive. Over the last few days, I've learned things about him that I never knew, and for that I am truly sorry." He swallows thickly, his eyes beginning to well with emotion. "If I had known I would have gotten him help."

I can only imagine how hard it was for Ray to hear half of the things he did about Wyatt. Including dealing cocaine, which is how Melissa was supplied for her drug habit.

I feel bad for him because even though I'm not sorry Wyatt is dead, I am sorry Ray lost him. As far as I know, Wyatt is all he had. Wyatt's mom died when he was a baby and Ray never remarried.

"I know my apology doesn't make up for what he did, nothing will. But I'd really like to take care of your medical bills, if you'd let me."

"No!" Jaxson says, his voice hard. "We don't need your money."

Ray shifts nervously, his eyes remaining on me. "Like I said, I know this won't make up for anything, but I'd really like to do something to show how sorry I am."

I think about it for a moment then nod. "Thank you for your apology. I accept your offer to pay for my medical bills."

"Unfuckingbelievable!"

I glare over at Jaxson, not appreciating his outburst.

"Thank you," Ray says relieved. "And thank you for hearing me out. Again, I'm sorry and I'm glad you and your baby are all right."

When he turns to leave, I call out his name, stopping him at the door.

He turns around, and my heart breaks when I see a tear trickling down his worn cheek.

"I just want to say that I'm sorry for your loss. I know this entire situation has hurt a lot of people, not just me."

He watches me for a long moment, his sad eyes looking at me differently than he usually does. "Thank you," he croaks then leaves out the door.

Silence fills the room as I stare at the closed door, my breathing heavy from the pain in my heart. Covering my face, I sob into my hands, hating the conflicting turmoil battling inside of me. Wyatt's death was unavoidable, even necessary, but I can't help feeling bad for Ray, knowing he's all alone. So many lives were affected from Wyatt's actions, not just mine.

A second later, I hear the door shut, then feel Jaxson come to stand in front of me. He hunkers down in front of me, resting his hands on my thighs while my face remains hidden behind my hands.

"I know you don't understand me taking his money, and I know you don't like it," I cry. "But he's hurting too, Jaxson. He didn't do this to me, Wyatt did. And if letting him pay for my bill brings him a small measure of peace, then I'm going to accept it."

He places a gentle kiss on the inside of my thigh, offering me comfort. "You're right, I don't understand it, and I don't like it, but that's because you're a better person than I am."

"I just want everyone to stop hurting, including myself."

"I know, Jules. You'll get through this. I'll help you."

He waits patiently as I release everything I need to, his warm hands rubbing my legs in a comforting gesture.

Once my tears subside, he takes my hand. "Come on, baby, let's go home."

It was past suppertime by the time I had been discharged, so we stopped at a drive-thru and grabbed a bite to eat. Halfway home Jaxson pulled over on the side of the road and blindfolded me, telling me he had a surprise for me. For the last few minutes, I've been dying of curiosity.

"I have to say, Jax, this is kinda kinky, we should try this sometime," I tease, wishing I could see his expression.

"Julia," he growls.

I chuckle and feel the truck come to a stop. "Are we home? Can I take it off now?"

"Just wait, I'll come around to get you."

I hear him exit the truck, slamming his door, and wait for him to come to my side. I'm close to bursting from excitement, dying to know what he's up to. I'm assuming this has to do with the sneaking around he did this week when leaving the hospital.

As my door opens, I turn to the side and feel his hands span my hips. I find his shoulders as he helps me down. Once my feet touch the ground, I wrap my arms around his neck and feel him stare down at me.

"Kiss me," I whisper.

His groan pierces the air before his mouth claims mine. I sigh against his lips, the small feather of a touch spreading through every part of my body.

"Come on," he mumbles, breaking the beautiful contact much too quickly. Taking my hand in his, he leads me across the gravel, the shale crunching under my flip-flops until we reach grass where he comes to a stop.

The little pieces of hair that have escaped my ponytail blow gently into my face from the warm night breeze as he comes to stand behind me. His hands move to my bare shoulders, and my pulse races as he leans down, pressing his lips to the base of my throat.

He flattens his hand on my stomach, pulling me against him where I can feel his erection.

"Are you trying to kill me?" I moan.

He chuckles, his breath tickling my ear. "I love you, Julia."

I smile, warmth invading my heart. I will never tire of hearing him say those words. "I love you, too."

I feel his hands move to the back of my head as he unties the blindfold. I blink several times, my eyes adjusting to the fall of night and I try to absorb what's in front of me. My heart understands it before my mind because tears immediately spring to my eyes, the sight before me taking my breath away.

A massive tree has been planted in my front lawn. Strings of white lights decorate it, making it look beautiful and majestic. But my favorite part of all, the one that has emotion flooding my heart, is the handmade wooden swing that's attached to it.

"I can't believe you remembered this," I breathe, tears spilling down my cheeks.

"I remember every word you've ever breathed, Julia."

My breath catches as I turn to him. "You did this for our baby?"

His response is a sexy smirk before he takes my hand and leads me over to the swing. I grab the rope that's on either side of me, lit with white lights, and sit down.

Jaxson kneels before me. "I did this for you, and when our baby gets old enough I will push them too, every night after supper."

A sob explodes past my lips, my face burying in my hands as I become overwhelmed with emotion.

He remembered every word.

"Look at me, baby." He pulls one of my hands away from my face and I gasp when I see he's holding a square cut diamond ring.

"Are you serious right now?" I ask through a fresh wave of tears.

"Julia—"

"Yes!" I answer before he can finish, then rein myself in quickly. "Sorry, continue."

He chuckles, amused by my excitement. "Marry me."

"You're supposed to ask, not demand it," I say with a broken laugh.

Another sexy grin tugs at his lips. "You know me better than that. I'm someone who demands, not asks. But if you say yes, I promise to love you forever, and push you on this swing every night for the rest of your life."

Warmth invades my chest, my heart soaring. "You're right, I do know you better, and I like you bossy. So shove that beautiful, shiny rock on my finger then come over here and kiss me."

"Now look who's bossy," he grunts, sliding the ring on my finger.

Taking his face between my hands I kiss him, long, slow, and deep, feeling it all the way to my soul.

"I'll take good care of you and the baby, Jules," he says, pulling back to look at me. "I promise to be what you guys deserve."

"You already are. You always have been." Grabbing his hand, I stand up. "Swing with me," I say, reversing our positions.

Our gazes remain locked as he sits on the swing, bringing me down to straddle him, his erection hitting me where I crave him most.

He groans, his eyes turning to fire as he grips my hips where my dress has ridden up. I grab the ropes on either side of his head, my eyes never leaving his as we begin to gently sway.

"How on earth did you get this tree here and planted?" I ask softly.

"The guys helped me. The lights were Kayla's idea, and I have to say it was a good one."

"Yes, it was," I agree, staring into his ice-blue eyes that are warm with need, yet fierce with restraint. "I miss you, Jaxson," I tell him sadly, knowing we need to have this conversation.

He frowns. "I'm right here, baby. I'm not going anywhere."

"You're holding back, you're not giving me all of who you are."

Realization dawns on him. "Jules…" He trails off, shaking his head.

"I need you," I plead quietly. "I need all of you, because you're the only one who can make me forget. He was the last one to touch me, and I hate him. I hate that I can still feel it. Make me forget. I want—"

He cuts me off with his mouth, his lips possessive, claiming me body and soul.

Moaning, I thread my fingers in his hair, holding him captive to me. I wiggle to get closer, grinding down on his erection.

With a growl, his hands cup my bottom, encouraging me further. He pulls his mouth from mine; trailing his firm lips down my throat. "You're mine, baby. Feel me. This is the only touch you're going to feel for the rest of your life."

"Yes, only yours," I whisper, pulling at his shirt, desperately needing more of him.

He leans back, swiftly discarding the material to reveal perfection. My hands explore his hot, naked skin, loving the way his muscles ripple and flex under my touch.

His fingers slip under my straps, dragging them down my arms until my dress is bunched at my waist. Thanks to the built-in bra, I'm completely bared to him. The warm evening breeze creating goose bumps to break across my fevered skin.

I feel Jaxson tense, fury raging in his eyes as he stares at my exposed skin. Looking down I realize he's seeing the faded marks on my breasts.

I force his eyes to mine. "Don't let him come between us. Erase them with your touch."

He buries his face in my chest, exhaling a deep breath. "I'll never let anyone hurt you again, Jules. I swear."

"I know," I whisper.

Gently, his lips brush every mark, healing some of my wounded heart. A harsh whimper leaves me when he takes a peaked nipple into his mouth. I clutch his shoulders, my back arching in pleasure as he does exactly what I need him to... *make me forget.*

"Jaxson, I need you inside of me, I need to feel all of you."

"Fuck, yes," he growls.

Grabbing onto the ropes on either side of me, I pull myself up while he fumbles to undo his pants. He pulls them open just enough to free his smooth, hard cock. His hands span my hips, shredding my soft yellow panties from my body before running his fingers through my wet flesh, sending pleasure to explode through me.

"Always so fucking wet and ready for me, Julia."

He grabs his cock and runs it where his fingers just were, coating it with my arousal, driving me wild with need.

"Please, Jaxson, now."

He lowers me onto him—too slow. Fighting against his cautious grip, I sink down on him, a cry of ecstasy leaving my lips as he fills me completely.

"Jesus!" His fingers dig into my hips with restraint.

"Stop holding back, please," I plead.

"Baby, you just got out of the hospital. I don't want to hurt you even more." Every word is delivered between clenched teeth.

"You won't. Just… please, Jaxson, fuck me."

With a growl, he pumps up into me harder and faster. It's still not all he's capable of but it's exactly what I need.

"Yes!" I cry out, pleasure whipping through my senses. "Don't stop!"

"Never. I'm never going to stop. I'm going to fuck you for the rest of my life. Sometimes it's going to be slow and gentle, other times it will be fast and hard but it will always, only, ever be me, Julia. Because you're mine."

"Yes, yours." I match him thrust for thrust, our rhythm so in sync I don't know who's driving it.

"That's right, baby. Fuck, you feel so damn good." He leans in, catching a nipple between his teeth as his hand moves between us, fingers seeking and exploring.

I whimper, feeling my impending orgasm build inside of me.

"That's it, baby, I can feel how close you are. Give me what I want, Julia. Let me feel your tight little pussy grip my cock." His husky, erotic words send me over the steep edge.

My head falls back on a cry, my gaze going to the dark night sky that's filled with stars, the bright spots blurring from the strength of my orgasm.

When I feel every last bit of pleasure leave my body, I bring my head forward and collide with Jaxson's fierce gaze.

"You're fucking perfect, and the best thing that's ever happened to me," he says.

I wrap my arms around his neck, bringing us chest to chest, our hot skin melding together as our hearts beat as one. My lips brush the corner of his eye as I deliver a gentle kiss. "You're the very best thing that has ever happened to me, too. And I promise, you're safe with me. I'll never leave you."

His eyes burn with too many emotions to name. A groan vibrates from his chest as I pick up pace again.

"Let go, Jaxson," I whisper, just before I lean down and sink my teeth into his shoulder.

"Fuck!" His cock pulses inside of me as his orgasm takes him.

I relax against him, my body limp with pleasure. His arms hold me close as we catch our breaths, our heartbeats slowing to normal.

"I have to say, Jules, I did not intend this swing for what we just did, but I'm sure fucking glad we will both be able to enjoy it."

I giggle against his shoulder. "I love it." Lifting my head, I look at him, our lips only a breath away. "Thank you, for everything."

"Thank you for agreeing to marry me."

"Well I thought I should give in, that tattoo on your back kind of ruins you for anyone else," I tease.

He doesn't laugh like I hoped he would; instead his expression sobers, his hand moving to my cheek. "Every other woman was ruined for me the moment I laid eyes on you. You have always been mine, and you always will be."

I swallow thickly, his words settling like a warm blanket over my heart. "I love you… forever."

Julia

7 Months Later

"N o fucking way, I will not wear pink at our wedding," Cooper says heatedly.

The four of us sit in my kitchen having dinner, discussing Kayla and Cooper's wedding plans. Clearly, they are still having issues over the colors.

Jaxson shakes his head vehemently, his expression panicked. "I'm with Coop, no pink."

"Oh stop being ridiculous," Kayla says. "You guys act like I'm asking you to wear a pink suit, it's a tie for crying out loud."

"I don't give a shit, Kayla, I'm not a pink kind of guy," Cooper exclaims, seeming more frustrated by the minute. "There's a thousand other colors out there, can't you pick something else?"

Kayla shrugs. "Okay fine, purple."

"For fuck's sake" he grumbles.

I giggle at Coop's signature move when he pinches the bridge of his nose.

As excited as I am for Kayla and Cooper's big day, because I know it's going to be amazing, this wedding planning business can be stressful. I am thankful Jaxson and I did ours the way we did.

It was very small. Jaxson is a private person and isn't one for being the center of attention, which was all right with me. Besides, neither of us wanted to wait that long to make wedding plans.

One month after he proposed, we had the small ceremony, at the very place I fell completely in love with him… our spot. It was only close friends and family; it was beautiful, intimate, and perfect. The beach was dotted with a thousand glowing tiki torches and further highlighted by the full moon and twinkling stars. We danced the night away with our bare feet in the warm sand and the cool ocean breeze on our faces.

We thought about going on a honeymoon, but decided not to. We were too nervous to be away from my doctor, just in case. So instead, the next night Jaxson planned a romantic night under the stars at the lighthouse.

It was perfect. It was…us.

"Fine! We'll wear pink ties, but that's it. I mean it, Kayla, don't push it on us anywhere else."

"Thank you, baby," she replies, kissing Cooper.

Jaxson drops his head in his hands, groaning in defeat.

"Well I think you guys are going to look incredibly sexy," I say, trying to ease their egos.

Cooper grunts. "More like fucking pretty."

Kayla and I burst into laughter and that's when I get a kick in the bladder. My hand drops to my stomach, rubbing comfortable circles. Jaxson and I found out we're having a girl, and both agreed to name her after my mother, Annabelle.

Jaxson is incredibly protective over her already, and Sawyer's comments never help either. The first thing he said to Jaxson when he found out it was a girl was, *Ha, ha, you're going to have a daughter, and she's going to grow up and be hot, just like Julia.*

Of course Jax didn't find it as funny as everyone else, and if there was ever a time I thought he would kill Sawyer, it was then.

I'm brought out of my thoughts with another kick that has me needing to use the bathroom. I push on the table to try and get out of my chair, but the struggle is real.

Jaxson jumps to his feet, pulling me to stand.

"I can't wait until I'm no longer too fat to stand," I grumble.

He pulls me against him, my round belly making it complicated for us to be too close. His head dips as he brings his mouth to my ear. "You're fucking sexy and once they leave, I'm going to show you how much."

I shiver in anticipation, loving how much he still always wants me. I head to the bathroom, turning my back on the group before Cooper and Kayla can see my flushed cheeks. Just as I situate myself, Annabelle kicks me so hard I gasp, and a ton of liquid gushes into the toilet.

What the… I look down in shock, realizing my water just broke.

Oh. My. God.

I'm thankful it happened now and not at the dinner table.

Okay, Julia, keep calm and think.

What did I read about? I guess the minor cramps I've been having today make sense.

After cleaning up, I walk back into the kitchen to the three of them laughing about something Sawyer did. It dies abruptly when they catch sight of me, obviously my expression saying everything I am not.

"What's wrong?" Jaxson asks, jumping out of his chair.

"Well, nothing's wrong, per say. It's just, well… my water broke."

"What?" He and Cooper bellow at the same time.

Then chaos erupts.

"Shit, the bag. I'll get the bag." Jaxson is quick, running around the table in a panic.

Cooper stands at the same time, colliding right into Jaxson's haste. "Shit!" he grunts, falling back into the chair. He waits until Jaxson passes before standing back up. "I'll drive, I can put the sirens on."

They both flee out of the kitchen, Cooper running out the door and Jaxson up the stairs.

Kayla and I walk to the kitchen entryway and watch the chaotic scene unfold. Jaxson comes flying down the stairs a moment later with his hands full of things, including my blanket and pillow that I don't need.

He trips over the blanket at the bottom of the stairs and stumbles. "Fuck!" he curses but recovers quickly, then he's out the door.

At the sound of Cooper's sirens, Kayla and I look at each other. "Did they just leave?" she asks, exasperated.

I shrug, unsure. Everything feels surreal at the moment.

She shakes her head. "Unfuckingbelievable! Don't worry, Jules, I got you. Let me grab my purse and we're out of here."

Suddenly, the sound of tires skid to a halt outside, and Jaxson comes running back inside. "Julia! Why aren't you in the fucking car?"

"Don't talk to her like that, you asshole. She's having your baby," Kayla snaps. "If you and Cooper would calm the hell down, you wouldn't have left without us."

Jaxson takes a deep breath, trying to calm himself, then strides over to me, his long legs eating up the distance between us. "I'm sorry, baby, can you please get in the fucking car?"

I nod, since I can't seem to speak, too many emotions swirl inside of me. Excitement, happiness, but most of all, fear. Lord, I'm so scared right now.

"Come on." Jaxson picks me up as if I'm not a giant pregnant woman.

"Jax, I can walk."

He shakes his head. "This way I won't lose you."

Kayla scoffs. "You won't if you guys would calm down."

"What the hell is taking you guys so long?" Cooper bellows out his open window as Jaxson walks us through the front door and down the steps. "Let's fucking go, I don't want to have to deliver this baby on the side of the road."

Jaxson picks up pace, as if concerned the same thing might happen. Climbing in the backseat, he situates me so I'm sitting on his lap.

Kayla hops in the front, her finger jabbing into Cooper's shoulder. You need to calm down. Julia is going to have a baby and you're only—"

"Oh, ow." I gasp and grip Jaxson's shoulder when a painful cramp tightens my belly.

"Oh fuck! Hurry, Coop," he says, as if the baby is going to fall out of me any second.

My breathing comes out short and fast as I try to remember the labor classes I took. "Jaxson…" I trail off when another contraction hits me, this one stronger.

"It's okay, baby, I'm here. Keep breathing, you're doing good."

Once the wave passes, I quickly try to get out words before another one hits me. "Jax, I really need you to stay calm, okay? Promise me you will stay calm. Because I'm really scared right now, and I don't want you yelling or scaring any of the nurses away."

He kisses my shoulder. "I'm calm, baby, and I'll stay calm. I promise I'll make sure you're taken care of."

"Thank you." I smile, excitement masking some of my pain. "She's coming, Jax. I can't wait to meet her."

He grins back. "Me too, baby. You're going to do great."

He claims my mouth in a mind numbing kiss, right when another one hits, my cry of pain exploding against his lips.

He freezes, scared to move. "Cooper… please hurry the fuck up."

Oh god, I have a feeling this is not going to go smoothly.

"Ahh! Oh god. Oh god," I wail, not caring in the least who hears me like I did when we first got here. This hurts so damn much.

"Deep breaths, Julia, you're doing great." The kind nurse reassures me, standing next to my bed as she watches the machine measuring my contractions.

Jaxson jumps up out of his chair that's next to me, glaring at the nurses. "Where the fuck is the guy with the drugs? He was supposed to be here two fucking hours ago."

"Jax, you promised," I plead, reaching for his hand.

"I'm calm, baby, I'm calm. Don't worry, I got this shit under control."

A laugh escapes me, even though I'm in excruciating pain.

He smirks. "All right, well maybe not totally under control."

"The anesthesiologist is on his way, sir. You have only been here thirty minutes, so no, he wasn't supposed to be here two hours ago."

He glares at her, not liking that response. "Well, it's thirty minutes too long. This guy should be prepared and waiting for this shit to happen."

I shake my head, laughing in disbelief when another bout of pain slices through me. Jaxson keeps hold of my hand, whispering words of encouragement in my ear that I'm really starting to find annoying, which makes me feel bad.

Thankfully, the anesthesiologist comes in shortly after and brings me peaceful relief. Though not before Jaxson ordered him to 'be careful' with the gigantic needle in his hand.

A few minutes later the nurse checks me again, watching the fetal monitor, and instantly I know something's wrong.

"Get the OR prepped, stat!" she shouts out the open door then looks back at me, her hand remaining inside of me. "Miss Reid, we need to do an emergency C-section. The umbilical cord is wrapped around the baby's neck."

"What?" I gasp, fear gripping my heart.

"What the fuck does that mean?" Jaxson bellows, looking ready to tear the place apart.

A flurry of activity explodes through my room as the nurse rushes to explain. "It's all right, this sort of thing happens more often than not. Try not to panic, I know it's hard, but trust that we will take care of you both. You're still going to have a healthy baby, just not the way you were anticipating."

"Jaxson?" I whisper, looking up at him for reassurance.

He leans down, pressing a kiss to my forehead, his expression looking much calmer than I feel. "It's going to be okay, Julia, you heard what she said. Annabelle is going to be fine, you're just going to have her a different way. Trust me, baby, I won't let anything happen to either of you."

Even though that's a silly promise to make, I trust him completely.

"Sir, follow the nurse as you will need to get scrubbed up before coming into the OR."

His hand drops to my cheek, his thumb soothing over my clammy skin. "I'll be right there, everything will be fine, I promise."

I'm rolled away before I can respond, feeling lost without him.

Thankfully, it's only minutes that we're apart. Relief swamps me as Jaxson comes rushing into the OR. He sits down by my head, grabbing my cold hand in his big, warm one.

Everything happens quickly.

"You're doing great, Julia, everything is good on this end. I almost have your daughter out," Dr. Bayer says.

Jaxson rests his forehead on mine, reassuring me through all of it. It isn't long before the sound of a baby crying fills the air, causing my own tears to fall.

"Here she is, your beautiful baby girl," Dr. Bayer announces, placing this teeny-tiny, naked thing on my chest.

Her skin is a warm pink, her eyes big and blue, and she has the perfect amount of brown hair. "Oh my god," I sob. "Isn't she beautiful, Jax?"

I look up to see his head casted down and his hands clutched in his hair. He lifts his head to look at me, his eyes wet. It's the second time I've ever seen him cry.

"Yeah, Jules, she's beautiful. Just like you."

I smile, knowing he's going to be the best father ever.

"Oh my god, you're so beautiful," Kayla coos, kissing Annabelle's tiny nose. "Seriously, she is. This is the best looking baby I've ever seen. Don't you think, Coop?"

"Yep, only because she takes after her mom," he teases with a smirk.

"Actually, I think she has Jaxson's eyes," Kayla says, but quickly points her finger at him. "Don't take that as a compliment, buddy."

Jaxson grunts.

"Auntie Kayla is going to buy you so many pretty dresses. Yes, I am. You're going to be the best-dressed kid around."

I giggle, watching her fawn all over Annabelle.

"All right, time's up. Give her back to me now," Jaxson says, reaching for her.

Kayla pulls her in closer to her chest. "No. I'm not done yet."

"Come on. Once Margaret gets here, I'm not going to be able to hold her until she leaves, and who knows when that will be."

Kayla rolls her eyes. "Fine. Sorry, kid, your dad can be a real pain in the ass. Be prepared for when he turns all green and spittin' mad. You will probably see it when you bring your first date over to the house."

Jaxson glares at her as he takes Annabelle. "There will be no dating," he grumbles. Leaning down, he presses a gentle kiss to her tiny forehead, the sight completely warming my heart. "The only man you need is me, baby girl. So don't go getting any ideas from your Auntie Kayla. I'm going to show you exactly what to do if any boy asks you out."

"Between you, me, Sawyer, and Cade we got that shit covered," Cooper replies seriously.

I shake my head with a smile. Even though I'm excited for the others to get here, I love that it's just the four of us right now. The way it has always been. Cooper and Kayla are the closest Jaxson and I have to siblings, and the four of us have been through a lot together.

I decide now is a good time to ask them what Jax and I discussed the other day. "Jaxson and I were talking, and we would really like for you both to be the godparents."

"Oh my god, really? Of course we will, we would be honored!" Kayla says, her eyes becoming emotional while Cooper wears a big smile. "All right, give her back now." She reaches out for Annabelle again.

"No way. I just got her."

"So what? You get to live with her and see her every day, I don't."

"What the hell are you talking about? You're pretty much over every day."

Kayla glares at him, looking ready to battle.

"Fine, whatever," he grumbles, reluctantly handing Annabelle off to her.

He moves to lie next to me on the queen bed. We got a private luxury room at the hospital since I will be here for a few days to recover. "How are you feeling? Do you need anything?"

"Just you," I tell him with a smile.

"That's something you'll always have." Leaning down, he rests his forehead against mine, blanketing us in our own intimate world. "You did real good today, Jules."

"Thanks, so did you. You only got mad at two people, I'm very proud of you," I tease, though I know it's something to be proud of.

"Anything for you, baby," he says with a smirk but his expression quickly sobers. "I love you, Jules. We're going to have a good life, I promise."

I smile, my heart skipping a beat like it always does when he says those words. But I didn't need the reassurance. We have come a long way to get to where we are now, and I know it wasn't for nothing. I know with every fiber of my being that our life together will be nothing short of extraordinary.

Thank you for reading my debut novel, *Fighting Temptation*, book one in the Men of Honor series. Feel free to follow me on my Facebook page for teasers and updates on this series or you can check out my website: www.authorkclynn.com for exclusive scenes and any additional information. Turn the page for a special bonus scene where you will read about all the men and their time in the hospital in Germany.

CONSEQUENCES OF HONOR

Bonus Scene

Alone in his hospital room, Jaxson stared up at the ceiling, lost in his guilt and the overwhelming despair that continued to plague him. The tortured memories continuously assaulted his mind, offering no reprieve from the hell he now called home. His body was broken, soul fractured and life irrevocably changed in a way that no human could fully comprehend.

Yet, there he was, heart still beating with vigor in his chest, air still pumping through his lungs.

Deep down he knew there was only one reason for that.

The light knock on his hospital door pulled him from his haunted thoughts. He was too weak to call out until he saw who it was. The nurse slowly wheeled Anna in, her face covered in scrapes, cuts and bruises. Some deep enough to leave scars for the remainder of her life.

His chest twisted with agonizing pain at the sight of the sad broken fourteen-year-old girl, adding to the suffering he was already experiencing.

"Hey, kid." He finally summoned enough words to greet her. They were weak and it hurt like hell to talk, but he'd found them anyway.

Anna's cracked lip trembled as she fought to hold her tears at bay. "Can I stay with you for a little while?" she asked, a tiny morsel of hope lying just beneath the fear in her voice. "I don't want to be alone. I'm scared."

The admission came as a shock to Jaxson. He couldn't understand why she felt safe with him. Not when he failed her like he did but he would not turn her away. He'd do anything for her. "Yeah, you can stay with me."

The nurse wheeled Anna closer to his bed. "I'll come back in an hour to check on you," she said, before leaving them.

Anna's cheeks hollowed and her chin quivered as she tried to hold herself together. "You look like you're in a lot of pain."

"Nothing I can't handle. How about you? Any pain?"

She shook her head. "I haven't felt much since they gave me the medication. I'm just... afraid."

"Don't be. No one can hurt you now. Your parents will be here soon to take you back home where you belong."

She swallowed thickly, her tears finally escaping down her cheeks. "Is it horrible for me to say I wish you were coming with me? I love my parents, but my dad isn't the kind of guy who knows how to use his fists or a gun. He's a surgeon."

"Well, I'll bet he's good with a scalpel and that shit can cause some serious damage to someone," Jaxson said, hoping to get a laugh from her.

It worked.

Anna busted into laughter and he couldn't help but smile but it quickly evaporated, the beautiful sound broke into a sob.

It killed him, like a cruel blade twisting in the center of his chest. No girl should ever have to go through what she has, especially one as young and innocent as her. "Listen, kid. I know we just got out of some crazy shit but you'll be safe with your parents. I'll bet your dad will take all precautions necessary to keep you safe."

Anna nodded and reached for the Kleenex next to his bed, dabbing her cheeks with it and erasing the tears. If only the pain on the inside could be wiped away as easily. "Maybe you can come visit me sometime?" she asked, hope thick in her voice.

"Yeah, maybe." Jaxson's reply was wary. He didn't know if he would be able to face her again. To look her in the eyes months from now and know his best wasn't good enough. "I'm going to a rehabilitation clinic for a while, but I'll come check on you when I'm out," he promised her in the end.

It was enough to bring a soft smile to her face.

Silence fell between them but their demons were loud, consuming the room.

Anna broke it a moment later. "Who was the girl that just left?"

Jaxson tensed at the question. "What girl?" He knew exactly who she was talking about. The pain was still fresh from the decision he made to send her away, the self-inflicted wound in his chest was as painful as the physical ones he wore on his body.

"The pretty one who was crying. The one your friend took away."

"Her name is Julia. She's my best friend," he answered, his voice as hollow as the organ in his chest.

"You didn't want to see her?"

"I did. I just didn't want her to see me," he explained. Even speaking of her hurt in a way he couldn't describe.

"Was she the one who gave you the necklace?"

Jaxson nodded, the fire in his chest growing hotter by the second.

"Are you in love with her?"

He glanced over at Anna, his eyes narrowing. "Do you always ask this many questions?"

She cracked a smiled, embarrassed by her curiosity. "Yeah, I do, sorry. I won't ask any more." A yawn escaped her, exhaustion slipping over her tired body and she laid her head down next to his arm.

"Why don't you go rest if you're tired? You can come back after. I'm not going anywhere."

"No," she mumbled, tiredly. "Please don't make me leave. I want to stay with you or I won't sleep."

Her plea had his burning chest tightening further. "You can stay as long as you want," he told her.

"Thank you." She reached for his hand, gripping it tightly in hers.

The feel of her small hand clinging to his shifted something inside of him. He held on tight, staring up at the ceiling, his thoughts fixed on Julia. "Can you keep a secret?" he asked her.

"Yes." she whispered.

"I'm in love with her. I have been since I was nineteen years old."

It felt good to confess that to someone. He wished he had been brave enough to tell Julia, but he knew in the end it was better this way. She was better off without him, especially now. There was no way he could drag her into this hell with him.

He was forever changed by this fateful week and she deserved so much more than what he could give her.

Anna never replied but her fingers squeezed his, as if she felt his pain, knew it. It wasn't long before her breathing evened out and she fell asleep.

When the nurse came back an hour later, Jaxson ordered for a bed to be brought in for Anna. The nurse obliged and woke Anna only long enough to get her situated. After she left, Anna grabbed Jaxson's hand once more and fell back asleep. He was glad he could offer her comfort. He wished he could find some of his own, or even a couple of hours sleep.

But sleep never came for him and peace was even further.

Jaxson spent the remainder of the night staring out into the darkness, wishing for a love he couldn't have, and remembering all the reasons why he didn't deserve her anyway. He stayed awake until morning came, until the promise of another day offered him a temporary escape from the demons that would continue to haunt him for the rest of his life.

Out in the hall Catherine and John Evans, along with their two daughters, ran up to the nurses' station, fear and agony plaguing the worried family.

"Excuse me. We're here for my son, Sawyer Evans." Catherine said, her voice thick with tears. Her heart had been in her throat since the phone call. Her entire world was in shambles and it wouldn't be righted until she knew if her son was still alive.

God help her if he wasn't. If she had come all this way to find out he didn't make it, she would not survive. Not without her only son.

John held his crying daughters close, feeling helpless and lost in his own grief. He'd been trying to stay strong for his family. He'd always been the rock they needed when times were hard but they'd never experienced anything like this before and the thought of losing any of his children or his precious wife frightened him more than anything else.

"One moment while I check with the doctor and make sure he's clear for visitors."

"Can you at least tell us if he's okay?" Catherine asked, desperate for answers.

The nurse gave her a sympathetic look. "Please, just give me a minute. I need to get clearance from the doctor first."

As the nursed picked up the phone, Catherine turned to her husband, sobbing into his chest. He wrapped his arm tight around her also, offering what little comfort he could. He knew she was just as scared as he was. Their children were their world and life without them would be destroyed.

"Mr. and Mrs. Evans."

Catherine stepped away from her husband and looked up at the stranger approaching them, the concern etched across his face matched that of their own.

The man extended his hand to them. "I'm Cooper McKay. I'm a good friend of Jaxson's. He was with Sawyer and Cade."

Another sob slipped from Catherine. "Cade too?"

Cooper nodded.

"Please tell me they're okay. Please," she begged.

Cooper seemed to hesitate before answering which made John's anxiety spike in fear.

"They're alive," Cooper finally answered, sending relief to sweep through them all. "I've spoken to your son but not Cade. He isn't seeing anyone at the moment. Both are in stable condition though."

"Oh thank God," Catherine cried, while Samantha and Jesse hugged one another.

Cooper cleared his throat and shifted on his feet. "I feel like I must warn you though. They are in very bad shape. It's not easy to see."

John could see it in the young man's eyes, what he saw of them was something he would live with forever. It brought his own concern back up to the surface.

Catherine shook her head. "It doesn't matter. As long as he's alive we will get him the help he needs. Both him and Cade," she added.

The nurse hung up the phone and turned to the family. "The doctor will be here shortly to speak with you. In the meantime, you are free to see your son. Please, follow me," she said, leading them away.

Catherine offered Cooper an appreciative smile. "Thank you so much."

Cooper gave her a nod and John reached out to clasp the man's hand, thankful for his help.

The family followed the nurse closely, except John. His steps weren't as fast as his mind had wanted them to be. His chest contracted, his worst fear making his feet feel like heavy anchors.

Once they arrived, he hung back as the nurse opened the door, watching his wife and daughters walk in. The sound of his wife's shattered sob pulled him closer, no matter how scared he was to see his son, he wouldn't leave his beloved wife to face it alone.

He stepped in behind her, his hands moving to her waist to steady her as her hand flew to her mouth. His own knees threatened to buckle at the sight before him but he'd remained standing by some miracle. His only son, his flesh and blood. The boy he raised to be a killer on the ice who went on to kill for his country, lay there motionless, his face almost unrecognizable due to his injuries.

Sawyer slowly twisted his head to the side, his swollen shut eyes making it difficult to see his family. His body was mangled, and it was obvious to everyone just how much pain he was in but he hadn't lost his trademark smirk or the playfulness in his eyes. "You all can thank me later for getting you a trip to Germany," his voice was rough as he breathed through the pain.

"Sawyer!" His name fled his mother's lips on a sob. She leaned over him, hugging his broken body carefully as she cried. His sisters fell on his other side doing the same, wrapping him in a cocoon.

"I'm all right, Mom," he choked out, his throat burning with emotion. His eyes lifted to his father's, where he stood rooted near the door. He was frozen. His mind still running through hundreds of scenarios on how his son ended up here in this condition. He'd always seen his son as strong, courageous, but not invincible. In his heart, he knew a day like today could easily become reality, which is why he never wanted him to do this in the first place. Seeing it with his own eyes broke him.

John couldn't stand there for another second. He turned and fled the room, his feet eating up the hospital floor as he found the nearest exit. Once his lungs took in the fresh air outside, he was finally able to catch his breath. He walked several feet away from the entrance where he knew he would be alone. It was there he was able to let go to feel the tremendous weight of what his son had gone through. It was there that John fell to his knees on the concrete, and cried for his son. It would change his family forever.

Cade lay silent in his hospital room. He ignored the nurse at his bedside as she diligently changed the bandage on his head. She again tried convincing him to take the pain medication but he declined, like he had the last several times. It wouldn't matter if she gave it to him anyway, nothing could take away the permanent ache in his chest.

His mind constantly conjured up the most unbearable things as he imagined what they did to her. The beautiful red head who had not only captured his attention but had somehow made him *feel* again. The knowledge hurdled through him, the revelation almost as painful as his tortuous thoughts. And when he wasn't thinking about her he was thinking about his little sister, the one person he could never save no matter how many times he's tried inside of his mind. So he wallowed in his guilt, burned there, convinced it was what he deserved.

"Sir, are you sure you won't reconsider about Miss Williams?" The nurse asked.

He refused to answer that question again, his response would be the same. He couldn't face her. Not now. Probably not ever. He couldn't look her in the face and know how much he had failed her. Or even worse, to see the fear in her eyes, fear of him, because she had got a glimpse at what exactly lived inside of him. It killed him, he ached to see her, to know she was okay. To watch precious air fill her lungs and know she was still breathing life into her beautiful soul. A soul so bright but was no doubt shattered from what those bastards did to her.

The nurse sighed at his silence. "Okay. What about family? Are you sure there isn't someone we can call for you? Anyone?"

"No," he spoke past the guilt and shame, his attention diverted to the darkened window. Night had fallen and with it came the promise of darkness, when his demons would swallow him whole. "I have no one."

The nurse sighed with sympathy then turned and left the room. Cade hit the button on the side of his bed, shutting out the lights, plunging himself into the hell he deserved. The hell he'd earned. The hell he called home. But it did not stop him from thinking about the woman who irrevocably changed his life. The little bit of light he was lucky enough to have for a brief moment before it was all stolen from him, thrusting him back into the dark where he belonged.

Faith's innocence had been stolen from her. She'd been tortured and abused in the worst way imaginable. But nothing broke her more than knowing that the little boy died for her or the man she fell in love with endured the same hell in order to save her.

Faith's attention drew to the door as the nurse stepped into her room, her face twisted in disappointment. "Did you tell him?" she asked.

The nurse nodded. "I'm sorry, I tried. But he's still refusing to see anyone."

Faith tried to keep the tears from falling but they slipped down her bruised cheeks anyway, betraying the broken state of her heart. She ached so much to be with him, to hold his hand, the sight of how badly he was hurt was still fresh in her mind. And it was all because of her. He suffered through it just to save her.

"Your parents will be here early in the morning," the nurse said, trying to make her feel better.

But it didn't work, her heart hurt too much and she knew how difficult it would be on her parents to see her this way or hear what she had been through.

"He asks about you," the nurse told her quietly.

Faith's tear filled eyes lifted back to her.

"He asks about you anytime one of us goes in to check on him and tells us to make sure all of your needs and wants are met. It's easy to see how much he cares for you."

That should have made her feel better but it didn't. If anything she longed for him more, to tell him how sorry she was for the pain he endured because of her. To thank him for saving her life and... to just be with him.

Faith's voice trembled as she thanked the nurse. The moment she walked out and closed her hospital room door, Faith crumbled. Turning on her side, she let go of all the sorrow that suffocated her. She cried for Cade, for his friends and for Aadil. She cried for herself and the shame she carried now in her soul. She cried until there were no more tears left and the loneliness sucked her into a deep slumber.

Unbeknownst to Faith, Cade changed his mind later that night and sat for hours next to her bed while she slept. He held her hand and watched her take in those precious breaths. Just one last time, he needed to see her. He stared down at her with longing and regret, wishing like hell he was worthy enough to hold her in his arms. Because if he had been, he'd never let her go.

Acknowledgements

Wow, where do I start? So many amazing people to thank!

First and foremost, I want to thank my husband. When I told him about my silly idea to write a romance novel, he encouraged me to do it. Thank you, Rob, for your support, for taking care of our kidlets, and running the household the last few months so I could finish a dream of mine. I love you with all my heart.

To my family, my parents, and mother-in-law. I love you. Thank you for always supporting me on this journey.

To my brother and sister-in-law, Jason and Shelley. Thank you for being so supportive during this journey and for encouraging me to follow through. I love you both.

Kayla—my good friend who's just as obsessed with dirty books as I am. You have been one of my biggest cheerleaders throughout this journey. Your support and input has meant the world to me. I loved all our massage sessions while talking for hours about my characters. Thank you for talking me down from all of my panic texts and second thoughts. I loved writing you into this story and giving you one hot book boyfriend. I can't wait to write a short story on "you" and Cooper. I love ya, girl.

Megan—oh, Megan, where do I start? We became best friends after the first day of grade six when I met the really smart girl who sat behind me and could read better than my parents. Lol! Then I found out you didn't eat meat and thought 'What's wrong with this girl?' Haha. The best part about writing this book for me is that we reconnected. One of my favorite things during this journey was all of our comments and arguing during this book—even your damn logical side that drove me nuts. I love you and cherish your friendship. Thank you for stepping up, helping me, and encouraging me all the way. This book would have NEVER happened without you. Thank you from the bottom of my heart for being my editor and the smartest friend I have. I can't wait to continue this journey with you. Just you wait—your book will come one day! And I am going to pair you with the biggest, baddest alpha around who will tame your feminist ass. :)

Katelyn Rae—I loved all of my appointments and discussions over this book with you. You started out as my esthetician four years ago and now are one of my friends. Thank you for your encouragement. Even though your part is small in this book, I can't wait to continue your character and show-case your business in the following books.

Cover To Cover Designs—Kari—thank you for making me one hot cover and guiding me through my first book. I cannot wait to have you make my others for me.

About the Author

K.C. Lynn is a small town girl living in Western Canada. She grew up in a family of four children—two sisters and a brother. Her mother was the lady who baked homemade goods for everyone on the street and her father was a respected man who worked in the RCMP. He's since retired and now works for the criminal justice system. This being one of the things that inspires K.C. to write romantic suspense about the trials and triumphs of our heroes.

K.C. married her high school sweetheart and they started a big family of their own—two adorable girls and a set of handsome twin boys. They still reside in the same small town but K.C.'s heart has always longed for the south, where everyone says 'y'all' and eats biscuits and gravy for breakfast.

It was her love for romance books that gave K.C. the courage to sit down and write her own novel. It was then a beautiful world opened up and she found what she was meant to do…write.

When K.C.'s not spending time with her beautiful family, she can be found in her writing cave, living in the fabulous minds of her characters and their stories.

Made in United States
Cleveland, OH
11 August 2025

19244399R00194